The Cigar Maker

Mark Carlos McGinty

Seventh Avenue Productions
Minneapolis

Also by Mark McGinty

ELVIS AND THE BLUE MOON CONSPIRACY

Seventh Avenue Productions
© 2010 Mark Carlos McGinty

ISBN-13: 978-0-615-34340-2
ISBN-10: 0-615343406
LCCN: 2009913688

Cover design by Lupi
Maps by Kevin Cannon
Author photo by Avery McGinty

Printed in the United States of America.

Contact the author at mmcginty_32@yahoo.com

www.thecigarmaker.net

For my grandparents, Carlos and Camelia Roque.

Author's note: The following is a work of fiction and is loosely based on real events. In some places, the actual history may have been altered to suit the story. An additional author's note at the end of the book will explain these historical discrepancies in further detail and also provide additional sources for reading about Ybor City's fascinating history.

Credit must be given to the following people who helped shape the book you are about to read:

Diane Salerni, Scott Dietche, Bill Durbin, Lloyd Lofthouse, Clayton Bye, John Peterson, Linda Evans, Dave Dykema, Arturo Fuente Jr., E.J. Salcines, Kevin Cannon, Gaye Grabill, Joe Roumelis, Meridith McGinty, Sean Beahan, Judd Spicer, Steve Marsh, the folks at IAG, Audrey Rañon, and Rodney Kite-Powell at the Tampa Bay History Center, the Ybor City Museum, Manny Leto at Cigar City Magazine.

Special thanks to Mom and Dad for the support.

And an especially big thank you to my friends and relatives in Tampa, both past and present, whose lives, stories, and great cooking were the inspiration for this book.

Finally, Ybor is pronounced E-bor, like eBay.

The Cigar Maker

YBOR CITY
1900
THE CIGAR MAKER

1. PASAJE HOTEL
2. YBOR CIGAR FACTORY
3. YBOR SQUARE
4. FIRE STATION
5. LA MORENA
6. GABRIEL MENDEZ
7. ARMANDO
8. LAS NOVEDADES

9. HOTEL HAVANA
10. CENTRO ESPANOL
11. LABOR TEMPLE
12. LAPÁR
13. CUESTA-REY FACTORY
14. JUAN CARLOS
15. OLIVIA FACTORY
16. ST. JOSEPH'S CHURCH
17. SANCHEZ BROS. STORE

18. SALVADOR ORTIZ HOUSE
19. VASQUEZ HOUSE
20. VASQUEZ FACTORY
21. CIENFUEGOS FACTORY
22. CHARLES THE GREAT FACTORY
23. LA RUBIA
24. TRAIN STATION
25. BREWERY

I.

SALVADOR
ORTIZ
1897

Chapter 1

Salvador had been in Ybor City less than one day when he saw a man bite the head off a live rooster. He had lost hundreds of dollars betting on cockfights in Havana, but after the factory cut hours and pay, no cigar maker could justify or even afford a rambunctious night of gambling and sport. It was not until he made it across the Straits to Tampa's Ybor City that Salvador realized what had devoured all those lost wages and hours. This young town was prospering while old Havana slowly died before his eyes. When Salvador arrived in the Cigar City and saw factories filled with workers and a rowdy nightlife colored by green American dollar bills, he knew he had found a town that would one day be famous.

Ybor was a man's city, clamoring with busy saloons, girls-for-hire, boxing matches, unending games of dominoes, and most of all hard work. Ybor was a town whose cigar workers were in demand, and everything seemed to be surrounded by rows and rows of shiny white tenement houses and the brick-oven smell of fresh baked bread. One thing was certain; this was no land of ancient sugar plantations and wealthy Spaniards. It was a cigar city ready for the Twentieth Century, and Salvador could smell them everywhere he went: in bars, on the street, in factories and restaurants, and on every neighbor's porch. Cuba was a land in disarray, but here was a place where Salvador and his entire family could prosper for a very long time. This was a town where he could happily lose a lot of money on cockfights.

"I have found my place," Juan Carlos told him. Friends since before they joined El Matón's crew, Juan Carlos was Salvador's oldest acquaintance. "I will die in this town," he told Salvador.

Salvador knew that a town filled with rugged, drunken cockfights and dime store prostitutes was a place that Juan Carlos would be delighted to call his home. During the first war, when they were a couple of penniless teenagers struggling to outlast the poverty of Cuba, Juan Carlos summarized their options. "We can engage in petty larceny in the city, rob people at knifepoint, and walk away with pesos and stale bread," Carlito said. "Or we can join the rebels and steal from rich sugar planters who live in cathedrals and pay hefty ransoms for the return of their kidnapped wives and daughters!"

Back in those days, before Salvador had a family or a future, these were his assets: a rusty old knife that had belonged to his father, a small box of matches, three cheap cigars, and a canvas backpack with a second pair of pants and a couple of worn out shirts. An orphan with little knowledge of even his relatives, it was odd that young Salvador, a man who valued honest hard work, would follow Juan Carlos into El Matón's rambunctious crew.

Years later, after El Matón and most of his men were decimated by Spanish soldiers, Salvador fled to Havana and learned the tobacco trade, while Juan Carlos lingered in town before he returned to the rebel lifestyle, fought the Spanish, and was eventually captured trying to rob a train. Juan Carlos was convicted and offered a choice by the declining Spanish government of Cuba: prison on the Isle of Pines or permanent relocation to Florida. Juan Carlos chose the place where so many Cuban men had already gone: Ybor City in Tampa.

It was there that Juan Carlos started serious work as a cigar maker, for it was customary for Ybor City *tabaqueros* to donate a portion of their wages to fund the rebels' efforts in Cuba. Juan Carlos continued to support the war from afar while he never tired of coaxing his friend to abandon the island and join thousands of Cuban and Spanish workers in relocating to the Cigar City. He paid the factory *lector* to write letters to Salvador and eventually his friend agreed to visit.

"Employment is sporadic in Havana," Salvador told Olympia, who hoped Salvador's trip to Florida would be more than a juvenile escape with his old friend. "With the war and all these cigar factories closing down and moving to Tampa, all the men are finding steady work in Ybor City. Maybe I should go there and see for myself?"

"I don't know what you're waiting for." Olympia said. "The Fuentes and Negro families have already moved to Florida, and Anna Fuentes wrote me and said they never plan to come back. And if there is steady employment there, like everyone says, then you will be able to work during your visit with Carlito, and can send money home each week. We have four children to feed and I do not have any more time to sweep floors in the factory while you are on vacation."

Salvador chuckled, knowing his wife was only half-serious. He held her and kissed her forehead. "It's not a vacation. But of course, I will send money each and every week." He wondered if she would make him promise not to gamble or attend any cockfights, but Olympia knew better than to try and keep a Cuban man away from his nightlife.

Salvador gathered his three boys, Javier, Lázaro and E.J. and knelt before them. "Papa has got to go away, boys, because there are no jobs here. I've got to travel up to Florida to see how we can do up there. With luck on our side, if we can make enough money, maybe I'll bring you up there too." He kissed each boy on the forehead; Javier, sixteen and an accomplished cigar maker, then fourteen-year-old Lázaro and finally young E.J. Then he held his oldest child, his eighteen-year-old daughter Josefina, who tried to smile while fighting her tears.

And so in the winter of 1897, Salvador Ortiz left Cuba for the first time in his life and took a boat to Port Tampa. Juan Carlos greeted him on the dock with a bear hug, a deep, mischievous laugh and his familiar odor of burnt tobacco and rum.

"Come!" Carlito grinned as he slapped Salvador's back, showing his crooked yellow teeth. For as long as Salvador could remember, Juan Carlos had a single tooth on the upper right side that was darker and more crooked than the rest, a single rotten fruit among a row of already stale teeth. "Let me show you my town!"

Salvador saw Ybor City as a promising young industrial town that had not yet hit its prime. It was a smaller version of Havana, where flat streets of sand surrounded dozens of brick cigar factories. But instead of Spanish flags, Salvador saw that Cuban red, white, and blue decorated every building. He sensed the revolutionary fervor was strong, and the abundance of activity and commerce suggested the city would one day mature into a vibrant industrial port and center of immigrant culture.

"You haven't stopped smiling since you arrived," Carlito noticed.

"What can I say, Carlito, you were right. It is what Havana should be, a thriving city with no Spanish soldiers."

Juan Carlos became serious. "Cuba Libre is very much alive in Ybor City, Salvador. There is almost no reason to return to Havana. Even after we win the war, Cuba will be wrecked. This is the best place to live. This is the new Havana."

Salvador followed Juan Carlos all over town, from the busy and commercial Seventh Avenue to the Cuban social club to the brick factory where Juan Carlos had learned to roll cigars. Juan Carlos pointed out the Pasaje Hotel. "A house of ill repute," he jabbed Salvador. "A place that supplies high class hookers to elite businessmen. For more middle class whores, one goes to La Rubia, but if you're really strapped for cash the worst in class can be found in the Scrub. But no right-minded cigar maker would ever venture into that part of town."

Salvador soon found himself behind a bar in the center of town under a cloud of cigar smoke, among a crowd of rowdy Cubans waving dollar bills and shouting at two angry gamecocks who chopped and clawed each other in a fight to the death.

When the match was over, Salvador had lost his bet, but he was among his people; surrounded by cigar makers of all ages, most of them in their twenties, thirties or forties, and wearing the pressed white shirts and ties they wore to work. Sleeves rolled up, facial hair, dirty fingernails, big smiles and loud voices. With no women around to keep them calm, the rambunctious group instantly made Salvador feel like part of the family.

Now a short man, plump and gruff, with half a cigar poking through his thick lips, appeared in the crowd carrying a metal cage. Juan Carlos slapped at Salvador's arm. "This is the match I want to see." He pointed at the man's cage where an aggressive black rooster fluttered its wings and bit at the cage bars trying to gnaw his way to freedom.

Juan Carlos started counting his money, trying to decide on his wager, and explained. "Fortunado and his lucky gamecock named Picchu. This bird is a champion in Key West, Ortiz. Specially bred on the island and undefeated, he was so feared that Fortunado could no longer get a match. No one in Key West was willing to wager their birds against his, so he brought Picchu to Ybor to face a new pool of brave and foolish challengers. Tonight is his Ybor City debut!"

Fortunado removed Picchu from his cage, gripping the fierce bird tightly in his pudgy hands, and held him above his head for the crowd to see. The black rooster had tiny divots and bald spots where he had been nipped and plucked by other roosters, and his beak was marked with chips and scratches, his badges of victory. The bird's claws looked menacing on their own, but each of them had been armed with a leather bracelet and a razor sharp steel spike called a short-spur.

Picchu ruffled his feathers and kicked his feet as Fortunado held him before the drunken crowd. Cheering and hollering provoked the bird, signaling an imminent fight. Picchu's head snapped left and right looking through the crowd for a brave challenger, and when the bird's shiny black eyes seemed to fall on Salvador, the cigar maker was so startled by the gamecock that he actually looked away.

Juan Carlos slapped his arm again. "Here comes the challenger!"

A yellow and brown rooster named Contusiór was held above the crowd by his owner and the bird reacted violently, chopping his short-spurs and fluffing his feathers proudly, showing his own scratches and pockmarks to the rowdy gambling crowd.

"This one looks just as fierce as Picchu," Salvador said.

"Then place your wager on that weak little bird," Juan Carlos said. "I'm going to bet on black." Juan Carlos disappeared into the crowd to place his bet, and Salvador followed, betting a small amount on the legendary bird from Key West.

Now Picchu and Contusiór were lowered into the wooden cockpit and held beak-to-beak by their owners, further agitating the birds. They thrust their beaks out and tried to pick and jab at each other, but their owners held them just out of reach. Then the men took their places at opposite sides of the wooden pit and lowered their birds to the dirt floor. On the count of three, they were unleashed.

The crowd erupted into a drunken frenzy as the gamecocks attacked each other under a cloud of dust and feathers. Salvador cheered as the birds stabbed each other with their spurs and pecked holes with their beaks. Blood splattered across the dirt, the bird's piercing shrieks blended with the cheering. Contusiór slashed Picchu's neck with his spur, cutting Picchu and forcing him onto defense. Contusiór sensed victory and moved quickly with one brutal chop after another until Picchu was a

5

bloody mess of black feathers pinned underneath. The fight was over in seconds, a stunning upset of Fortunado's bird.

Contusiór's owner jumped into the ring and pulled his champion from the fray, raising him above his head with a triumphant smile at the cheers and boos alike. Salvador and Juan Carlos tore their tickets and tossed them aside as Picchu collapsed. Fortunado jumped into the ring to recover his dying bird knowing the gamecock could not be saved.

Fortunado had bet a considerable sum of money on Picchu and was so angry that the bird had lost that he took the rooster's head in his teeth and, with the certainty of a man chomping the end from a cigar, bit Picchu's head clean off. Blood spurted. Fortunado spat the head onto the ground where it rolled across the dirt like a baseball and rested against the wooden wall of the cockpit with the black eyes locked open. Then Fortunado kicked the dirt and tossed Picchu's body aside like a crumpled candy wrapper into the trash. He pulled a black feather from his lips and wiped away a mouthful of blood before he stomped angrily into the crowd.

Salvador was astonished. With eyes bulging he slapped at Juan Carlos. "*¡Coño!* I can't believe he did that! Did you see it, Carlito?"

Juan Carlos was laughing. "How could I miss that?"

Salvador was so excited about Picchu's brutal and comical beheading that he told a group of cigar makers about it the next morning, and then recounted the story in the afternoon to another group, and several times that night he told the story to anyone who would listen, never tiring of the tale.

In the days that followed, Salvador found work at the Vasquez and Company factory where he rolled cigars at a wooden bench beside Juan Carlos. They spent their nights gambling in taverns with the cigar workers until they tired and passed out at a boarding house on Twelfth Avenue, where for three dollars a week Salvador received a room, a bed and two daily meals. He was happy to be back with Juan Carlos. Though many years had passed, it often seemed like old times.

Orphaned at the age of fourteen, when his parents had been accused of aiding the Cuban insurrectionists during the Ten Years' War, Salvador distinctly remembered armed rebels passing through their home, stopping in for a small meal or a bed and talking quietly with his father.

A quiet peasant farmer, Ernesto Ortiz had been promised by the rebels that the farming village of Herrera would be protected from the Spanish army. Salvador's father had told him, "Fruits and cattle raised by our village should feed the peasants, not be redistributed to Spanish soldiers."

Salvador was learning the farming trade, but his father quickly gave him an education in politics. "Spain is draining Cuba of its natural resources," Ernesto told his son. "They are giving nothing back. All the wealth generated by Cubans is feeding the Spanish. They own our government and our property and leave us no opportunity for self-determination. Shouldn't every man have the right to decide who enjoys the fruit of his own labor?"

One morning Ernesto's lessons abruptly ended, and Salvador was forced into the world to find his own education. When shots rang out in the distance and the sound of approaching horses grew louder and louder, Ernesto frantically woke his only child and ordered him to run across the fields and hide in the forest. "Go now, boy! Step lively and don't look back!"

Those were Ernesto's last words to Salvador.

The boy ran until he was hidden by a giant Ceiba tree. Watching from afar as Spanish soldiers on horseback trampled through the village and set the modest *bohio* homes ablaze, Salvador saw the fragile shelters of wood and palm fronds collapse into flaming piles as many of the villagers, including Salvador's mother and father, were captured by the soldiers and executed.

The image of his mother and father on their knees before a gang of Spanish troops, with his sobbing mother begging God's mercy before rifles exploded, became seared into his memory. Salvador fled into the forest carrying nothing but his father's rusty dagger and a hatred and complete mistrust of anything Spanish.

When he finally made it to the western city of Pinar del Río, and met Juan Carlos on the streets begging for food, it became easy for them to steal from the aristocrats responsible for their plight. For Juan Carlos had also lost his father and a brother at the hands of Spanish soldiers. Young, vengeful Carlito carried a pistol and a machete in a canvas duffle bag and hoped to join a band of rebels but had little luck finding an army that would lead him into battle against the Spanish.

"I like you, Ortiz," Juan Carlos told him the day the teenagers met on the street. "Your story is like mine. It seems as though we're the last of a dying breed." The truth was that Juan Carlos could use another man to help him rob a local Spanish bookkeeper he had been watching for over a week.

"You have a knife, I have a gun and this man is a Spaniard. Not only that but he has money. I have been watching him for many days now. Every night after he locks his office, he walks down the block to the Spanish bakery where he has a cup of coffee and a pastry before heading home. We go in right before he locks up and split our earnings right down the middle. If we're successful, we come back next week and rob the bakery."

Salvador, as if transfixed with the unending memory of his mother's head being blown apart by a Spanish rifle, nodded and gripped the wooden handle of his knife. Normally he wouldn't consider stealing, and would rather work for his daily meals, but he had been numbed by grief.

"Yes, we are stealing," Juan Carlos said. "But we are stealing back little pieces of our own country. We are reclaiming what is ours."

Salvador thought of his father's blood, spilled on Cuban dirt. "Let's go."

On Carlito's signal the boys entered the bookkeeper's office and less than a minute later were running from the scene with enough pesos to eat for several days. It was easier than Salvador thought it would be. The bookkeeper was a man used to the confines of his office and did not compare to the menacing Spanish soldiers Salvador had eluded in the countryside. "You've got guts," Juan Carlos seemed to admit later on, as they divided their money in a secluded alley. "If you were afraid, the bookkeeper couldn't tell." Carlito was satisfied that he had found a partner and the duo spent the next weeks robbing aristocrats, begging for food and eluding the authorities. When Juan Carlos decided it was getting too hot for them in the city, he introduced Salvador to Victoriano Machín, the charismatic young ruffian who would eventually become the legendary bandit El Matón.

They became part of his crew, joining with a group of young men like themselves who acted like rebels. They were not part of the organized resistance but saw themselves as part of the same struggle. For years the band roamed the province, eventually on horseback, and terrorized the aristocracy while managing to evade the Spanish army. They were loved and considered heroes by the local peasants but loathed and denounced as bandits by the Spanish authorities. Poor as they were, Juan Carlos had found his army and Salvador had found a family.

Good looking by working class standards, Juan Carlos was a brash instigator, always challenging the men to arm wrestle, or race on foot, or compete to shoot the most squirrels. But Salvador seemed to always be sitting and thinking, often late into the night long after the rest of the group was asleep. He didn't read, hardly drank and thought carefully before he spoke. He was notorious for observing the scene, forming an opinion and then speaking thoughtfully to those who would listen.

One night as the men were settled around the fire cleaning their rifles and counting pesos paid to them by a local Spanish landowner in exchange for protection, they listened as one read from a Havana newspaper. When he was finished Juan Carlos explained how current political affairs related to the rebels. "General Maceo will never accept the terms of the Zanjón treaty. An armistice that does not provide for complete and total Cuban independence is no treaty that any Cuban can accept. When Maceo refuses to lay down his weapons, hostilities against Spain will continue. We should not relax so quickly."

The men nodded their agreement. "Maceo will never surrender," remarked one.

Another raised his fist and said, "Long live the Bronze Titan!"

They silently considered their roles in Cuba's long struggle for independence, a conflict with no stand-up battles, only surprise attacks and destruction of property, for which they were all guilty.

Salvador finally spoke. "The decision is not Maceo's to make. His influence on Zanjón is insignificant."

He received unanimous indignation from the men. As Salvador was jeered, Juan Carlos stood and laughed and resentfully taunted his friend. "The farm boy from Herrera thinks he knows more about politics than the rest of you warriors. Explain yourself, Salvador. How can you insult the great general when you may one day wear a true soldier's uniform and fight in his army?"

El Matón rested quietly off to the side, a red kerchief tied loosely around his neck, pretending to nap with his hands clasped over his belly but with one eye half-opened.

Salvador said, "Maceo is a field general with only 1,500 men. He cannot rally the support of Cuba. He is an asset on the battlefield but has little clout in national politics."

"Ha!" said Juan Carlos incredulously. "Listen to him!"

"This is the way it is," Salvador said simply. "I wish it was not."

When the treaty was ratified a few days later, and the protesting Maceo and his men were forced into exile, Salvador never mentioned that he had been right about the general. But he had quietly earned the respect of the men, including Juan Carlos and more importantly, El Matón.

Years later, as Salvador matured and realized his good fortune in surviving his days of rebellion, he denounced his rambunctious past, married a good woman and became a cigar maker in the city of Havana. His children, his family seemed poised to prosper, if not for another war nearly two decades later, the final battle for Cuban independence.

It brought Havana into a state of depression. The city became overcrowded with the constant arrival of peasants relocated from the warring country. Food shortages and sanitation problems resulted, yet Salvador maintained his faith that the island would overcome its problems. But with unreliable employment in Havana, and a trip to Ybor City that sent Salvador home with a pocket full of cash, the idea of joining Juan Carlos in Florida became more attractive.

When Salvador returned to Havana after his month long visit to the prosperous Cigar City, he saw city streets filled with garbage, homeless families, and Spanish soldiers. He had grown accustomed to the fragrance of tobacco and fresh bread that hung in the Ybor air. Now, stepping over the legs of people huddled on the sidewalk outside his apartment building, the odor of unwashed bodies seemed especially oppressive. The heat and humidity only made it worse.

Carrying a bag of rice he had purchased for his family, Salvador moved quickly towards his apartment and cradled the bag close to his chest. Beggars saw Salvador was neither filthy nor starving and cursed him when he would not give them money. If he had the means he would invite them all into his home for a feast, but instead he kept his head down and moved quickly.

Stray dogs roamed the street in small, pathetic little packs and Salvador encountered a group of four near his apartment building. He didn't know what breed they were, but they looked like brothers, skin and bones, each with a layer of black fur that pressed tightly against their ribs. Salvador wished he could set aside a few chunks of bread from his meager dinner and feed these dogs. He imagined himself tossing a bowl of rice and beans into the middle of their pack and watching the dogs devour it instantly but he did not want to divert even the smallest portions of food away from his family.

When he arrived at the door to the Ortiz apartment, there was an old woman down the hall, sitting against the wall apparently suffering from cholera. Her face was shrunken and dehydrated and the puddle she sat in reeked with the awful smell of diarrhea. She groaned from abdominal pains and tried to say something to Salvador as he stepped over her and hurried to his door thinking this would never happen in Ybor City.

Once he was safely inside, Salvador closed and locked the door and then noticed his heart was pounding, his forehead beaded with sweat. This was no place for his children, he thought, and wondered if Olympia knew about the sick woman outside. He decided not to mention what he had seen but waited instead for Olympia to bring it up.

She did, while Josefina helped her fix a small meal of rice and beans for the boys and Salvador. With her attention on her pots and her black hair surrounded by steam Olympia said, "There are sick people right outside that door." Salvador said nothing, wishing instead to discuss the matter privately with his wife.

After dinner Salvador and Olympia left the apartment and went walking along El Malecón, the waterfront promenade built along Havana's northern shore. A salty mist sprayed the sidewalk as waves crashed against the seawall forcing Salvador and Olympia to sidestep the saltwater puddles that crept inward as far as a city block. In the harbor, the giant U.S. battleship *Maine* quietly protected American interests from the long-standing civil disobedience.

Along the avenue wandered destitute peasants and homeless families, relocated from the warring countryside or ejected from their homes in Havana. Morro Castle, the picturesque stone fortress that guarded the entrance to Havana Bay was a tangible reminder of the Spanish dominance responsible for Cuba's plight. Salvador hoped that once the war was over, the castle would be torn down or razed by rebels. The obliteration of their most famous landmark in Cuba would be a symbolic and fitting end to Spanish rule.

A begging child approached but Salvador had nothing to give. A woman cried nearby and Salvador saw anguish in the faces of the people who sat on the street with their children and their bags, refugees from the war. His faith in his country had been dying for years. Now, with little work in this city and hardly enough food to feed his children, Salvador wondered how long it would take for Cuba to recover.

Olympia coughed and wiped her nose with a small handkerchief. The conditions in the city had been slowly affecting her health.

He said to his wife, "I'm taking E.J. out of school."

Olympia nodded as they walked. "He's only seven."

"Old enough to work," he said. "An able bodied boy in school is a waste. No need to learn facts and figures when he can be sweeping floors or sorting tobacco leaves."

"It is hard for anyone to find work in this town, especially a seven-year-old boy."

Even a master cigar maker like Salvador had not been able to rely on steady employment for many months. His sons Javier and Lázaro could sometimes find work stripping the stems from tobacco leaves, or rolling inferior cigars but there had been no reliable employment for them either.

Olympia and Salvador walked quietly along the boulevard. The night was quiet and the February air was crisp and salty and smelled of burning garbage. Olympia wanted to talk about Salvador's trip to Florida, to get the details on the Cigar City that seemed to be attracting every cigar maker in Havana.

"What about Ybor City?"

Salvador was quiet for a moment. "It was a promising town, no doubt. Easy to find work there."

"And how much longer until all the jobs in Ybor City have been filled?"

He shrugged. "I saw dozens of cigar factories under construction. I also heard the Don Pedro factory will be closing its doors in Havana and relocating to Ybor City."

Olympia found it irritating that Salvador could not admit to the obvious. She saw a family sitting against the seawall, their faces dirty with grime from several weeks without a bath. The worried looks of two small boys made Olympia fear that E.J. and Lázaro could soon be on the streets begging for bread. "Isn't it time we left this place and moved to Ybor City?"

Salvador sighed deeply. "Martí and Maceo returned from exile and died in battle. It is time to fight!" He pointed to the battleship in the harbor. "Don't you want to be here to see Cuba celebrate her victory?"

"I couldn't care less at this point, Salvador." She sniffled and wiped her nose, looking at him crossly, expecting him to come to his senses and deliver his family from this terrible situation.

"I'm not sure we should leave just yet; the war will be over soon. Leaving now would be an insult to my parents."

Olympia finally lost her patience. "Will you get over it? What in the world is the matter with you? It's been almost thirty years since they died, Salvador. Our family is starving! Get us off this island before we're all sick and dead!"

Salvador disapproved of Olympia's lack of respect but he merely said, "Your ties to your family are different than mine."

Olympia rolled her eyes and stopped walking. Now, practically pleading with Salvador, she jabbed him in the chest. "If you want to honor your father, then do what is right by your children and give them a happy life! Do you think your father would have wanted his grandchildren to shit themselves to death? Would your mother have thought it better to be dead than American?"

Despite her weakened state, Olympia remained polished and feisty. With four children, she was eternally more active than her husband. She rarely talked about politics or world events, had no close friends except for Salvador and her oldest child Josefina, and never ever spoke of her parents. Once, at Olympia's insistence, Salvador attended a church service with his wife. During the Mass he sat still and reverent like the statue of Mary and said nothing. He spoke few words of it afterwards and rarely set foot in a church again.

Salvador taught his sons the practical skills of cigar making, along with Cuban history and leisurely games like rummy and dominoes. Salvador told his boys, "Cigars are society. They are the food you eat and the bed where you sleep. They are the clothes you wear and the shoes on your feet. Cigars are, at the very least, responsible for everything you and I have."

Olympia made sure her children knew the Bible. The boys listened out of obligation, but Josefina read the Bible all the way through to the end and became extremely critical, which angered Olympia and made her defensive. "The ages of these people are ridiculous," said Josefina. "If history unfolded the way the Bible says, most of these people, or at least their children and grandchildren, would be alive today!"

Olympia replied simply, "The Bible is a book of faith not arithmetic."

Josefina considered herself to be a true believer but enjoyed a thoughtful discussion with her mother. "Faith in God." she said.

Olympia nodded curtly. "Faith in God, faith in your family."

Josefina glanced through the window of their damp apartment to the dirty streets of Havana. "Faith in your country?"

Olympia was awakened from her daydream when a terrible explosion shattered the calm evening air and knocked her to the ground. Salvador crowded over her and covered her head with one hand while shielding her with his body. With their faces pressed to the ground, they could taste the saltwater that soaked the pavement.

"Are you hurt?" he asked.

The ringing in her ears made his voice sound distant. Olympia was dazed, the smell of soot felt heavy. She shook her head. "I'm fine."

They looked to the harbor, where the USS *Maine* was engulfed in a fireball of swirling smoke and debris. The explosion had come from inside the ship and the entire front half had been obliterated. The deck had erupted into a mess of fire and twisted metal parts that threw wreckage across the harbor in all directions. Down to the water rained blocks of wood, steel railings, chunks of cement and fragments of grating. Among the mess, faint cries came from the water. In the dim light, from the fires from the ship, Salvador could see the bodies of American sailors floating on the water.

He could hear spare ammunition popping and crackling on the ship while sailors who remained on board hurried to the deck and jumped overboard. Pandemonium broke out in the harbor as people on land shouted and pointed towards the wreckage while rescue boats were dispatched to evacuate the survivors. Salvador saw the commotion and was certain that more chaos would come. A line of blood ran down Olympia's temple and reminded Salvador of his mother's death. The war had arrived in Havana; the United States would soon enter the conflict.

Despite his desire to remain in Cuba and see the end of the war, another excuse to stay would be hard to come by. Salvador, a man who wanted to do what was right for his family realized Olympia was correct. It was time to abandon the country his father had died to save.

II.

OLYMPIA CANCIO
de la SERNA
1880

Chapter 2

The seeds of Cuba Libre were sprouted by men like Olympia's father, Testifonte Cancio, who transplanted his Spanish empire to Cuban soil and built a booming sugar market on the back of slave labor. Testifonte moved his family to the plantation in the Pinar del Río province when Olympia was only three, just two years before a long revolution erupted and brought social and financial disarray to the island. The Ten Years' War ended with a treaty between Cubans and Spaniards but some who continued to fight threatened Testifonte's sugar estate. He fortified his property with armed guards, but not enough to protect Olympia from every danger presented by unstable, post-war Cuba. In 1880, soon after she turned seventeen, Olympia was kidnapped by the bandit group headed by the charismatic Victoriano Machín, known among the peasants as El Matón.

A son of plantation slaves and the oldest of six children, Machín saw himself as the charitable benefactor of his peasant siblings. War meant the Machín family was homeless and unemployed as business owners hired only Spanish workers. Victoriano was forced to slip into town to pick pockets and rob Spanish bakeries in order to feed his starving brothers and sisters. He was a charitable brother who blamed the Spanish for sinking Cuba into a dreadful depression.

Machín's deeds were not limited to his family, and he generously shared the fruit of his exploits with neighbors and fellow peasants. As the rural proletariat starved and vagrancy became a permanent feature of the landscape, Machín became a feared thief of Spanish aristocracy who supervised a redistribution of wealth in the province. He was no longer just a nice-looking low-class teenage hood but a benevolent outlaw who looked after his people. His popularity grew. He attracted recruits and built a small army, outfitted first with machetes and then guns. They saw themselves not as bandits but young rebels in the mold of Cuban generals like Calixto García and Antonio Maceo.

Machín stood among his men like a young captain wearing black pants with a black vest over a half buttoned white shirt. With a red kerchief tied around his neck, a belt of bullets slung over each shoulder and a pistol holstered on each hip, he stood confident and ready to announce their most daring raid yet. His long black hair seemed to shine in the morning sun, but when the wind blew wisps of dirt and dust from his locks it became obvious that Machín had shunned the luxury of a bath for many days.

He said to his men, "We will go in the dead of night, after the house and surrounding quarters have fallen asleep." His army of twenty sat around a campfire and listened to their leader. Machín's magnetic nature impressed young rebels like the peasant boy Salvador Ortiz, who was nervous to hear the details of the raid but anxious to collect the payoff that Machín had promised.

Now the bandit leader picked up a small log and held it before him like a club. He wrapped an old tattered rag around the end and showed it to his men. "What is this?"

The wily Juan Carlos answered, "It looks like a stick with a towel wrapped around it."

"Wrong." Machín grinned; in another life he could have been a stage actor or an entertainer. He took his club and held it into the fire, and when he pulled it out, the tattered rag was balled in flames. "This is our weapon. We will descend on the plantation like thunder and leave the sugar fields burning."

Storming a giant sugar plantation was a greater crime than any of them had ever committed, but the rebels thought of their families and the starving people of Piro. The Spanish had given these men no other choice.

The revolution was underway.

Machín's men gathered on a hill to the south of the plantation overlooking Testifonte's forty acres of sugar cane. North of the cane field, standing like a stone fortress and dwarfing the plantation buildings, was the immaculate mansion of the Cancio family.

The gray and white manor was surrounded by brick storage huts and wooden worker's dwellings. Dozens of tiny figures were speckled across the plantation, chopping cane in the field and hauling it to the mill on horse-drawn carts.

"Let's move around to the north," Machín instructed. "I want to get a closer look at the mansion and try for a headcount on the workers and guards."

The group moved into the forest and positioned themselves on the north side of the plantation. Here they had a closer view of the small village within the estate. Two of Testifonte's men patrolled the perimeter with rifles and both were so far away that the bandits had little reason for concern.

Machín actually snickered. "Two guards? That's all he has? This won't even be a challenge." He pointed towards the mansion. "See that stone building there? That's the mill which houses a press for extracting sugar and a boiling room where the sugar is heated into molasses. If it is destroyed then the whole plantation will shutdown. That must happen only as a last resort. If this plantation is making no money, then we will be unable to take our share of the wealth."

Salvador pointed to a pair of brick buildings beside the mill. "What's in those two buildings over there?"

"Storage," said Machín as his eyes moved across the entire plantation. "Cancio will be hindered but not out of business and more important, we will have the attention of the entire province."

Including the attention of the Spanish army. None of the men fooled themselves into thinking their task was without risk. Even if they did make it back to Piro, under a banner of victory, they were at the mercy of the peasants. Betrayal could be more disastrous than finding themselves face to face with Spanish soldiers.

"Yes, it is an act of war," Machín explained. "But this is *our* country."

They observed the plantation until it became as quiet as a lake in the dead of night. After the sun set, the sweet smell of caramelized sugar and dying coals wafted from the boiling room.

Lamps burned inside the mansion and illuminated the rooms for Machín and his men, who crouched in the weeds just outside. Testifonte could be seen in the dining area with his son and daughter while a plump mulatto housemaid circled the room and tended to the family dinner.

It was the first time any of the rebels and seen the wealthy sugar planter in person. Testifonte was dignified but informal, rarely wearing a suit and tie, and tonight he dined in a thin white shirt with an opened collar. Dark hair was lined with streaks of gray and he wore a small moustache like a man from a Greco painting. His skin was smooth and youthful, unblemished by hours in the sun like his workers and characteristic of a career spent almost entirely behind a desk.

Known as *caciques* in Spain, men like Testifonte held the power and ruled politics, agriculture and real estate. They considered themselves family people who prided themselves on the purity of their race. Testifonte often told Olympia and her older brother Hector of the myths of Don Pelayo, who lead Gothic nobles to victory against Moorish invaders at Covadonga. "Asturias is the only real Spain," Testifonte would say. "The rest is conquered territory."

While Testifonte's father and brother were captains of finance and government, he'd made his fortune in sugar. And since most *peninsulares* hired only Spaniards, thousands of Cubans remained unemployed. Testifonte tried to shield his children from the prostitution and robbery that resulted and even hired a bodyguard to accompany his daughter between the plantation and her school. Victims of poverty were attracted to crime and banditry and until now, Testifonte had been lucky to avoid confrontation with these clever and mischievous men.

As he inspected the family from afar, Machín said, "The son should be dealt with cautiously and appropriately."

Beside the planter was Hector, a healthy young man in his early twenties who looked athletic and near his physical prime. He resembled his father in every way, including the moustache, open collar and flawless skin.

At the opposite end of the table was Testifonte's seventeen-year-old daughter Olympia, whose appearance was pure and untarnished. The girl's black hair was wound in perfect braids and she had clean, olive skin like the wealthy women of Southern Spain. Machín smiled when he saw the pretty, young girl. "A clear child of the indoors," he remarked. "Her father will pay a fortune to have her returned safely from the cesspool of peasant society." He laughed and imagined tens of thousands of pesos in ransom, enough to purchase a horse for every one of his men and feed all of Piro for a month.

The bandits returned to camp and the following morning the rebel leader gathered his men and reviewed the plan. "We'll wait until dark. Once the guards are eliminated we'll storm the mansion like a hurricane. For the rest of the day, we rest."

And so they rested, until dusk when they formed a column and marched down the hill to the Cancio plantation. Once it was dark, they formed a perimeter around the north side of the property and on Machín's signal, they lit their torches.

Testifonte was in bed and drifting towards sleep as faint voices called him into a dream, and then the sound of ceramic pots shattered on the cement outside and forced his eyes open. Men were shouting and Testifonte realized the voices and hollers did not belong to his staff. He knew instantly that his plantation was in terrible trouble.

When he sat up, he looked through his bedroom window and saw orange flames down below. The fields were on fire! He threw his sheets away and jumped out of bed.

Machín's men moved swiftly across the plantation and illuminated the night with their flames. Torches were thrown upon the palm-thatched roofs of the storage huts and into the workers' dwellings. The guards had been immediately ambushed and neutralized with a pair of gunshots and the bandits carried their fire into the cane fields, which became a curtain of white light.

As he torched the sugar cane Salvador thought of his parents and remembered the sight of the family *bohio* crumbling under an orange fireball. Now Salvador carried the torch and was invigorated as he turned it against the same aristocracy that had murdered his parents and made him an orphan. The sweet odor of simmering sugar and ash overtook the estate and Salvador felt great satisfaction watching the Cancio empire burn into worthless curtains of smoke.

A plantation that had been silent and sleepy just moments ago now clamored with commotion. Men with machetes and torches screamed and yelled like true warriors and ran every direction smashing flower pots and useless, petty trinkets that seemed to be the height of self-indulgence. Gunshots echoed across the hills as the bandits fired their weapons and torched plantation buildings before the inhabitants had time to react.

Testifonte moved quickly for a man over fifty. Once out of bed he hurried across the hall to Olympia's room. The girl was awake and sitting upright in bed, frozen, waiting anxiously, knowing that someone would soon arrive. She gasped when she saw a man's shadow in her bedroom doorway and relaxed slightly when her father came forth.

Before Testifonte could say anything there was a terrible crash from the first floor, like a bull had charged through the front door at full speed and then ran headfirst into a dining room table set with plates and glasses for morning breakfast.

Machín and his men charged into the house and shattered windows, torched the curtains and carpet, and used their machetes to hack at the furniture and smash every breakable object of affluence in sight. Wine glasses and fancy pottery flew across the dining room and exploded against the walls with bursts of glass and debris. The downstairs was filled with dust, dirt, and smoke almost immediately as the bandits ran through every room like rabid wild animals, energized by the hot blood of war and revolution.

Testifonte's son Hector appeared on the grand staircase with rifle in hand, but before he could load a shot, he was overwhelmed by men and his rifle confiscated. Two men held him down while Machín led a charge up the stairs and found Testifonte in the hallway shielding Olympia, who huddled terrified behind him. The sugar planter stood defiant, his arms angled back to form a wedge around his daughter. His chest swelled as he looked down his nose at Machín.

The sugar planter and the rebel leader stood face to face.

Machín signaled to his men to halt behind him as he smiled at Testifonte. His grin was captivating, almost as if he was ready to sit down with Testifonte and discuss business. It became a quiet scene with the sounds of crackling embers downstairs and the flickering yellow flames outside reminding everyone of the emergency they faced, yet Machín was relaxed. He said to Testifonte, "Good evening, sir. We did not mean to wake you and your family from their quiet slumber, but as you can see, your property is in danger and we have come to rescue your daughter from the fires."

Machín extended his left hand for Olympia as if expecting Testifonte to be so charmed as to step aside and surrender his daughter.

Instead, Testifonte puckered his lips and spat towards Machín's hand. The rebel leader smiled. "Good sir, you have no time for these juvenile antics, for the fires desperately need your attention."

"You are heathens!" shouted Testifonte. "Thugs! Beggars with rifles! Get out of my house and return to the alleys and live off the filth from which you were spawned!"

As smoke filled the hallway and obstructed their vision Machín said, "Neither of us have time for discussion. Salvador! Take the girl!"

Salvador appeared beside Machín and saw Olympia Cancio de la Serna up close for the first time. As she peeked out from behind her father, Salvador first thought she looked frightened. He instantly remembered his parents and thought of how he must have looked when the Spanish burned *his* house. But then a fleeting look of calm passed over her and made Salvador question his assumptions. There was something inquisitive and searching about her, as if she could just as easily have been watching him through her window.

Testifonte stepped forward to challenge Salvador. "Take me instead."

Juan Carlos unsheathed his machete and held it under Testifonte's chin. "Cooperate and you will save your family and possibly this house."

Testifonte froze under the blade as Salvador reached behind him and grabbed Olympia by the wrist. The girl yelped but offered little resistance as the bandits disappeared with her into the smoke. They ran from the burning house and escaped into the night with Testifonte's most prized possession thrown like a bunch of bananas over the shoulder of Salvador Ortiz.

Chapter 3

The village of Piro was less than two miles from the Cancio plantation. Olympia was taken to a small *bohío* where she was watched by one of Machín's men. Unable to sleep and not wanting to touch her bare feet to the dirty floor of the hut, she kept her legs coiled beneath her as she sat on the hut's uncomfortable cot and slapped at the bugs. She remained awake until morning.

When sunlight broke Olympia got her first look at Piro and the dreadful Cuban peasant lifestyle. There had been an obvious absence of occupancy in her hut. Smaller than her bedroom, it consisted of shaky walls made from wooden boards that supported a rickety, thatched roof. The dirt floor was littered with sticks, leaves, old bottles and empty cans. A few empty wooden boxes were cluttered in the corner as if someone had thrown them in from outside, and there was a wooden table covered with rusted pieces of farming equipment and dirty rags. It was an entirely depressing scene devoid of clothes, jewelry boxes, a comfortable bed, or the many perfumes arranged on Olympia's dresser at home.

The small village was scattered with huts of similar style and size. Most had small gardens, and some had a horse or an ox tied to a post or a tree outside. A small creek ran through the village and there was a single stone well in the center of Piro where a pair of peasants filled water buckets. Olympia couldn't imagine drinking water that came from a well shared by a hundred people or living in a house so small.

She realized then, as she observed their dirty faces and shoddy clothes, that the bandits were not rogue wanderers merely passing through and using Piro as their base. They were the sons, fathers, and husbands of these peasants. Banditry was the economy of this village. A way of life. Olympia was convinced that she was not prepared to relinquish her comfortable lifestyle. She wanted to go home.

Three days later Machín and his men returned to the plantation. The fire had burned several workers' huts to the ground, the brick storage huts had been blackened by flames, and their wooden roofs had burnt and crumbled. The mansion had survived the attack but most of the furniture from the first floor was sitting outside on the lawn in charred pieces. Windows broken during the assault had been patched with boards but worst of all was the cane field. Nearly an acre had been charred black and the stalks rimming the hotspot suffered from burns and smoke damage.

Machín and Salvador met Testifonte on the porch. Hector stood behind his father with rifle in hand, and Salvador noticed six new men had been hired as guards. Testifonte knew that somewhere in the wilderness, somewhere close, bandits watched and waited with Olympia.

"I will pay no more than ten thousand pesos," Testifonte announced. "And I want a guarantee that neither my property nor my family will be harmed again."

Machín somberly shook his head. Salvador was fascinated to see the young negotiator at work. "We can make no guarantee without tribute," said the rebel leader.

"I am a landowner and will not be bullied. I should send my men to invade your village and take my daughter back by force!"

Machín laughed. "I count six guards, Don Cancio, whereas I have twenty men and the protection of an entire village."

"The Spanish army should raze that settlement!"

"Choose your words carefully," Machín warned. "For the Spanish could easily mistake your daughter for one of us."

Testifonte scowled and glanced at his son, who waited for his father's next move. The sugar planter reached into his pocket, removed a small leather pouch and handed it to Machín. "That is five thousand pesos. Return my daughter and I will pay the rest."

"Fifteen thousand is our price for your daughter. For another ten I can guarantee the safety of your family for one year, and I will ensure that your plantation is protected."

Testifonte scoffed. "What is this, a criminal demanding a tribute?"

"Or we can take your daughter back to camp and you can send your men to remove her by force."

Testifonte glared at Machín for a long time. The planter saw a young man who believed that his deeds were noble, who considered himself a hero among his people and to his society. Testifonte was not just dealing with men who held his daughter, but with an entire social order opposed to his success. The Ten Years' War had ended at Zanjón, but the conflict continued, humbling the sugar planter and leaving him no leverage.

Machín and his men returned to Piro like lords of the mountains with bags of money in their hands. Machín distributed payment to his men and gave the rest to the villagers, making him an instant hero and celebrity in Piro. Word of his success and generosity spread throughout the province, along with a humorous story of how Testifonte Cancio had referred to Machín's men as thugs.

"The people are happy to have among us such a generous fellow!" an old man happily told Machín. The rebel leader was faced with an influx of new recruits and had enough money to buy a horse for every member of his army. As his power and prestige increased, Machín was dubbed El Matón del Pueblo, the People's Thug, and began his stint as the most popular, most respected bandit in all of Pinar del Río.

Olympia returned to her home forever changed. For during her short time with the peasants, and through no fault of her own, Olympia Cancio de la Serna, age seventeen, had become pregnant.

Chapter 4

She hid it from her father for as long as she could, but after six months, Testifonte could no longer ignore that his daughter's once graceful walk had become an awkward waddle. He was reminded of how Olympia's mother had walked when she was carrying. "You are pregnant," he finally said.

"Yes," Olympia responded wearily, fearing the invective she knew she was about to receive but relieved at no longer having to hide her belly.

"You are seventeen and unmarried! Who did it?"

She would not tell. At first Testifonte suspected it to be one of his hired hands who would surely crave a pure and pleasant girl like Olympia. For days he interrogated her, and named man after man, until he had gone through every employee, every associate who had been to the house, even certain men from town, and concluded none were responsible. Then Testifonte pinpointed the conception to the time when Olympia had been in the hands of bandits, but she stole away to her room and locked herself inside.

Testifonte pounded on the bedroom door. "Which bandit is the father of this child? Name him or I will throw you out!"

Olympia shouted through the door. "You would renounce your own blood!"

"My blood has disgraced not only this house but the Cancio family name!"

The impregnation of Testifonte's unwed daughter at the hands of a Cuban bandit meant for catastrophic social and financial implications. Testifonte thought of his business associates and his fellow sugar planters. What would they think if they knew his first grandchild was a child of the peasant class? How could he have allowed his daughter to breed with such filth?

Olympia remained in her room and watched the busy plantation outside. The roofs of the storage huts had been replaced and the cane field had started to grow where it had been torched by the bandits. Men of the plantation were back to work in the field while donkeys hauled carts of sugar down the road to Pinar del Río.

But everywhere was evidence of the bandits' raid. Black streaks on the brick walls of the storage huts marked where the fires had burned. There were stumps of sugar cane topped with black ashes speckled throughout the field, scars left by Machín's men. Scars like the one she carried in her belly.

She considered hiding in a cart bound for the city and seeking refuge in town where her baby could be born without the scrutiny of her father. But she did not know how to support herself. She did not know how to be resourceful like the villagers from Piro and conserve every last crumb. She didn't even know how to cook.

Now Testifonte returned to Olympia's room and quietly knocked on the door. "Olympia, please talk to me."

The door opened, and his daughter stood before him, her face a mess of stringy hair matted by tears. "I was not corrupted by choice. It was their leader, the one called Machín. He took me into a hut and forced himself upon me. And if you disown me because of this, then my baby will only know the story that I tell. That one day my father died before my eyes and that I was orphaned and forced to find my own way."

Testifonte was devastated. A rape and unwanted pregnancy was disastrous, a pure tragedy. His youngest child had been corrupted by the men who descended with torches from the hills. If the local sugar planters knew Testifonte was raising a child of bandits, he would be outcast and ostracized. The men responsible had to pay. Testifonte vowed to get back at Machín's men in due time, but first the blood of heathens could not reside on his estate.

He pointed a finger at Olympia. "You will stay, but this bandit-child will not! You cannot bring the blood of delinquents into this home."

"So instead of cutting off one of your limbs, you will sever one of mine!" Olympia retreated into her room and slammed the door.

Testifonte could hear her struggling to push her nightstand across the room until it finally thumped in place behind the door.

He left her alone.

In the weeks that followed Olympia avoided her father whenever possible. At night, she locked her bedroom door, afraid that men would sneak in and take her away. When she summoned the courage to join her family at dinner, she was forced to endure her father's reproachful stare. Sometimes she would skip meals altogether, only to steal food from the kitchen in the middle of the night when she could no longer tolerate the hunger.

Word of Olympia's pregnancy began to leak to the plantation's employees and soon, as the gossip spread throughout the province, Testifonte's business associates began inquiring about Olympia's pregnancy. He downplayed the situation and denied the father was a Cuban bandit while he simultaneously offered a bounty of fifty thousand pesos for the head of Victoriano Machín. Testifonte's rage nearly drove him mad. He feared what the *caciques* in Spain would do if they learned of the situation, and conjured outrageous scenarios of Spanish elites banishing the Cancio family from their circle the way Adam and Eve were sent from the garden by God. The thought that his first grandchild would be the product of rape drove him to consult with a local Spanish doctor.

"I know of several abortifacients," said Dr. Sanchez. "Some are more gruesome than others."

"What if I wanted it to be a secret?"

The doctor was surprised. "I do not understand. How could it be a secret?"

Testifonte explained the situation. "I see," the doctor said. "In this case, I would recommend an herbal remedy. Some have used black snakeroot, but its smell is unpleasant and would be difficult to administer. I would suggest something with a more attractive taste. A tea of pennyroyal and brewer's yeast yields a peppermint taste but the pennyroyal herb is highly toxic. It is a safe and certain abortive. The tea will initiate menstrual flow and induce labor."

"Very well." Testifonte decided on the herbal tea which he purchased from Sanchez that day. A week later, as Olympia stood at her window and watched the plantation, the portly housemaid Gloria knocked gently on her bedroom door and cracked it open. "Señorita Olympia, I have brought you a refreshment."

Gloria set a tray with a teapot and cup on a small table near the door. Without another word, Gloria turned and left, closing the door behind her. Olympia watched the plantation, where her brother supervised a group of workers who cut sugar cane and loaded it onto an ox-drawn cart. Across the property near the sugar mill, Olympia saw two men load another cart with bags of sugar that were ready to be taken to Pinar del Río for sale. Again she considered running away to live in the city by herself.

She left the window and poured herself a steaming cup of tea that smelled pleasantly of peppermint and lemon. Taking her cup to bed she relaxed with a book, *Beyond the Sierra Morena,* a Spanish tale of romance and adventure, and rested one arm over her belly as she sipped her drink. It warmed and relaxed her and by time she had finished the cup, Olympia was fast asleep.

She awoke an hour later with pain in her abdomen and dampness between her legs. She reached below the covers and when she pulled her hand out, it was completely covered in blood. Olympia was struck by a purely animal terror and in her horror she screamed – for the servant, for her father, for God. She tried to get out of bed but collapsed onto the floor. Testifonte, who had been in the house awaiting the results of the tea, burst into the room and saw the bloody mess that was his child's bed, and her slumped body curled into a ball on the floor.

"My child!" he called out as he rushed to her side. Though it was something he should have expected, the sight of bloody bed sheets made Testifonte physically ill. All of the money he had amassed in Cuba, his contacts within the Spanish government of Havana, his reputation in Madrid seemed worthless if his daughter was to die. Olympia screamed hysterically. Her breathing was heavy, and she was soon drenched in sweat.

Testifonte knew he had gone too far. He realized how desperate her unexpected pregnancy had made him and now he prayed his selfishness had not caused the death of his daughter, so weak and so vulnerable. But buried deep in the back of his mind, in the darkest corner of human reality, was the thought that it may be possible to save Olympia without saving the baby.

"Doctor," he said as a horrified Gloria hurried into the room. "We must take you to a doctor!"

"No!" Olympia cried and shook her head. "Do not take me to a butcher!"

Testifonte was desperate. He pleaded, "I will bring a doctor here!"

Olympia shook her head, but the shock was so intense that she passed out.

Testifonte rushed out to find Dr. Sanchez. He cursed the man whose potion seemed to be killing his daughter, but the doctor explained defensively that there were side effects and that since he had not been there to administer the tea, he was not responsible for the reaction.

"Please come to the house and examine her," pleaded Testifonte.

Testifonte, Hector, and Gloria watched the doctor's examination from the corner of Olympia's room. Olympia was back on her bed with clean sheets; the bleeding had stopped, and she had been sedated considerably. When Dr. Sanchez was finished, he asked to speak privately to Testifonte. "If I were to leave right now, both the baby and mother would survive. However, if you still want to go through with your original intention, arrangements can be made. Your daughter could find herself in a situation where she had simply lost the baby."

A chance to terminate the pregnancy was an opportunity to regain the respect he had lost in the business community and to save his reputation. But was it worth the cost of his daughter's happiness? The girl had already been devastated by the circumstances, and Testifonte feared the loss of the baby would injure her further and simply drive her mad.

Testifonte reached into his pocket and handed Dr. Sanchez a few coins. "Thank you Doctor, but I will care for my daughter."

Olympia recovered quickly, and her baby was born a healthy girl. Olympia omitted the surname of the baby's father and used only her own, naming her daughter Josefina Cancio. And though the baby was born at the mansion, her father chose not to remain inside the house during the delivery but sat outside on the porch and smoked a cigar. He visited Olympia's bedroom afterward, took only a quick glance at the baby, and turned and walked out.

Testifonte had been overwhelmed with guilt. He could hardly look his daughter in the eye and the sight of the baby, a fragile and innocent child he had tried to kill, made Testifonte feel like the villains from the hills. His reputation had been damaged, and his relationship with his daughter was beyond repair. He spent that night in the church, begging for God's forgiveness.

Once the shock of the incident had passed and the pain of childbirth subsided, one thought lingered in Olympia's mind. A peppermint tea was unlike anything she had ever tasted, and only one time had it ever been served. She asked Hector if he had ever tasted the mysterious concoction but he hadn't. The connection was obvious: the tea had made her sick.

She had been poisoned by her own father.

Instantly Olympia became sick to her stomach, an illness that lasted for days. She remained in her bed, outraged and unable eat. What man would deliver poison to his own child and attempt to abort her firstborn? The evil that lurked in her home drove Olympia to decide that men like her father; men of land, men of riches and money, bankers, planters and politicians – all of them were men that she hated.

Olympia then confronted Gloria who said, "I knew your father brought the tea from a doctor, but I thought it was something to help you rest, since your belly was causing pain in your back and chest."

Olympia pressed her for the truth and Gloria finally admitted that she suspected the potion could be harmful, but that Testifonte insisted it was for Olympia's own good. "I am only a servant of your father." Gloria shamefully hung her head. "I have little influence over his mind."

The act of betrayal by Gloria convinced Olympia that she could no longer live at the plantation. Her father would never accept Josefina as anything other than the disgraceful product of Olympia's corruption. The baby of a bandit. Yet Olympia did not know where else she could go; in her father's house they were fed and bedded. She needed to be where the baby could be cared for. Again she considered running away to live in Pinar del Río or going as far as Havana. As she fed Josefina through her breast, she wondered constantly which direction to go.

Her fate was decided, days later, by the return of El Matón.

*   *   *

The gunshots erupted in the early morning, just as the sun broke over the eastern hills but before any of Testifonte's workers had awakened. The bandits stormed the property on horseback, surprising and overwhelming Testifonte's modest contingent of six armed guards, and killed two before the rest surrendered. Olympia barricaded herself in her room and watched from the window as twenty-five horsemen surrounded the mansion like a cavalry of desperados, rifles and shotguns in hand, with machetes hanging from their belts.

El Matón's army had grown in the last year. They were more numerous, more organized, more disciplined. He still wore a red kerchief around his neck but it was now leather instead of cloth. The bullets that crisscrossed his chest seemed brighter, the bandit leader's hair was longer and shinier and he looked more confident than ever before. Sitting atop a healthy black horse El Matón fired his rifle into the air and defiantly called for Testifonte to emerge. "Señor Cancio! Come forth and renew our pact or watch your plantation burn!"

At that the bandits produced unlit torches, and prepared to carry fire across the property. Olympia cracked her window open and held Josefina in her arms as she knelt below the windowsill to listen. It was the first time since the birth that Olympia had seen Josefina's father, and she was tempted to broker some kind of introduction between them. His smile, his charisma, those dark emerald eyes, though evil as they were, had become part of Olympia. She saw those features every time she looked upon her child.

Now she saw her father and brother emerge from the house and start shouting at the bandits. She could not make out her father's words but El Matón laughed and said, "Who knows how many of your guards we have bribed already? If we were to torch your fields, could you rely on your foot soldiers to avert an army of horsemen?"

"You," Testifonte pointed at El Matón. "Have a price on your head for what you have done to my daughter! All of you have been branded outlaws by the Spanish authorities, who will execute the people of Piro until none remain except old women and children!"

Olympia pulled her window closed and moved out of view.

Down on the lawn, Machín shouted to Testifonte. "You cannot risk more damage to your crop. Agree to another tribute, good sir, this time twenty thousand pesos in exchange for a promise that we will ignore your sugar fields for another year. This agreement will protect your next harvest."

With great reluctance, knowing Machín had the advantage, Testifonte agreed.

The bandits rode from the plantation with El Matón at the front and Salvador Ortiz guarding the rear. The young bandit was not five minutes from the mansion when Salvador saw a sudden, frantic rustling in the bushes beside him. He halted his horse while the others trotted ahead, and reached for his rifle, but was startled when a young girl wearing a white dress jumped onto the path ahead of him. Her black hair was damp and messed about her face, with leaves and tiny sticks caught in the strands, and she was out of breath. Panting with her face flushed, Salvador noticed she wore a sling around her neck like a bandolier that cradled a tiny infant. It took only a moment before he recognized this girl as Testifonte's daughter.

"Why not take the path?" He said. "It will be much easier on your feet."

Olympia took a moment to catch her breath. Then, almost pleading she said to him, "Kidnap me!"

Salvador laughed incredulously. "What?"

"Kidnap me now, you fool!"

He laughed again and leaned down to speak directly to her. "That is ridiculous."

"I have run away from home and have nowhere else to go!"

Salvador glanced back to the mansion and realized he could be caught in a trap set by Testifonte. The planter sends his daughter into the brush to confront the bandits, seemingly by herself, but armed men wait in the bushes ready to strike. Salvador gripped the reins and kicked his horse. "Run back home, I am sure your father misses you."

He tried to maneuver his horse around her but the girl stood in his way, so he circled her, his eyes constantly scanning the surrounding bushes.

"I am not going home!" she insisted. "If you will not take me, then take my baby!" She began to untie her sling.

Salvador wondered if the girl was a bit mad. He relaxed a bit, no longer threatened by Testifonte's imaginary men. "Señorita, I hope you realize that there is no way I will take your baby with me."

"My father will kill her if I return!"

"You are exaggerating. What father would murder his daughter's child?"

"He has already tried to kill both her and me."

The girl was emotional, her eyes welled with tears and her face desperately waited for him to take her. Behind her fear, underneath the cosmetics of affluence responsible for her smooth skin and healthy hair, Salvador saw an attractive and appealing girl nearly his age. He said, "I find it difficult to believe that a man exists who does not completely adore his grandchild."

"Please," she begged. "I will pay you for a ride to Pinar del Río."

Salvador realized that the girl was adamant to escape from whatever drove her into the forest. When Olympia saw Salvador was not convinced she said, "Take me back to your camp, you fool! My child and I are worth a fortune!"

He admired the idea. This was a girl who thought like a rebel. "Are you suggesting we ransom you back to your father? I thought he didn't want you."

"Perhaps he will come to his senses after I disappear."

"But will you want to return?"

"You're going to have to gamble." She smiled slightly, with a subtle twinkle. "Kidnap me."

It was quite the gamble. Salvador surveyed the line of trees before him for any signs of an ambush. The rest of his rebel gang had continued along the path and were far ahead, leaving Salvador alone and virtually defenseless. The daughter of Testifonte Cancio stood before him, baby in arms, her lower lip nervously mashed between her teeth. She had no intention of returning home. But Salvador thought about the people of Piro, the money he could raise if they were able to ransom the girl and her child. Salvador would be a hero, revered by the people, canonized in legend like El Matón.

He offered a hand to the girl. "Have you ever ridden a horse? I named her Chani, after my mother."

When Salvador's horse trotted into Piro, the young brunette sitting atop was quickly recognized as Olympia Cancio, the planter's daughter who had been with them a year ago. The rebels cheered Salvador, who tried to explain that she came to him by chance but the men dismissed Salvador's modesty and praised his catch. They gathered around Chani and when they saw Olympia carried a newborn baby, they calculated a fortune in Salvador's impossible deed. He had brought back two prizes to be ransomed instead of one!

El Matón appeared in the crowd and came forward to greet Olympia, bowing graciously before her. "It is a pleasure to welcome you back to Piro, Señorita. I promise this visit will be pleasant."

Olympia averted her eyes and did not respond. As Salvador helped Olympia and Josefina off his horse, he saw Josefina's face up close for the first time. He knew instantly that those dark, friendly eyes belonged to El Matón. He had suspected the rebel leader to be the father – El Matón had told him about the night he had shared with Olympia over one year ago, and Salvador could tell from Olympia's defensive posture that it was not a memory she cherished.

She stayed with Salvador and remained in his *bohío* for many days, emerging only in the morning and at night for fresh air. Salvador waited with her, fulfilling her unspoken wish to be guarded from El Matón, but the couple hardly interacted. When Olympia wasn't tending to her baby, she curled up in the corner of the cot and read from an adventure novel she had brought with her.

One morning, Olympia could hear men talking outside the hut and then Salvador entered with El Matón and Juan Carlos in tow. The rebel leader stood in the doorway with Juan Carlos while Salvador sat on the hut's single chair. El Matón eyed the baby with a curious smile. "What is her name?"

Olympia held her close and rocked her gently. It took her a moment to decide, but finally she said, "Josefina."

"Olympia," said Salvador. "We have come to discuss the conditions of your return."

She shuddered. Since stealing away from the mansion several days before, Olympia had not entertained the idea of returning to live with Testifonte. "I will never return."

El Matón was not bothered by her sincerity. "You must return to that big, stone mansion, Señorita, for we plan to abduct you again next year."

Salvador said, "Doesn't a girl your age belong at home with her family?"

Olympia was insulted. "This coming from a man who runs through the countryside cheating and stealing! Don't lecture me on Spanish family values, Salvador. I am no child. I am old enough to be on my own. Now take me to Pinar del Río and leave me there!"

El Matón said, "Your mother will miss you."

"My mother died from smallpox when I was four."

They were silent for a moment. Then Salvador said, "Perhaps an arrangement can be made that will accommodate both parties. We will ransom Olympia and the baby back to Testifonte, and then take them into the city."

The others were confused. Juan Carlos asked, "How is that possible?"

Salvador explained, and once an agreement had been reached, Juan Carlos and El Matón left Salvador and the girls alone. Salvador reached into his pocket and produced a cigar. He sat back on his chair and crossed his legs as he struck a match and lit the end. He blew smoke into the air. "Being an outlaw is no easy profession."

She laughed. "It is no profession."

"Oh, but it is hard work to stay alive when legitimate employment is scarce. We do not rob and ransom for pleasure, you see. There are times when we are so poor we do not eat for days. Or we travel the countryside foraging for scraps, unable to cultivate land like your father. The growth of plantations like your father's has driven the peasant farmer off his land. I was forced from my parents' farm when I was just a boy. That expensive mansion where you rest your head has shielded you. From your bedroom you cannot see the depression that has ruined Cuba. You cannot see the peasants who are forced to wander from place to place in

41

search of livelihood. If men like your father would hire Cubans instead of closing the ranks to Spaniards and slaves, things would be different."

He sat back and puffed on his cigar. Olympia watched and listened, feeling almost humbled to hear a bandit's version of her father's battle. Salvador continued, "Cheating and stealing has become an adequate means of survival. To your father, we are outlaws, but to the destitute we are nobles who plunder from the wealthy to provide for the poor. This village could not survive without us. In our society, the bandit is a hero, a man who, with the peasants, shares the same enemy."

"Then we also share the same enemy, Salvador. For my father is mine." She looked to Salvador and though neither of them said another word, Olympia felt strangely safe.

A week later, El Matón and his men rode to the Cancio plantation to arrange Olympia's ransom but returned with complications. "My daughter returns," Testifonte had said. "But without the baby."

"You see?" Olympia said when she heard the news. "He has not repented. He would rather have me dead than to let my child sleep under his roof. What did you say?"

Salvador and El Matón shrugged their shoulders. "What could we say?" said Salvador. "We refused on the grounds that we will not intervene in a family affair. We are ruthless scoundrels, as your father says, but we will not separate mother from child."

"What are you going to do?" she asked.

"I will take you to Pinar del Río," said Salvador. "But first, I am asking for your trust."

"What do you mean?"

He explained and after a long hour of negotiation, Olympia agreed to go back to the mansion, without her baby. The next day, El Matón and a group of his men returned to the Cancio plantation on horseback. Like the last time they had bartered Olympia for ransom, she remained guarded at the edge of the property while El Matón and Juan Carlos rode forth to collect the money.

Testifonte saw that his daughter was safe and without the baby. He did not ask about the infant but instead handed El Matón a pouch filled with money, nodded curtly and waited as Olympia was brought to him.

Her eyes did not meet his and were instead sullen and filled with tears; she was clearly devastated by her decision. As the bandits rode away and disappeared into the woods, Testifonte followed his daughter into the house.

"I am pleased you have come to your senses. The baby would only face ridicule and disgrace, as would our entire family, my dear. Now I can once again claim you as my own." He tried to reach forward and hug her, but Olympia moved away and said nothing. With her eyes on the floor, she shuffled away like a sick woman living her final days. She climbed the stairs and disappeared into her room. As he watched her go, Testifonte realized the damage to his daughter was significant but repairable with time. He was happy that she was home and relieved that he would not have to admit the folly of his ways.

Parting with Josefina was the most painful thing Olympia had ever done. It left her colorless, like after her mother died. The worry she felt was beyond imagination. Could this child survive in the hands of an outlaw, even one like Salvador who she oddly trusted? She made the sacrifice knowing Josefina would be better off and would grow up in an environment free of Testifonte's threats. It was also an act of nobility, Olympia convinced herself. She was not aiding the outlaws but helping the poor and starving people of Piro.

But Olympia was miserable. As she sat in her bedroom and thought of the possibilities, the knot in her stomach drove her to bed where she remained sobbing and unable to move. How could she have left her baby in the hands of a bandit? She could hear her mother's voice, chastising her from heaven, scolding Olympia for her terrible decision. By now they could have sold the baby, or taken Josefina back to Piro to be killed.

Olympia hollered in despair, her cries were heard throughout the halls of that great stone mansion. Testifonte, knowing they were sobs of sadness, hoped it would soon pass.

She rolled onto her back and stared at the ceiling, said a prayer and begged for God's forgiveness. She would need to see a priest when the ordeal was over, to confess her sin of leaving Josefina. God might forgive her, but would she ever be able to forgive herself?

The sun set outside and when Gloria brought dinner, Olympia refused. She had no appetite and even if she did, she did not deserve to eat. Finally she heard the family turning in for the night and when she heard her father's bedroom door close, she was tempted to jump from her bed, run outside and retrieve Josefina but she resisted the urge. She needed to wait until all were asleep or risk being heard and followed.

Another unbearable hour passed and finally Olympia rose from her bed, packed a bag and checked herself in her bedroom mirror. It would be the last time she saw herself in the wide glass that sat atop her cherry brown credenza, a mirror bordered with dark brown birch wood and lined with gold. Her face was soaked red with tears; she was unable to look herself in the eye and instead used a silk handkerchief to wipe the smudges of moisture from her face.

She hated herself for what she had done, but it was time to go out now, time to leave this house and never return. She took her bag, slipped out of her room and tiptoed down the hallway.

Salvador was hunched behind a row of bushes near the rear of the mansion with Josefina bundled in his arms. As he watched the child rest, he remained fascinated that Olympia had trusted him. She had done what she needed to do to escape her father's hate and Salvador admired the young woman's bravery. With the bloodline she possessed, how could Josefina grow up to be anything but a valiant and fearless little girl?

Salvador heard the sound of light footsteps fluttering across the grass. He looked to the mansion and saw it was completely dark with only a single lamp flickering in one of the downstairs windows. He held the baby close, ready to flee but soon saw Olympia emerge from the darkness wearing a nightgown and sandals and carrying a small knapsack.

She moved quickly and silently, her eyes overflowing with tears and fixated on the bundle in Salvador's arms. She cried uncontrollably as she snatched her baby from Salvador and held her close. Relieved to have Josefina back in her arms and unable to forgive herself, Olympia sobbed and kissed every inch of her baby's face.

"I'm so sorry, Fina!" she cried as she hugged her baby. Apologizing over and over again, she lost herself in her own arms; the baby became her universe and nothing else existed.

Finally she felt Salvador tugging her arm. "Come, Olympia! We must be swift!" He took her bag and helped her to her feet. Still holding Josefina close and without looking back to the mansion, Olympia mounted Chani and held onto Salvador as he gripped the reins and kicked off.

Piro greeted them with a celebration. Testifonte's ransom money had been used to prepare a feast for peasants and rebels alike. They dined together on long wooden tables setup in the center of town – a pair of *bandidos* strummed guitars and sang folk tunes as the crowd toasted over roasted pork, beer, wine, cigars and rum.

When Salvador and Olympia appeared atop Chani, the crowd cheered and El Matón approached them with a bottle of rum in each hand. He raised the bottles to Olympia and proclaimed, "All hail the daughter, and granddaughter, of Testifonte Cancio!" The crowd cheered again and Olympia, daughter of the hated Spanish aristocrat, became the guest of honor.

As Salvador jumped off his horse and helped Olympia and Josefina to the ground, El Matón handed him a small leather pouch filled with coins. "Here are one thousand pesos, a well-deserved bonus for the work you have done."

Salvador snatched the money and a bottle of rum from El Matón and joined the party. The feast lasted long into the night, and the men got rowdier the more they drank. Salvador remained at a table with Olympia and Josefina and tended to them while they dined. Olympia, who had been given a well worn dress by one of the peasant women, was relieved to be free of her father, but frightened at the unknown future that waited. Nonetheless she was comforted to be with a man she could trust, at least for now.

When the roast pig had been eaten to the bone, the mugs and bottles were empty, and the smell of charcoal lingered in the air, the people began to drift back to their homes to make love or pass out into inebriated slumber. As Salvador walked Olympia back to his *bohio* where she would sleep, he heard the sound of approaching horses.

Salvador had heard that same sound seven years ago, before his father rushed in and begged him to run for his life. Salvador could hear

Ernesto's voice shouting, "Go now, boy! Step lively and don't look back!"

Moments later a group of Spanish soldiers on horseback burst into Piro. Bandits ran for cover and reached for their rifles, but bloated bellies filled with food and booze made them sluggish, and almost useless defenders of their town. The Spanish had timed it perfectly, aided by a tip from Testifonte Cancio.

"It's an ambush!" Salvador shouted as he grabbed Olympia and pushed her towards the hut. Gunshots exploded all around, pulverizing Olympia's ears and nearly knocking her to the ground. She held Josefina against her breast and tried to cover the baby's ears while Salvador yanked at her arm and pulled her into his *bohio*.

He grabbed a shotgun and stuffed his leather money pouch into his belt as Piro became a loud melee of stray bullets and screams. The smell of gunpowder grew thick in the air and stung their eyes and lungs. "Keep low," Salvador said as he peeked out of his hut. Chani was just yards away, but the town seemed to be swarming with dozens of horses carrying Spanish soldiers every direction.

He saw his chance and took it, yanking Olympia out of the hut and to his horse; he had her off the ground and on the saddle in seconds. With remarkable speed Salvador was in place behind her, and with a sharp kick, Chani shot away and darted into the woods.

"Hold on tight!" he yelled as he placed the reins in her free hand. Using his legs to steady himself on the bumpy ride, he brought his shotgun to bear and aimed it at a Spanish soldier that gave chase at his flank.

Just twenty feet apart, Salvador's horse and the Spaniard's ran side by side as their riders aimed their weapons. Salvador looked down the barrel of the Spaniard's rifle and into the soldier's eyes to see a young man not much older than himself or any of the rebels in the crew.

Hardly taking the time to aim, they fired at the same time. A bullet whizzed by Salvador's ear with a snap, and his reflexes made him flinch. He hoped he would not need to fire a second shot but the soldier fell from his horse, and his steed trotted aimlessly into the woods. Salvador looked back at the fallen boy and saw the blast had hit the soldier in the face, sending him dead to the ground without a twitch. Ready to fire another shot Salvador reached around Olympia with one hand and took the reins. He watched all around for more soldiers but there were none. They were free, escaping into the forest while the sound of gunshots echoed behind them.

El Matón had been so drunk he had hardly been able to stand. When the soldiers arrived the bandit leader was slow to react, caught in the middle of them, helpless with no chance of escape. Six Spanish soldiers on horses formed a semicircle around the stumbling rebel leader and aimed their rifles.

He smiled and held a bottle of rum into the air. His red kerchief was tied clumsily around his neck and even at his final moment, the legendary outlaw was happy and defiant. He shouted, "Long live the torch!" and the soldiers fired their weapons.

Victoriano Machín, El Matón, the greatest bandit in the province of Pinar del Río, fell dead to the ground.

Salvador's horse sprinted farther and farther into the country until she could run no more. Now far from the action, Salvador halted Chani and brought her to a brook for water. Looking around them, trying to pick any evidence of Spanish soldiers out of their dark surroundings Salvador said, "The authorities are trying to purge all rebel elements from the province. We should suspect they are looking for you too."

Olympia checked Josefina and saw the baby was unhurt. "Such a brave child," she whispered. Then she looked over her shoulder to Salvador. "How long before you can return to Piro?"

"Never," Salvador said. "We must stay on the move and try to get into the city. If we reach Pinar del Río, perhaps we can masquerade as a simple peasant family. I have a thousand pesos in my pocket; maybe we can ride farther north to Havana and hide out there. Unless there's some place you have to be right now?"

The idea of hiding out as a peasant family intrigued her and charmed her sense of adventure. She had nowhere to go, no agenda, and no obligations except for the safety of her baby. It was a freedom she had never felt before, would never feel again, and a moment she would always remember.

She reached back and patted his leg. "Very well, Salvador, take your humble peasant wife and child to Havana."

Salvador nodded and kissed her cheek then tightened the reins and raced away with the planter's daughter and her child, headed for Havana as a wanted man.

Chapter 5

They rode for hours until every muscle in their bodies ached. At dawn they stopped at the base of a hill near a farm outside of Pinar del Río. Salvador tethered Chani to a tree and held Josefina while Olympia climbed to the ground. Sore all over and lacking sleep, they collapsed on the grass to rest.

As Olympia leaned her back against a giant buttress root of a Ceiba tree, she noticed that her ears still rang from the gunshots the night before. She held Josefina close to her chest and began to breastfeed the infant hoping that the child's ears had not been damaged. Salvador looked away from Olympia's exposed bosom and decided to count the pesos in his sack. He knew they would soon be out of money and would need a way to survive once they reached Havana.

He thought Olympia was engaging, and her adventurous nature appealed to Salvador, but reality soon took hold of him. An outlaw in possession of a young Spanish runaway and her baby would be executed upon capture. He considered abandoning the girls and going to Havana on his own, keeping all one thousand pesos for himself. Or he could attempt the unthinkable and ransom them back to Testifonte.

It would never work, Salvador quickly told himself. A foolish idea since it meant entering enemy territory, and having to convince Olympia to return home. He turned and saw Josefina was now sleeping in Olympia's lap; the mother had buttoned her gown and was dozing lightly with her head resting against the Ceiba root.

He asked, "Have you reconsidered?"

Though her eyes were closed, Olympia wrinkled her nose in annoyance at the question. "Reconsidered what?" She knew Salvador was taking a huge risk in transporting them to Havana and didn't expect him to stay for long.

He chose his words carefully. "Now that you are free from the confines of the plantation, you will soon see that depression and destitution are all around. The land is in ruin, the cities are filled with beggars and vagrants, no place to raise a baby. You are young. Perhaps you should return to the plantation where you will be safe?"

She sat up and snapped, "How can you say it is safe there when my father poisoned me and tried to kill my baby!"

Salvador held up his hands. "Be calm!"

Olympia sat back and closed her eyes.

"Did he really do that?"

She sat up again. "No, I made it up, you fool. Of course he served me a poisoned tea disguised with peppermint. It caused me to bleed down below and I almost lost my baby."

Her voice trailed off and seemed to grow sadder with each word. Salvador finally believed her tale. "It sounds awful."

"It was," she whispered and rested against the root and again closed her eyes.

They were quiet for the next minute. Then Salvador said, "I shouldn't have kissed you. It was uncalled-for. I'm sorry."

Olympia shifted a bit but kept her eyes closed and said nothing.

Salvador said, "I have been on my own since I was fourteen."

Olympia wanted to answer coldly and tell him to be quiet so she could rest, but there was something about this bandit that made her hesitate. He was comforting and treated her with more respect than her father made her believe she deserved. Pretending like she didn't care she asked, "What happened?"

Salvador thought back to the day his parents were killed. He said, "My father was a good man, you see, a very poor farmer like his father. And my mother had no enemies in this world. Her only crime was her marriage to a man suspected of being a rebel agent. Back then, when the Ten Years' War was raging, this was a Spanish colony even more than it is now. Cubans have since learned to fight back, to struggle for the sovereignty of their island. We never were very high on the social ladder, you see."

Now she got cold, "I know the history, thank you very much."

He rolled his eyes. "My father did not try to hide me from social injustice and taught me the value of hard work. He educated me on agriculture and hunting and even taught me how to roll a cigar on my knee with a single leaf of tobacco. But war was all around us. I remember Cuban insurgents passing through Herrera; some of them even stayed overnight in our home and dined with us the next morning. These men were heroes in my eyes, true freedom fighters."

He paused and collected his thoughts, speaking slowly, reflectively. "One night while we slept, torches were thrown into our house. My mother and father were dragged outside and both were executed by Spanish soldiers. Our home burned to the ground and I was left with nothing."

Olympia cracked an eye open, a look that told Salvador he should continue.

Salvador reached to his belt and revealed a small rusted knife with a wooden handle. "This is all I have from my father. I took it the night before he was killed. He never had a chance to notice it was missing."

Olympia watched as Salvador inspected the knife, seeming to lose himself in the intricacies of the blade. "How did you get away?"

"I ran, then I hid. I watched the entire exchange from the woods nearby. My parents were forced to their knees and shot in the head, the both of them. I ran to Pinar del Río and did what I could to feed myself. And if you can say one thing about a raggedy illiterate man like me, it is that I am a survivor."

He told more of his story: his first petty theft with Juan Carlos, meeting El Matón, their exploits as bandits. Olympia found herself fascinated by his tales and thought they were more interesting than any adventure story she had ever read. "So your father," she said. "I guess he aided the insurgents against the Spanish?"

Salvador nodded. "Of course he aided the insurgency. Like I said, my father was a good man."

"Do you still hate the Spanish?"

He looked at his shoes and nodded slowly. "Most of them."

"You killed that Spanish soldier back there, didn't you?"

Another quiet nod. "I think so."

"How many others have you killed?"

"Aside from yesterday? Only one other. A young man in Havana when I was about eighteen. I had been with Victoriano and Juan Carlos for a few years and one day we tried to rob a bakery. It didn't go so well.

Perhaps I was frightened or just plain stupid. I shot the owner and ran away."

Olympia watched him closely for any sign of remorse. She thought she saw a genuine sadness. "It is a sin to kill. Do you ever think about that?"

He shrugged. "My mother was Catholic but my father often whispered against the church and the priesthood."

"Then where do you stand with God?"

He laughed. "Who in the world can answer that question?"

Olympia straightened her hair. "I know where I stand."

"Of course," said Salvador. "You have been confined to mansions and raised by maids. I was grown in the wild. We subscribe to an entirely different creed."

Olympia became defensive. "The shelter of money did not protect me from hate or fear or arrogance."

He knew she spoke of Testifonte. "I'm sure your father will accept you if you return."

"I am sure you are a fool."

"Most Spaniards think that way of Cubans."

Olympia sat up straight and looked at him directly. "I seem childish to you, don't I? Like a foolish little girl. I have been sheltered but I am not stupid." She rose to her feet, cradling Josefina carefully as she stood. "And I am smart enough to demand that you take us to Cabo Corrientes because I would rather swim to Panama with my baby on my back than spend any more time with you!"

Salvador knew he was in trouble when he realized that he did not want her to return to the plantation, or to be anywhere that he wasn't. He shook his head and tried to appear nonchalant. "Now you are talking nonsense."

"Then we will go alone." Olympia started to walk away but Salvador called her bluff.

"There are Spanish troops out there who will return you to your father; or perhaps some of my rebel brothers will find you. Either way you will be dealing with reckless men who cannot be trusted around a young woman like yourself. And that baby..." He let his voice die as he shook his head.

She stopped and turned to glare at Salvador. "I told you, I am not stupid."

He waved his hand towards the grass. "Then be smart and let the baby rest. This area is quiet except for a few peasant farmers nearby. It is safe for now."

Faking reluctance, Olympia returned and sat on the grass with Josefina resting across her lap. Moments later both mother and child were asleep with Salvador standing guard. He paced around the Ceiba tree with a close eye on his surroundings but stole frequent glances to the young Spanish princess and her child. He knew that he could climb on his horse and leave them at that moment and be free for his own pursuits, but he didn't want to go.

There was a moral responsibility to protect the runaway, and something else was holding him back. Leaving meant being alone and without a family. He shook his head as he leaned against the tree and reached into his shirt pocket for his last cigar.

After a short nap they started moving again and at midday stopped at a farmhouse where Salvador purchased a bunch of bananas and some bread from the farmer. Hardly satisfied by her meager meal, Salvador assured Olympia that they would stop again soon. With Olympia sitting behind Salvador and Josefina resting between them, Chani trotted along a flat dirt road that stretched into the country as far as they could see.

Circumventing the city of Pinar del Río, they were soon on a straight shot to Havana and Olympia realized how far she was from home. Periodically she would turn to look around them and absorb her surroundings realizing Salvador had been right about the poverty. Outside of the plantations, Cuba was sparsely populated with shantytowns and rickety wooden huts, peasant farmhouses that were falling apart, and depressed people wearing dirty brown clothes.

Once she turned to look behind them and noticed a single man on a horse, far behind but traveling at a pace so rapid he seemed to be gliding towards them on a cloud of dust. A moment later she looked back again and saw he had closed the gap, his horse still kicking up a brown haze. "A man is following us," she said.

Salvador turned quickly and gripped the rifle that lay across his lap. He saw the rider fast approaching but said nothing so as to not alarm the girl. He turned back to the road, keeping one hand on his rifle, and formulated a plan for defense and escape.

A few minutes later the rider was just fifty yards behind them. Olympia was almost angry. "Aren't you going to do anything?"

Salvador turned again and when he got a better look at the rider, he smiled and slowed his horse to a halt. Bracing for another shootout, Olympia gripped Salvador's shoulders and hugged herself against him, hiding her eyes and protecting Josefina below. "Good to see you survived, my friend!" she heard Salvador say. She looked up and saw the rider was Juan Carlos Alvarez, marked by his crooked yellow smile and the outlier, a single dead tooth on top.

Salvador waited for Juan Carlos to catch up. "Have you heard from the others?"

Juan Carlos moved his horse alongside Salvador's and the two advanced at a slow trot. "Machín is dead," Juan Carlos said to him.

Salvador swallowed hard and thought of Josefina. The baby was now officially without a father. He wondered what Olympia would say when the child asked about him. Olympia, for the first time, wondered the exact same thing.

Juan Carlos said, "So are Reyes, García and Fuentes. The rest were captured or scattered and I am lucky to be alive. *Coño.* I suspect the Spanish were tipped off by the girl's father." Juan Carlos glanced back to Olympia, who kept her eyes hidden.

"That is a possibility," Salvador said. He turned back to Olympia. "Olympia, this man is famished, give him some food."

Reluctant but compliant, Olympia reached into the bag and tore a banana away from the bunch and handed it to Juan Carlos. He devoured it in seconds and tossed the peel aside.

"I lost my weapon," he said to Salvador.

"Take mine," Salvador said and handed his rifle to Juan Carlos, a gamble that infuriated Olympia and caused her to scold Salvador later on. He would explain that it would be easier for them to masquerade as peasants if they were unarmed. It was better to let Juan Carlos be the bandit and assume the risk.

Juan Carlos pointed to Olympia. "Let's take her back to her father. He will pay ten thousand pesos, Salvador. We will split it fifty-fifty, just like old times." He grinned and showed Salvador his single rotten tooth. Endearing at first, the dead tooth was now the mark of a ruffian, a tiny devil inviting Salvador back to the lifestyle from which he fled.

"She refuses to go."

Juan Carlos raised an eyebrow and glanced at the girl. "She is very independent."

Salvador nodded and focused on the road ahead.

"So you will feed two more mouths along with your own? Why not let her go on her own if independence is what she desires?"

"She also desires an escort."

Juan Carlos did not know what to make of such a frustrating situation. Salvador held a prize worth a fortune and was refusing to share. Now that Juan Carlos held the rifle he considered turning it on Salvador and taking the girl and her baby as his own but something told him to do nothing. He would be on his own with the girl, and would have to ride back to the Cancio plantation without the protection of Machín's rebel army. He would have no clout and would be laughed at by Testifonte – if he wasn't arrested before reaching the property.

"Very well," said Juan Carlos, suspecting his friend had grown attached to the girl and her baby. "Then if there are no protests, I will accompany you on your travels for now."

Salvador nodded and kept his eyes on the road.

"Where are we going?"

Salvador pointed ahead to the flat road that disappeared into a point on the horizon. "Havana."

When they reached the city Olympia saw that the destitution in Havana was even worse than the country. Poverty existed in staggering numbers and when Olympia saw throngs of people shuttling their belongings from place to place, their faces tired and dirty and desperate for work, she began to understand Cuba's banditry and social unrest.

Salvador reluctantly sold his comrade Chani upon entering the city and rented a shoddy apartment in the middle of town. Juan Carlos did not stay around long and soon disappeared into the city to pursue the life that he knew.

As the days became weeks, Salvador and Olympia quietly established a simple, covert routine and he was lucky to find sporadic work sweeping floors at a local cigar factory. But as time passed they began to consider a life apart. Olympia, a runaway estranged from her father, could never return to the plantation and would be virtually alone in the big city without Salvador.

Meanwhile, the young rebel was a loner with no family to run from. Protecting Olympia and her baby had become his mission and without them he would have no purpose or place. Their relationship, once based on survival, had become one of mutual respect. Olympia trusted Salvador. A warrior in a giant city facing war and depression, Salvador made her feel safe. For him, providing for this runaway and her child made him feel as if he had transcended the poor peasant orphan he had been his entire life.

They stayed together.

Time passed, the economy slowly improved and Salvador became apprentice to a cigar maker and began to learn the craft that would become his family's trade. He quickly developed a passion for the art and completed his apprenticeship. Thus began his career as a cigar maker; a proud artisan of hand-rolled high-quality Havana cigars.

He would later tell his sons, "A good cigar is a work of art."

During the evenings, while Josefina learned to walk and feed herself, Salvador and Olympia played dominoes or cards and learned that they knew many of the same games. She taught Salvador how to dance, a pastime they would enjoy for the rest of their lives, and he told her about cigars, farming and politics from the Cuban perspective. Olympia's upper class education had taught her etiquette, reading and music but she never thought she'd need to know how to cook or do laundry. She had watched Gloria move about the kitchen but never paid much attention to what the maid was doing.

Olympia soon found herself quizzing the female neighbors on cooking instructions. The other women knew Olympia was different; her teeth were white and shiny, her hands soft and unblemished, her walk graceful and proper. They were surprised that Olympia, a young woman claiming to be a Cuban peasant, knew little of basic domestic functions.

A neighbor gave her a secondhand cookbook titled *La Cocina de Anna*, a ratty old thing with brown pages falling out of the spine. Each recipe was splotched with oil stains, evidence of the book's constant presence beside the stove during the preparation of hundreds and hundreds of meals. Olympia made many mistakes at first. She didn't steam the rice long enough and served wet, crunchy grains. And there was a time when Olympia forgot to pick the rocks out of a bag of black beans and Salvador cracked a molar. He hollered in pain and cursed Olympia, causing the baby to cry, but apologized hours later after several shots of bourbon had dampened the sting.

During times like these, Olympia missed the comfort of her father's mansion. Salvador feared she would leave him and return to the plantation but she never did. It took awhile to admit that she had taken a serious liking to this interesting bandit. He detested his criminal past, worked honest hours that he enjoyed, loved his country, and brought home enough money to feed this small, unlikely group one could call a family.

She wondered why he had yet to make a physical advance. Was he keeping his distance because he was respectful of her traumatic ordeal with El Matón? Or did he simply find her unattractive?

One night, while Josefina was asleep and Olympia and Salvador played cards and drank red wine, she asked him. "What are you waiting for, Salvador?"

He knew what she was referring to. He smiled.

Salvador had wanted to kiss her again since their escape from Piro, he was merely waiting for her consent. They slept together that night and began bedding together regularly. In 1882, Salvador's first child was born. A son named Javier, a handsome little boy with black hair like his mother and strong hands like Salvador.

"He will be a cigar maker," Salvador said as he held his firstborn, hoping his son would have an easier life, free from the wandering hunger that Salvador had known since adolescence.

Later that same year, as a cool air from the north swept inland and began Cuba's short and mild winter, Olympia was visited by her brother

Hector. Though she had cut all ties with her father, she had written secret letters to Hector, letting her older brother know that she was alive and happy and living in Havana. He met her at the apartment while Salvador was away at the factory and embraced his sister while little Josefina, now almost three, clung to her mother's dress. The toddler was beautiful, with her mother's grace and big black eyes that watched Hector curiously.

"We want you to come home."

Olympia backed away and shook her head as the taste of peppermint flooded her mouth. Josefina, still clinging to Olympia's dress, backed away with her. "I will never return."

"You are a member of the Cancio family. Come home where you can live comfortably in healthy surroundings." He glanced around the apartment and saw only two rooms: a bedroom and a living area with a small kitchen.

They sat on a pair of chairs in the kitchen while Josefina remained close to her mother and watched the uncle she hardly knew. Olympia said, "I like it here."

"I see," he nodded. "The young woman goes out into the world to prove herself and becomes…what? A house servant?" Then he noticed a crib in the corner of the room where a baby slept. "Another?"

Olympia smiled and nodded. "Javier."

"You did not mention him in your letters. Who is responsible?"

"I am responsible," she said sternly.

Hector saw that his sister was happy to be free. She was stubborn and determined to prove that she could make it on her own. "Who is the father?"

"A good man."

"An educated man?"

"In many ways his education is superior to both yours and mine."

"Who is he? One of the men from Piro?"

"He is a cigar maker. Respected and admired among the working class."

Hector sighed and watched Josefina, who lurked beside her mother and held the fabric of Olympia's dress above her face as a shield. He smiled at the child and then turned back to Olympia. "Do you love this man?"

She spoke with confidence. "Of course."

"Why give up everything to live in poverty?"

"I would not trade the riches in this apartment for all the sugar in Cuba."

"Father forgives you; he never meant to harm your baby."

Now Olympia was outraged. "Father forgives me? It is not his place to forgive anyone!" She lowered her voice. "He poisoned me, Hector! Have you forgotten? He did an unthinkable thing!"

"He suffered a lapse of reason."

"And now I am a young mother with two babies from different fathers, a whore in his eyes. If I were to return he would denounce me as exactly that. Admit that I am right!"

Hector shook his head and slid his chair a bit closer. He took her hands and lowered his voice. "Olympia, we are set to inherit a fortune when he dies."

She lowered her voice as well. "I am not safe on the plantation as long as banditry runs like a plague. Our father is the lord of his land, but these men are the lords of the mountain and when they descend on his property like locusts, they do not deal in forgiveness."

"Piro has been purged and Father has reinforced the compound with armed guards."

"I would not be safe there, Hector."

Hector sighed. "Your inheritance will be forfeit."

"He can't buy my love. That has already been forfeit."

Hector saw that she was certain in her desires and he believed that she truly loved this mysterious man. He stood to say goodbye. "I look forward to reading your letters." Before he left, he turned to ask one last question. "This cigar maker, he treats you correctly?"

Olympia nodded convincingly. "He is a good man."

"An outlaw."

She smiled. "His name is Salvador."

"Have you married him?"

Olympia blinked, not expecting this question. She shook her head. "You should."

She did. Marriage for Salvador meant making peace with himself and coming to terms with his hatred of the Spanish. He could not stop himself from resenting Olympia for being a Spaniard, even though it was his choice to stay with her. He even resented his own children from time to time, especially when they were disagreeable and displayed Olympia's brash exuberance. He often considered how marriage to a former Spanish aristocrat could avenge his parents' death, and tried to find ways to justify the deed, instead of knowing he had insulted his father's soul.

Olympia took the name Olympia Cancio de Ortiz and insisted that Josefina and Javier be baptized in the Catholic Church and given Salvador's surname. They became Josefina and Javier Ortiz Cancio. Josefina would consider herself a true child of both parents as she had arrived in Salvador's care during her infancy and knew no father but him. He was her one and only Papa.

Though Salvador could often see Josefina's charming resemblance to El Matón, he was always quick to point out Olympia's features. "You have your mother's eyes," he would say as he held the young child close. "You have her nose...her ears...her chin..." Salvador grew so close to her that he often forgot he was not her blood, or chose to bury the secret so deep that he believed himself to be her true father.

Only when Josefina tried to charm him with a playful smile did Salvador catch a glimpse of the bandit leader; the crafty gleam in Machín's eye, the boyish dimples on his cheeks and chin. Memories like these stirred a minor discontent in Salvador's feeling towards Josefina. He remembered that her past was slightly tainted, her origin far from noble. Olympia never shared the details of the rape with anyone – those memories were deeply personal – and she decided early on that Josefina could never know her true origin.

Fearing that Josefina would learn of her tarnished past as a bastard and product of force, Olympia decided to protect Josefina from the truth by completely assimilating herself into Cuban culture and becoming part of their class. Hector could never understand why she had renounced her wealthy Spanish background to raise her children in poverty. How would the children react if they learned their veins flowed with a mixture of blood that had almost always been at war?

There was no reason for young Josefina to try and comprehend her mother's trauma and it would be unfair for Josefina to live with lifelong knowledge of her impure beginning. Perhaps one day, when Josefina had matured, Olympia would tell the story of the father's true identity but at a young age, it was a burden the girl need not carry.

Olympia made Salvador promise he would never reveal the details of Josefina's past. "I promise," he insisted but Olympia commanded him to place a hand on the Bible. At first Salvador refused the ridiculous gesture but a glare from Olympia convinced him to comply. So as Olympia presented the word of God, Salvador placed a palm on the book and swore he would never tell a soul. He didn't see it as a pledge to God, but a promise to Olympia.

Two years later, a son Lázaro was born, and when the boy was barely six and his brother Javier only eight, Salvador took them both out of school and taught them the cigar trade. Whenever any relevant jobs were available, Salvador sent his boys into the competitive throng of men looking for work and considered the family lucky if they were able to sweep factory floors or remove trash, or found the fortunate job of sorting through tobacco leaves. When times were tough, even Olympia would venture into the humid factories and work a few hours a week sweeping floors.

Salvador was always happy when his boys came home dirty with sticky fingers caked with tobacco residue. He told them, "Boys your age should be earning wages for the family. Work hard, boys, or die like a lazy dog."

On Javier's tenth birthday, Salvador named him his apprentice. The economy was still recovering from the Ten Years' War and employment as a cigar maker was sporadic so Salvador taught Javier how to roll cigars using the inferior leaves that were normally thrown away by the sorters. He taught Javier the art of blending tobacco to balance the flavor of the leaves, and instructed Lázaro to salvage scraps of floor sweepings and bring them home so Javier could practice.

"Soon you will be a master cigar maker," Salvador told Javier. "And you will be able to work in the factory with real leaves, rolling cigars that will be smoked by rich men all over the world. Your cigars will be tasted in every major city from Mexico City to London to Madrid. Imagine that!"

After E.J. was born in 1890, rumor began to grow of a new cigar city in Tampa and many Cubans began to leave for Florida to work in these brand new factories. But Salvador's sense of nationalism was strong and kept them planted firmly in Havana. "My father died for this island," he would remind Olympia until it made her sick. "I have killed for this land and you have given up too much to just walk away."

But when the city became overcrowded with peasants and beggars and the Spanish-American War started with the explosion and sinking of the *Maine* in Havana Harbor, everything changed. The Ortiz family packed their belongings, left the land of Salvador's father, and settled in Ybor City. Salvador wondered if Olympia ever regretted her decision to leave the plantation behind. One time when they were alone in bed, he asked her how she felt.

"Do I miss the comforts of affluence?" she replied. "Of course I do. Who wouldn't dream for someone to cook your daily meals and wash your clothes? The food was divine and I loved the clothes and perfume. But I have learned that the necessities of that lifestyle are nothing more than luxuries meant to satisfy the very desire they create."

She never told Salvador about the times she wished she could drop everything and return to Cuba to be with her brother and sleep in her giant bedroom. It didn't happen often – only when food was scarce and the family sank into lulls of depression – but there were times Olympia wished she could run away like before, and be free once again.

III.

YBOR CITY
1898

Chapter 6

Ybor City, the premiere cigar manufacturing center in the world was founded on a nearly inhospitable plot of sandy palmetto scrubland east of Tampa Bay. The soggy, scorching climate bred so many insects that Juan Carlos jokingly told Salvador, "We are forced to wear mosquito nets to keep the bugs from our eyes!"

Yet the climate was perfect for cigar making.

By the time Salvador arrived with his family in 1898, the Cigar City had become a vital port town with a bustling urban economy built almost entirely upon the manufacturing of hand-rolled cigars. Hailed as the Queen City of the Gulf, cargo vessels sailed from brand new ports, railroads connected Tampa to the rest of the country, hotels waited for visiting investors and businessmen, waterworks pumped fresh water throughout the city and a trolley service carried passengers to every corner of the urban landscape.

The industrial enclave was a sanctuary for Cuban and Spanish workers who had fled the tumult of revolution in Cuba. So successful was Ybor City that it spawned the copycat neighborhood of West Tampa, which became an immediate success and placed downtown Tampa in the middle of two industrial bookends. Ybor City and West Tampa became the limbs that nourished the city; the skilled immigrant workforce was the blood and oxygen of the one-industry town.

Salvador and his family arrived in Port Tampa with no formalities and without anyone asking where they were going or how long they intended to stay. Juan Carlos met them at the dock and greeted Salvador with his famous bear hug and kiss on the cheek. "I am so pleased you have decided to move!" he exclaimed then bowed politely to Olympia and the children and pointed them to a train that would take them into Ybor City.

The family huddled together and listened as Juan Carlos vibrantly described the city. "The train ride lasts eight minutes and takes us through downtown Tampa and past the lavish Tampa Bay Hotel." He pointed out the window where a Moorish luxury hotel capped with silver minarets topped a Tampa skyline speckled with brick buildings and palm trees. The train entered Ybor City from the west and Olympia was relieved to see that the immigrant community was like a smaller, cleaner version of Havana.

As they stepped off the train, Juan Carlos held his arms open and spoke to the city. "The Cuban influence is everywhere! In the architecture, the language, the music and the food." The family saw sandy streets lined with brick and lumber buildings, with wrought-iron balconies so close together that people could lean over and whisper the gossip of the streets to their neighbors. Palm trees and cast-iron streetlamps lined the roads and electric streetcars navigated the town, their bells ringing as they passed.

"Seventh Avenue is the main attraction," Juan Carlos said. "It is the only street paved with bricks, where one can find tailor shops, restaurants and markets, all with signs written in Spanish." Salvador met the smoky smell of black beans and roasted pork outside the restaurant *Las Novedades* and everywhere was the grind and clomp of vendor carts pulled by horses. He gathered his children and proudly pointed to Cuban flags hanging from flagpoles and draped over windowsills. It was comforting to see that Ybor City had been electrified by rumors that the United States would intervene in the war and liberate the island but Salvador wondered if a post-war Cuba could ever achieve the energy and excitement of the fresh, prosperous Ybor City.

"Wait until you see *La Gran Séptima* on Saturday night," Juan Carlos told them. "A walk down Seventh Avenue is the crowning event of the weekend. Everyone will be here, bumping into each other and talking to people sitting in chairs, or shouting to their friends on the balconies. This is a social magnet for Latinos. You can hardly stand on the sidewalk without being knocked over by the mob of pedestrians."

Juan Carlos squatted down to eight-year-old E.J. "And for you, the *heladeros* have fruit flavored sherbet!"

He looked to Javier and Lázaro. "For the older boys, Seventh Avenue is where you go to gaze from a distance at the local girls." Then he turned to Josefina, who was eighteen. "But beware of the bachelors, who whisper in hushed tones as the ladies pass." Josefina blushed.

Juan Carlos took Olympia by the arm. "There is always a group of men congregating in front of the social clubs, discussing politics and world events. They become silent when young, beautiful ladies walk by, and their conversations mysteriously resume after they pass."

After a lunch at *Las Novedades*, the family rode a streetcar to the northeast side of town, where the red brick Vasquez cigar factory stood three stories high on Twelfth Avenue and Twenty Second Street, its twenty-five thousand gallon water tower topping the building, a skyscraper amid rows and rows of identical white tenement houses. The cigar workers' homes all bore the classic design of the shotgun style. Made entirely from Florida pine, box-shaped, with high cedar-shingled roofs and glass windows, they stood on short brick pillars to keep them from the creatures, the heat, and the wet ground below. There were few luxuries besides a picket fence, window blinds and an outhouse. The houses were so close together that neighbors could converse window-to-window and family secrets had to be whispered lest they be heard by all. Salvador was pleased to see the Cuban flag flying from nearly every one of these homes.

"Vacancies are limited," Juan Carlos said. "There has been a steady arrival of immigrants since the explosion of the *Maine*. But you can find the most affordable housing near the factories."

Olympia asked if Juan Carlos owned a house.

"Not me. A single man is better off living in the boarding houses." He smiled and took Salvador aside. "You should have stayed single, my friend. Marriage and Ybor City don't always mix!"

Juan Carlos helped Salvador make arrangements, and later that day, the Ortiz family had purchased a house on credit, interest-free, on the east side of Nineteenth Street between Twelfth and Thirteenth Avenues. The cost was seven hundred and fifty dollars, payable in weekly installments of five dollars. There was a Spanish neighbor named Songo on one side and an Italian family on the other.

As the Ortiz family moved in, white haired Songo watched from his porch. Salvador walked over and introduced himself. "My name is Salvador Ortiz." Songo rose and they shook hands. Salvador noticed a small dog pacing between Songo's feet. He reminded Salvador of the dogs outside the apartments in Havana, completely black except for a spot of white at the end of his tail, which wagged happily as the dog watched Salvador. Unlike the dogs from Cuba who showed their ribs, this one was round and plump. Songo kept him well fed.

Songo introduced the young beagle. "This is Pano."

Salvador squatted and patted Pano on the head. Later, Salvador would save the last of his dinner, some rice and black beans, which he placed in a pie tin and brought outside for Pano. The dog demolished the offering, which quickly became a daily ritual for Salvador and his newest friend.

Behind the house stood the thin, brown trunk of a young avocado tree, its leaves a healthy arrangement of dark green ovals. A banana tree stood nearby with giant leaves that flopped downward like elephant ears. Salvador gazed at the small back yard they'd share with several neighbors and found a spot where he could plant an herb garden: mint leaves, oregano, cilantro, green peppers and onions.

Later that day, Juan Carlos and Salvador took Javier, Lázaro, and E.J. down the street for a tour of the Vasquez factory while Olympia stayed with Josefina to settle into the house. So far Olympia had been satisfied by the new city. The neighborhood, the entire town, was very friendly. There had been nothing but warm welcomes all around. Neighbors smiled and waved, the grocery man arrived with his cart and gave Olympia enough produce to fill the icebox, then refused to accept payment until next week, after the family was settled and secure.

She looked east to the Vasquez factory, where her husband and sons would work; the young E.J. would join his brothers as an apprentice. Only Josefina would finish her education and would be the first in the family to do so. Nicknamed Fina by her mother, it was a name Josefina tolerated but disliked, allowing the greeting only from her mother and father. Whenever anyone outside of the family called her Fina, she would politely say, "My name is Josefina Ortiz, thank you very much."

Olympia glanced at her daughter. Josefina's long black hair was curled and eternally decorated with ribbons of blue or white. At age eighteen she was already independent, attractive in both mind and body, with a charisma unlike that of either parent. Olympia thought back to when Josefina was a baby, when the idea of a tenement house in Ybor City was a possibility she had never considered.

"Do you think we will be happy here?" she asked her daughter.

Josefina nodded. "It's bigger than that damp, three-room apartment in Havana and everyone is so nice here. There are no crowds fighting over the toilets."

Olympia laughed while Josefina helped her unpack. There were four rooms in the house, all of equal size with two bedrooms, one for the parents and one for the boys to share. Josefina would sleep on a couch in the front parlor. Olympia slid the windows open to create airflow in the hot and humid dwelling while Josefina went to the back of the house where the outhouse and water pump were located. Workers' houses were all around and many of their neighbors would share the same facilities, sacrificing privacy for convenience. Josefina frowned at the single outhouse. It looked like she would have to fight for the toilet after all.

Across from the Vasquez factory stood a house unlike the others. It was twice the width of a worker's house, with three floors and a yard that was large enough to hold four tenement homes. Surrounded by orange trees, it was clearly the home of one of Ybor City's most privileged. Olympia would soon learn that it belonged to cigar manufacturer Antonio Vasquez, owner of the company that bore his name. She was reminded of the mansions that stood on the sugar plantations of Pinar del Río, like castles of Spanish royalty. It seemed so long ago, a time long forgotten, the life of someone else.

Salvador's boys found no surprises at the Vasquez cigar factory. It resembled any of the factories Javier and Lázaro had worked at in Havana. A basement gave the factory a fourth level where bales of tobacco were stored, sorted according to quality, and moistened for pliability. At ground level a pair of loading docks accepted incoming tobacco leaves, and sent finished cigars out for sale after they had been banded and boxed.

After new leaves were treated they were sent to the top level to have the stems removed by a team of mostly women and children known as strippers. Salvador brought E.J. to this area to show him where he would be working. "You see, E.J., after the stems are removed by the strippers, the bundles are passed to the *resagadores,* who sort through the tobacco and separate the leaves into piles according to quality and color." E.J. nodded, his brown eyes opened wide, intimidated by all the activity and the speed that the strippers worked.

The second floor was the galley, with rows and rows of wooden workbenches filled with busy *tabaqueros.* They were mostly men who worked diligently by hand, rolling the leaves into dolls, slicing the ends with their round *chaveta* knives and placing them into wooden molding blocks, where the cigars would take and hold their cylindrical shape. The workers wore aprons over white shirts and ties. Many of them smoked cigars while they worked, in near silence, while they listened to the words of the factory reader. As Salvador watched the workers, he recognized many of them from his earlier visit to Ybor. He smiled and waved to Alberto Segundo, who Salvador had rolled cigars with several years ago in Cuba. Alberto returned a smile and a nod as he rolled a cigar from his bench. The familiar faces were comforting.

At the *tribuna,* a raised platform in the center of the factory floor, sat Sando Peña, who read from *Les Misérables.* His booming voice thundered across the factory floor and echoed off the walls. The Victor Hugo novel was a favorite among the workers – its revolutionary themes resonated long after the workday was complete, when many of the workers went home to update their families on the tale of romance and redemption. The workers cheered for Jean Valjean, booed Javert and fell silent to hear the escapades of Cosette and Marius.

Chosen by a popular vote cast by the workers, the *lector* read from a novel every afternoon. The previous winner had been *Treasure Island,* and next in line was *The Three Musketeers.* "One can never emphasize how important the readers are," Salvador told his sons. "They are often the only education a cigar worker can find."

During the morning break the men sat outside on the low brick wall that surrounded the factory to drink coffee and smoke cigars. The *cafetero* and his assistant were already positioned outside with two giant enamel coffeepots as the cigar makers poured out of the building. One pot contained hot, black Cuban coffee and the other had hot, sweet milk. Cigar workers purchased either black coffee or a mixture of both coffee and milk for three cents. Sometimes the *cafetero* would provide fresh sweet rolls which he sold with a cup of coffee for a nickel.

Salvador and his boys followed and mingled with the workers, a group of men with the camaraderie of a sports team or a fraternity, and Salvador instantly became part of the group. They discussed politics and local issues, and the conversation was usually dominated by Juan Carlos.

In the mornings, the *lector* translated national news stories from the competitive New York newspapers of Pulitzer and Hearst, and by midmorning the *lector* was reading literature from the local proletariat. This consisted of writings that promoted labor causes and sometimes touched on radical and even anarchistic ideals. The social agenda was clear, as the workers demanded readings from *El Boletín del Obreros* (*The Workers' Bulletin*), a local Spanish-language paper produced by the young Cuban journalist Gabriel Mendez.

Mendez was the protégé of Sando Peña, the latter being a man who Mendez idolized and emulated in every way. Peña had been a reader at a cigar factory in Cuba. When Vicente Martinez Ybor brought the cigar industry to Tampa in 1886, the trilingual *lector* had been one of the first to follow. Born in Córdoba in 1830, Sando was the son of a school teacher. An assiduous instructor, his father helped Sando learn the Spanish alphabet while most fathers helped their sons learn how to walk. By age eight, Sando could recite poems by Gustavo Adolfo Becquer and quote his favorite writer, Miguel de Cervantes.

Peña was tall and heavyset; his demeanor was clean and handsome. He dressed elegantly, always in a coat and tie, his shoes always shined and his hair always in place. He wore black rimmed glasses, smiled often, and had a presence that would absorb the attention of whatever room he had entered. Sando was notorious for greeting all acquaintances with a hearty double-fisted handshake and a friendly kiss on the cheek.

Although most of the workers were illiterate, and would remain so their entire lives, they were far from ignorant. They so desired to stay up to date on current events that they contributed a portion of their wages to ensure the factory *lectors* would be paid and present every day.

It provided Sando with a comfortable salary of thirty dollars a week – much more than any cigar worker. But most rewarding was the attention of the crowd. The duty of the *lector* was that of an entertainer. Sando's powerful voice could mesmerize the workers, and he took great pleasure inventing his own voices for characters. He loved to read the antics of Don Quixote and make the factory floor explode with laughter.

But Sando was nearly seventy and his voice was not as strong as before. Retirement loomed before him, and Sando longed to return to Spain, to make one last pass through Europe and live his last days on the peninsula. For several years he had groomed a replacement, the young writer and newspaper publisher named Mendez.

With a pudgy, round face and glasses that seemed to match his shiny, slicked-back hair, Mendez exuded an intellectual confidence that some interpreted as arrogance. Usually dressed in a three-piece suit, and carrying a stack of books, he so resembled a young Sando that the cigar workers playfully began calling him Little Sando or Sandito.

Sando told Mendez, "The *lectura* is a system of education in politics, labor, literature and international events. You must view the reader's platform as a pulpit of liberty. That's what Martí once said. The reading is a way to reflect the democratic spirit of the workers. They want content that's close to their hearts, that focuses on themes of freedom and class struggle."

Mendez had been recently elected *Presidente de la Lectura*, head of a committee that nominated and auditioned candidates for the reader's position. Mendez acted as an agent who negotiated the reader's salary and collected contributions from the workers as they left the factory.

But factory owner Antonio Vasquez was so uncomfortable with the leftist rants of the readers that he forbade Mendez from collecting money on the factory floor and insisted business be conducted outside with the vendors.

Don Antonio knew he was powerless to control the content of the readings. He knew of one factory owner who had tried to ban the *lector* completely but the workers quickly reacted with a walkout and did not return until they were promised fulltime readings of any material they chose.

Mendez was not only defending the workers' cherished rights, but his own writing. As Cuba Libre became more popular, so did the works of Mendez, whose perspective was heavily influenced by José Martí and the anarchist writers of Havana. Many local workers considered Mendez to be one of the most important voices of their society. Readings from *The Bulletin* had sometimes enraged Don Antonio, and nearly caused him to close his factory for the day but the foreman, Pipi Capecho, urged him to remain open. "It is better to have happy workers with leftist ideals than no workers at all."

Mendez was eager to take Sando's place as *lector*. His voice was adequate and he was able to translate the English language papers into Spanish. He shared the same literary tastes as many of the workers; his favorite novels included *Don Quixote*, *Robinson Crusoe*, and *Moby Dick*. His writing was already popular among the working class, and Sando had given Mendez a powerful endorsement.

Juan Carlos told Salvador, "I will introduce you to Mendez. He can be a bit stuffy, as most scholarly types are, but we share a common cause. Mendez is a big fan of Martí, and is exactly the type of person we want fighting for us."

When Salvador and his boys finally left the factory with Juan Carlos, they encountered a group of reporters on the front steps who were in town to cover rumors that Tampa was to be a staging point for the inevitable war with Spain. The reporters gathered around a tall Spanish businessman who addressed them with a smile behind his thick black beard. "That's Armando Renteria. He's a big name in this town."

"What does he do?" Salvador asked.

"He is a partial owner in several cigar factories, an investor in local business and a controlling force among the *bolita* games. In fact, Armando nearly owns the Tampa *bolita* business. Aside from that he is a wealthy Spaniard," Juan Carlos said scornfully. "He is rumored to have close ties to the mayor and the chief of police."

Salvador raised an eyebrow.

Juan Carlos nodded. "They say that if you don't act right, the man with the beard will come see you."

"*Bolita*," Salvador grinned. "I am anxious to participate in a throw."

They paused on the steps to listen as Armando's deep voice addressed the reporters. "What have the cigar factories done for Tampa?" Armando said to no one in particular. "For starters, they have turned two hundred acres of worthless land into valuable tax-paying real estate, worth over two hundred dollars an acre! They have erected nearly a half million dollars worth of buildings, employing hundred of laborers and mechanics, and have built a city of ten thousand! They maintain our ship line to Central America and the West Indies, which adds special importance to our port, and advertises Tampa throughout the Union, bringing hundreds, if not thousands of visitors to our city! Is there anything so promising in Cuba?"

A reporter asked, "Señor Renteria, as a man of Spanish blood, where do you stand in the possibility of a war between the United States and Spain?"

Armando continued to smile. "I stand with the cigar industry!" The reporters laughed. "A war with Spain will be good for Tampa, and if it's good for Tampa it is good for cigars. Though I am a Spaniard by birth, I consider myself to be an American. But if you'll pardon me, there are matters that need my attention." He excused himself from the reporters and entered the factory to meet with Don Antonio Vasquez.

La Rubia was a carnival. Loud, crowded, and filled with cigar smoke. A bar along the left was packed with men drinking beer, bourbon and rum. Some played cards, others argued over the coming war; their opinions danced along the bar in Spanish and Italian. The rest of the room was filled with tables where men played dominoes in groups of four, or rolled dice for money, or ogled the women of the tavern – none of whom appeared to be wives or girlfriends but were in fact, on the job.

Again, Salvador saw the familiar faces of men he had worked with in Havana.

Juan Carlos was greeted by a short, stocky man with glasses, who held a smoking *robusto* size cigar in one hand, and a mess of crumpled *bolita* tickets in the other. Juan Carlos introduced him as Gabriel Mendez. Salvador smiled sincerely and took Mendez's hand. "I've just arrived in town and already I've heard a lot about you."

74

Mendez nodded subtly as he inspected Salvador. The young writer was more serious than Salvador had expected and on the surface, not very friendly. Juan Carlos said, "Salvador and his family just arrived from Havana." Then Juan Carlos winked at Mendez and whispered, "Salvador and I were good friends in Cuba, Mendez, an acquaintance of El Matón."

At this, Mendez became genuinely interested. "You fought alongside El Matón del Pueblo?"

Salvador became uncomfortable. He had made every attempt to abandon his violent past and his association with the rebel leader Victoriano Machín. "It is not something I talk about very often," Salvador admitted. "But yes, I was there with Carlito."

Mendez was impressed. "Welcome to Ybor City."

"Thank you."

He offered a cigar, which Salvador gladly accepted. It was local; a short, fat *robusto* from a premium brand rolled in Ybor City. It tasted of coffee and vanilla, sweet and smooth with a tangy finish, just as Salvador preferred. Juan Carlos produced his own cigar, one he had hand-rolled from his own personal provision of tobacco. Cigar workers were given a daily allowance of leaf for their own use and many rolled these into cigars for consumption later on. Others tore them into little pieces and chewed the leaf, spitting the juice on the floor or ground, or into spittoons, when they were available. Some even sold their personal cigars on the street, or from their homes. It was a fringe benefit deeply cherished by all workers.

Now Juan Carlos pointed them into a room in the back where a crowd shouted and waved dollar bills. Standing on a platform, the object of the crowd's attention, was a curly-haired, foul-mouthed Spaniard known as Gallego, the master of Ybor City's *bolita* game. A business partner of Armando Renteria, Gallego accepted money and wrote tickets on little slips of paper he filled out with short pencils. Gallego had a second pencil behind his ear and another handful in his shirt pocket. With the amount of money gambled nightly on *bolita*, and the generous eighty to one payoff, Gallego went through pencils like cigarettes.

Behind him was a chalkboard with a calendar for the month of February. Beside each date was a number between one and one hundred – the results of previous *bolita* throws. Seeing the trend of prior results prevented players from betting on a number that had appeared with unusual frequency, and gave them a better idea of which numbers were due to be cut. Beside the chalkboard was a painting that told players how to bet according to their previous dreams. If a player dreamt of a horse, he should bet #1, #4 for a cat, #19 for a cow, #44 for a bull, and so on.

Next to Gallego was a table where one hundred clay balls stood on display, each one white and the size of an average radish, with a black number painted across the face. While Gallego cursed and shouted playful insults at the patrons, Salvador followed Juan Carlos and Mendez to the table. Juan Carlos reached into his pocket and removed a small gray stone tied to a leather band, a necklace.

Juan Carlos held the object so Salvador could see. "An alligator tooth for good luck." Then he waved the tooth over ball twenty-nine and bought a corresponding ticket. Salvador looked across the table and saw a man waving a clenched fist above the seventy-eight ball. In his fist was a small leather pouch. Salvador asked what was inside.

"Sand."

"Sand?"

The man grinned. "Magic sand!"

Salvador glanced around him and saw nearly all the men had a good luck charm or ritual of some kind. There were dice, bird feathers, and dried flowers, one man had a photo of a young woman, and another had a brown, dead lizard. Salvador spotted a tiny man, older than any man he had ever seen, holding the seven of diamonds over ball number seven. Salvador's good luck charm was his father's knife, which he did not always carry.

He reached into his pocket for change. "I will bet a dime on fifty-nine, the year of my birth, and a dime on sixty-three, the year of Olympia's."

The Spaniard Armando Renteria lurked in a dark corner in back of the room and supervised the game that he owned; his black beard helped him blend into the shadows.

Gallego announced that all bets were in and the crowd became hushed. All one hundred balls were placed into a brown potato sack, which was tied tightly, and the throw began. The sack was handed from person to person. Nearly everyone who handled it shook the bag and hexed it with a good luck charm. It traveled all the way around the room and back to Gallego, who grabbed one ball through the outside of the sack and tied it off with a string. The crowd murmured and buzzed in anticipation while Gallego used a knife to cut the bag above the string. The ball with the winning number dropped into his hand.

The crowd took a collective deep breath as Gallego looked at the number and revealed jagged yellow teeth under his bushy moustache. He held the ball above his head, so that only he could see the number then flipped it to show the crowd. He shouted, "Forty-seven!" and the crowd groaned and tore up their losing tickets but one man yelped with joy and shouted that he had picked the winning number. The room parted and saw the winner was a skinny man with short hair and big round ears, known locally as La Chihuahua.

"*Coño,*" Juan Carlos muttered. "Let's find a table for dominoes. I do not care to hear the triumphant howling of La Chihuahua."

They tossed their losing tickets aside and headed to the front room and settled at a table. Mendez produced a set of dominoes while Juan Carlos recruited a fourth, a man with dark, sunken eyes known as Ojos Negros. As they setup a game of dominoes, Juan Carlos said to Mendez. "So tell us, Mendez, the latest from the world of politics. How soon until the United States enters this war and obliterates the Spanish Navy?"

Salvador and Ojos listened to hear the answer.

Mendez said, "McKinley has ordered a Court of Inquiry to investigate the cause of the explosion aboard the USS *Maine*. It will be some time until they reach a conclusion."

Juan Carlos was agitated. "I'll tell you what sank that ship right now. It was sabotaged by Spaniards who want no U.S. presence in Cuba. They plant mines in that harbor, you know. They likely directed the ship to precisely where a live mine happened to be."

Mendez was reasonable. "It could be any number of things, Carlito. It could have been an accident, an internal explosion. It could have been Cuban rebels for all we know, trying anything that would bring the U.S. into the war with Spain."

Juan Carlos dismissed it with a wave. "The rebels have no means to sink a battleship. I tell you, it was the Spanish. I don't know what McKinley is waiting for. Court of Inquiry? It's a bureaucratic waste of time, if you ask me. Remember the *Maine*, and to hell with Spain."

"Questions abound though," said Salvador.

Juan Carlos concentrated on the dominoes. "Questions? Like what?"

"Should the United States decide to drive Spain from Cuba once and for all, it leaves the future of our island in question."

Mendez nodded. "Salvador is right. We should ask ourselves: would we rather have an ally in the United States than an enemy in Spain? Spain as an enemy gives us cause to rally, to band together in a fight for independence. But the United States will not enter the conflict with hopes to be Cuba's ally, but their surrogate mother. I fear that if we do not claim our island, Cuba will always be somebody's colony."

Juan Carlos flipped a domino hard enough to shake the table. "Let the Americans rid Cuba of Spain, then we can decide what to do about imperialism."

Ojos said, "Martí declared Cuba an independent republic before he died. I don't see how anyone has any business there."

Salvador puffed on his cigar as he inspected the dominoes. He spotted Armando behind with bar with Gallego counting money and sorting through *bolita* receipts. "But the U.S. will care for Cuba in a way that Spain never did."

"That may be true," said Mendez. "But once the U.S. is in Cuba, what will get her out?"

La Chihuahua came into the room, his pockets heavy with cash, and he approached the bartender. "Manuel, pour a drink for every man inside the building. And they can thank the number forty-seven, which has sponsored this event, and this round of drinks!"

The crowd booed playfully, until Manuel poured rum for everybody, then they cheered and raised their glasses to La Chihuahua, who had climbed to the bar. "*¡Salud, mis amigos, salud!* And to Cuba, may she live long, and live free, so that we may return to our homeland, and prosper there as we have prospered here. *¡Cuba Libre! ¡Cuba Libre!*"

And the crowd shouted along with him and toasted their home country. Salvador thought of his father, who would approve of the unity and strong sense of nationalism for Cuba. Salvador and his friends drank long into the night, celebrating an imminent victory in the Cuban War for Independence.

Chapter 7

Javier Ortiz thought he was macho. Vasquez and Company paid better wages than the cigar factories of Havana, and after Javier gave half his earnings to his parents, he had plenty left over for himself. He saved for two months until he had enough for a new black suit, a watch and a matching vest, a getup that he decided to test on the young women of Ybor City.

He dressed in the new outfit and placed the small gold pocket watch in the vest pocket, wore a matching black hat and shined his black leather shoes. With a black hat and a shining gray tie, sixteen-year-old Javier thought he looked as impressive as any of the American soldiers who roamed Seventh Avenue. He knew he was definitely more handsome than those boring bankers and accountants who always hurried home at five o'clock.

As Javier strolled down the boulevard with a cigar between his fingers, he walked tall through the busy Saturday evening crowd. Though he was an attractive young man, his suit was no fancier than those worn by the local businessmen and politicians. He halted in front of the Centro Español building on Seventh Avenue and leaned against the brick wall where two young ladies his age were about to pass. Though they pretended not to notice him, both watched Javier from the corners of their eyes.

"Good afternoon, Señoritas," Javier greeted them with a smile and a tip of his hat. "Care for an escort to the store, or perhaps you'd like to accompany me to a dance tonight?"

One jeered from the corner of her mouth, "Buzz off, creep." The other one laughed, and then both girls hurried away snickering. Javier was amused and somewhat embarrassed but he was not discouraged. His father had taught him that failure was inevitable and quitting was unacceptable. He'd keep trying on the ladies and knew eventually he'd win one over.

Ybor City had plenty of other distractions. The United States had declared war on Spain, and the attack on Cuba would be launched from Tampa. The military used the palatial Tampa Bay Hotel as its base. The city became hectic and overcrowded as thousands of troops and tourists wandered the streets of Tampa. Javier saw how the generous visitors delighted the Tampa businessmen with exceptional profits and booming business. Vasquez and Company was injected with a powerful shot of cash flow as the news coverage of the military buildup helped popularize Tampa cigars, which quickly became world famous and caused further economic surge. There was no shortage of work at the benches for Javier and his brothers. And he saw how proud his father was to be working, happy to be able to provide regular meals to his family.

But Javier figured another way to benefit from the economic activity.

"Here is my idea," Javier pulled his little brother E.J. aside one hot Saturday afternoon in May. They watched a parade of soldiers stroll through sunny Ybor City, tugging at the collars of their uniforms and wiping sweat from their foreheads with white handkerchiefs. Javier said, "To satisfy these thirsty soldiers and journalists, we will set up a refreshment stand on Seventh Avenue. For a handful of pennies and nickels we can buy ourselves a dozen lemons and a pound of sugar and make lemonade!"

E.J. welcomed a chance to earn favor with his older brother. "But I don't have any money."

Javier straightened his tie and pointed to his shiny black shoes. "Do I look poor? I'll provide the expenses from my share of factory wages, as long as you squeeze the lemons and mix the sugar. We split the profits right down the middle."

"Shouldn't we give some to Mama?"

Javier scoffed. He was entitled to the proceeds from the lemonade, since it was his idea and his money. He was a little resentful that E.J. had reminded him of his duty to help his family but figured there was no sense in arguing with his little brother.

"Sure, we can give some money to Mama," Javier said. "It'll make her happy and we will be repaid with food and good will."

"What will we use for cups?"

"We can use Mama's from the kitchen. As long as we bring them back before supper she won't mind. Deal?"

They shook hands and ran back to the house to gather their supplies. Salvador and Juan Carlos were on the porch smoking cigars and they quietly watched the boys come and go with amused smiles. Salvador said, "We've been in America for four months and already they have become capitalists."

The afternoon was sweltering, which guaranteed success. The boys sold dozens of cups of lemonade to friendly soldiers and journalists for a nickel apiece. They could not help but admire the soldiers who would soon leave to liberate Cuba. E.J. asked Javier, "If America wins the war will we be able to return home?"

Javier shrugged. "Maybe. Stop asking questions, we're running out of lemonade." Javier sent E.J. to a nearby vendor to purchase more lemons so they could mix another jug. To a small boy like E.J. the soldiers were taller than houses, with elegant blue uniforms and buttons that sparkled. Especially awe-inspiring was Teddy Roosevelt and his colorful Rough Riders, who fast became the darling of the press and the envy of every young Tampa boy. E.J. was inspired by Roosevelt's charisma and enthusiasm. With a handkerchief tied loosely around his neck and a pair of round spectacles above his bushy moustache and gleaming white teeth, Roosevelt was a captivating man who brought hope to those praying for victory in Cuba.

At the end of the day, Javier and E.J. had earned a profit of more than five dollars and as promised, Javier gave one dollar to Olympia and split the rest with his brother. E.J. saved one dollar in a small leather pouch that he hid under a pile of clothes and though Olympia had already been paid, E.J. secretly gave his other dollar to his mother.

Javier planned to spend his entire share on card games and booze.

That night the Ortiz family dined together in their kitchen and E.J. told them excitedly about his day selling lemonade to soldiers. "There were hundreds of them walking through town and some of them even had guns! And one time this soldier bought a cup of lemonade and gave me a dime and even let me keep the change!"

Salvador smiled. "It sounds like you had a lucrative day."

"I don't like him being around those soldiers," Olympia said. "But I'd rather my boys sell lemonade to soldiers than have them begging for food on the streets."

Josefina said, "I heard they created a volunteer army, and thousands have already enlisted, including several local boys from Ybor City."

Lázaro looked up from his meal, "Which boys from Ybor City?"

Salvador tried to hide his concern. "You're crazy if you think you're about to enlist in the U.S. Army. You're only thirteen."

"There are boys my age helping the rebels in Cuba," Lázaro said.

"Hardly," said Salvador. "It is completely different in America. This army has different rules; number one being that you must be eighteen. You could pass for sixteen, maybe, and would certainly be of help to the cause. But the American army has rules. They will not take you."

It was true that Lázaro looked older than he was – Javier had often been mistaken for his younger brother. Salvador knew that Lázaro could probably pass for eighteen but he didn't want the boy to have any misguided ideas about war.

Lázaro poked at his dinner. "I don't care about those stupid soldiers anyway." He was at the age where he was no longer a boy but not yet a man and he often became envious and irritable around adults.

Salvador, trying to reassure his son, said to his family, "The Americans will make short work of the Spaniards. This will not be like the Ten Years' War, which is something we should all be thankful for. Less than a year, six months perhaps, and Cuba will be liberated. Besides, Lázaro, you are well into your apprenticeship. Concentrate on your work; this family needs your wage."

Lázaro had been Salvador's apprentice in the cigar factories for over a year, after spending four long months sweeping the factory floor. It had taken Salvador less than three months to pass the basic skills to Javier; so he was naturally disappointed with Lázaro's slow progress. When it came to cigars, the boy hadn't the drive or even the brains of his older sibling.

But Javier was a natural. He kept his knife sharp and concentrated on his work while listening to the *lector*. When the knife sharpener would come by, Javier would hand over his *chaveta* and sit back with his hands clasped behind his head, listening to *Moby Dick* and chomping on a piece of tobacco leaf. When his *chaveta* has been returned sharpened, Javier would seamlessly resume his work at the bench needing no assistance from his father.

Earlier that day, Salvador had inspected one of Lázaro's sloppy, uneven cigars. One end was loose and the other was tight and covered with bumps. Salvador shook his head. "It's a good thing they only give you the inferior leaves. You'll be back to sweeping floors if these don't improve."

Lázaro felt awkward at the work benches. Learning to roll cigars required patience; the craft had a certain finesse that Lázaro had not yet grasped. It was hard to roll a high-quality cigar and the men who did it well, men like his father, were proud of their work. Lázaro watched how hard Salvador concentrated when a handful of tobacco leaves was before him. His father was a perfectionist at the workbench, falling into an unbreakable rhythm and making sure that every cigar was just right.

Lázaro hadn't the patience or the desire to sit at a bench for hours rolling cigar after cigar. He was happy to have been taken out of school but had little interest in finishing his apprenticeship and perfecting his trade; he persisted with his lessons only to quiet his father.

He had a shy personality and was dubbed Silent Sam in Ybor City, as he rarely spoke and seldom said more than a few words when he did. He lacked Javier's good looks and the maturity of Josefina. Even his younger brother E.J. could compete when it came to wit. But none of Lázaro's siblings could match his temper or his pride.

Notorious for brawling with the boys of his youth, and often hitting both of his brothers, Lázaro used fighting as a social crutch. When he was teased by the schoolchildren, Lázaro quickly stopped caring about friends and decided not to have any. His physical bravado made up for his intellectual shortcomings, something that made Lázaro grudgingly proud. He had been an intimidating presence on the schoolyard and had just begun a growth spurt that gave him the confidence to challenge boys three or four years older, so it came as no surprise to Salvador when Lázaro went too far one summer night and found himself in a fight he could not win.

The war with Spain was delayed, and as May became June, the temperature rose along with the tensions inside the Army's rank and file. Inactivity rotted troop morale and caused the soldiers to release their tension upon those around them. Fights broke out in the camps, drunken soldiers caused disorder throughout city, and a series of robberies and assaults made the people of Tampa view their visitors as a mixed blessing.

Salvador and Olympia experienced this during their weekly Sunday night dance at the Cuban Cantina on Eighth Avenue. The metal chairs and tables of the modest restaurant were pushed against the walls, leaving a cramped but cozy dance floor for a dozen couples. A four-piece folk band was setup in the corner with a guitarist, a percussionist who played congas and maracas, a trumpet player and a tall, lanky female singer known around town as Claudia.

Salvador and Olympia danced an upbeat timba with few worries. No longer were they concerned about how their children would eat or if sanitation problems would make them sick. Here they could enjoy the night and dance carefree long into the night.

But outside the cantina, two American soldiers became involved in a heated exchange. One soldier was pushed through the doorway of the Cuban Cantina where he fell against a table and onto the dance floor, breaking several bottles and halting the music.

The dancing stopped. Olympia, with her arms around Salvador, looked over his shoulder to the fallen soldier and said scornfully, "The *yanquis* have become a nuisance. How much longer will they be here?"

Salvador was not as concerned. "Patience, my love. They'll soon be gone."

There was yelling and commotion outside the cantina where several troops had gathered. After much hooting and hollering, gunshots broke out and Salvador and Olympia ducked for cover along with the rest of the dancers and the band. When the blasts were followed by rowdy, drunken laughter, the couples inside the cantina relaxed and realized the group of soldiers had used the avenue's electric streetlamps for target practice. Flying glass and stray bullets had become an imposing danger to anyone walking the streets.

"This is what I'm talking about," said Olympia. "It has been months since the *Maine* exploded. These troops are paid to fight, not to drink and buy *bolita* tickets in our taverns."

E.J. suddenly appeared beside them. His face was flushed and sweaty, and he was out of breath. Salvador flinched, startled by the sudden appearance of his young son. "E.J. what are you doing here?"

E.J. caught his breath. "Lázaro is hurt."

Josefina was angry at her brother. He had tried to impress some girls he did not know, had picked the wrong battle, and did not walk away when he had the chance. She was angry with herself for not being able to stop him. She knelt at her brother's bedside, wrapped ice in a towel and held it to his broken nose. The blood had stopped flowing but was smeared and dried across his lips, chin and neck. Dark spots would form under his eyes and he'd have a pair of black eyes tomorrow. "You're going to look like a little raccoon," Josefina said. "*Un mapachito.*"

Javier stood near his sister and watched as his brother rested stiff with pain. "Stupid fool," he said.

"Shush, Javier!" snapped Josefina. Her eyes flared toward her brother. "He needs no further scolding. Let his wounds be his lesson."

"I warned you," she said, turning to Lázaro. "I told you to go home."

Lázaro kept his eyes closed and pretended not to hear his sister. He had no desire to engage in a sparring match. Already embarrassed to be bedridden and under her care, the pain in his face seemed to worsen whenever she spoke. Not only was there a sharp, biting pain in his nose, his head hurt and so did his fist. It was possible one of the bare knuckle punches he'd landed had broken a bone in his hand. But he would not tell anyone about that. A broken nose was more humiliation than he cared to endure.

A clamor of footsteps arrived on the front porch, the front door opened and people entered the house. The feet halted at the bedroom doorway and Lázaro opened his eyes to see his mother and father at the threshold with E.J. When he shut his eyes again and turned away, he tried to make his movements appear slow and involuntary as if he were drifting off to sleep.

Everyone started talking at once. Olympia herded everyone out of the room and demanded that Lázaro recover in peace. When Salvador saw his boy was not critically wounded, that he needed a bed instead of a grave, he followed the group to the parlor. Olympia made coffee and everyone settled so Josefina could tell what happened.

"I was riding the streetcar to Eighth Avenue with my friend Esmeralda; we were going to a dress shop to look for outfits for Elsa Roque's wedding next month. When we stepped off the streetcar, we saw a soldier talking to two Spanish girls. They couldn't understand him so they walked away but he followed. He didn't appear very threatening; Lázaro the fool was just looking for another excuse to fight."

Josefina sighed and appeared suddenly irritated. "He came strolling onto the scene, rolled up his sleeves, and stepped between this soldier and the girls. He had words for the soldier, who laughed and tried to push him out of the way."

Salvador interrupted. "How old was this soldier?"

Josefina shrugged. "Not much older than Javier. Eighteen maybe. He probably saw Lázaro and thought they were the same age, and that it would be a fair fight. I called to Lázaro but he ignored me and held up his fists like he was some kind of prize fighter."

"Who were these girls?" Olympia asked.

"Nobody," said Josefina. "Two girls twice his age who would never give him the time of day. The soldier even started to walk away but Lázaro, showing off, went up behind him and grabbed him by the shoulder. The soldier whirled around and pushed Lázaro to the ground and that's when Lázaro lost his temper. I yelled for him to go home, but he tried to tackle the man. The soldier somehow caught Lázaro by the collar and Lázaro spit in his eye. Then the soldier pulled back and socked him square on the nose.

"The fight was over but he kept hitting Lázaro, for no apparent reason other than to blow off steam! He ran away when he saw what he did and so I gave Lázaro a handkerchief to stop the blood. Then we helped him to a streetcar and brought him home." She crossed her arms disapprovingly as if expecting her parents to be as angry as she was.

Salvador shook his head. "Young fool. The boy wanted to prove himself."

Josefina said, "He even tried to blame me for distracting him and said I should mind my own business. Can you believe the nerve of this child?"

Salvador excused himself and went to the bedroom to sit by his boy.

Josefina had noticed that Lázaro had an instinct for fighting. He didn't cower but stood his ground, protected himself and tried to fight back. Josefina later shared this with her mother, who waved her away quietly, not wanting to hear the truth, and changed the subject.

Salvador entered the boys' bedroom and saw Lázaro in bed holding a bloody towel over his nose. Lázaro's eyes were closed but he didn't have the deep breath of a person at rest. Before Salvador could address his son, Lázaro moved the towel and began to speak.

"I know I am only a boy. But I am old enough for an American soldier to beat me to the ground and break my nose. I may be stupid in your eyes, but did you expect me to run? They came here to fight, so I challenged one to a fight. Who says I am not old enough? I could take any one of those puny *yanqui* dandies."

Salvador replied gently. "That is fine if you are a character from the books that Sando reads, but in real life there are consequences, many of which are not so romantic. You thought you could take any one of them, sure you could. But look what your heroics have done. You're in bed with a broken nose."

Lázaro opened his eyes and looked to his father. "What have you taught me? Fight back and never let yourself be bullied. Who will be here to protect our family if you or Javier should disappear?" He could see faint admiration from his father. Lázaro wanted his father's approval and understanding. He no longer wanted to be thought of as a kindhearted child, but a man ready to fight in wars.

"I am not afraid," Lázaro said. "Soldiers, guns, bayonets, Spaniards and Americans, all the men of the world; I fear none of them."

Salvador wondered if the wound was responsible for this unusual confidence. "What is wrong with being a cigar maker?"

"A cigar maker? What does that amount to?"

Salvador sensed Lázaro's drive for authority. The boy's eyes seemed darker, icier, and for the first time, the boy looked dangerous. Lázaro was not interested in an honest worker's wage. He wanted glory, to lead men into battle like José Martí, Calixto García and Teddy Roosevelt.

Salvador said, "A man should not measure his success in life by the type of work he does, or by the medals he has won, but by the impact he has had on those around him, especially his family."

Lázaro said nothing. He closed his eyes and turned his head the other way. Salvador lightly patted his son's forearm and left him alone to rest. Lázaro slept long into the next day and onto a quick recovery. His eyes were blackened for weeks, his nose forever crooked.

Two things resulted from the incident with the American soldier. The first was that Lázaro started to carry a knife. He chose one small enough to hide in his pockets, and to avoid the attention of his parents. The second result was that Josefina, in a move that surprised her father but not her mother, announced to the Ortiz family that she had volunteered to become a nurse for the U.S. Army. She would be assigned to a hospital ship bound for the war in Cuba and would be leaving soon to begin her training. She was eighteen years old.

Chapter 8

A busybody like her mother, Josefina took a supervisory role over her brothers, ensuring they left for work on time, caring for them when they were sick, and threatening to tell their mother when obligations were not being met. Old enough to comprehend the political forces shaping Tampa and Cuba, Josefina approved of how her father and brothers supported the Cuba Libre by donating a portion of their wages to the war effort each week. She even offered to quit school and go to work like her brothers but Olympia would not allow it.

"No daughter of mine will sweat herself to death in a cigar factory. Finish your education," she insisted. "You will be the first of this family to do so. Look at your father, he can sign his name but barely knows the alphabet."

"But I am eighteen and I already know how to read. I want to work."

"Unheard of," Olympia shook her head. "Get an education. A smart girl will marry a smart man." Olympia knew Josefina would not be content to remain in her parents' house. The girl possessed a sense of curiosity that could not be contained.

When Tampa became infested with soldiers and the excitement of war, Josefina completed school but decided she was more useful as a nurse in the U.S. Army. At first Olympia was uneasy with the news but understood her daughter's decision. "I have not been able to participate in the war effort like the cigar makers," Josefina said. "I have no wages to give. The men who are fighting in Cuba are not only being killed by bullets, Mama, but by yellow fever. The Army has high demand for nurses who are immune, and I can help."

Olympia saw Josefina, eighteen years old and struggling for an identity separate from her mother's, with the adventurous nobility of a familiar bandit leader. Olympia thought back to when she was Josefina's age and that moment of freedom she encountered atop Salvador's horse.

She could not run away from home and then expect her adult daughter to remain obediently by her side. Reaching out and squeezing her daughter's hand she said, "You have my blessing."

Salvador protested when he heard of the agreement. "Why would you want to return to a war zone? You are no soldier!"

Olympia defended her daughter. "The Army needs nurses to care for the soldiers."

Salvador waved a hand dismissively. "She has no experience!"

"They will train her and pay her thirty dollars just to volunteer."

Salvador gazed upon his daughter, young and poised, a calm woman grown up and sure of herself. "Trust me, Father," she smiled, and he couldn't resist. Josefina had always been rational and he trusted her to make a wise decision. He admired his daughter, for she saw the other girls of Ybor City who went nowhere without a chaperone, and decided they were not who she wanted to be. To escape their parents and the shadow of supervision those girls married young but Josefina was not interested in weddings or matrimony. She yearned to be useful outside of the home and an asset to the world at large.

What more could Salvador do with a daughter so passionate about Cuba Libre than allow her to return and liberate his father's land? He gave her his blessing and before she departed for her training with sixteen other aspiring nurses, Salvador pulled her aside and slipped a five dollar bill into her hand. "It might come in handy," he winked. Josefina smiled, showing her dimples, and kissed her father's cheek.

In the summer of 1898, Josefina was sent to the floating hospital ship *Solace* which brought her to the theater of war. The ship could accommodate two hundred patients and was fitted with a large operating room and a canvas-enclosed contagious disease ward built on the hurricane deck. The sight of the soldiers and the guns made Josefina realize how serious this was. The ships they sailed with were not heading to Cuba with passengers destined to visit old friends, or to visit their favorite market. Men were being sent to kill, and Josefina would be right there with them.

She looked to the mast where the Red Cross flag of Geneva flew, and remembered that she was doing humanitarian work. When the first men wounded during the bombardment of San Juan were collected,

Josefina had her first personal experience with war. Bleeding men hollered in pain while others slept so quietly they didn't seem alive. Some lived, and others died but Josefina trusted her faith in God and knew that He had a plan for all of them.

It was during the surgery of a young man who'd been shot through the leg that Josefina worked closely with a young Spanish doctor named Andres Domínguez from Tampa. A thin young man with a pointed nose that held wire-rimmed glasses upon a nearly bald head, Josefina took a liking to him immediately. Andres had come from Asturias in the Spanish peninsula a decade ago, practiced medicine in Tampa and had volunteered to help with the war effort. Josefina found it odd at first that a Spaniard had volunteered to help the American military in a war against Spain but the approachable doctor clarified. "I am an American citizen. I have considered myself an American since my father moved us to Florida in 1888."

His father had been a political activist in Spain, identified as a radical by the opposition Spanish government, and had been pressured to leave the country in order to stay alive. Andres harbored a bit of animosity towards the peninsula, but he did not reject his heritage. He was an active member of Ybor City's Spanish social club, Centro Español, and had urged the club to build their own private hospital.

"The social club pays injury benefits and death benefits," he explained, "but they are against the construction of a hospital. They cite concerns over the cost but I believe they are afraid to forge into such unknown territory."

Josefina liked to sit and listen to the doctor as he described the health situation in the South, and especially the field of medicine in Tampa. Once, after the *Solace* had unloaded a boatload of sick and wounded soldiers – both Spanish and American – at Hampton Roads and turned to return to Cuba, Dr. Domínguez and Josefina had a long discussion.

"In the early days of Ybor City, the immigrants died like flies. The men who built the city battled mosquitoes and alligators but most of all, the unsanitary conditions, and especially the water. Even today, water is not considered safe unless it is passed through filters, but ten, fifteen years ago Ybor City was as dirty as an outhouse. And though it still has a long way to go, progress has been made."

Josefina listened quietly as they sat on the ship's deck. Andres said, "Immigrants faced a challenge, one that we still face today, a challenge that I know you have experienced. A social and linguistic barrier that separates the immigrant community from Anglo Tampa. White doctors rarely understand our language or the tropical ailments common in Cuba and Central America. Thus, there is a pressing need for health services in the Latin community. The cigar factories have always been a dangerous place to work."

"My father and my brothers work there. My mother too, from time to time."

Andres spoke sternly. "The factories are a breeding ground for tuberculosis. The workers chew tobacco all day and then spit on the floors, rarely using spittoons, and the windows remain closed in order to preserve the moisture of the tobacco leaves. In a hot, humid environment like that it is a blessing every cigar worker has not become stricken by disease."

Josefina thought of her family who were virtually uneducated in the health conditions of the factories. Then Dr. Domínguez continued talking, and her attention was back to him.

"The mutual aid programs and benefits administered by the factories are not enough. Like I said, they represent progress, but more must be done. Your father and brothers probably pay about thirty cents a week into some kind of fund and in return receive the services of a physician."

Josefina shrugged. She had no idea.

Andres nodded. "There are a couple of clinics in Ybor City, but their services are limited to the capabilities of two or three doctors. There are no hospital beds, not enough for immigrants, with insufficient operating rooms and no pharmacy. Anglo Tampa has these things, why not Ybor City and West Tampa?"

Josefina agreed with a nod.

"If the cigar workers can organize massive work stoppages, support Cuba Libre, conduct labor demonstrations and operate soup kitchen, if they can pool their funds to aid out-of-work families, what is stopping them from organizing a full scale mutual aid society? Contract medicine?

Hospitals, funds and scholarships to educate more doctors and nurses? A Tampa college of medicine!"

Josefina laughed knowing the doctor was only dreaming of the possibilities. He grinned and then became serious. "The Hillsborough County Medical Society is against people like me. They have already labeled mutual aid as socialistic and un-American. It is almost as if they are prepared to wage war against any physician whose desire is to serve the Latin community.

"The Medical Society petitioned the War Department and claimed Tampa was the healthiest city in America. This was one reason, along with its location, that Tampa was chosen as the staging point for this war. With all the troops coming into town, the overcrowding led to an outbreak of diseases. Half the soldiers suffered from heat stroke as they marched through Tampa in their wool uniforms with no food or water. Have you been to their camps?"

"No," she shook her head.

"Dismal. Water supplies are contaminated, sanitation is poor, and the problems spill into the civilian community. The summer rains will most definitely bring with them an outbreak of malaria. Though the Army brought its own doctors, civilians such as me are needed wherever we can help." He turned to her. "It is very honorable for you to volunteer your services."

She shrugged, "I was useless in school and jealous to see my younger brothers handing their wages over to my parents."

"And I could not stand to see these troops, enlisted like pawns to fight against my home country, brought to a city that was wrongly advertised as the healthiest in the land."

"You are being harsh," said Josefina. "You make it sound as though this is an unjust war, a corrupt war."

"I have not condemned the war, nor have I questioned its legitimacy. The body that governs Tampa's health care is my opposition. There are many like me, Asturians within Centro Español, who have talked about building a hospital. That is my objective. Call me radical, call me a socialist, but I believe the Spanish and Cuban immigrants in Tampa deserve their own hospital. If Anglo Tampa will not help us, then we must help ourselves."

Josefina vowed silently that night, to help Dr. Domínguez in his fight. She was a nurse, a Cuban nurse, and part of the Latin community that Anglo Tampa refused to help. Josefina knew her father struggled against similar forces in the cigar industry. This war between Cubans and Spaniards would be settled on the battlefield but another battle was brewing in the factories.

The shooting war ended after four months, but it was not until Josefina was stationed at Stenberg Field Hospital at Camp Thomas in Georgia that she was faced with a true test of her mental and physical limitations. The military camp where ailing soldiers recovered from malaria and typhoid fever had sanitary conditions worse than anything she could imagine, where dysentery and diarrhea were so abundant – and Josefina became so used to the odor – that she choked on the smell of fresh air.

When she first saw the thirteen unfinished board huts that stood for the hospital Josefina knew she was in for a challenge. With holes cut for windows and no screen to protect the patients from the swarm of flies and mosquitoes that constantly streamed in, the nurses were faced with a choice: cover the openings with wooden boards and eliminate all ventilation, or leave them open and deal with the insects. The weather seemed to be ninety degrees all day and if the windows were closed the huts became ovens filled with humid air soaked with soldiers' sweat and diarrhea. So they left the windows opened and invited swarms of insects that tormented the hospital as if they had come directly from the Bible

After only two days moving about these crowded shacks Josefina considered deserting the camp and returning to Tampa. Only one lantern hung in the middle of each hut for light and the little iron beds were so close together that Josefina was constantly tearing her clothes and scratching her legs on the bed wires. There was no laundry soap, cleaning supplies were scarce and cold water was such a rare commodity that it was reserved only for sick soldiers, and those who needed it most. Hot water did not exist.

Most horrifying to Josefina was the hygienic situation. The camp had three toilets for two hundred nurses, located five hundred feet from the sleeping quarters. There was nowhere to bathe and the heat was so bad that Josefina's clothes seemed to be constantly soaked with sweat. Her shift lasted more than sixteen hours and by the end of the day Josefina would fall asleep with no concern over whether she would ever wake up again, so tired that she regularly skipped her evening prayer.

But it was exactly what she had been searching for. This was just the type of experience Josefina had wanted, something her brothers could never top, so when one of her young counterparts threw her nurse's cap aside and abandoned the camp, Josefina stayed. She had a duty to these men and though she often found herself wishing an illness or injury would send her home, the grace and appreciation of the soldiers kept her on her feet.

There were times when a soldier would succumb to disease and die wailing for his mother, or choke on a final breath while his bowels relaxed and emptied on the wooden floor below. In moments like these, Josefina forced herself from looking away, and saved the tears for bedtime when she would be alone, too anguished and exhausted to cry.

Even her strong will and fortitude, and her dedication to the sick, could not withstand the camp's terrible sanitation problems. She soon had her own stomach pains, then diarrhea and vomiting. She tried to ignore her own illness and blamed her fever on the intense September heat but her intestines had become inflamed with bacteria that thrived in poor conditions. Diarrhea and sweats brought dehydration that Josefina could not fight. While tending to a soldier sick with malaria, and swatting mosquitoes from her blurred vision, Josefina collapsed onto the dirty hospital floor.

Now bedridden like the wounded, Josefina was diagnosed with dysentery and given water and chloride of lime – the same solution the Army used to sterilize the sewers of Havana. It tasted terrible, and Josefina prayed that God would deliver her from this camp and take her back to Tampa. Blessed with a strong immune system, Josefina's situation stabilized, and as soon as she was able to travel, she rode a train from Chickamauga to Atlanta to Tampa. Instead of returning to the Ortiz house, discharged from her duties and fifteen pounds lighter, she went to the clinic of Dr. Domínguez in West Tampa, a small house west of the Hillsborough River where he lived with his patients.

He was surprised she had come to him first and was happy to see her. "You don't look well," he said as he greeted her at the front door, noticing the outline of her clavicle and bony shoulders. "Please, come inside."

She stepped into a small parlor and sat on the couch. Andres hurried to bring her a glass of water with some ice and then sat beside her. She told the story of Camp Thomas and he listened quietly until she was finished. Then he asked, "If you are sick why haven't you notified your family?"

"Because I do not want them to worry."

Andres understood. He knew Josefina well enough to know that the eighteen-year-old girl was protecting her pride. "Do they know you are home?"

She shook her head. "When they learn I am home, they will throw a giant party and invite the whole neighborhood. Right now I need to rest, for a day or two. I can return when I am healthy and ready." She finished her water and handed over the empty glass. Her black eyes said more than her words. "I can go to a hotel."

"No," he shook his head, reading her mind. "You need medical attention. Stay here."

Josefina stayed at the clinic for a week and used one of the small hospital rooms like a typical patient. She recovered and returned to the Ortiz house, greeted by the faint smell of cigars and the sound of a Spanish guitar strumming somewhere across the street. After dinner that night she sat on the porch swing with her mother, savoring the familiarity of home. Her brothers E.J. and Lázaro played baseball on the street corner with the neighborhood children and Songo and his dog Pano returned from a walk next door.

Olympia saw a smile unlike any she had ever seen in her daughter. It was not the playful, charming grin Josefina flashed when she was being coy but rather a glow, an emotion she had rarely displayed. Olympia was a grown woman of thirty-five who recognized the look. "What is his name?"

"Dr. Andres Domínguez," Josefina said after a brief pause. "We are getting married!"

Olympia patted her daughter's leg. Her oldest child, the half-peasant grandchild of a wealthy sugar planter was going to marry a Spanish doctor. Olympia wondered what would have happened had she remained at the plantation. Would Josefina feel so happy and proud? Would Salvador have been captured by Spanish soldiers and executed like his parents? Or would he have joined the rebel army and marched to glorious victory in the final war against Spain? And what if Olympia had run away but ditched Salvador and attempted to swim to Cabo Corrientes with her baby on her back?

She pondered these questions while she watched the children play on the sandy street – her son E.J. stood on a pile of Spanish moss used for second base. Olympia was proud of her family and knew that in her battle with Testifonte, she could finally celebrate her own personal victory.

IV.

VASQUEZ AND COMPANY
1899

El Boletín de los Obreros
(The Workers' Bulletin)

Vida Después de España
(Life After Spain)

by Gabriel Mendez
December 11, 1898

The surrender of Spanish forces has brought forth a significant change for the Cuban workers exiled in Florida. Spain has been vanquished – her flag no longer waves above our island, but what does this mean for the peaceful society of Cubans in Florida? After having been preoccupied for so long with the struggle for an independent Cuba, the end of the war with Spain forces us to ask: are we really better off?

Cuba is free of Spanish colonialism but is now faced with Yankee imperialism. Will this be a welcomed change, or will the US simply resume the persecution of the working class that began under Spanish rule?

It is clear that the war benefits the American financial situation more than it helps the Cuban worker. Teddy Roosevelt, the darling of the war, was recently elected governor of the State of New York. Clearly his victory in Cuba (and his success in the newspapers) will be the spark of a triumphant and lucrative political career.

Victory in Cuba has also helped to repair and unite the United States, which is still healing the fractures of her own civil war. President McKinley was recently cheered in the South, to the sound of Dixie, with the old Confederate General Joe Wheeler at his side.

I wonder what the US victory in Cuba can do to mend our damaged island, and if American leadership in the Cuban War for Independence has made Cuba any more independent?

Cuba faces an uncertain future. The nature and function of exile has changed. With our island nearly destroyed, and 50,000 Cuban soldiers emerging from the jungle to try to find jobs in an exhausted market (there are currently 200 sugar mills in Cuba, compared to 1,100 before the war) the exiled worker's enthusiasm to leave Florida and return to Cuba has died. There seems to be little point in resuming a life on a war-torn island, when our homes and our children are here.

If Cuba Libre has taught us anything, it is that we were able to build a large, powerful revolutionary society through dedication and hard work. And it is to our movement, our society in Tampa and Ybor City that our attention must shift. The approaching wave of US investment and political power in Cuba cannot be avoided. Thus, we must insulate our society from the impact of American corporate efficiency.

Cuban workers in Tampa will not be completely emancipated until they realize that social liberty is more beneficial to an exiled worker than a liberated Cuban republic. Independence in Cuba cannot be ignored or opposed, but it brings no benefit to the exiled worker. Only harm.

The goal of Cuba Libre was the greatest possible amount of freedom for all – to do as we wish without harming others, and to have equal access to the resources of the world. American money will soon take over these resources in Cuba, and the worker will soon feel its effects here.

Can anyone deny that the rich Spanish cigar manufacturers, and the powerful American corporate tycoons and politicians, have access to the best of the world's resources? This argument can be made with respects to housing, health care, education, leisure, and any aspect of everyday life. Is this why the blood of our sons has been shed? Is this why the cigar worker has dedicated his relatively modest wages? Was Cuba Libre purely for the benefit of the American political and business elite?

The Cuban worker must not succumb to imperialism or the pressures of American business. He must embrace his social liberties and remain a large, revolutionary body, unwilling to surrender to the slavery of capitalism. The worker must remain as united as he was in the face of Spanish tyranny; otherwise he is not worth the tears spilled over his fallen soldiers.

The worker must take control. He must be sure it is he who rides in the saddle. His fight has not been to further the financial and imperial aspirations of the United States. The corporate hierarchy will not determine his freedoms; instead, the Cuban worker will be his own master. It was his war, it is his island, and this is his social liberty. He will be his own master. In the words of the Apostle Martí, 'With all, and for the benefit of all.' And long live Cuba!

Chapter 9

"A good cigar is judged by its taste, color, and aroma, but a *great* cigar possesses other qualities that are more elusive. Its elegance must fit the expectations of the cigar sophisticate who promises himself that he'll light one up as soon as he finishes dinner. He may have whiskey, wine, coffee, cognac, it doesn't matter. There are no rules that say this drink must accompany that cigar. Nor does the setting matter; it is up to the taste of the smoker. In this sense, smoking a cigar is an act of independence. To enjoy a fine cigar is to savor one's freedom.

"The elegant smoker has his drink in hand before he begins smoking, so he won't have to worry about getting up again once he has settled into his chair. Before he lights his cigar, all his attention is devoted to examining its craftsmanship. The color and shape should be uniform, a perfect tube with no soft spots or bulges, identical to the brothers it was packaged with. The wrapper, whether *claro* or *maduro*, should be free of blemish. It should have a subtle aroma of chocolate, vanilla, spice, perhaps even coffee or roasted nuts.

"An experienced gentleman can tell whether a cigar will be good or bad simply by smelling it, but *excellence* cannot be determined until after it has been lit. It may have a perfect color, layered flavors, and a pleasant aroma, but burn badly. If the body heats unevenly and becomes jagged, or if the wrapper begins to peel, the cigar loses its integrity. It becomes a nuisance, something the smoker must tend to rather than savor. A great cigar retains its beauty and symmetry as it is consumed.

"Like this one, it is our best." Don Antonio Vasquez, son of the legendary tobacconist Florentino Vasquez, placed the cigar on a silver tray and pushed it across the dining table to his seventeen-year-old son, Antonio Junior. "The Vasquez and Company Don Florentino with the *maduro* wrapper, considered by many to be without peer. Notice the beauty of the wrapper. It is dark and even, almost black. Take special note of the quality. The leaf has been cured and fermented to perfection. This is a gentleman's cigar, not like the refuse smoked by the workers."

Antonio Junior inspected the cigar as instructed while Don Antonio watched his son. "No life form on this planet undergoes such a slow and graceful death as the tobacco leaf." Don Antonio paused for emphasis. "The leaves of our cigars are handpicked from the best *vuelta* in Cuba. I have visited these farms many times and we buy a product that is grown on the best soil and cured through the most careful, painstaking process. Tobacco leaves are like women, Antonito. They are complicated, they must be cared for, caressed and loved, and kept under close watch, otherwise they will take you for all you're worth!"

Vasquez produced a box of matches. "Lighting the cigar is the best part. Watch what happens." He placed the cigar in his mouth and struck a match then rolled the end of the cigar in the flame until it burned with a perfect red coal. Vasquez exhaled a long, cone-shaped puff of smoke and the room immediately took on the aroma of fine tobacco. "Notice how it does not smell like smoke?"

"It smells like tobacco," said Antonio Junior.

"Which is exactly how it should be! Light yours!"

Antonio Junior lit his own cigar and sat back, blowing his smoke upwards and over the table. He was a younger version of his father, the latter being a heavyset fellow, always dressed in a three-piece suit with the gold chain of a pocket watch strung across his belly and a company brand cigar dangling between his fingers. Don Antonio's black hair was thinning on top, a contrast to his son's healthy head of full black, and both wore thin moustaches – Antonito's was thinner and not as gray as his father's.

The Vasquez men smiled rarely, and the father seemed to be eternally preoccupied with matters of business and was always quick to solicit input from his advisors before making a decision. His father Florentino was the mastermind who had built Vasquez and Company, and Don Antonio was aware that he lacked his father's brilliance in conducting business affairs. Decisions had been instinctual to Florentino who possessed a natural business acumen that made his management seem whimsical and without serious consideration. After he died three years ago, Antonio took over and moved the company to Ybor City, carefully laboring over minor details of the transition, second-guessing himself and delaying decisions until opportunities had expired.

Antonio Vasquez knew he was not as effective as his father. Although Vasquez and Company cigars were still regarded among the best in the world, their reputation had been waning as more and more cigar manufacturers entered the market. Vasquez often felt he was guiding his father's company into a slow, dismal failure that would have shamed Florentino. He hoped to pass the business onto his son and continue a family tradition but the Americanization of the cigar industry threatened that dream as small cigar companies began to be swallowed by American corporations. The quality of Vasquez's product had kept the company afloat, and Don Antonio needed to be sure his son understood the old world traditions that defined their brand.

He said to Antonito, "As you draw the cigar, there should be slight resistance, and it should be smooth throughout. If the cigar is heavy with leaves, rolled too tight, the draw will be plugged and you won't be able to pull much smoke. If the draw is too easy, the cigar was not rolled with enough leaves and will burn much too quickly. The perfect cigar will draw somewhere in the middle, not too tight, not too loose but consistent throughout the entire experience."

Don Antonio switched his cigar to his left hand and watched it burn. "After you take the smoke into your mouth, keep it there for a second or two and blow it out slowly. Then take the tip of your tongue and brush it along the roof of your mouth." Don Antonio showed how. "And *that's* how to enjoy the taste of the cigar!"

Antonito tried as his father had instructed and nodded to signal it worked. They smoked in silence for a moment. Antonito let his cigar dangle from his mouth while he rested his arms over his plump little belly.

The rest of the guests lit their cigars. Among them Armando Renteria said, "This business of tobacco has always been a family affair." The men nodded in agreement.

Also at the table were Pipi Capecho, the Vasquez factory foreman and financial advisor, Rolando Ragano, an Italian-Spaniard who owned a small share of Vasquez and Company as well as half the *bolita* and all of the prostitution in Tampa, and businessman Arlen Kincaid, sole owner of the *Tampa Daily News*, partial owner of Vasquez and Company, and the only member of the dinner party not of Spanish blood.

When Armando said the business of tobacco was a family enterprise, he spoke of his own history. The Renteria and Vasquez families had been partners in the cigar business for over forty years. Before he died and left Vasquez and Company to his son, Florentino Vasquez was the owner of a successful bank in Spain, and an avid smoker and aficionado of the hand-rolled, clear Havana cigar. In 1858, when Antonio was only seven, Florentino sold his institution, moved his family to Havana and purchased a small, floundering cigar factory. Florentino financially resurrected the company and renamed it Vasquez and Company. He paid premium salaries, and hired experts to run the operation and his cigars quickly gained international recognition for their high quality and superior taste.

After the Ten Years' War, when several cigar factories in Cuba relocated to Florida, Don Antonio moved his father's operation to Ybor City and Armando, a man that Vasquez considered to be a close cousin, soon followed. While Vasquez concentrated strictly on cigars, Armando found ways to diversify his enterprises in Ybor City. He had invested in Vasquez and Company and owned nearly twenty percent of the company, but Armando also controlled the other half of Tampa's *bolita* racket. A rival of Rolando Ragano, Armando's interest in the illegal game produced an enormous amount of cash flow from the immigrant cigar makers, so much that the police were willing to ignore these escapades. For their tolerance of *bolita*, Armando and Rolando diverted ten percent of their profits to Tampa's chief of police.

Vasquez said to Armando, "Our fathers worked together to start this enterprise over forty years ago. And now, as we begin a new era, Vasquez and Company will lead the tradition of the finest cigars into the Twentieth Century."

The dinner meeting at the Vasquez mansion was for the owners of the company to discuss the long term prosperity of their business. They were among the Tampa elite, and Antonio Junior was honored, and a bit intimidated, to be sitting in one of his father's high-level business meetings for the first time. Now Vasquez poured cognac for his guests, including his son, and the men sat back to puff their cigars.

Vasquez said, "The arrival of the American military in town brought the attention of the world and resulted in record revenue for Vasquez and Company. Now that the war is over and life has returned to normal, we stand at a crossroad, my friends. Spain has ended its time in this part of the world; we have lost control of Cuba and face a decision. Many of our countrymen have sold their interests to American corporations and returned to the peninsula. Others have chosen to stay and keep their homes in Tampa, Havana or Key West. What will be your decision? To remain players in this competitive cigar industry or to cash in your interests and go your own way?"

Vasquez feared he'd be abandoned by his investors and left to return their investments or worse: to lose his partners and have no choice but to sell his factory to an American corporation.

Arlen Kincaid answered first. He was the only American at the table, relatively young in his late thirties, with clean features and wire rimmed glasses that suited his intelligence. He was a forward-thinking man with his mind dedicated on building and cultivating relationships that could one day be profitable. "It is clear to me that the Cuban workforce is not going anywhere as long as there are cigar factories in Tampa. This is the cigar capital of the world and the *Daily News* will report on it every day. My life is here. I have no desire to leave, Don Antonio."

Vasquez nodded and smiled at the American. He had never doubted Kincaid's loyalty; the Spanish partners were the real concern. Vasquez looked to Armando. "You own twenty percent of this company, and hold a small stake in several factories throughout Tampa. Your father and your brother still operate a tobacco *vega* in Cuba that supplies nearly all of my raw materials. Though you are Cuban born, you are Spanish by blood. Tell me Armando, how long will your family remain in this part of the world? What plans have they to return to Spain?"

Armando poked his cigar into his black beard and blew smoke. "I am here to stay, Don Antonio. As long as money flows into *bolita*, neither I nor Rolando has reason to leave town. Even if you were to sell your majority interest in Vasquez and Company to an American corporation, I would remain."

Armando let his gaze fall on his rival, and Rolando nodded respectfully. Tall and lean, with a receding hairline and a dapper suit,

Rolando Ragano presented himself as a businessman but often bragged each week of having new prostitutes to offer out of the Pasaje Hotel.

The *bolita* business was strong and Armando had slowly taken control of all games played on the east side of town. He was competing with Rolando for complete ownership of the entire industry. Complete control of *bolita* with interests in several factories and continued support of the Tampa police would make Armando the most powerful entrepreneur in Tampa.

Then there was the female issue. Armando had said before that his relationship with Elena, his former wife, was over, and that the burning coals were now cold and sopping wet. Still, Vasquez suspected that a small spark, an invitation from Elena, could pull Armando out of Tampa and yank him back to the peninsula. Such was love. A man could be told, over and over again that love was dead and lost, yet the slightest hint of a renewal, real or imagined, had been known to turn wise men into fools.

Next Antonio turned to Rolando Ragano. Ragano was half Spanish, half Italian and rumored to have ties to the mafia in Italy. Born of a wealthy family in Cuba, Ragano had been accused of plotting to murder a Spanish official and successfully fled the island. He settled in Tampa and with the backing of his friends from Italy, Ragano became involved in *bolita* and prostitution in Tampa which gave him multiple sources of steady cash flow. He purchased shares of several legitimate businesses, including five percent of Vasquez and Company and fifteen percent of Banco Tampa, where his influence helped him be appointed president.

Armando watched closely as Ragano waved his hand toward Don Antonio, dismissing any thoughts of selling his interests and retiring. "I have no desire other than to remain in Tampa and grow my businesses."

Vasquez said, "Now that all the company's owners have pledged their support, our partnership remains intact. It is time to decide our company's future." Vasquez looked at Capecho, the factory foreman who also kept the company's books. A short Spanish man with a small frame and short black hair, he moved and spoke quickly, was excellent with numbers and had over twenty years experience in accounting and finance. Capecho was an industry expert originally hired by Florentino Vasquez.

Don Antonio said, "Tell us, Pipi, have we arrived at the time to execute our long term goal, to expand Vasquez and Company with branch operations in Jacksonville and Key West?"

Capecho replied, "It is no secret that our competition is fierce, profit margins are low, costs are high and cash is depleted. Though an influx of capital during this last year provided temporary relief, as you have said, the troops and reporters have left town and taken the hyperbole. As a result, the market has stabilized and we find ourselves struggling in a very competitive and modernizing industry. Sure, we can expand, but we must modernize and we must cut our costs."

Vasquez asked, "What is the best way to do both?"

"The easiest way to cut costs is to cut wages, but I advise strongly against this."

The others shifted uncomfortably. Armando said, "The workers will strike instantly and will only return for their original wages or better."

"I agree," said Capecho. "So we must attack this opportunity from the supply side. Currently there is no limit on the amount of tobacco a worker can use, and they are allotted as many as five leaves a day for personal use. This amounts to nearly a thousand cigars leaving the factory every single day for free. A tremendous waste! The introduction of quotas and weight restrictions on tobacco leaves can mitigate this loss and significantly reduce our overall costs."

Vasquez cursed himself for not considering this option – his father would have thought this through weeks ago. "Free tobacco leaves have been a fringe benefit to cigar workers for years. Any restriction on personal consumption would be viewed by my workers as an encroachment on their basic rights. There is a near certainty that quotas and restrictions on tobacco consumption will lead to a strike."

Armando spoke before anyone else could. "We have all agreed, Don Antonio that we find ourselves committed to modernization. A restriction on tobacco consumption is merely a measure of cost savings that is being employed across the industry. And I think that as owners, we can offer no further investment without results."

Vasquez looked to Ragano and Kincaid, who nodded their agreement.

Capecho said, "The workers could be persuaded to stay at work if only their *lector* did not have them on constant alert. Has anyone read what Mendez has been writing lately? He practically calls for a strike on principle!"

Vasquez said, "We can do nothing about Mendez. Now that Sando has retired, it is Mendez who was elected *lector* by the workers. He is an anarchist and a malcontent, but his newspaper is what the workers want to hear, not just in my factory but throughout Ybor City. I do not see Mendez sitting silent while the workers are faced with quotas."

"And we cannot do away with the *lector*," Kincaid added.

"Never," said Capecho. "We've learned that without the *lector*, the workers strike. And I do not blame them. The *lector* is as much a part of their society as Centro Español is to ours."

Antonio Junior spoke next and said something that shocked the rest. "What if Mendez was prohibited from arguing against the restrictions? What if he was *forced* to support the quota?"

The men were quiet for a moment, and then Armando began to chuckle, a deep bellowing laugh of approval. "Your son is shrewd, Don Antonio. His sense of business is bold, almost harsh. It could take him a long way." Armando held up his cognac and toasted Antonito.

Vasquez said, "My son is inexperienced and a bit naïve. Taking Mendez out will not guarantee that our workforce will be subdued and compliant with new standards. And if Mendez were to go, there are dozens who would take his place."

"I don't think Antonio Junior is proposing the use of force," Armando said with an eyebrow raised towards the boy. "Perhaps Mendez can be persuaded. Let me approach him as a businessman. Let me talk to him and perhaps an agreement can be reached."

Vasquez held up a finger. "Mendez is not a man who can be bought."

Armando pulled from his cigar and sat back. "I am surprised that you would underestimate me, Don Antonio."

*　　　*　　　*

112

After dinner Armando and Rolando traveled by streetcar into Ybor City, headed for the Pasaje Hotel where they would have a late night drink and possibly a couple of prostitutes. As the streetcar rolled through Ybor City, Rolando said, "The fat man is having a hard time dispensing with the old world traditions of a cigar factory. He is putting up too much resistance to modernization for my comfort. I fear our investment dollars may be at risk."

Armando was not as concerned. "Do not worry about the fat man. He'll do what is right once his current accounts go past due and he sees his competitors adjusting for the new century. I want to show you the plans I have for a new string of cigar factories!"

Rolando raised an eyebrow as the streetcar screeched to a halt at Ninth Avenue and Fourteenth Street, outside the two-floor, redbrick Pasaje Hotel. Though the men were rivals in the world of *bolita*, their financial interests were intertwined, and they often consulted each other in matters of the cigar industry. Armando led Rolando beyond the Pasaje and west on Ninth.

Rolando followed Armando across Thirteenth Street, where there was nothing but vacant land and palm trees. This was the far west end of town, an empty plot of land between Ybor City and the Hillsborough River. The sounds of streetcars and wagons had faded into the nighttime chirpings of insects and the brushing of the warm, Florida breeze.

Armando opened his arms to the vacant land. "Imagine, Rolando, a string of brand new, modern factories between here and the river, with easy access to the port and railroads. State of the art equipment, the most talented workers using tobacco shipped directly from my father's *vega* in Cuba. Imagine the name, my friend, Renteria and Ragano Cigars, world famous and impossible to resist!"

Ragano smiled as he imagined a row of brick cigar factories capped with American flags. A streetcar line expanded into the new development, new businesses opening close to the factories, bars and taverns that he could control. Mountains and mountains of *bolita* dollars in his pocket.

He grinned at Armando. "Renteria and Ragano, eh? You are proposing a partnership in this new enterprise?" He extended his hand for Armando to shake. "Fifty-fifty, and we discuss it over brandy?"

Armando did not smile, his face was unusually serious. Instead of shaking Rolando's hand, Armando grabbed his rival's wrist. Before Rolando had time to react, Armando pulled Rolando close and swung his right hand upwards from below, digging a knife into Rolando's chest.

"On second thought," Armando said as he twisted the knife under Rolando's sternum. "I don't need a partner. All I need is your business."

"You son of a bitch," Rolando gasped. The blade had entered his abdomen just below the rib cage and had pierced him with such surprise that Rolando went into shock almost immediately. He was able to take one short breath but Armando had dug the blade upward into one of Rolando's lungs and the wounded man quickly lost the strength to fight back.

As Rolando slowly slumped to the ground, he grabbed onto the collar of Armando's suit but his rival continued to twist and turn his blade, slicing Rolando's insides. Rolando knew he was a dead man and realized he had been lured from the city into this remote spot, away from any eyewitness, hidden by the cover of night. As he choked on his final breath, he wondered if his body would be discovered before it was devoured by the critters of the wild.

"Rot in hell, Spaniard," Rolando gasped as his dead body slumped facedown to the dirt. Armando pulled his blade away and squatted, using the back of Rolando's coat to wipe the blood from his knife.

Armando noticed his collar was crumpled where Rolando had clung for balance, and a splatter of blood tarnished his sleeve. "One of my best shirts. Do you know how much this cost?" He reached into Rolando's back pocket and removed his wallet, took all the cash, and tossed the rest aside. He left the rings and jewelry and then hurried back to town, ducking into the Pasaje Hotel to bide his time.

He ventured to the top floor, known as a house of ill repute operated by Rolando, and paid a visit to the young prostitute Gisela. Gisela was twenty-one years old and almost completely blind. Orphaned as a small child, the malnourished Gisela arrived at a mission in the Bahamas and was cared for entirely by Catholic nuns. The girl was sick, vomiting constantly and covered with rashes, and it was quickly discovered that she suffered from scarlet fever. She was treated but showed little improvement and soon developed viral meningitis. Her vision suffered, becoming blurred and foggy, until she lived in total darkness, sensitive only to powerful direct sunlight.

As she healed, Gisela's vision problem set her apart from the rest of the girls at the orphanage and at age thirteen, she ran away with another girl, another misfit, and quickly turned to drugs and prostitution. For eight years she had been living hard and was not sure how much longer she would last. She knew she was slowly killing herself and was resigned to a slow, drawn out death.

Though she was blind, Gisela was considered to be quite attractive with her slim figure and long black hair, and was popular among the hotel's clientele, which included top businessmen from Tampa and elite visitors from out of town. The most recent dignitary rumored to have spent an evening with the bordello's madam was Teddy Roosevelt. Some say he only spent a few hours upstairs and shared nothing more than a drink with the club's top call girl, a dark and attractive woman from the Azores who called herself Madam Kitty. Others claimed Colonel Roosevelt enjoyed all the benefits of the club and returned many times to visit the madam.

Armando usually stopped at the Pasaje after hours, when the taverns had closed and most men had gone home. Gisela always recognized his long strides and heavy footsteps – Armando made his presence known even as he walked down the hall. When the door to her room opened, she sensed his bombastic presence. The smell of cigars and alcohol was typical in the brothel but Armando usually drank bourbon before he came to see her, and the odor took over the room.

He took his time with Gisela, who thought of Armando as an intimidating man but one who made for tiresome work. He was slow to start, difficult to sustain, and finished only half of the time. He treated her carelessly, no differently than the rest of her patrons, and rarely paid extra for her service. When she heard his powerful footsteps clomping down the hall, she shuddered, tensed and drank two shots of rum before he arrived in the room.

It was a typical visit for Armando. He took his time getting started and went for nearly half an hour before he finally gave up and collapsed beside her exhausted and displeased. She sat up in bed and reached to the nightstand for the bottle of rum, poured herself a glass and handed the bottle to Armando. "Your mind again?"

He grunted and took the bottle. "My mind, that's usually the problem, isn't it?"

"So what's new?"

Armando swung his feet over the edge of the bed and took a gulp of rum as Gisela brought her knees to her chest and coiled her arms around them. The night was silent except for a streetcar dinging in the distance.

Gisela heard voices on the street below. Two men calling to each other; she swore she heard one shout, "Get help."

Armando stood and went to the window to view the commotion outside. He peered down to Fourteenth Street where two Cuban men in work clothes jogged towards the city, away from the scene of the crime.

Rolando's body had been discovered.

Gisela said, "What's all that yelling about?"

Armando wanted to tell her, "Your boss is dead."

He imagined her reaction would be minimal. There was no love between a prostitute and her pimp, and Rolando's death would be inconsequential to Gisela. She would have nothing to do but keep working until another took his place.

It would be foolish for Armando to reveal his knowledge of the murder to the prostitute. She remained sitting up on the bed with her arms wrapped around her knees and her head cocked slightly, training her ears on the sounds outside.

"Nothing more than two drunken Cubans," Armando said as he opened his wallet and tossed a few bills – Rolando's bills – onto the bedspread. Gisela listened to him leave then finished her rum and drifted into a tired, drunken sleep.

As he walked to his apartment, Armando thought of his ex-wife, somewhere in Spain. After nine years of marriage Armando was surprised she had tolerated him for as long as she did. One source of conflict was her longstanding desire to return to Spain versus his love of his career and the Americas. But even more significant was their inability to have children, for which Elena did not think she was to blame. Even when Armando was able to finish their lovemaking, his wife had never become pregnant. When she became thirty-five her desire to breed was overwhelming. Though Armando tried, it seemed to Elena that his heart was not there and he didn't seem to care if they had children or not.

Though the marriage existed on paper, it died slowly in their hearts. Armando started to go out more often at night, making regular visits to the Pasaje. Prostitutes were harder to disappoint.

Suspicious of his late arrivals, which became more and more frequent, Elena confronted Armando on his adultery. They fought an intense battle where all grievances were revealed. Secret thoughts and brutal accusations were levied until Armando lost his temper and struck Elena. He quickly went out and when he returned the next morning, Elena was gone. After three months of silence Armando was contacted by a lawyer from Spain.

When Armando struck Elena, she finally realized his deep disrespect for women. His father was a wealthy landowner and Armando had grown up on a plantation populated by slaves. He had often talked of how he and his brother had taunted and abused the female slaves and even bragged about losing his virginity to a young worker who was little more than a child. Armando had never been taught about the need for scruples and was used to getting everything he wanted. Elena had known this all along, but it took Armando's fist to force her out of denial.

He reached his apartment and went straight to his bed. Before he slept he thought of Gisela and how she reminded him of those young slaves he used to harass. Armando knew that Gisela was an orphan, perhaps a child of slaves, and he saw her the way he saw the young workers from his father's tobacco plantation. She was a lowlife to be used at his discretion, one step below the city's filthy cigar workers. It mattered little that he was unable to sexually function in her presence.

Armando suspected that Vasquez knew about his violence toward Elena, but other than his former wife, only Gisela knew of Armando's sexual failures. There was no way Vasquez or any of his partners could know these unflattering details; Elena had not been the type to associate with businessmen. And what chance was there that Gisela had talked to Vasquez? Or Mendez? None.

But if somehow, by strange chance, someone did learn the truth, Armando's reputation in Tampa would be tarnished. He would no longer be known as an admired industrialist who was supported by Tampa's top levels of business and government. He would be a laughingstock, the Impotent Investor. Short of respect and out of business.

His secret was safe and now that Rolando was dead, Armando could proceed with the next phase of his plan: assuming control of Rolando's *bolita* racket and owning the game citywide.

Chapter 10

The next day was Saturday, and Armando set out to collect the skim from the previous night's *bolita* games, starting at La Rubia where he met El Gallego at the bar.

Gallego handed Armando his share of the cash. "I've been working on something pretty goddamn interesting. Come see." Gallego took Armando to a small office behind the bar and held out a blank, white *bolita* ball.

Armando took the ball in his hand and noticed immediately that it was much heavier than it should be. "It's heavy, like a ball from a black powder rifle."

"Lead," said Gallego. "It will sink to the bottom faster than an old coon trying to swim, so I can feel for it during the cut. We track the bets before the throw and paint this ball with the number that has the highest odds, or arrange side bets on the weighted number. When I reach through the sack to tie off a ball, I choose this heavy one. We can change the number for every throw and fool those Cuban pricks every time. What do you think?"

"Thoughtful," Armando admitted with a nod. "What's the risk?"

"Are you worried that Mick cop will start flapping his balls over this crap? The risk is minimal. Someone will hit the same number sooner or later. It won't reduce our payouts, but they can be offset. Think of it as a hedge."

Armando smiled. "And you're thinking like a Jew. I expect a taste."

Gallego nodded. "Of course, old bastard, count on that."

Armando patted Gallego on the shoulder. "There might be some more business coming our way."

Gallego raised an interested eyebrow but Armando only nodded and left the bar, leaving El Gallego guessing.

Next Armando went to the Sanchez Brothers General Merchandise store where he met up with the twin brothers. Benny and Eddie Sanchez had moved from Spain to Cuba with their family in the 1870's. Their father had opened a shop in Havana called Sanchez General Store, where his sons worked until the war drove them away from the island and to the thriving community of Ybor City. After their father passed away, Benny and Eddie changed the name of the shop and established themselves on Eighth Avenue and Eighteenth Street, three blocks from Centro Español in the heart of town.

The Sanchez brothers were not small men. Their twin frames were husky and healthy, intimidating to strangers, but the brothers came off as good natured to those who knew them well. They moved quickly for their size, and were graceful and gentlemanly, especially around their friends and inside the store, where their deep voices could often be heard politely helping customers. Both of average height, their arms and legs were stout, their hands large and powerful. The brothers suffered whenever the local cigar factories shut down and wages ceased. Hence, their relationship with Armando was more than cordial.

Partners in Armando's *bolita* enterprise, the brothers sold chances out of their store, where it was customary for customers to purchase a ticket along with a bag of sugar or bar of soap. Armando often hired the brothers, using their size to his advantage, when he needed to collect from a past due colleague.

As he met the brothers in the store that morning, Armando grinned and leaned against the counter. "You boys want to make a little extra money?"

Their first stop was the Gonzalez Bakery on Eighth Avenue where they were greeted by the pleasant smell of baking bread and sweet pastries. Proprietor Porfirio Gonzalez was behind the counter arranging a tray of *pastel de guayaba* behind the glass display case. When the bearded one entered the store flanked by the heavy Benny Sanchez, Porfirio instantly knew something had changed. The lanky and balding Gonzalez stood at attention behind the counter as Armando smugly approached him.

"We're here to collect last night's skim."

Porfirio was visibly surprised. "Where is Rolando Ragano? I thought he owned the game."

Armando leaned against the counter and smiled gently. "He did, my friend, but he has left town permanently."

They visited three more businesses that had sold *bolita* chances under the backing of Rolando, and claimed the proceeds for their own. Rolando's murder had hit the morning paper and many of his partners wondered what to do about the game. When they were visited by the man with the beard, they quickly complied with his demands, not wanting to upset the *bolita* racket and fearing they'd suffer Rolando's fate. Once their rounds were complete, Armando paid the Sanchez Brothers their share of the skim, then returned to his office on Fifteenth Street.

A small, tidy office with the words "Renteria Investment Capital" painted on the window in Spanish, Armando had an apartment upstairs where he lived alone. He sat at the office desk and started counting the morning collection. A few minutes later the front door opened and in walked chief of police Sean McGrath.

The chief was in his late fifties, tall and slim with red hair and an Irish accent that he had brought from the island as a teenager when his parents had immigrated to the States. The chief had a newspaper under his arm and after he walked to Armando's desk, he tossed the paper on top of Armando's pile of cash.

"Our friend was murdered," said the chief.

Armando glanced to the headline of the *Tampa Daily News*. It read "Bank President Found Stabbed." Armando looked up to the chief and waited.

McGrath said, "Where were you last night?"

Armando sat back and said, "Let me ask you this: how much did Rolando pay you to ignore the *bolita* syndicate?"

McGrath was stone-faced, "Ten percent."

"And what do I pay you?"

"Ten percent."

Armando moved the newspaper and counted off a handful of bills. He handed them to the chief. "Here's fifteen. Come see me next week. We'll make it a regular thing."

"Grand," said the chief with no emotion of any kind. "Now I must be on my way. A respectable Irishman like me can't be seen fraternizing with a reputed lawbreaker and suspicious person like you, can I?"

Armando chuckled, making the chief smile. A nod of the head and a curt salute with his forefinger and the chief was on his way. Armando locked his cash in a safe under his desk. Next stop: lunch, followed by a visit to Vasquez factory *lector* and local radical journalist Gabriel Mendez.

The office of *The Workers' Bulletin* was located in Mendez's two-story house on Tenth Avenue, between Thirteenth and Fourteenth Streets. The first floor housed a small, cast iron printing press and an office in the front, which Mendez used as a meeting place and reception area. There was also a small bookcase library where Mendez kept the works of Mikhail Bakunin, Peter Kropotkin, Errico Malatesta and his own personal collection of novels by Hugo, Cervantes, Dumas and others. The rest of the items on the shelves were small, inexpensive pamphlets with essays on various political topics. Mendez, always believing in promoting his fellow writers, carried works by local talent and newcomers from Key West and Havana.

The building's backdoor led to an alley where Mendez had constructed a small loading dock from plywood. Each Monday Mendez paid pennies to schoolboys who picked up his publication and circulated it throughout town. The paper was also delivered by train to Jacksonville and New York and by boat to Havana and Key West.

Mendez was very serious about his work, and if he wasn't reading to cigar makers from the *tribuna* at the factory, he could almost always be found in his house laboring over his next issue, attending to business matters, or supervising twenty-year-old Guillermo, an aspiring *lector* and Mendez's one-man staff who ran the press and shipping operations. A year under thirty, Mendez was constantly busy and had never married. Like Juan Carlos, he felt that marriage did not mix with his daily aspirations.

As Armando approached the building, he saw Mendez sitting inside by himself shuffling through papers at his desk. Armando let himself into the quiet office and greeted the writer with a pleasant hello. Mendez was shorter than Armando by almost four inches, and was fifteen years younger. His recent promotion to *lector* had vitalized the writer and his

122

attempt to emulate the great Sando Peña was apparent in his attire and demeanor. He wore a tie and white long sleeves under a blue vest, with his black hair gelled straight back, breaking into a wavy part along the left side. A local *robusto* cigar burned in an ashtray beside him and the printing press was frozen silent.

Mendez was immediately suspicious of Armando. A visit from the man with the beard was usually never welcomed and Mendez knew Armando would expect him to be intimidated. Mendez's revolutionary spirit prevailed and he sat calmly and watched Armando enter.

Armando took a seat across from Mendez, smiling under his beard, and placed a box of Vasquez and Company Don Florentino cigars on the desk. Mendez could see a gold chain hanging from Armando's neck with some kind of pendant attached – it looked like the top of a cross. Mendez set his papers aside, picked up his *robusto* and eyed the cigar box. "If you're here to purchase space for an advertisement, the paper accepts cash and credit."

"These cigars are a gift to you and your staff."

Mendez said. "From Don Antonio Vasquez."

Armando smiled. "Correct. For entertaining his workers and keeping them productive with your persuasive readings. I have not yet congratulated you on your recent promotion to *lector*. Sando Peña will be a hard man to replace but I have no doubt of his endorsement. He claims that there is no better man for the job."

Not a blink from Mendez, whose face remained passive and unaffected by the flattery. "To what else do I owe this pleasure?"

"Mr. Mendez, your paper has been a favorite among the cigar workers since before the Cuban war. As you know, your work is read from Havana to New York City. You've been inspired by Martí, as we all have, but now that his war has come and gone, it seems your rhetoric has become unnecessarily, more and more, shall we say, *extreme*?"

Mendez raised an eyebrow. "Extreme?"

"It seems you're pulling the Ybor City workforce towards some inevitable confrontation with management. A confrontation that Vasquez and Company feels could be disastrous to the cigar industry and would undermine the very community you are trying to protect."

Mendez sat back and crossed his legs. "I'm listening."

123

"What sense is there in disrupting the balance of this city? The people of Tampa have come to rely on the status quo, and you've taken…"

Mendez interrupted. "The working class of this city has never had a status quo to rely on. Their situation has historically changed day by day. They don't live in the same world as you."

"We both go to work, we come home, we eat, and we sleep."

Mendez became more agitated. "As anyone who earns a living has done for centuries! How can you come into my print shop and expect me to digest a Spanish perspective on the Cuban struggle?"

Armando paused and waited until Mendez was calm. Then Armando said quietly, "All citizens of this city want good jobs and happy lives for their families."

"Yes," Mendez nodded. "But the Cuban working class must adapt to a different post-war situation than the Spanish elite. Our fight is different from yours."

Armando smiled. He looked suddenly friendly. "I did not come here to fight."

"What can I do for you, Armando?"

"Why do you promote anarchy?"

Mendez sat back in his chair with ice in his eyes. "Anarchy makes no promises, my friend. Anarchy breaks no promises."

"A profound observation," Armando said. "But I am here to compromise. Your writing is sound, its message is clear. You read to the Vasquez company workers – that is something we will never attempt to prevent. The workers pay you to read what they desire and we both know what happens when the workers do not get what they want."

Mendez shrugged. He agreed.

Armando held up a hand. "I am not a censor. I desire a peaceful work environment, just as you do. Without a *lector*, how would the workers hear your wisdom or stay up to date on current events? They deserve to be informed on the state of world affairs as much as anyone!" He produced a copy of *The Workers' Bulletin*. "But in your latest article, you called on the workers to take control of the factories. You practically called for an armed revolution, right in the middle of a workday!"

"There is a reason the workers become agitated by what they hear."

"But why stir them up? Another strike will cripple our city!"

Mendez sat forward. "And what reason would they have to strike?"

"None!" Armando said. "So why would you give them one? The workers are the backbone of this city. I depend on them as much as you."

Mendez leaned a bit closer. "What do you *want*?"

"I'm not asking that your words take the side of management, but be careful what your paper says about modernization. The workers are a volatile group, and any disruptions could be harmful to the factory, or to anyone involved in said disruption."

"Neither I nor the workers will back down to threats."

"Threats?" Armando gestured to the cigar box. "I brought a gift!"

"Do you think you can bribe me with a box of cigars?"

"Bribery? My good friend, I came here today as a gesture of goodwill!"

Mendez sat up and shouted, "Get out of my office! Take your cigars and tell your boss that Gabriel Mendez is his own man! He will not be intimidated into submission by Spaniards. If Antonio Vasquez feels threatened by a strike, the problem is not me, but the way he runs his factory. He should remember that his workers keep the roof over his head. Tell him I said exactly that!"

Armando stood and caught the box of cigars that Mendez flung back to him. "You are overreacting!"

"Do not expect me to negotiate. My position stands. My articles will continue as they were. And if you think taking my words off the *tribuna* will end your labor troubles, you will learn the Cuban workforce is its own machine. It runs without influence from you or me. It is not something you can easily overcome in a fight. It was their solidarity that defeated your home country of Spain. And now the workplace belongs to them. Nurture the worker, or management will be their slave."

"Think about what you are doing! The factories are losing money, they must modernize."

"I will think very hard about that, Armando. Leave now, otherwise your *bolita* rackets and your partnership with the Tampa police will be the subject of my next issue."

Armando laughed. "That is a weak argument, my friend. *Bolita* is tolerated by nearly all citizens of this city, white, Cuban, Spanish, and Italian. An article exposing any connection between *bolita* and the police will be considered old news. Your readers will see you teetering on the brink of obscurity."

Mendez said, "Then perhaps my publication can do a story on your failed relationship with your wife. Were you unable to satisfy her, Armando? What secret sent her back to Spain?"

Armando said nothing for a moment. Though his blood boiled, he managed a cordial smile. "I thank you for your time this morning, Señor Mendez. You have been a fine addition to the Vasquez factory. Unfortunately my interests dictate that I will be forced to side with management in any dispute that may arise." Armando did not look back as he let himself out.

He reported back to Don Antonio in the late afternoon, finding the fat man on his porch with a glass of lemonade, sitting beside Maria and watching the Vasquez factory. Down the street, a group of children played baseball at a sandy intersection.

As Armando approached, he noticed that Antonio Vasquez and his wife Maria looked so alike that they could be cousins. They were both portly types with the same dark, thinning hair and sat still and silent, side by side, and wore matching reflective frowns.

Armando bowed politely to Maria. "Good afternoon, Señora Vasquez." She smiled and nodded and then dismissed herself, as she knew the men were about to discuss business affairs. Armando took her place beside Don Antonio.

"Care for a glass of lemonade?" asked Vasquez.

Armando waved him off. "Ragano is dead."

"I know," nodded Vasquez. "One less partner."

They were quiet for a moment. Then Armando said, "I also went to see Mendez about his writings."

Vasquez inspected Armando and thought he saw frustration. "The meeting did not go as you had expected."

"Mendez will not be persuaded."

"I expected that he wouldn't." Vasquez pointed across the street to the three story brick factory. "My father built this company on old world beliefs and 1840's technology. As we are about to enter the Twentieth Century, I realize the factory must be modernized if it is to remain competitive. Efficiency has become the concern in the industry, and I am afraid these quotas and weight restrictions cannot be avoided. I have talked with some of my counterparts at competing factories and many of them are upgrading their systems to include measures of cost control. Cuesta-Rey has revolutionized their marketing and compensation programs. They even go so far as to pay incentives to their most productive workers! Oh, how quickly the industry is changing!"

Armando said, "Mendez is the wick to the dynamite of the working class."

"Then tell me, old friend, how many sparks flew at your meeting today?"

"Mendez is an agitator and a powerful voice, but he does not determine the will of the workforce. They will likely oppose modernization, regardless of what Mendez says. However, the faster the fuse can be smothered the sooner the workers will accept the quotas. Mendez cannot be bribed. I doubt he can be blackmailed."

Vasquez sighed. "Regardless of what Mendez does, the loss of our friend Rolando will be felt. It will be difficult to modernize without his steady investments and almost impossible to survive an inevitable strike if we are to move forward with the quotas."

Armando agreed. "Sell me his interest."

Vasquez was surprised. "What?"

"Rolando Ragano owned five percent of Vasquez and Company. I am prepared to purchase his interest outright. For cash. You want to modernize? You want to survive a possible strike? I have the cash not only for that, Don Antonio, but for expansion of the entire company."

Vasquez knew Armando's money came from illegal activities, including *bolita* and possibly prostitution. He also suspected Armando would be taking over Rolando's businesses, though he stopped short of considering Armando's involvement in the murder.

He knew Armando was moving in on his company, trying for a slow methodical takeover, and there was nothing Vasquez could do to stop him. The company's financial position was weak and heading towards bankruptcy. Armando would provide a welcome injection of cash and use his investments in the cigar company as a method of laundering money and diversifying his profits.

He would save the company and seize it at the same time.

Vasquez nodded, agreeing to sell Armando another five points, bringing the investor's ownership to twenty-five percent. One fourth of his father's company had been mortgaged in an effort to keep it alive.

Vasquez sat in silence and watched the children play.

Chapter 11

Don Antonio never expected his workers would strike so quickly. Mendez had taken a planned fundraising trip to Havana and Vasquez decided to introduce the new weight system during his absence, while the factory floor was free of his agitations. Vasquez thought the timing was perfect.

Vasquez was wrong.

The day the new restrictions were introduced, the cigar workers in Tampa already knew about the scales. The tobacco strippers and sorters had been busy at work when the scales arrived. They had been instructed to use the scales and allocate the leaves accordingly, so that each worker received a fixed amount sufficient for the factory to produce 25,000 cigars a day. Word of this new requirement quickly spread among the workers, and the cigar makers knew what to expect a day in advance.

They arrived in the galley that day in anxious silence. They had heard the rumors from the strippers and selectors, but wanted to hear the news from the manufacturer himself. Don Antonio watched from his office as Capecho stood above the galley on the *tribuna* and explained the new system to the workers. "Based on your individual production requirements, you will be given a specific amount of leaf and responsibility for a daily quota. Two other cigar factories in Ybor City have introduced quotas and weight limits and two more are moving ahead with modernization later this week. In West Tampa, three factories are set to introduce similar requirements. Modernization is sweeping the industry. Production will rise, costs will fall, and Vasquez and Company will continue to be a leader in this competitive market. I do not want to take away any of your valuable time so I will leave you with your work."

As the workers began to murmur amongst themselves, Juan Carlos did not hesitate to take action. He began to tap his *chaveta* against the wooden counter where he sat. Slowly and rhythmically the cutting knife made a distinct click-click-click against the wood. He looked down the row where Salvador sat a few benches away. Salvador picked up the signal and started to tap his *chaveta* as well. He nudged his son Javier beside him and motioned to Lázaro to do the same. Soon a dozen workers were tapping the edges of their metal *chavetas* against the counters in unison. They began to pick up speed and soon the clicking became a pounding as more and more workers joined the fray. They pounded the counters with their knives, used their free hands to slap against the wood and stamped their feet on the hardwood floor.

Don Antonio returned to his office without turning to watch the commotion. The reaction was already out of his hands. Soon the entire factory floor was a clamor of pounding, stamping and yelling. Workers started to throw their knives aside and overturn their tobacco bins as they reached for hats and jackets. Juan Carlos rose to his feet and Salvador did likewise. Others followed, and the galley became an orderly stampede of agitated workers, a complete walkout, so abrupt that Vasquez could do nothing but watch his workers file out of the building without looking back. He was left alone with his staff and an empty factory floor.

Outside, the workers gathered at the base of the factory's steps like an angry mob. The group formed a semi-circle around the end of the building as a frustrated Juan Carlos found himself in the center of the commotion. He spoke mainly to Salvador but raised his voice loud enough for anyone to hear.

"Quotas and weight restrictions! Do they think we will accept this misuse of our skills? We are artisans, not laborers! We create high-quality cigars, we do not mass produce! This weight requirement, this output requirement, this exploitation of our function in the factory, treats us as if we are machines!"

Salvador and his sons listened closely as others mumbled their agreement. Juan Carlos continued his sermon. "The weight restriction will rob us of a benefit that has been known to cigar workers for decades! It means the end of the tobacco we take home for our own consumption. That will be a benefit no more! There will be no extra worker's tobacco, because now you must account for every leaf! Now they will brand you as a thief if you take as much as a pinch of crumpled filter! Are you willing to give up this basic right?"

The crowd shouted a collective *No!*

Someone yelled, "We are not slaves!"

"This country abolished slavery decades ago!" shouted Juan Carlos. He raised his voice even louder, "It is as if we are fighting Spanish tyranny once again! And again we will prevail! We will not return to this factory until the scales have been removed and management has dispensed with these ridiculous quotas!"

The crowd shouted an affirmation that quickly died when Pipi Capecho appeared atop the steps and clapped his hands together several times to draw their attention. Pipi descended into the crowd as Juan Carlos mocked him with open arms. "Look who has decided to come crawling out of his castle! Our brave factory foreman! But where is the king? Why has he sent only his jester?" Juan Carlos smiled at Capecho. "Tell me, Jester, who told the king to insult his subjects with these new rules and regulations?"

Capecho pretended to ignore the question. He stopped on the fourth step and stood slightly above the crowd. "Now that you've had your demonstration, we invite you to return to work or else we will lock the doors. Your families cannot survive without your wages."

Juan Carlos said, "There are a dozen factories in Ybor that would hire skilled artisans like us!"

Capecho shouted above the applause. "Vasquez and Company is not the only manufacturer in town with weight systems and scales. This is happening throughout the entire industry. There is no avoiding it. Wherever you decide to work, you will face modernization."

"Wrong, since we have recently *rejected* modernization!" Juan Carlos declared. He stood before the mob with his arms crossed and his head cocked defiantly at Capecho. Then Juan Carlos pointed to the factory's second floor window where Don Antonio stood watching. "Tell your king that it will not be easy to convince us to return."

"Very well," said Capecho. "What choice do I have? You want me to lock the doors, so I will lock the doors." He turned and made his way to the empty factory, closed the doors, and locked the workers out.

The Weight Strike of 1899 had started.

*   *   *

The crowd eventually dispersed. Some went home; others headed into town, but most lingered on the streets and sidewalks in front of the factory. They talked and occasionally looked up to the factory windows where Don Antonio still watched. Inside the factory, the manufacturer finally turned away from the crowd and walked back to his office. The hollow echo of his footsteps in the silent galley made him realize that the company his father had built had suddenly stumbled to its knees. It had not been the first strike levied against Vasquez and Company, but it was the first with Don Antonio at the helm. His first big test and his father, Florentino, now years passed, would be disappointed if his son did not prevail.

Capecho and Antonio Junior were waiting for Don Antonio in his office. Capecho sat in one of two wooden chairs opposite the Don's desk. Antonio Junior was at a small writing table against the wall. Vasquez entered and slumped in his chair. "Antonito," said the Don. "Go find Armando and bring him here as fast as you can." Antonio Junior nodded and disappeared.

Capecho was silent. He had endorsed these weight restrictions and had helped to push the system on Don Antonio. Now that it seemed to have backfired, Capecho felt the burden overwhelm him. He sat quietly and braced himself for Don Antonio's reaction.

Vasquez was surprisingly gentle. He gazed at the ceiling of his office, lost in thought. Finally he spoke. "I did not think that if there was to be a strike it would happen so abruptly and with such certainty. But I suspect the objection is not limited to our company and is typical of every factory that has introduced new restrictions this day." He looked to Capecho. "Forgive me for saying this, but I almost hesitate to ask for your counsel. One mishap can be overlooked if you can tell me the best way to recover from this predicament."

Capecho replied quickly, having already considered four possible remedies to a complete strike. "The first and easiest course of action, which is also the most foolish, would be to do away with the scales and to forget about quotas completely."

132

"This defeats our purpose."

"We would still face high costs, and we would also give the workers reason to believe that they are in control."

"That must never happen," Don Antonio said.

Antonio Junior returned with Armando. They took the empty seats in the office.

"That was fast," remarked Don Antonio.

Armando said, "I was on my way. There is news from the Olivia factory. Their workers have refused to return to work until the quotas and scales are abolished. They have also been locked out and are gathered on the street. One of your workers I believe, Juan Carlos Alvarez, is busy outside stirring up commotion. He has attracted a crowd down the street and is agitating them, practically instigating revolution."

Capecho said, "Juan Carlos is a ringleader among the workers. He's vocal, like Mendez only not as thoughtful. The man was an insurgent in Cuba who advocates violence before reason."

Armando said, "Men like him could be eliminated."

The others were silent and suddenly aware of the void left by Rolando Ragano.

Vasquez waived his hands. "Enough of this nonsense. Agitators will be dealt with appropriately. Pipi was busy proposing solutions."

Capecho continued. "The second solution, which is not as costly and possibly only a short-term fix, is to import strikebreakers from Havana or Key West, possibly Jacksonville. They can fill the benches and force our regular workers to fend for themselves until their will has been broken."

Vasquez fiddled with his moustache. "How will this city – which has such an abundance of cigar workers – react to an influx of foreign labor?"

"The city will be oversaturated," Capecho said. "But our production will not be hurt and costs will fall since strikebreakers will agree to work for less and will comply with scales and quotas. Local business will be satisfied that money is still coming in, foreign labor or not."

Vasquez asked. "What else?"

"Third and also my least favorite, is to raise our prices and let the customer absorb the extra costs. This means giving in to the walkout and risking our position in the market. Our survival would depend on increased prices across the entire cigar industry, Don Antonio, the probability of which is slim. We are confronted with a major setback to our plans for expansion."

Vasquez sighed and lit a cigar. "What else?"

"Fourth and final, is to remain firm in our stance. To concede nothing and outlast the cigar workers with the help of the city."

"What do you mean?"

Capecho glanced to Armando who said, "In the past, businessmen and concerned citizens of Tampa have formed their own groups, with the help of the Tampa police. They can take to the streets and become a presence in Ybor City, a force to convince striking workers that the safest choice would be to return to work."

Vasquez said, "You're suggesting a posse take to the streets? That squads of vigilantes intimidate the city's cigar makers and scare them back to work?"

Armando nodded, "I am proposing precisely that."

"You have experience organizing these committees?"

Armando closed his eyes and nodded. "These groups of law abiding citizens have been very effective in the past. It is something Vasquez and Company can initiate with the support of the city. The chief of police will certainly be willing to clean these vagrants out of the alleys and send them back to work. The mayor also holds an interest in the cigar industry. Neither of them will be difficult to persuade."

Vasquez exhaled and leaned back in his chair to ponder his options. Abolish the scales, import strikebreakers, raise prices, or intimidate the workers. It was a difficult choice. He wondered what his father would have done.

That night dozens of cigar workers convened at the Labor Temple on Ninth Avenue. Presiding over the meeting was the forty-eight-year-old de facto leader of the Tampa labor movement, Angelo De la Parte, one of the most respected Cubans in the cigar industry. A cigar maker during his youth, he studied mathematics and writing independently and eventually became a teacher, then a factory *lector*. Known in Ybor City as Lapár he would introduce himself elegantly as Lapár De la Parte. An articulate man who had learned to speak English, German, French and

Italian in only four years, Lapár could translate almost any written work into Spanish.

He was tall, with thin hair tapered short with a weekly trim, and elegantly good-looking, like the politicians who appeared briefly to give speeches at street corner rallies, only to disappear and resurface in black and white newspaper photos the next day. He was a friendly and charismatic personality and a natural leader. In another life, he could have been governor of Havana or, years later, a U.S. Congressman. It was rumored among some that Lapár would eventually run for mayor of Tampa.

Lapár De la Parte devoted nearly every minute to the labor movement but always reserved time for his family. He was a busy man who would rush back and forth between cigar factories and labor meetings, usually with two or three books under his arm. He had started his own debate club and was often seen on Seventh Avenue on Saturday nights, walking with his wife and two young sons. Among the workers, Lapár was a likeable man, approachable, and known to have settled many disputes among the workers. Every time he had encountered Lapár, Salvador thought of a friend from his past, El Matón, who had the same engaging quality that persuaded people into his cause. Since he knew there were some among the Tampa elite who might view him as a threat, Lapár never took to the streets without carrying a small, four-shot .22 revolver in his pants pocket.

Now Lapár stood at a podium at the front of the room and called the meeting to order. "Of course we now face a matter of money," his *lector* voice boomed across the room. "The question is can we hold out longer than the manufacturers? And then there is the city of Tampa. Any disruption in the flow of cigars out of this city sends a shockwave through Tampa businesses. If we decide to continue this strike, the whole of Tampa will feel its effects. For this reason, neither the Tampa city council nor the chamber of commerce will support the cigar worker. They will turn against us. We will be on our own. But if we spend money and continue to function as consumers in the Tampa economy, we can shift the burden to the factories, who have decided to lock their doors and halt production. Many of us can find employment elsewhere, even if it means leaving town and sending funds home to our families. I know there are some of us who are willing to travel as far as Key West and Havana to secure their wages. This is only to our advantage."

Many voiced their agreement. Juan Carlos said, "Like Martí and the People's Revolutionary Committee who once financed Cuba Libre, any Cuban cigar worker who is still employed should donate a portion of his wages to support the cause we face today."

There was a brief applause and Juan Carlos continued. "Those of us who can read and write should begin to draw up papers that we can distribute on the street and deliver door to door. We must do this until Mendez returns from Cuba."

"Where is Mendez?" shouted a voice from the crowd.

Another said, "Who has time to write hundreds of copies by hand? If this strike is to have an impact, why not wait for Mendez to return and turn on his printing machine?" There was general agreement from the group and then the questions shifted to time.

"How long should we expect this strike to last?"

"For how long can we expect to obtain credit in the Latin stores?"

Lapár held up his hands. "We must hold out until Vasquez and Company and the other factories submit to our demands. We stand on the side of righteousness. The quotas are not correct. We have the resources we need to triumph but solidarity is the key. We must remain united!"

"We must vote!" a voice shouted.

"Yes," said Lapár. "We must show the manufacturers that this strike is not the work of a few but the collective policy of the entire workforce. And the vote should be carried out as soon as possible by all workers who have been forced from their workbenches this day."

A second meeting was scheduled for the next day to plan a campaign with hopes that a citywide vote would occur by the end of the week. Lapár closed the meeting. "We must enlist the rest of the city's cigar workers by gathering the labor leaders, and forming an organization. Then we should hold a massive demonstration, outdoors, including every cigar worker in this city."

*   *   *

The next morning the mayor of Tampa called a meeting in his downtown office. At his side was Chief McGrath. Both men were investors in the local cigar industry, owning shares in several companies. The mayor was also part owner of a small shipping company that imported tobacco leaves from Cuba.

Representing the manufacturers were Antonio Vasquez, Carlos Ramos, owner of the Olivia Cigar Company, and from the Cienfuegos Factory, owner José Cienfuegos. Finally there was Arlen Kincaid, owner of the *Tampa Daily News*, and Vasquez and Company partner Armando Renteria.

The meeting began with a statement from the mayor. "Half of this city's workforce is now on strike. Even the factories that have not introduced quotas are facing walkouts by workers who support their so-called greater cause. My primary concern is to get them back to their benches as soon as possible. If this lockout continues, all of Tampa will feel it and I don't want a few angry Cubans to start an economic civil war in our city. I want them back to work right away. Not next week, not tomorrow. *Today!*"

"Today is out of the question," said Vasquez. "The popularity of this walkout has set us back at least a week. Working conditions can be changed, wages can be altered, but the Cuban worker possesses an untamed will."

"There are plenty of ways to weaken their resolve," the chief said. "A side-effect of every strike and something we will use to our advantage is the vagrancy of the striking cigar worker. Any able bodied man who is not at work will be arrested. Those who resist will be punished – harshly. Agitators and labor leaders should be intimidated, even threatened. Soon there will be no vagrants, as they will prefer the factories to jail."

The mayor waved a hand towards McGrath. "There are not enough police to round up all of the strikers, and putting the workers in jail is no solution. There may soon be thousands of them crowding our streets. Police patrols and street squads will help, but more should be done."

"The people of Tampa already complain about these Sunday circuses held by the immigrants." said McGrath. "No one approves of how these Cubans amuse themselves in the saloons on Sundays until long after dark. I see it as a clear flaunting of the Sabbath."

Kincaid smirked, "When was the last time a Cuban man set foot in a church?"

Vasquez explained. "In Cuba, the church is ruled by the Spanish. As bizarre as it may sound, Cubans see the church as something to fight or, now that the war is over, to ignore completely."

"What about their newspapers?" The mayor asked. "What can be done about these radical publishers who distribute that infuriating anarchist literature among the workers?"

Vasquez answered. "The top *lector* at my factory, also the most popular writer in Ybor City, has traveled to Cuba, but we expect him to return shortly. In my opinion he should be treated no differently than the labor leaders. Among the working class, Mendez is the loudest voice."

Armando asked, "What novel is he currently reading to the workers?"

"*Les Misérables*," answered Vasquez. "The novel is a favorite among the Cubans. They identify with the French Revolution and think Jean Valjean is some kind of saint."

"There is also Juan Carlos Alvarez from Don Antonio's factory," said Armando. "He is also an associate and a co-conspirator of the writer Mendez. And Angelo De la Parte, a very persuasive leader, and very intelligent. These men should not be ignored. They will surely fan the flames of dissent."

The mayor said, "I expect widespread results. The anarchists, the strike leaders, the empty benches must not hinder the city's aggregate production of cigars. Your chief of police will back you, and you have the support of the city council, the chamber of commerce and the mayor's office. Use any methods deemed appropriate to put these people back to work."

The police chief pointed at Vasquez. "Perhaps you and the other manufacturers can produce a list of troublemakers. For the safety of our streets."

Vasquez nodded. "Juan Carlos Alvarez and Gabriel Mendez are perhaps the two worst that I know of." He looked to Armando. "What about the man I always see with them? Salvador?"

Armando squinted. "I don't know this man. Our biggest trouble will come from Juan Carlos and Gabriel Mendez. But do not worry; I will take care of them." Armando glanced to McGrath who caught the look and nodded subtly. The rest of the men noticed this exchange and looked away, not wanting to consider the sinister activities they sensed would soon be plotted.

Vasquez said to the mayor. "Allow me to make a proposition to my counterparts in this room. From now on, the factory owners in this city can no longer function as independent, isolated businessmen. Our landscape has changed and we face new challenges, the type that threatens not the individual manufacturer but our entire industry. Would it be wrong to assume we should form our own sort of association? The labor leaders have called on the cigar workers to unite. Although their rhetoric is dangerous, can we not learn from their wisdom and embrace an alliance of factory owners?"

There was unanimous admiration for Don Antonio's proposal. His father would be pleased with the thoughtful act of diplomacy. Vasquez promised his counterparts that whatever the outcome of the strike, their brotherhood of powerful cigar factory owners would not be threatened or controlled by striking cigar workers.

It was Vasquez's way of countering Armando's consolidation of power. Armando had strengthened his position on the factory's balance sheet and on the streets of Ybor City while Vasquez improved his position among the manufacturers and the city of Tampa. Vasquez wondered if Armando actually *wanted* the strike. Was it another tactic in Armando's plan to take over the cigar factory? To bankrupt the company so he could swoop in like a vulture and buy it cheap?

Regardless of the motives, Vasquez knew he was fighting a two-front battle with striking workers on one side and an ambitious investor on the other.

Armando left the meeting and started his morning rounds, canvassing the new territory he'd taken from Ragano. With all of Ragano's *bolita* games under Armando's influence, he had almost complete control of the business and expected his income would double. He was happy to see that all of Ragano's subordinates easily kicked their skim his way, but he was surprised that even with the new business, the take was about the same.

With the cigar makers out of work, *bolita* activity had fallen dramatically as the workers were saving their money, hunkering down for what they expected to be a long struggle. The Sanchez brothers' store paid an especially low draw. "Business has suddenly died," said Eddie Sanchez. "Whenever these cigar makers are out of work, this becomes a ghost town."

Armando leaned against the counter and said in a low voice, "My business today is more than financial. I have a proposition for you and your brother, a chance to earn some extra money and ensure this work stoppage is settled in our favor." He motioned for Eddie to lean in close, and then placed a quarter on the counter. "I'd like to buy one bottle of glue."

The SS *Olivette* returned to busy Port Tampa the following evening. Freighters loaded with cigars set sail for Texas and Mexico while cargoes of fresh produce arrived from Honduras, and tobacco from Cuba. A young American boy sold the last of the day's newspapers to passengers that debarked from the *Olivette*, but he ran out before Mendez could buy a copy. Instead, Mendez chased the man who had purchased the last paper, an Italian man with suspenders and a black hat, and offered to buy his paper for a dime, twice the regular price. The Italian agreed and Mendez saw that the front page of Kincaid's *Daily News* bore the headline *Cigar Workers Strike*, with a photograph of the Vasquez factory. Beside the picture was the smaller headline: *Decree to Workers: Return to Work Now or Face Employment Blacklist*.

His eyes moved quickly across the page. According to the article, nearly a thousand had walked out of six factories but the paper claimed the strike was expected to end quickly once the workers had gone broke and hungry. The strike had clearly gained momentum during the past few days and he felt a sudden need to reacquaint himself with the rest of the workers.

He hustled into Ybor City and went straight to La Rubia, where he knew he'd find his friends. The tavern was filled to capacity and buzzing with talk of the work stoppage. Juan Carlos rushed to greet him almost instantly upon his arrival. They embraced briefly and Juan Carlos said, "The Vasquez workers voted unanimously to continue the strike."

Mendez nodded his approval and took a moment to survey the tavern. He caught the eyes of some hopeful cigar workers and imagined them rejoicing the return of a savior, like so many did when Martí had returned from exile.

Mendez sat at the table with Juan Carlos and Salvador. "This news has caught me by surprise. Forgive me for being away but my fundraising trip was lucrative."

"You are here now, my friend," said Juan Carlos and promptly updated Mendez on recent happenings. No workers had returned to their benches and had spent the day grouped together on street corners, in bars, or at their homes. They were a unified body and many factories besides Vasquez had voted to continue the strike. "Some workers have walked out on principle! Their factories have introduced absolutely no new quotas or restrictions yet they strike in support of the greater cause."

Salvador added, "Spanish workers face the same troubles. Management can't expect to walk away from this with a victory."

Mendez thought for a moment. "Have you considered what you hope to get out of this strike?"

Salvador answered. "We want them to remove the scales and do away with quotas of course. We want to protect the rights that cigar makers have enjoyed for decades." Juan Carlos agreed with a nod.

"You can get more," Mendez's certainty was inspiring. "First, demand removal of the scales and the end of these output requirements. Then, you will demand higher wages for all and you will get them. Stop wasting the last of your money on *bolita*. Save every penny and gather as many donations as you can. And we will rally, this week. Tomorrow, if it can be organized."

Juan Carlos smiled. "Perhaps you should put that in print. I will help you with this, my friend. We should get started tonight."

"Come," Mendez tugged at Carlito's sleeve. "There is much to do!"

Salvador remained at La Rubia to mingle with the workers while Mendez and Juan Carlos jogged along the sidewalk on their way to the print shop. "I have asked my cousin Helio in Havana to organize a collection from the workers down there. He will raise cash to get us started. Many of you will have to leave the city and find work elsewhere."

Juan Carlos nodded. "That will not be a problem."

Mendez reached into his jacket pocket and removed his keys as they rounded the corner. His office was just ahead. He intended to print pro-strike pamphlets that night and distribute them throughout the city the next day.

When they arrived at the front door, Mendez thrust the key towards the keyhole but it was deflected by something hard. He tried again but the hole had been sealed. He kicked the door. "Can you believe this?"

"What is it?" Juan Carlos looked closer.

"Someone put glue in my keyhole!"

"Maybe we can chisel it out."

Mendez looked through the front window. "My shop has been trashed!" Inside, the printing press was on its side surrounded by a mess of papers and pools of ink. The bookshelf had been toppled and the library of books was spilled across the floor. Mendez frantically rattled the doorknob. "Someone will pay for this!"

"What about the back door?"

They ran around the corner to the alley. Mendez told Juan Carlos, "They're playing dirty already. I'm almost frightened to consider how they plan to have us defeated." They arrived at the rear exit to Mendez's house and were relieved to see the keyhole was untouched.

Behind Mendez a voice called out, "Welcome home!" A giant boot swept Mendez's feet off the ground and brought him to his knees. Hands grabbed Juan Carlos at the neck and then down came wooden clubs. Mendez was struck on the side of the head by a board that sent his glasses flying and knocked him to the ground and nearly unconscious. His ears rang and the sting was so bad that Mendez thought he tasted charcoal.

Juan Carlos struggled inside a blur of fists, boots and splinters. The thugs were quick and precise; their bats cut flesh and bruised bones. They threw their weapons across their victims' battered bodies and their low voices faded as they escaped down the alley. Juan Carlos swore he heard laughter. The goons were easy to identify: a cop, the stocky twin frames of the Sanchez brothers, the black beard of Armando Renteria. Mendez was curled into a ball. Juan Carlos tasted a mouthful of blood. He spat, cursed and vowed revenge.

Chapter 12

Mendez awoke with dried blood caked in his hair. An hour since the attack and he remembered little except a shot to the head that put him down. Still trembling, his tongue fiddled with a loose tooth and he tried to ignore his shaking hands, blamed it on adrenaline.

Juan Carlos had a face full of blood that dried one eye shut. He'd been clubbed several times and his neck was so sore he wondered if it was broken. Armando Renteria was the foremost thought on his mind.

Retaliation.

After they struggled to pull themselves inside the shop, they remained on the floor just inside the back entrance. Juan Carlos fought the pain and pulled himself into a chair next to the door.

Retaliation. He already had an idea.

The Sanchez brothers were a couple of brutes who took a payoff. The other guy looked like a police officer from Tampa. Juan Carlos did not care about the supporting players. Armando, despite his connections and circle of influence, was the target. If Carlito could find a way to get close to the *bolita* tycoon he could settle the score directly. They would be even inside of two weeks.

Like his toppled printing press, Mendez lay on his side, a messed up wreck. He looked to Juan Carlos who was on a chair scowling at the floor, thinking hard, formulating a plan. Mendez gathered his strength and spoke, "Can you walk?"

Juan Carlos nodded. His plan took shape.

"Upstairs," Mendez said. "Ice."

Relying on the railing for support, Juan Carlos hobbled up the stairs to Mendez's apartment. He returned with a block of ice, a pair of towels, and a bottle of brandy. He smashed the ice on the floor and sent pieces in every direction. Mendez grabbed a chunk and held it against his temple where the first shot had landed. Juan Carlos wrapped a handful of ice in a rag and wrapped it around his neck, using the corner of the rag to clean the dried blood out of his eye.

Carlito opened the brandy and both men downed hearty gulps, speaking little for the next hour; their only interaction was the passing of the bottle back and forth. As their bellies filled with alcohol and the pain subsided, they began to take perspective on the attack.

Juan Carlos said, "If only I had the strength."

"To what?"

"Nothing," Juan Carlos said quickly. He respected Mendez for his brilliance but would not include the intellectual in his plan. He needed a fighter, someone who understood the importance of retaliation, that the fight in Ybor City was no different than their struggles in Cuba. Armando symbolized the Spanish colonial power Juan Carlos once fought. He needed a man who was not afraid to confront this danger.

Someone he trusted.

Salvador.

His brother from Cuba, a true rebel who had lived by the machete and torch. When Salvador saw what had become of Juan Carlos and Gabriel Mendez, he would be overwhelmed by loyalty and would acknowledge that the class struggle, the fight he'd waged since his parents were murdered, had extended to Tampa.

"This assault," Mendez began as he iced his head.

"Is humiliating."

"But it has placed us upon moral high ground. We must not let the cigar workers be intimidated by these gangs of thugs. We must carry on with our protests and inform the rest of the workers of what happened outside this shop tonight. It will only strengthen their resolve."

"Certainly," said Juan Carlos. "We will not return to work under these circumstances. The manufacturers will not be made to think they can beat us back to the benches."

They nursed their wounds late into the night until they fell asleep, Juan Carlos in his chair and Mendez, still curled in pain, on the floor.

Early the next morning the alcohol had worn off and the pain was even worse. Mendez's face felt like it had been stomped and crushed by the steed of Death himself. Juan Carlos took another shot of brandy to ease the throbbing in his neck and then let himself out the back. His body ached but he could walk and was determined to set his plan in motion right away.

He caught a streetcar and headed north to Salvador's house.

The white tenement was a silhouette in the dim morning light. Juan Carlos hobbled around the side to Salvador and Olympia's bedroom window where he found the curtains drawn and the window half-opened. Carlito parted the curtains and peered inside to see Salvador and Olympia asleep in bed. He whispered, "Ortiz." Then again, louder. The couple stirred and then Salvador awoke and saw his friend's eyes watching him from between the curtains. Carlito's dark and crooked tooth was just barely visible in the dawn light, his face a shadowy, disturbing appearance.

"Who's there?" Olympia murmured in a half-trance. Salvador shushed her and told her to go back to sleep as he slipped out of bed.

Juan Carlos met Salvador on the porch where the latter came out yawning with messy hair, buttoning his *guayabera*. It was not until Juan Carlos was eye to eye with Salvador that the morning sunlight exposed a lacerated face covered with dried blood, and eyes swollen black and blue. Salvador was jolted suddenly awake. "*¡Coño!* What happened to you?"

"Mendez and I were assaulted after we left the bar by Armando Renteria, the Sanchez brothers, and some lanky weakling cop. They attacked us from behind like cowards and beat us to the ground without giving us a chance."

Salvador couldn't believe it. He waved Carlito towards the house. "Come inside, my friend. I will help you wash."

"No need. It will take more than a few hoodlums with sticks to put me out of business."

"How is Mendez?"

"Worse. I don't know of a single bookworm who can put up a fight, and I still don't after watching what they did to him. They broke into his shop before we arrived and vandalized his printing press. The shop is a mess, littered with ink and papers. An obvious attempt to intimidate all of us."

Salvador looked closely at the cuts on Carlito's face. "Will he need a doctor?"

"Probably not. Salvador, I need your help." Juan Carlos explained his plan, which silenced Salvador and made him pace. After a moment he sat on the steps to think. Juan Carlos joined him, eager for his friend's decision.

Salvador thought for a moment and said, "You do not feel it is important to show the people of Tampa, especially the Americans, that we intend to abide by the law?"

"Of course. I would never do anything to harm the good of the cigar workers. But this goes beyond the workforce. Think big, Ortiz. Armando must be dealt with outside the realm of this labor dispute."

Salvador shook his head, not liking his friend's intentions. "Armando is a powerful man, Carlito."

"But only a man."

"This will only inflame the situation."

"Just think about it," Juan Carlos tapped Salvador's knee. "Mendez would help, but he is not suited for this type of activity. Don't ever forget your roots, my friend. I am going home now to change clothes and clean up but I will be back later."

Salvador rose. "I am sending my boys Javier and Lázaro to Key West to find work. Once they leave town, perhaps we can talk."

Juan Carlos nodded, satisfied that Salvador would come around.

Later that morning a crowd of workers gathered in front of the Martinez Ybor factory on Fourteenth Street to proclaim their intention to proceed with the boycott. Police arrived as the crowd grew into the hundreds but the handful of officers stood virtually unnoticed by the mob.

Mendez was only two blocks away in his office. He could hear the growing commotion outside and felt obligated to summon his strength and hobble to the event. Soon his young assistant Guillermo arrived to start his shift. Mendez stood and opened the front door from the inside and let the boy into the office. Guillermo was appalled when he saw what had become of the press and frightened to see his boss's wounds.

"Don't worry about me. My loud voice is responsible for the trouble that I attract. It is the equipment that should concern you. Guillermo, how long do you think it will take to repair it?"

146

Guillermo looked at the press. "Let's stand it upright so I can see."

Despite the pain in his ribs and arms, Mendez helped the boy lift the heavy printing machine. When it stood in place, Guillermo took a walk around and inspected it from all sides. "It appears they just pushed it over. I can see some damage, though only a few pieces are broken. I can get started today and should have it up and running sometime tomorrow."

"Whatever it takes," Mendez said. "Money is no object. I am willing to pay whatever the cost but that press must be running by noon tomorrow. That is your deadline and I am not flexible on that."

Guillermo understood. "I'll get started right away."

"Good," Mendez grabbed an umbrella, which he used as a cane and hunched awkwardly to the front door then pointed at the keyhole. "Those bastards filled it with glue. See if you can chisel it out or else we'll have it replaced. I will be back in a few hours."

He left and headed south for the crowd. More police officers had arrived, including Chief McGrath, and were greeted by indignation as the cigar workers booed, spat, and kicked sand at their feet. McGrath raised his pistol and fired a shot into the air, instantly quieting the crowd who stood and watched the chief holster his smoking revolver.

He shouted, "By order of the Mayor of Tampa, and for the good law abiding people of this city, it is my duty to inform you that any and all striking cigar workers who do not return to work will be arrested! We will give you one hour to return to the benches or face time in jail!"

To his embarrassment, his decree was greeted with a mixture of laughter and jeers. Crumpled copies of the *Daily News* were launched from the crowd and rained down on the insignificant police force. The presence of McGrath and his men only intensified the worker's resentment.

Mendez limped over to the chief. The arrival of the bruised and beaten Gabriel Mendez, who walked with a cane, calmed the curious crowd.

"I am Gabriel Mendez!" he shouted for all to hear. "Last night I was attacked outside my own home along with my friend Juan Carlos Alvarez!"

The crowd booed, and many demanded the identity of the perpetrators. Mendez held up a hand to keep them calm. "It does not matter who did this, as we will not seek retribution." He looked directly at the chief. "The workers of this city are law abiding."

McGrath hollered to the crowd, "Then abide by the law and get off the streets before we arrest you for vagrancy and loitering!" More booing and cursing arose, and a second barrage of crumpled newspapers exploded from the crowd.

Mendez said to the chief, "They will return to work once they have regained their rights. Threats of arrest will not persuade them. Only after the manufacturers correct their injustice can arrangements be made. Perhaps you should inform the mayor of this, and quickly, as this city cannot sustain a prolonged work stoppage."

McGrath was still, the droopy wrinkles of his face locked into a frown. "They have one hour to return to work, lad." The chief produced a pocket watch and held it so Mendez could read the time. "One hour, and then we start making arrests."

With that, McGrath called the police away from the scene. Mendez convened with the crowd and decided they should save their energy and disperse. A large demonstration was planned for the end of the week, and Mendez invited any volunteers to join him in his office, where they would draft and print a counter-manifesto to deliver to the manufacturers.

Many inquired about the beating, and some demanded the identities of those responsible but Mendez declined. "It is a personal matter. Focus your efforts on the rally and on winning this battle. That is your retaliation – a demonstration of our solidarity and your desire to stand up to the unfair business practices of your employers."

Juan Carlos was back at the boarding houses on Twelfth Avenue. He had bathed and cleaned his wounds and applied a bandage above each brow. After a shot of bourbon, he fell to his bed to nap. The lumps in the mattress reminded him of a secret that not even Salvador knew. It dated back five years, to when José Martí had led the revolution against Spain. The Cubans of the city of Tampa had given crucial support to Martí's independence movement, most noticeably in the form of money collected at the cigar factories each week. Most workers knew their donations had paid for supplies, including weapons and ammunition used by the rebels in Cuba. Some of these weapons had been purchased in the United States and then smuggled to the shores of the island.

Juan Carlos had been a player in this trade, using his own dwelling as one of many secret storage depots in Ybor City. Weapons would arrive from out of town, and Juan Carlos would hide them under his mattress until the time came to hand them off to a loyalist who would take them to the Cuban shore and into the hands of the rebels. Hundreds of firearms and thousands of rounds had passed through Carlito's hands. The vast majority made it to the island, but there was a small supply that Juan Carlos had kept and had tied in place under the mattress where he slept.

He had justified his personal arsenal as necessary for his own protection. Under his bed, tied to the springs were four pistols, one bolt-action Krag carbine, an old machete, a razor-sharp hunting knife, two dozen boxes of bullets, and a tin can filled with gunpowder.

The weapons needed to be cleaned so after his nap, he nibbled on some bread and fruit, washed them down with more bourbon, and got to work. He reached underneath the wire bed frame and found a .38 caliber Colt revolver. He held it in his hand to inspect it and then placed the weapon on his bed. One by one he removed the weapons from under the mattress and set them on the bed and then knelt beside them. He was busy for the next two hours. He polished and oiled the firearms and sharpened the blades with Armando Renteria the foremost thought on his mind.

The Ortiz family had been living in Ybor City for a year and a half before they needed to ration their food. Olympia was reminded of the poverty of Havana – the small portions of rice and beans, the sporadic work, the sad faces of her children. Salvador barely had enough to feed his friend next door, the little beagle named Pano.

Olympia was outraged that Salvador would donate a single spoonful to Pano. "Don't waste food on the dog!"

He shrugged. "It's just a little rice."

149

The look Olympia gave him showed how much she disapproved. She was concerned that the current work stoppage would last for months and that their struggle would be no different than their time in Havana. How long would she have to hear E.J. complain about being hungry? The streets were not yet lined with the poor but Olympia feared her children would soon be at Port Tampa, begging newly arrived travelers for spare change.

"The situation in Havana has improved," Olympia said to Salvador. "Perhaps it is time to return?"

Salvador had considered this, but he was not willing to abandon his fellow cigar workers. His commitment to them was strong, and he wanted to teach his children to stay and fight.

"This strike will be over in no time," Salvador assured her. He did not mention that without his daily tobacco allotment, he had not tasted a cigar, or any tobacco, in several days. The withdrawal was starting to affect him with minor shakes and sleepless bouts of anxiety.

Olympia did not fault Salvador for supporting the strike but the Ortiz family was nearly broke. The family had one option, which Olympia easily approved.

Salvador took Javier and Lázaro into the room shared by the boys and invited them to sit on the bed. "The next boat to Key West leaves on Saturday and I'm sending you down there to find work. The island has not been affected by the strike, and work is abundant but not for much longer. We must be swift. There will be dozens of workers on the boat with you, plenty of familiar faces but plenty of competition. Gabriel Mendez, our *lector*, is a friend of mine. He will be on the same boat and can help once you arrive in Key West. I am confident in the both of you as long as you stick together. You will need to earn enough to house and feed yourselves, but the rest must be sent home. Josefina's nursing wages are not enough. This family, E.J., your sister, your mother and me, will depend on the money you send. I do not expect you to be there for long and I will summon your return as soon as possible. Now, what questions do you have?"

Javier shook his head. He understood the severity of the financial situation and the role he needed to play for the sake of his family. Lázaro asked, "Why won't you come with us, Papa?"

"Because." Salvador sat between his boys. "Someone needs to stay here and take care of our mother and your younger brother. I also have a responsibility to our fellow cigar workers. The two of you are more flexible than me. If you can't find work as cigar makers, it is easy for young men to find work stripping leaves, or sorting them, or making deliveries, or any number of support functions. While I am needed here, our family is depending on you to send money from Key West." He put his arms around his sons. "If you feel you are not up to this task, then now is the time to say so."

The boys were silent. Salvador looked to Javier and saw confidence in the boy's upright posture, attentiveness in his eyes. Salvador would not need to worry about his eldest. Then Salvador turned to Lázaro, whose eyes flickered with apprehension of his uncertain task. Salvador said, "Lázaro, your apprenticeship is complete. You are a cigar maker and I am depending on you. I do not doubt that once you return from this courageous trip, you will laugh at yourself for being nervous today."

"I am not nervous," Lázaro said quickly.

Salvador smiled proudly. "I almost forgot that you once defended yourself from the drunken petulance of an American soldier. Nothing should frighten you."

Guillermo fixed the printing press in under two hours and by Thursday afternoon the press feverishly printed handbills and pamphlets with Mendez's latest message. They would be distributed on the streets and left on the doorsteps of local homes and businesses. The press ran for most of the night and Mendez enlisted a volunteer staff to distribute the literature and spread the message that the striking cigar workers would rally tomorrow.

Mendez felt like a general directing his army. He thought of Martí rallying the cause of Cuba Libre, sending Juan Carlos, Salvador, E.J., and a dozen others throughout town with stacks of handbills advertising the rally.

Volunteers who were literate stationed themselves on the busiest street corners in Tampa and shouted Mendez's proclamations and the grievances of the workers. When possible, they did so in both English and Spanish. Crowds gathered to hear these street corner orators. The

Latinos nodded in agreement with Mendez's words while some of the Americans voiced their disgust. To protest the striking cigar workers angry white citizens shouted, "Get back to work!" or "Lazy bum!"

Mendez took it upon himself to contact *lectors* from the operating factories and insist they read his message to their workers. He went so far as to urge other factories to either strike on principle, or to support a common struggle with a redistribution of wealth: organized donations for their out-of-work comrades. And if neither were a possibility then the least they could do was to attend Friday's rally in Ybor Square.

The publicity campaign was successful. Over four thousand attended the morning rally in front of the idle Martinez Ybor cigar factory, nearly half the city of Tampa. Most of the attendees were Cuban workers, both striking and employed but united under a common cause. The camaraderie of Cuba Libre had endured beyond the war and became a fight for better working conditions and quality of life in the United States.

There were Spanish and Italian cigar makers at the rally along with Cubans, and besides the proletariat, most of the city's cigar factory owners were there, including Don Antonio Vasquez and his staff. Members of Tampa's interested business community had dropped by to observe the commotion, with a sizeable turnout of curious white-Anglo Tampa citizens, police officers, the chief of police, newspaper reporters and the mayor.

The rally started as the gathering cigar workers started chanting, "Strike! Strike! Strike!" More handbills were distributed by Mendez and his volunteers and police officers orbited the crowd with their clubs and rifles on display – a warning to the strikers to behave.

The first to appear at the top of the Ybor factory steps was Lapár De la Parte who officially launched the rally. He wore a three piece suit and held a newspaper coiled into a cylinder that he waved at the crowd. He looked very much like a young politician running for mayor or even the U.S. House. Once the crowd calmed, Lapár began to speak. "What would you do if I told you that some factories pay higher wages for the same amount of production?" The crowd started to boo but Lapár retained his momentum and spoke louder.

"What would you do if I told you that *some* factories show workers more respect and give them better treatment? What if I told you that in *some* factories workers still enjoy the basic old-world traditions you enjoyed in Cuba? What if I told you *some* factories still allow their workers to smoke at the benches, to come and go as they please, to work the hours they wish to work, without the detriment of scales and weight restrictions and quotas? What if I told you that at *some* factories workers can still take home up to five cigars a day? What would you do if you learned that all of these things were happening...but not at your factory?"

"Strike! Strike! Strike!"

"These things are certainly not happening at the Vasquez factory! Not any longer! The Vasquez factory and every factory with weight restrictions has insulted your ability and violated basic customs! What would you do if you were in this position, as so many of you are?"

The crowd cheered and the chanting continued. Lapár waited until it died before he went on. "The cigar maker risks being reduced from a respected artisan to a manual laborer akin to a slave, over which a financial cost has been levied. The focus is shifting from worker well-being to profits and productivity. Basic freedom is being replaced by scales and unreasonable quotas. Is this what you want?"

The crowd responded with an angry, "No!"

"In some factories, the cigar makers are subject to unfairness and infractions such as brittle tobacco, breaches of etiquette towards the *lector*, closed windows and tepid drinking water. For the sake of healthy tobacco leaves, you are expected to sacrifice your own health and work in those hot and humid buildings, with no cross-ventilation, during the warmest time of day, in order to meet a quota! This is not how it was in the old-world and it does not have to be this way today!"

The crowd applauded again and Lapár waited for them to finish. Among the crowd, Juan Carlos stood with Salvador. They caught a glimpse of Don Antonio and Armando standing among the people. Juan Carlos thought of his injuries and the weapons under his bed but turned his attention back to Lapár. "And since you, the cigar makers, face injustice in the factories, you have chosen to strike. Since you are faced with unfair quotas and tobacco weight restrictions, you have chosen to strike. This is a standard procedure, and the *torcedores* have evinced no signs of hostile action, despite an act of violence against two Cubans."

There arose a wave of murmurs and concerned whispers from the crowd. "This strike will not end quickly. Not until the manufacturers revert to old-world tradition and remove scales from our workplace. They must *increase* your wages before you return to work! Cigar workers earn three-fourths of the income in this city. You must use your financial might and defeat the hostility of the factory owners, who are reverting to slavery – a practice this country defeated in its own civil war over thirty years ago! Let us not return to the days of forced labor but retain our honor and win back the rights we enjoyed just last week. And then let us fight for more. We must let the manufacturers know, that in a fight against the Cuban worker, victory will not be easy!"

He stepped away as the crowd cheered and Mendez took his place. With a bandage still covering his nose and jaw and a cane in his hand, Gabriel Mendez was another reminder that a threat of violence and retaliation hovered above the dispute. It also provided a hint of sympathy to the cause. "My friends, we are meeting here today, not to look back but to move forward. With the changes brought upon our work force by modernization we are at the mercy of the dollar. We must adapt to the change before the change forces us to adapt. We must prepare ourselves for future struggles, not against Spanish ownership, but against American control. It is important to remain united as one and that is why I call upon all cigar makers, Cuban, Spanish and Italian, to begin a formal union: an organized effort that will protect your rights and resist the unfair changes of Americanization.

"I have been in contact with our friends in Havana and we should all continue our relationship with the island. They have pledged their support to this current dispute. I believe in my heart that we will prevail. My concern is the future."

He paused while the crowd applauded briefly. "We are passing out information today and more will be delivered shortly through your factory *lector* and through my periodical, *The Workers' Bulletin*. I invite all workers who desire involvement in the organization of our union, to contact me or your local leaders. And I want to thank everyone for coming, especially the manufacturers and members of the Tampa government. This struggle affects them as much as the workers. I trust that a fair agreement can be reached, one that will protect the security of the cigar industry. Thank you all, and continue to work hard – you are the backbone of this city!"

An enthusiastic applause followed. Even Vasquez and the other manufacturers reluctantly clapped with the crowd. In the center, Mendez stepped aside and Lapár returned to address the people. "Whether we are American, Cuban, Spanish, or Italian, we are all vital components of a city that finds itself in a crisis. While these labor disputes burn unsettled, we are all faced with the same question: how will we survive? As a city? As a culture? As a family? What can we do, aside from waving a magic wand and satisfying both sides of this conflict?

"We must decide whether or not to continue this strike, despite its detriment to the economy. Will you take this as far as it needs to go? Judging by your presence on this day – hundreds of faces lining these streets, instead of filling the factories – it would appear that this labor strike has your complete support. Am I wrong?"

The crowd shouted, "No!" There was brief applause and then Lapár called for a vote. "The Vasquez factory recently voted unanimously to continue the strike. Do you agree with them? Let's vote!"

Ballots and pencils were distributed to the striking workers, who had a simple choice: yes or no. The workers murmured to each other during the voting and looked over flyers that promoted the labor union once they submitted their ballots.

Once all ballots had been collected and counted, Lapár appeared before the crowd. "I am pleased to announce the results. As further evidence of your solidarity, the cigar workers of Tampa have voted 2,815 to 116 in favor of continuing the walkout!"

The workers cheered. The poll was terrible news for the manufacturers and investors who observed from a distance. The message was clear: unless management backed down, the strike would continue indefinitely.

Lapár said, "Now that you have decided, a shortage of money is inevitable. I call upon local merchants to extend credit and to donate food, clothes, and money to families that will surely suffer from this lockout. And to cigar workers who remain employed, I call upon you to do the same. Remember, these are your brothers, your countrymen, and this is their time of need. They would extend the same compassion to you.

"Restaurant owners, do what is ethically inescapable, and open soup kitchens to feed these hungry families. I call upon you to start these kitchens today. And most important, beyond donations, charity, or solidarity, what must happen, for the sake of the city of Tampa, is for cigar factory owners to do away with these frustrating quotas and weight restrictions that have forced the workers from the floor and caused them to meet here today. End the quotas now and this strike will end. Please, for the good of all, reinstate the old-world tradition that made Tampa the cigar capital of the world. May God bless us, may we remember the law, and may we all go in peace!"

The program ended but the crowd did not disperse. Many mingled in little groups and discussed the topics that had been presented. The police remained on hand to monitor the crowd, though they did not urge anyone to return to work, as they had done all week, for fear of starting a riot.

Salvador and Juan Carlos found Gabriel and Lapár, to shake hands and praise their speeches. "This has been a success," Juan Carlos said. In the distance he saw Antonio Vasquez and Armando Renteria leaving the scene, probably heading east to their empty factory. Salvador smiled. The workers had the upper hand and it appeared they could force the manufacturers to react to their demands. There was energy in the square, solidarity, and a clear plan for victory.

The next morning, with their bags packed, the eldest Ortiz brothers ate breakfast with their family. Olympia served rice and the family shared two fried eggs. Javier and Lázaro indulged in the meager meal not knowing when they would next sit and enjoy their mother's cooking.

E.J. pleaded with his brothers to take him to Key West but Salvador insisted it was a job for the oldest boys and that E.J. was helping the family by staying in Tampa to help his mother. Olympia and Josefina sat quietly, their eyes watery from a mixture of gratitude and worry. The thoughtful mother packed a small lunch for the both of them to share on the boat – Cuban bread and the last of the family's ham. When breakfast was finished, the boys bid farewell to their mother, sister and E.J., and then rose to gather their things.

While Olympia had her back turned, Salvador spooned a small bit of his fried egg and some crumbled Cuban bread into his handkerchief and brought it outside to feed Pano. The dog lapped up the food in seconds then looked up to Salvador as his tail wagged and his eyes asked for more. Salvador patted the dog's head, satisfied that his secret was safe.

Then Salvador accompanied Javier and Lázaro into town to meet Mendez and together the four of them rode the train to Port Tampa. Mendez planned to visit cigar workers in both Key West and Havana to raise funds to donate to striking workers' families in Tampa. He discussed his strategy with Salvador during the ride.

Once Javier and Lázaro arrived at the port, the city of Tampa seemed far away. The smell of the sizzling eggs their mother had cooked that very morning now felt like a distant childhood memory. The brothers could no longer hear E.J. playing outside, or feel the salty breeze blowing through the opened window of their bedroom.

Javier and Lázaro boarded the ferry. Gabriel Mendez followed like a newly initiated uncle while Salvador watched from the dock. By the next day, his sons would have traveled a great distance. It was with that thought that Salvador waved goodbye and returned home.

Chapter 13

Free soup houses popped up all over Ybor City and West Tampa in the form of tents or tables setup along the sidewalk, or in the yards of the tenements. The Latin merchants and bakeries donated bread, rice, beans, pots, bowls, spoons, and other cooking supplies to the workers, whose families contributed what they could. On almost every menu was a Spanish soup of garbanzo beans and sliced potatoes and some Cuban bread, which the workers felt fortunate to have.

Even when no meal was being served, the soup houses became gathering places for striking workers. When they weren't busy eating, with nothing better to do, men would linger around these tents to discuss the situation and denounce the manufacturers.

Salvador could hardly avoid these volatile groups, who gesticulated passionately while engaged in wild arguments, so he stood quietly in the soup line with E.J. while Olympia and Josefina waited on a blanket nearby.

Standing in line behind Salvador was Lapár, his tall and dark-haired wife Esmeralda, and two young sons. Salvador greeted them with a polite nod and a smile and said, "Great speech."

Lapár smiled, never modest about praise. "Thank you very much, Salvador."

The cigar maker blinked, surprised that the illustrious labor leader knew his name. Now genuinely wanting to talk Salvador said, "Your assertion was difficult to retort. You spoke in simple terms that both the workers and manufacturers could appreciate. Few are fit for such a task."

Lapár nodded appreciatively. "You are friends with Juan Carlos Alvarez and Gabriel Mendez."

Salvador nodded. "That's right. Juan Carlos and I grew up together in Cuba. We are practically brothers."

Lapár shook his head sadly. "Terrible about that incident in the alley." Then he bent over and smiled at E.J. "And what is your name?"

"Emilio José."

Lapár patted E.J.'s head. "How nice of you to stand in line and help your father!"

Salvador noticed Lapár's remarkable charisma. The soup line moved a little and the men took a few steps closer to the pots.

Lapár introduced Salvador to his wife and sons and then asked, "How long have you lived in Ybor City?"

"Just over a year. My wife and daughter are there." Salvador pointed to a blanket where they waited.

A young boy handed Salvador a pair of empty tin bowls and another filled them with a thick, steaming stew. When Salvador's bowls were filled, two more were handed to E.J. Lapár held out his own bowl and said to Salvador, "Politics was a way of life during Cuba Libre. Perhaps some are not interested in debating policy, but all should care about the good of their people. Is that not why Martí led the insurrection and Maceo and Gómez continued his fight?"

Salvador smiled politely. "Of course."

Lapár smiled back, understanding that Salvador wanted to deliver a meal to his family. "I enjoyed talking with you, Salvador." He smiled at E.J. "And farewell to you, young man!"

Salvador picked up a quarter loaf of bread from the next table and joined Olympia and Josefina with E.J. in tow. The family began to eat. Josefina asked, "Who was that man you were talking to?"

Salvador smiled at his daughter. He was happy to have her home and proud of her effort to serve her country. It had been little more than a year since she had first left for the U.S. Army but she had grown so much. She was more confident than ever before, a wise woman of the world, and a professional nurse about to marry a Spanish doctor.

"That was Lapár, our labor leader. He comes on a little strong up close."

Lapár looked exactly as Josefina had imagined: impressive and good looking but arrogant, with a swagger that made her suspect he was out to achieve more for himself than for his people.

They were suddenly startled by shouting, a loud, metallic crash and the clanking of aluminum pots being overturned and thrown to the ground. They turned to look and saw a gang of twenty uniformed police officers invading the soup kitchen from all sides.

A raid!

The police overturned soup kettles, kicked out cooking fires, and threw the donated bread to the ground and stomped it into the dirt. Most workers rose and cleared the scene, but others fought back. Some harmlessly cursed the police officers, but a few brave men attacked the officers with punches or kicks until they were thrown aside, or wrestled to the ground and arrested.

Salvador rushed his family away from the scene as the raid deteriorated into a brawl. *Tabaqueros* threw their soup bowls at the officers; those who threw stones were beaten down by clubs. As he looked back at the fracas, Salvador saw several cigar workers face down on the ground in handcuffs while the police chief orbited the scene.

"Come on," Salvador nudged E.J. "Let's hurry home."

"But I'm hungry," E.J. protested.

"I'm hungry too."

Josefina said, "I'll fix something for you once you're back at the house."

E.J. sulked "Rice and stale bread?"

"Be thankful you're not on the streets begging."

When they arrived at the house they learned there was no rice or bread remaining so Josefina sliced a green pepper and an onion and fried them in the pan.

"This is for all four of us?" pouted E.J.

"Hush!" said Olympia as she handed him a plate. "You're lucky to have anything at all!"

After a tiny meal that only made them crave more, Salvador stepped outside to sit on the porch and was greeted by Juan Carlos, who still had a small bandage on his forehead and blue crescents under each eye. Carlito's wounds made him look like a true warrior. He grimaced when Salvador appeared. "I am at the point where most men would break!"

They started walking. Salvador hurried to keep up with his friend's brisk pace. "What happened, Carlito?"

"You haven't heard? The police have been raiding our soup houses all over town. There was a raid near the boarding houses and another on Seventh Avenue."

"I know," Salvador said. "We were at one just a few blocks away when police chief himself came and arrested several of our men."

Juan Carlos picked up a rock and hurled it in the direction of the Vasquez factory. "They are trying to destroy our morale, and I am frightened because it is working. I am strong, Ortiz, and you are strong, but can we speak for the rest of the workers? I fear their resolve will break and that there is nothing you or I can do to stop it from happening."

"Do not forget, Carlito, that the manufacturers are also close to a breaking point, otherwise their actions would not be so harsh. We just need to hold on for a few weeks. Money will soon be arriving from Havana and Key West."

"There are times I believe we live in a town without rules. Why should we show the people of Tampa that we are law abiding when the law is not recognized by our own police? They send their goons out to surprise us with clubs and beat us until our blood soaks the ground. Police show up every time we are gathered in groups of three or more. They destroy our soup kitchens, threaten our families, arrest us and treat us like the blacks who were once their slaves. All because we desire to be treated fairly at our jobs. We are dogs, Salvador, mongrels."

"We are not mongrels."

"This is the same fight we waged in Cuba. Class warfare, rich against poor, the affluent versus the working class. And my good friend Armando, I suspect he has played a part in these raids today."

"You make him out to be some dark villain who drifts through the night and whispers in the ears of all the powerful men of Tampa."

"That is exactly what he is! An investor in the cigar trade, sure. His father was close to Don Antonio's father, yes. But this man has been directly affected by the strike. The cigar manufacturers are not buying tobacco from his father so there is no money there. *Bolita* is virtually out of business. When was the last time you bought a ticket?"

"It has been awhile," Salvador admitted.

"No money coming in there either. Armando controls maybe eighty percent of this city's *bolita* games. He's dried up and going broke. He's in with the mayor, the police chief, Kincaid and Vasquez. Why else would he assault me, Salvador? Why?"

Salvador became nervous. He knew Juan Carlos was about to proceed with his plan. "I agree, Carlito that Armando Renteria is key player in this struggle, but this battle is different than any of those we faced in Cuba."

"How is it different? They are both struggles for survival!"

Salvador stopped walking and Juan Carlos paused to listen. "My sons are working in Key West. We'll soon have money coming in and we'll soon be back to work."

"It sounds as if you have renounced your roots, Ortiz."

"I left that past in Cuba."

Juan Carlos scoffed. "So then I cannot count on you?"

"I need a better reason than revenge."

Juan Carlos grabbed Salvador's sleeve and stopped him. "Is that what you think this is about? Revenge? This is not personal."

"Call it what it is, Carlito."

Now Juan Carlos was angry. "When I knew you before, you were not a man who would turn his back on a brother."

"When I became a cigar maker, Salvador the Outlaw retired."

Juan Carlos looked him in the eye. "You have disappointed me, Ortiz. This man ambushes me and Mendez in the alley, and you would let him walk away like nothing happened."

"You are only asking for trouble, Carlito. You know how powerful this man is."

"He will be so humiliated he won't say a word!"

"I think you are wrong. I'm sorry, my friend. Perhaps when I was younger and had nothing to lose, I would have joined you. But now, my family is more important."

"I thought I was your family," Juan Carlos scowled. "I see that is no longer the case."

Salvador scoffed. "Don't overreact."

"Enjoy them while you can, Salvador." Juan Carlos walked away and headed for the boarding houses.

Salvador wanted to call to him and tell him to be careful but instead he said nothing, turned and walked home. He wondered if he would see Juan Carlos again.

As Salvador returned to the house, he heard a rustling in back; boys whispering the sneaky sounds of mischief. He walked around the side and saw two teenage boys raiding his vegetable garden. One carried an armful of green peppers while another was looting Salvador's avocado tree.

"Get out of here!" Salvador grimaced as he stepped forward to shoo them away. The hungry boys dropped their plunder and disappeared between a pair of houses like two frightened bunny rabbits. Salvador retrieved the produce. Except for the peppers and avocado that he carried, his vegetable garden had been depleted, only a few herbs remained, and they were useless without the complement of a hearty meal.

"A total of six soup kitchens were raided yesterday, and three the day before," McGrath told the mayor. "These workers are an aggressive bunch. There has been brawling and assaults on my police officers. My jails are full, yet vagrancy has not decreased, nor has hostility against the badge. These cigar makers are defiant. When they aren't at their benches, they pollute the streets like homeless dogs. Any visitors who come to town see these crowds of loitering Cubans and wonder how safe the streets are. We can clean them up, but I need more men."

The mayor considered it for a moment. He looked at Vasquez. "What can you tell me?"

"Production has ceased and most of the factories have shut down completely. Inventories are nearly depleted, and total losses to the industry are approaching half a million dollars. Even the *bolita* receipts have seen a significant decline. Worse news is that this is not temporary. Hundreds of workers have left town, and word from Key West and Jacksonville is that the Tampa workers are easily finding employment. We have stepped up our efforts to persuade them back to work but with no success. We seem to have learned the hard way that their reaction to violence is to solidify their unity and fight harder."

"Well," said the mayor. "Commerce cannot survive if these factories remain closed. I must ask you Don Antonio, if there is any chance that the manufacturers' union will consider opening its doors?"

Vasquez had been looking for a way out and needed to find it with dignity. With limited financial resources and mounting debt, Vasquez and Company was on the verge of bankruptcy. He simply could not sustain the lockout any longer. He also could not just open his doors, allow the workers to return, and let them think they had defeated Don Antonio. His investors would never allow it. But he could preserve his prestige if the mayor *forced* him to submit.

"Mr. Mayor," Armando spoke unexpectedly. "I am sorry to say, that as the head of the manufacturers' union, Vasquez will tell you that we cannot do away with the quotas."

Vasquez was startled that Armando had boldly spoken on his behalf but he did not care to contradict the powerful *bolitero* in front of the others, so the Don said nothing, a silence that validated Armando's position.

The mayor was dissatisfied. "If this crisis doesn't end the city may never recover."

The police chief said, "We'll form an armed brigade that will take to the streets and confront these lazy workers. We can no longer frighten them. From now on, our only choice is to force them back to work. We shall deport the dissenters and castigate those who resist. This committee will need backing from the city of Tampa, under your name, Mr. Mayor."

Armando added, "If possible, Mr. Mayor, you can attach endorsements from the governor and our representatives in the U.S. Congress."

"Perhaps we are not yet to this point," the mayor said. He clasped his hands thoughtfully before his face and wedged them below his chin. "I know that two of the strike's top agitators have already been, shall we say, visited by this type of committee?"

All present knew he spoke of the assault on Gabriel Mendez and Juan Carlos Alvarez. The mayor continued. "Those men were not deterred by the confrontation and violence only strengthened their resolve. The initial focus here, before this lockout had ever occupied our thoughts, was to increase the profitability of the cigar business. We all have financial interests in these factories, some of us more than others, but the bottom line is this strike began because we wanted to decrease the costs. But instead of focusing on decreasing the costs, if I may state it plainly, what is wrong with increasing prices and passing the costs along to the consumer?"

The men looked to Vasquez for a response. When he was silent, the mayor asked, "Perhaps you can deliver my suggestion to the manufacturer's union?"

Vasquez nodded. "Perhaps."

"See to it," said the mayor. "And you can put your vigilante committee on hold."

"There is no way any manufacturer can afford to raise prices!" argued José Cienfuegos. Don Antonio hosted another gathering at his house, this time to relay the mayor's proposal to Tampa's top cigar manufacturers. Drinks were served and the men, ten in all, sat in the parlor of Don Antonio's mansion and smoked cigars while discussing the mayor's suggestions.

Cienfuegos felt that he spoke for many of the manufacturers when he disagreed with the mayor's ridiculous idea. "Not only will a price increase drive our customers into the arms of our competitors, it sends a clear message of resignation to the *huelguistas*."

Olivia Cigar Company owner Carlos Ramos said, "The mayor is not asking for a complete submission, only an adjustment, before we are faced with certain defeat. Do any of you doubt that the consumer will pay a few extra pennies for a quality product?"

"Natural that you would say that, Carlos," said Cienfuegos. "As your factory has been on the brink of insolvency since before the war. Let's face it, these men are starving, yet they refuse to return to work."

Vasquez grew impatient with the lack of agreement. "Then what do you propose, José?"

"I believe it is time to import strikebreakers from Havana. The Cuban labor force is robust and seeking employment, as many soldiers returned from battle to find plantations destroyed and factories relocated. And the Tampa police will protect them once they arrive. Am I right, Armando?"

The men looked to Armando, who quietly lurked in the corner, sipping brandy and smoking a mild half corona. He nodded. "Indeed."

Cienfuegos turned to Vasquez. "With all due respect, Don Antonio, the mayor is out of his mind to propose a price increase."

Vasquez said, "The mayor only wants what's best for the city."

Juan Costas, owner of a pair of factories in West Tampa asked, "How many strikebreakers can we expect to import from Cuba?"

"Certainly not enough to fill all of our empty factories," said Cienfuegos. "But enough to make a significant impact in the short term. And we'll need a place to house these people."

Armando suggested to Vasquez, "Perhaps you can rent some of the vacant tenements north of Fourteenth Avenue for our new arrivals."

This was an enormous expense that Vasquez could not afford. He wanted to curse his most generous investor and chastise Armando for making such a bold suggestion before their peers. Vasquez thought of his father, who often spoke in terms that projected financial strength. Vasquez knew he could not pay for these houses, yet he did not want to risk the appearance of weakness in front of the manufacturers. Trying hard to mask his reluctance, Vasquez nodded and said, "That can be arranged."

Armando's face was passive, but he was satisfied that he might have pushed Vasquez deeper into the hole.

"Thank you, Don Antonio," Cienfuegos raised his glass as a tribute to Vasquez. "If we can pack these men into the vacant houses like hogs, and have the rest pitch tents and camp out, this just might work. How will we advertise this opportunity?"

Armando said, "I will place advertisements in the Ocala and Jacksonville newspapers and also make a trip to Havana personally to spread the word and bring back as many recruits as I can."

Cienfuegos smiled. "Then I will plan to have these men in my factory by the start of the following week. We only need to make sure Don Antonio takes his fair share of the labor and leaves some workers for the rest of us."

The men laughed and Vasquez said, "We have all seen how these workers stick together. We will all be better off if we do the same. But something bothers me: once the strikebreakers arrive they will certainly become a source of trouble. The regular workforce will not stand to see immigrant workers walking into their factories. I expect there will be violence."

"I think we all expect violence," Armando said as he stepped out of the corner. "I will speak with Chief McGrath. The police have served us well so far. They can be made to accommodate us."

Through the window of his second-floor apartment, Juan Carlos could see the roof of the idle Vasquez factory standing above the tenements five blocks east. It was past eight o'clock but the August days were long and the sky would be light for another hour.

He waited.

He sat in a chair near the window and watched the city, imaging that Seventh Avenue was noisy and crowded. But this was no time for nightlife. On his bed: a hunting knife freshly sharpened, his .38 Colt revolver, two feet of rope, an overnight bag and forty eight dollars in cash. More than enough.

Juan Carlos held no grudge against Salvador. The man had grown tame with age; his views had become more moderate. His immediate family had become more important than his close friends. Juan Carlos could not hold it against the man. Salvador's intentions were just and Juan Carlos could handle the job by himself. He would do it alone, just him and Armando, on the streets of Ybor.

Armando left the Vasquez mansion and headed south through the rows of tenement houses. The cigar manufacturers had agreed to enlist strikebreakers from out of town and the influx of paid workers would mean Armando would continue to make a living off *bolita*. Meanwhile Vasquez would be cutting costs and producing an inferior product — Armando wondered if the factory owner would fulfill his obligation to house the imported workers. If he did, it would bleed the resources of Vasquez and Company until they required another injection of new capital. Armando had saved a considerable fortune and would be ready to react when the company requested another bailout. No longer would he have a twenty-five percent share in the company. By the time this strike ended, Armando would be close to owning half of Vasquez and Company.

And once the strike was over, *bolita* would resume throughout all of Tampa and the money would begin to pour into Armando's hands. He would soon be more than a *bolitero* – he would be a respected man of prestige. Perhaps he could run for mayor.

Salvador had no money to spend on gambling and he hardly drank. He didn't even have enough money to afford a nice meal with Olympia so he did like every other loving husband in Ybor City and took his wife dancing. Olympia eagerly accompanied Salvador to the Cuban Cantina, where they danced with other cigar workers and wives to the stripped down music of a piano player and trumpeter.

Olympia gingerly moved across the dance floor with her hand in Salvador's, smiling at him, enjoying being together despite the circumstances. She turned a pirouette and then fell into his embrace as the music slowed.

They rocked back and forth in tempo with the music.

Juan Carlos headed south towards the Pasaje Hotel. A black top hat was pulled over his eyes and he wore glasses and a tie, looking very much like a Spanish bookkeeper or banker returning home from a late night at work. He kept his head down as he walked, aware of the streetlamps that flickered to life as the sky dimmed to the odd purple light between dusk and darkness.

He could hear activities buzzing from Seventh Avenue and knew most of his friends were there. Shops and taverns would be closing soon. He leaned against a lamp post a lit a cigar.

There was a vacuum in Ybor City prostitution. After the loss of Rolando Ragano, ownership of the city's most famous female workforce had been in question. *Bolita* was securely Armando's but prostitution was another question. He guessed that a lot of hands were entering the trade, with some of the money finding its way to the chief.

To get a better read on the situation, Armando stopped at the Pasaje and sat at the bar. He ordered bourbon and let his mind wander. The club wasn't very busy; Armando saw only a handful of customers and even less call girls. He wondered if prostitution was a business where he could succeed. He'd need the support of the police, which he already had, but prostitution was not like *bolita*. *Bolita* was out in the open, a famous game enjoyed even by the most fragile little old ladies.

Prostitution was a dirty business where he'd need to be a more aggressive manager. And he'd need a strong partner. Not the chief of police, but someone to supervise the call girls, to run their business and ensure they paid their skim. Armando didn't have the reach to be influential in this business. Not yet. But if he was going to survive all types of financial hardship and truly become the most powerful man in Tampa, he needed to diversify his enterprise.

He finished his bourbon and ordered another.

An hour of dancing was enough and Olympia's feet were tired and crying for rest. Though she'd enjoyed a wonderful night with Salvador, there would be plenty of time for dancing on other nights.

"Let's hurry home," she said to Salvador as they left the cantina. "Josefina is downtown with E.J. We will have the house to ourselves!"

Salvador grinned and took her hand. "Then we must be swift!" He pulled her to a waiting streetcar, dropped a pair of nickels into the slot and held on as the trolley took them home.

Armando finished his third bourbon of the night and left his cigar in the ashtray to die on its own. He slid out of his chair and stumbled when his feet touched the floor – the alcohol made him wobble at the knees. He thought of Spain, the land of his parents and home of his ex-wife Elena. Perhaps he could pay a visit to the peninsula. She would welcome him, but the meeting would be futile and without much purpose for her.

He shuffled down the hallway to Gisela's room and knocked on the door. There was no answer so he tried the doorknob, but it was locked. A moment later, he heard the latch click from the inside and the door opened a crack. As he entered he was instantly greeted by the odor of rum and stale sex. Gisela felt her way to the side of the bed and sat down. She wore a white corset and white underpants, a pair of white stockings formed two snakelike coils on the floor.

"I'm finished for the night, Armando," slurred the blind prostitute as she lit a cigarette. "Come back tomorrow."

"You look tired," Armando instinctively loosened his tie, the first thing he always did upon entering her room. "I would have thought business would be slow."

She waved her hand drunkenly. "This business is never slow."

He unbuttoned his shirt. "Now that your boss is dead, who is responsible for you and the others?"

Gisela sat silent, annoyed, with her glassy eyes pointed to the bare wall of her room. She took a long drag from her cigarette and blew a cone of smoke into the air. "Why are you getting undressed? You're not going to fuck me tonight."

She was right. He had no plans to be with her and was undressing out of habit. He buttoned his shirt and noticed her defiance; an insulting display of courage rarely attempted on Armando. He asked again, "Who is responsible for you?"

Gisela sat back on the bed, her cigarette dangling loosely from her finger. If she had any worries, they were not on her mind tonight. The absence of a boss seemed to have given Gisela new confidence, like a great burden had been lifted.

"You're wondering who is in charge," she said with a hint of rebelliousness. "Ms. Kitty has instructed all of us to keep our pay until she works out a deal with the owner of this hotel."

Armando took a step closer. "I'm here to work out my own deal."

The heaviness in his breath finally jolted Gisela and for the first time that night, she was intimidated. She took a quick puff of her cigarette and sat up a bit straighter. Armando did not give her a chance to argue. He climbed onto the bed and mounted her, whacking the cigarette out of her hand as he pinned her legs down with his knees. A hand reached for his face, but he swatted it away and clamped a powerful fist around her frail, defenseless neck.

"Work for me and I won't hurt you."

Gisela gasped, "I work for myself."

He squeezed a bit harder and moved in close so their noses were inches apart. He could smell the rum and cigarettes on her breath, and she caught a whiff of bourbon on his. "I don't think you understand how serious I am. Your boss is dead. You need protection."

Gisela was frozen underneath, tense and waiting for him to hit her, or rape her on the spot. When he did nothing but pause, she said, "On the dresser, a little white porcelain case."

Armando released her and his weight disappeared and with it, the odor of bourbon. She heard him move across the room and rummage through the jewelry and knickknacks on her dresser. He found the little porcelain box and the money inside. He counted a total of $110.

"You've been quite busy," he remarked as he paged through the bills.

Gisela started to sit up in bed. She rubbed her neck and patted the bedspread for her cigarette case. "Leave enough for me."

Armando took eighty dollars and tossed thirty onto the mattress. "Sleep well," he said as he reached into his pocket for a lighter. Gisela found her cigarettes and slid one into her mouth. Armando flicked his lighter and held the flame under her smoke. "I'll see you next week."

She scoffed as she inhaled her new cigarette. "I can't wait."

He stuffed the cash into his pocket as he let himself out, happy that he had added another business to his stream of income. As he left the hotel he noticed that Ybor City had fallen asleep. It was late, there were no afterhours gambling matches and all of the taverns had closed. The trolleys had stopped running and most of the city's inhabitants were long in bed. Only the flicker of streetlights kept the town from complete darkness.

Armando was still tipsy and tired from a day of work and a night at the Pasaje, and he planned to pass out the instant his face hit the pillow. Taking a shortcut to his apartment on Eighth Avenue, he cut through the alley behind the Eden Theater. It was so quiet he felt like the only man in the city.

A sudden blow to the back of the head knocked Armando to the ground. He tried to breathe but found his wind was gone. He was suffocating, and as his face dug into the pavement, he felt a rope around his neck pull tighter and tighter until his vision blurred and he slipped into unconsciousness.

He awoke face down in the alley with a thundering pain beating his head. He was groggy, drunk, and confused and then felt a weight flatten his body against the ground. He tried to push himself up for air but noticed his limbs would not obey. His hands were tied behind his back with rope. The weight was someone's body pinning him down, with a knee wedged between Armando's shoulder blades.

Armando gasped, "Who is it?"

"Shhh," whispered a man's voice.

A crumpled pair of pants dropped to the pavement before him and Armando quickly realized they were his pants...his buttocks were completely exposed. He struggled and fought against the weight on his back, but his attacker had him pinned.

"You'll pay for this," Armando said. "Do you have any idea who I am? You will pay dearly for this, *hermano!*"

His wallet was thrown on top of his pants, empty. He heard the attacker folding paper money and stuffing the bills into his pocket. Then a punch to the left kidney forced Armando's face to the ground. He spat dirt and struggled uselessly.

Another punch to the right kidney. Then another. The last of Armando's strength disappeared and then to his horror something cold and metallic pushed against his backside. It tore its way inside and Armando wailed in pain.

"Fuck you," Armando hissed. The sound of a pistol being cocked made Armando freeze and hold his body tense. The barrel of a handgun was two inches inside him.

Then a voice that he recognized. "I see why your wife left you. Your pecker is the size of a bullet."

Juan Carlos Alvarez.

Armando said, "You're nothing but an out of work Cuban attempting the most courageous deed of your life."

Juan Carlos dug the pistol in farther and then leaned close and whispered gently into Armando's ear. "Be careful what you say, I have a jumpy personality."

"Kill me now, Juan Carlos. Trust me. Do not leave me alive."

Juan Carlos laughed, "Do you think I'm afraid of you, Spaniard? You run a few *bolita* games, so what? I have killed greater men than you."

One more punch to the kidneys and Juan Carlos yanked the pistol out of Armando. He stood, picked up Armando's pants and used them to clean off his gun. "What are you worried about? You still have your shirt."

Juan Carlos took off running with Armando's pants coiled under one arm and a small knapsack thrown over his shoulder. In his pocket he had forty-eight dollars plus more than eighty looted from Armando's wallet. He rounded a corner and ditched Armando's pants in a trash basket and then headed south for Port Tampa. The next morning he was on the first boat to Key West.

Armando lay struggling on the ground for nearly twenty minutes before a young Cuban tenant from one of the apartment buildings above the alley came down to help. Armando was humiliated. Being found tied, beaten, and bottomless in the middle of an alley was no way to begin a campaign for mayor of Tampa. He knew the story would get out and he would be held accountable almost instantly. The damage to his reputation could be immeasurable.

"I saw the whole thing," said the young Cuban tenant with wide-eyed wonder as he untied Armando and handed him a pair of shorts. "Who was that man?"

Armando slipped on the shorts and tried to sit up. His back was sore from the punches; he had a bump on his head and a sting in his butt. He was barely able to talk. Politics could wait. Right now, "Find a doctor."

Chapter 14

Key West had been a pleasant surprise for Javier and Lázaro Ortiz and especially for the younger brother – for it was that first visit to Key West which offered Lázaro his first intimate encounter with a woman. The brothers had been working hard at the García and Sanchez cigar factory and had saved money to send home but Javier had also gathered a recreational fund: a small pool of cash they used for gambling and other taboo activities young men engage in while away from home.

There was a prostitute named LaBraza that Javier had learned of from factory cigar workers; she owned a house on Duval Street in the heart of Key West. "For two dollars," Javier told Lázaro, "she will give you thirty minutes. And for five dollars, a whole hour."

Seventeen-year-old Javier was confident and at the age where he did not give it a second thought. The young man was ready to go. It wouldn't be his first time, and Javier already considered himself to be a gift to the females with his designer clothes and shined shoes.

Lázaro was understandably anxious as he had never been with a woman. Fifteen and just entering the curious and awkward phase of his life, he was forever aware of his crooked nose and the slight slouch in his walk. Lázaro was shy and self-conscious around women, lacking the charm and swagger of his older brother.

"What does she do?" Lázaro asked.

"Don't be such a prude!" laughed Javier. "Anything you ask for, *hermano*!"

Lázaro knew he could not say no to Javier. His older brother had already made up his mind and would not accept the thought of Lázaro staying home. The younger brother had virtually no choice in the matter. Javier would demand Lázaro's company.

"Don't worry," Javier assured his brother as they walked through a canyon of classic pastel-colored wood frame bungalows along Duval

Street. Mule-drawn streetcars provided a noisy clomp and clatter along the city's busiest street. "I will wear her out so she won't be aggressive on you."

They arrived at the location: a small, yellow two-floor house set on foundation piers, with a peaked metal roof and a covered porch tangled with a colorful variety of flowers and plants. The vivid arrangement outdid any porch Lázaro had ever seen. Javier instructed his brother to wait outside while he went inside by himself. As Javier disappeared up the wooden porch steps with a brisk, cocky strut, Lázaro leaned against a tree and bit his fingernails.

Lázaro still hadn't convinced himself that he would go through with the deed and it was not too late to run away. Lázaro knew he only had precious minutes until his brother reappeared at the base of the steps. He could run back to their boarding house, or disappear into Key West, a city more populous than Tampa, but would never be able to avoid Javier or fight his brother's jeering ridicule.

While Lázaro was stuck in this internal debate, he lost track of time and was soon faced with a smiling Javier, who greeted him with a hearty slap on the shoulder. "Your turn!" Javier buttoned his shirt and ran a small black comb through his hair.

He saw that his brother remained expressionless and did not move. "What's the matter, Silent Sam? Hurry up before someone else has their way and knocks her out for the night."

Lázaro hesitated and stared blankly at his brother.

"Get on with it!" Javier took Lázaro by the shoulders, whirled him around to face the steps and pushed him forward. Propelled by the momentum, Lázaro's feet kept moving and slowly pulled him up the steps and to the front door. He took a breath and, almost possessed by another force, he knocked.

The door opened and the lanky LaBraza leaned into the doorframe and looked him up and down. A Basque from Iruñea on the Spanish peninsula, she was in her mid-thirties, tall and slim with wiry arms and legs like a spider. Long black hair hung over her shoulders and her black negligee shadowed her dark, purple eyes. She sipped from a tiny, metal flask and when she spoke, crooked yellow teeth appeared and emitted a strong odor of whiskey and tobacco.

LaBraza squinted at this young man standing in her doorway – her eyebrows formed a disapproving purple V. She wondered for a moment if she was looking at the same boy who had left just minutes ago. "How old are you?"

Lázaro straightened up to appear taller. "Nineteen." He knew he probably couldn't pass for that age, but this woman was clearly drunk and could not tell either way.

She pointed a long, boney finger his direction. "You have money?"

He nodded so she pulled him inside and shut the door. When he entered the house, the odor of whiskey and tobacco instantly disappeared and Lázaro was hit with an overwhelming stink of cats. He saw two gray hairballs sleeping on the front windowsill, and another white feline streaking under a pile of clothes on a couch in the front room.

The rest of the small bungalow was littered with clothes, piled on the floor and draped over furniture. As LaBraza led Lázaro into her bedroom he noticed a variety of liquor bottles decorating a dresser cluttered with knickknacks and perfume bottles, and two more cats lounging on the purple bedroom rug.

"How many cats do you have?"

LaBraza smirked as she closed the bedroom door behind them. "More than you'll be able to count in the time that you're here."

She sat on the bed and invited Lázaro to stand before her. He handed her a wad of dollar bills which she snatched and set on the bed beside her. He noticed a field of cat hair covering her bedspread. Without a word she reached for his zipper but stopped and squinted at him again. "Have you ever done this?"

He nodded stupidly and tried to stop himself from shaking, knowing that Javier had probably given this prostitute an experience Lázaro would never be able to match. She smiled knowingly at the novice before unzipping his pants and dropping to her knees.

Like his brother it took Lázaro only a few minutes to finish, and like his brother he sprang down the steps and onto the street feeling like he could conquer the city. Javier waited outside with a cigar in his mouth, smiling and flirting with the ladies who passed by. When his brother emerged, a proud Javier welcomed him with another powerful pat on the shoulder and snatched a few cat hairs off his back. "How does it feel to finally be a man?"

Lázaro felt better than he could ever remember.

They had not taken five more steps before they were suddenly face to face with Juan Carlos Alvarez. "Boys!" He greeted them with open arms and a grin that revealed his discolored front tooth.

Javier, always happy to see the man he considered his uncle, greeted Juan Carlos with a customary hug and kiss on the cheek. "Carlito! How long have you been in Key West?"

"A few days," Carlito said. "Some business in Tampa brought me down here." Juan Carlos knew of the whorehouse nearby. LaBraza's house was well known to the local cigar makers, and Juan Carlos had already inquired about such accommodations. Seeing the boys outside made him suspicious. "Where are you coming from?"

"Nowhere," Javier said quickly as he nudged Lázaro. "Just touring the city before dinner."

Juan Carlos smiled. He could tell from the dazed grin on Lázaro's face that the boys had been with the prostitute. With a knowing smile he sent them on their way and then stood outside the yellow bungalow realizing that LaBraza had just been visited by the Ortiz boys. If Salvador's sons had just been with her then Juan Carlos no longer felt the need. He kept walking and found a tavern with a card game.

Juan Carlos was reunited with Mendez later that night when the young writer walked into the Duval Street saloon where Juan Carlos played cards with three other cigar makers. Mendez had been raising money in Key West for the last two weeks and was preparing to leave for Havana. When Carlito saw Mendez he nearly jumped out of his chair and rushed across the bar to greet him with a firm embrace. Juan Carlos held a newly lit cigar between two fingers and his breath smelled of beer.

Juan Carlos looked over his friend and saw Mendez still had a small purple bruise under his eye but had otherwise healed. "It's good to see you, Sandito. How goes the fundraising?"

Mendez raised his voice above the piano music and chatter. "Better than expected. The workers in Key West have been generous to our friends in Tampa and needed little persuasion. One can only hope the Havana workers will treat us so fortunately."

Mendez had made several visits to the Cuban social club in Key West, where after making his case, he would pass around a *jipijapa* – a woven, brimmed hat – and collect donations from the workers.

Juan Carlos grinned and squeezed Mendez's wrist with appreciation. "Well done, Sandito. And there is news from Tampa about our friend, the man with the beard." Juan Carlos used his hand to mimic brushing his imaginary beard.

Mendez was interested and leaned in closer to hear. Juan Carlos put an arm around Mendez and proudly whispered the tale of his revenge directly into the writer's ear. Mendez was not impressed and clearly disapproved.

"Stupid move, Carlito," Mendez scowled.

"Rubbish!" the incensed Juan Carlos pushed Mendez away and forcefully pointed at him. "You are avenged! You should be thanking me for fighting in your place!"

Mendez spoke gently to try and calm Carlito's anger. "It was unnecessary, my friend. You have embarrassed Armando and sent him home in disgrace, but he will return and he will come after you again."

Juan Carlos stepped back. "I do not fear some arrogant businessman."

"He does not ask you to. He will not forget what you have done, and he will not let you get away with it."

Juan Carlos waved him away in disgust. "You sound like a Spaniard."

"Just be careful, Carlito. Armando Renteria has powerful surrogates. There are many who would do his bidding in his absence. His influence is vast. They could be looking for you here in Key West and are certainly awaiting your return to Tampa."

Juan Carlos straightened up as if the news had invigorated him. "You are talking to a man who fought beside El Matón, who shed blood with Cuban rebels. A man who has mastered the machete and the torch."

Mendez dismissed Carlito's claims. "The war is over, my friend. Grow up."

*   *   *

Antonio Vasquez stood at a second-floor window of his empty factory and gazed at the tenement houses below. The workers and their families were having an elaborate picnic along Twelfth Avenue. Tables draped in white cloth and covered with food sat amid a hundred people who mingled in the sandy streets and joyfully gossiped of local events and politics. Children swarmed around them, running between tables chasing each other and livening the street with their games. It was a cheerful scene and – more than just a show of strength for the families – it was an all out taunt to the cigar manufacturers.

Vasquez paced from window to window as he watched the antics below. Behind him the galley was a dead zone of endless, vacant workbenches. In the office, Capecho met with an officer from the Bank of Tampa to discuss repayment of the company's past due loan.

"How is this possible?" Vasquez muttered as the rejuvenated families smiled and laughed as if their pockets were filled with cash.

Salvador and Olympia sat at a table on their front lawn with their neighbor Songo and chatted while they ate fresh fruit and watched the children play. There was a baseball game on the wide, sandy flat where Twelfth Avenue met Twentieth Street, and E.J. was currently awaiting his turn to bat.

There was a feeling of triumph at the picnic. Mendez had been well received in Key West and Havana and had returned with enough money to fund Ybor City soup kitchens for at least another month. Many Tampa workers were in Havana and Key West rolling cigars and sending excess funds home to their families and Salvador could not wait to get back to work himself. He never felt completely satisfied unless he was working, whether it be at the job or around the house.

Olympia was pleased with Javier and Lázaro's success and had been able to put an adequate meal on the table every night since they started returning wages to the household. She was especially proud of Lázaro who was struggling to find his way through life and would struggle even more as he grew older. Seeing the workers fight through this strike and ultimately prevail would help build his confidence and sense of worth.

Now E.J. took the plate, and Olympia and Salvador applauded and cheered as he waited in the batter's box for the first pitch. The pitch came from a boy a few years older than E.J. but when Salvador's son swung the bat, he connected and sent a wooden crack echoing across the tenements.

Salvador stood and applauded. E.J.'s nine-year-old legs became a circular blur as the boy raced to first base and beat the throw. Olympia shouted happily for her son and clapped her hands above her head as E.J. stood quietly on first base with his hands on his hips catching his breath, already watching the next batter and ready to head for second.

The sound of the parents' cheering resonated in the empty galley as Vasquez stood in the window watching the baseball game and wondering what to do. The workers were incredibly resourceful and were sending a direct message to the manufacturer that they were far from surrender.

Renteria was out of town, the subject of a violent and embarrassing attack that sent him to the hospital and caused a wave of gossip related to the size, or apparent lack thereof, of Armando's most vital component. After a day in the hospital, Armando had traveled to Cuba to recuperate at his father's tobacco *vega* without giving anyone a planned date of return.

Before Armando had gone, he had visited Arlen Kincaid and paid the editor to print an article in the *Tampa Daily News* that portrayed Armando in a positive light. Damage control, an obvious attempt to protect his reputation while his body healed offshore. Gallego had taken over *bolita* in Armando's absence and had consolidated all games into a single throw held four nights a week at his tavern La Rubia.

More damaging to Armando's reputation was his plan to import strikebreakers, which died with the absence of its champion. Now Vasquez stood in an empty factory while a healthy and invigorated workforce waited patiently for him to open his doors. Scales and quotas were meant to be a cost-saving improvement but had been rejected by the workers and forced the company to the brink of insolvency.

Capecho returned from his meeting and approached Vasquez, who didn't look away from the baseball game. The Ortiz boy had advanced to second base on a ground ball and stood with hands on hips ready for the next pitch.

"What news do you have?" Vasquez asked his accountant.

"We're broke, dangerously in debt and unable to secure credit."

Vasquez said nothing and tightened his lips. The company his father had owned outright and passed to Don Antonio was now owned by several investors. Vasquez's personal stake was down to less than seventy percent while Armando's had increased during the strike. Now the *bolitero* had an option to purchase another two percent should Vasquez and Company default on the loan Armando had granted.

"What do we do?" Vasquez finally asked.

"The choice is simple," said Capecho. "Open the doors or file bankruptcy."

Vasquez dropped his head and let his eyes fall to the factory floor. He searched for answers in the sandy, wooden floorboards and recognized the chain reaction his decision would cause. If he did away with quotas and weight restrictions, he knew the other factory owners would have to follow. Preparing to be despised among the manufacturers, Vasquez looked to Capecho and placed a gentle hand on the foreman's shoulder. "We can no longer deny the mistake we've made. Open the doors."

Capecho nodded and quickly hurried away.

Vasquez turned back to the ballgame. The inning had ended and the players crisscrossed on the sand as one team filtered towards their side while the other fanned across the field and took their positions. Vasquez and Company was back in business, but Don Antonio was out of money and deeper in the hole than ever before.

El Boletín de los Obreros
(The Workers' Bulletin)

Unidad Después de la Huelga de Pesa
(Unity After The Weight Strike)

by Gabriel Mendez
December 5, 1899

The Weight Strike was a decisive event in the history of Ybor City's labor relations. At first glance, it would seem a great victory for the cigar workers, who have won higher wages, a uniform pay scale, and the removal of scales and quotas from the cigar factories. The workers held out and were rewarded. The manufacturers gave in to worker demands and ended the lockout in a position worse than where they began. An outsider would say that the cigar workers have placed themselves in a position of power where manufacturers must meet their demands or face prolonged and financially disastrous walkouts. But with a closer look, we begin to understand why the cigar worker must proceed with caution.

The Weight Strike was important for the workers because it established a vital labor union, La Sociedad de Torcedores de Tampa, known to its members as La Resistencia. The organization, created and managed by immigrants, has seen eager enrollment and elected as its president Angelo 'Lapár' De la Parte. As this century comes to a close, La Resistencia boasts three times as many Cubans as Spaniards. It is a denial of the American Federation of Labor's narrow brand of unionism, which emphasizes work-related issues such as wages and hours, a simplistic approach that is harmful to the goals of the cigar worker.

La Resistencia aims to organize all cigar workers to resist the exploitation of labor by capital. It is not an advocate of the partial strike but is convinced that the general strike is a revolutionary maxim. So it would seem that our new labor union has become the new protector of the local cigar worker. This is not the case and we must not become overconfident in our practices! Because of the Weight Strike, there exists an opposing force. A manufacturers' union has been established in direct opposition to La Resistencia.

The Cigar Trust is a union of cigar manufacturers determined to never let another labor dispute disrupt their drive for efficiency and industrial domination. The Cigar Trust is an agent of financial power and greed. It exists not to support the greater benefit of a healthy workplace but to further the corporate profit machine and squeeze every penny out of its workforce. Though slavery has been abolished on paper it smolders and flickers at our lowest levels, waiting to reignite and burn with the endorsement of corporate America.

These are changing times and the Cigar Trust will surely fan the flames of oppression as we enter the next century. Only through continued dedication to La Resistencia, and mindful remembrance of our struggles, past and present, can we ensure a way of life that is our own, and not the result of a corporate profit margin.

The Weight Strike is over and the cigar worker is better off, but tensions are high in this war of cultures. I call on all workers, Cuban, Spanish and Italian to stand ready, and be prepared, for another clash is inevitable!

V.

YBOR CITY
1900

Chapter 15

Lázaro hated 1900 from the moment the clock struck midnight. He hated the optimism and patriotic celebrations that ushered in the new century. He hated President McKinley and his running mate Theodore Roosevelt. He hated the Rough Riders and the Spanish-American War. Most of all he hated the tobacco business and almost everything about the Cigar City, which still reigned supreme.

He hated the new labor union *La Resistencia* which formed after the Weight Strike of the previous year and he hated when his father would proudly proclaim that he held union card #389 out of a pool of 2,000. He hated his little brother E.J. who had become Salvador's apprentice, and seemed to be the darling of the factory, hogging all the attention.

Lázaro Ortiz hated almost everything about Ybor City, everything except boxing. Hardly active in the city's social life and considering himself a pariah among the cigar workers, Lázaro spent his free time at a smoky, indoor boxing club on Ninth Avenue that hosted fights three times a week.

Tables and chairs had been pushed against the wall to house a makeshift boxing ring constructed from plywood and ropes. Lázaro stood among the rowdy, drunken men in the crowd and watched the fighters bob and weave like dancers rehearsing a fluid but rugged number with punches that exploded in sweat. It was invigorating for the sixteen-year-old to watch these men beat and pound each other over and over, fueled by the cheering crowd and bursts of adrenaline.

Lázaro had been in many fights during his short life, and although not an experienced boxer, when he saw a poster hanging on the club wall advertising an open contest for the next week he decided to enter. The entry fee was fifty cents, but when Lázaro tried to pay the club's owner, a lanky fellow with a thin black moustache known around Ybor as Lapiz, he was refused.

"You are probably too young," Lapiz shook his head. Everything about Lapiz was thin. His slicked-back hair had dwindled to a few shoots of black and gray and his eyes formed narrow little slits as they watched Lázaro. Even his eyebrows and lips seemed to have been drawn onto his face with a single line of ink.

"I am eighteen," Lázaro lied with great defiance.

Lapiz chuckled, not convinced. "We already have enough lightweights."

"What if one of them drops out?"

The boy had a point. Lapiz considered the young man who stood before him with a mouth that curved to the left and a crooked nose that had obviously been broken once before. The boy's shoulders slouched forward tiredly and made him look like he would struggle for balance in the ring. If the boy had not spoken, Lapiz would have suspected him to be slightly retarded, but the boy had the proper fee and a presence that swelled with confidence and certainty. And he probably could pass for eighteen.

"Have you fought before?"

Now Lázaro stood tall, his shoulders thrust back like a soldier coming to attention. "I have fought many, including an American soldier."

Lapiz raised a skeptical blade of eyebrow. "An American soldier you say?"

"My father said he nearly killed me."

Lapiz squinted and tried to match the boy's face to any of the hundreds of men who visited his club. "Who is your father?"

"Salvador Ortiz Nerón from Nineteenth Street. He works at the Vasquez cigar factory and fought in the wars in Cuba."

"He was an insurrectionist?"

Lázaro nodded even though he had no idea what his father had done during the independence wars.

Now Lapiz smiled and patted Lázaro on the shoulder. "You are a courageous boy but foolish, I think. There are men entered to fight who are stronger and more practiced. Do you own a pair of gloves?"

"I need no gloves. I will fight bare-knuckled if I have to."

The owner laughed again. "Buy yourself a pair of gloves. And show up early, as early as you can. We'll want to get your fight out of the way before the crowds arrive and embarrass you."

The night of the fight Lázaro arrived early as instructed, with a pair of cheap boxing gloves he had purchased from a used goods dealer on the outskirts of town near the Scrub. The gloves amounted to nothing more than padded mittens but they were approved by Lapiz who waved Lázaro towards the ring where a crowd had already started to gather and place bets, and where Lázaro met his competition.

"Lazaro Ortiz, meet Abe Brown." Abe was another lightweight of similar size, a black boy who looked only slightly older than Lázaro and not much smarter. One of his eyes was focused intently on Lázaro, but the other was glazed and watery, and seemed to stare slightly over Lázaro's shoulder.

They nodded and sized each other up, both with an ill-mannered sneer. Abe had his shirt off and wore a pair of ragged shorts. He had a lean upper body with definition that was intimidating, and he wore gloves of only slightly higher quality than Lázaro's shabby mittens. At the moment, Abe unworriedly shifted his weight back and forth between each leg, and his dangling arms loosely practiced their punches.

Lapiz asked Lázaro, "Who is your second?"

"My what?"

Lapiz laughed. "You have no attendant? No one to back you up during the fight?"

Lázaro gazed behind Abe and saw an older black man who carried a washed out towel and a grimy leather bag. His clothes were worn and like Abe's and their droopy faces shared a resemblance; he was probably a cousin or uncle.

Lázaro said, "I usually come and go by myself."

"Well, if you're on your own, you have only a few minutes to find someone before the fights get underway. Your names are the first on the bill." Lapiz disappeared into the crowd and left Lázaro alone.

More and more men arrived until there were nearly a hundred, and the room became clouded with shouting and cigar smoke. It was not the primetime full house Lázaro had experienced in the past but there were

189

certainly more men than he expected. Suddenly Lázaro felt a hand on his shoulder. When he turned he saw Javier gawking.

"You old fool!" Javier said as he reached down and touched Lázaro's boxing mitts. Javier wore a white suit and black tie with a matching white vest and a white fedora. There was a black handkerchief in his breast pocket and a cigar dangling between his fingers. He looked foolishly debonair. "Don't tell me you are entered in this thing!"

Lázaro said nothing. He stared at his brother and calmly practiced his punches the way Abe had done, trying to look tough but succeeding only in making Javier laugh. Lázaro could smell bourbon on his brother's breath. Then Javier slapped him hard on the back, still trying to contain his laughter. "You're lucky Papa isn't here to see this!"

"Where is Papa?"

"He is down the street playing dominoes." Now Javier stood up straight to look his brother in the eye. "Seriously little brother, I do not think you realize what you are getting into. These fighters are unforgiving."

Lázaro shrugged. "So what? I have never forgiven a soul."

Javier said, "You'll come home with a mouth full of blood and no teeth. Who are you fighting?"

Lázaro pointed to Abe. Javier dangled his cigar between his fingers and then popped it into his mouth as he watched the young black fighter hop from foot to foot in the corner of the ring. Javier puffed his cigar and pulled it out of his mouth as he put his arm around his brother. "He's blind in his left eye."

"How do you know that?"

"That's Abe Brown. Haven't you seen him up close?" Javier said. "One eye watches you but the other seems stuck like a marble in the mud. Watch out for his right hand, and stay to his left if you can."

Lázaro didn't think anything of Abe's eye when he first saw him, and Javier seemed to know more than a thing or two about this fighter. Lázaro said, "The bar man told me I need a man in my corner."

Javier puffed his cigar. "Not me, little brother. I am here to gamble and am not someone you'd want in your corner since I'm here to bet against you."

"You're betting against me?"

"You've never fought and Abe Brown is three-and-two, soon to be four-and-two."

"Who did he lose to?"

Javier chuckled. "Someone much more talented than you." He patted his brother on the back, wished him luck and hurried off to place his bet.

Now a bell sounded and the murmur in the room subsided. Lapiz appeared in the center of the ring wearing a black jacket with tails and hovered over the crowd like a smiling villain. He raised his arms above his head and began to announce the night's matchups. "Place your bets! Place your bets! We'll be starting shortly! The main event is between Archie the Menace and Stomping Stan DeMartino." Lapiz paused while the patrons cheered and jeered the two fighters. "But before the heavyweights take the ring, we have a three bout ticket for the lower weight classes. Up first, a five-round fight featuring, Abe Brown, the Slugger from the Scrub!" The men cheered, though quietly, reserving their energy for the main event. Abe danced to the center of the ring and raised a glove to the crowd. As Lázaro awaited his introduction he heard men behind him snickering and laughing, using words like 'puny' and 'pathetic.'

"Versus," Lapiz pointed to Lázaro, "a newcomer, the Son of Salvador, Lázaro Ortiz!" Lázaro heard booing from the crowd and a trickle of laughter. Lázaro waved to the crowd, spotted Javier's white hat among the fans, and saw his brother smiling at him. He almost smiled back until Javier raised a white ticket in the air and pointed at Abe Brown; a clear taunt to his younger brother. Lázaro ignored it and turned his attention to the ring.

The opening bell rang and the two fighters began to circle each other. Abe, compensating for his spoiled left eye, circled clockwise and Lázaro moved with him. The crowd cheered and provoked them, while cigar smoke swirled and formed a cloud above the ring that immersed the fighters' heads in a white haze.

They circled for half a minute, Abe looked for an opening and Lázaro waited to react. Finally, with the speed of a rabbit, Abe attacked and jabbed for Lázaro, landing a stunning punch squarely on Lázaro's chin. The sound of cheering was lost as Lázaro's feet fumbled and tried to stay on the mat. His head vibrated and his vision became a foggy blur. His chin stung where it had met Abe's knuckles; the thin boxing gloves did little to pad the effect of a head-on punch. Before Lázaro could recover, another left-hand punch landed on his ribs and then a right hook caught him on the cheek and sent him to the ground.

It wasn't a knockout blow, and Lázaro was surprisingly fast to return to his feet. He was amazed at how hard he was breathing, and by the amount of sweat dripping from his face. He'd need to increase his stamina if he was ever going to have a chance to last into the late rounds.

The cheering and booing that arose from the crowd after Lázaro went down did not let up when he got back on his feet. The referee separated each fighter and then chopped the air with his hand to signal the all clear. Again they circled while the crowd cheered for more. Lázaro knew he should take advantage of Abe's blind spot and he moved in for a jab but Abe countered with his own. Neither landed a punch, and the two fighters locked up. Lázaro pushed Abe away and then aimed a right hook at Abe's left cheek but his fist met empty air as Abe was already out of the way. Before they could circle again, the bell sounded that Round One was over.

Lázaro wavered and looked around. Then he saw Javier's white suit in the corner and Javier waving to him and pointing to a stool he'd placed in the ring. Lázaro stumbled over and sat down. Immediately Javier leaned over his shoulder and dabbed at his brother's cut lip with a handkerchief.

"You're circling the wrong way, fool! His left eye is blind, remember? So he circles to watch you with his right. Force him to circle the other way and you'll stay in his blind spot. Then move in and hit him with a right hook. And hit him hard, aim for the jaw. Punch with your legs, your body. How do you feel?"

Lázaro nodded. He was nearly out of breath and hoped the one minute break would be enough to recover. He looked across the ring where Abe received similar attention from his second. Javier rubbed his shoulders and said, "Good luck and keep the pressure on him. I didn't mean what I said about betting against you."

Before Lázaro could ask what he meant, the bell sounded and Round Two was under way. Abe sprang from his stool and came directly at Lázaro but a quick sidestep sent them circling the direction that favored Abe's eye. Lázaro moved in quickly and jabbed with his right hand but Abe, watching with his good eye, swatted it away with his mitt. Again, Lázaro attacked, and again and again, and finally he landed a punch against Abe's left temple. The crowd cheered, and Lázaro's confidence surged. He tried to attack with a left hand body blow but Abe saw an opening and landed two quick punches on Lázaro's face. He felt blood welling in his mouth but stayed on his feet and was able to lock Abe in the center of the ring. Finally, the bell rang to end the second round, and Lázaro collapsed onto the corner chair exhausted and surprised by how much energy boxing required.

"Your lip is swollen," said Javier. He had removed his white jacket and his vest – they hung on a chair beside the ring – and he had rolled up his sleeves to dab at Lázaro's bloody lip with a towel instead of a handkerchief. "You look tired. Maybe you should lie down during this round?"

"Quit?" Lázaro said incredulously.

Javier shrugged. "I take back what I said before. I really did bet against you, for you to fall in the third round. So cut us both a break and don't let this guy beat you any worse than he has. When Mama learns what you've done tonight, she'll never stop slapping you."

Now Lázaro was angry. Had his brother come to his aid only to keep him on his feet long enough to lose at the right time? And how could Javier bet that his younger brother would lose to a one-eyed Negro from the Scrub? It was so infuriating that Lázaro hopped to his feet determined to defeat Abe Brown for no better reason than to lose his brother's bet. When the third round bell rang, Lázaro became as aggressive as a lion in the wild. Lázaro the Lion is what they would call him, as soon as he made a name for himself by defeating the Slugger from the Scrub.

Abe was just as determined to improve his own record. They met in the center of the ring and exchanged a fury of punches that energized the crowd, whose loud cheers inspired the fighters. It was an exciting circle: the faster the fighters punched each other, the louder the crowd cheered, and the more they cheered, the harder the fighters worked. Their knuckles were bruised, their blood was spilled and their skin swelled purple. Lázaro was pumped with adrenaline, and Abe drooled like a wild dog, spraying saliva across the ring with every jab and punch. It would become a famous exchange, and for weeks the spectators would talk about the Round Three of the opening match between that black boy from the Scrub and the Cuban from the Vasquez factory.

What made it something to remember was the way it ended. An even contest for the first half, Round Three turned bad when Abe surprised Lázaro with an uppercut to the chin and followed with a trio of hooks to the temple. Right-left-right. Groggy and off guard, Lázaro stumbled and backed into the ropes. Abe moved in for the kill and landed a right hand thrust square in the middle of Lázaro's face, shattering his nose. Blood gushed from his nostrils like a dam had broken and Lázaro's ears rang like a gun had exploded right beside them. As Abe cocked his fist for the finishing blow, Javier appeared between them to block the punch, effectively ending the fight.

Lázaro collapsed to the mat, his energy depleted and his head in so much pain that he did not care about the loss. No one would ever say that Javier intervened too early. Instead they would praise him for jumping in at the last second to save his little brother and for sacrificing the shirt and slacks of his treasured white suit. Lázaro was too dazed to realize the fight had been stopped. The frenzy of spectators celebrating their victory or cursing their loss faded behind the pain he felt over his entire body. He came to and found Javier before him, dabbing Lázaro's wounds with a towel. Javier looked worried, and Lázaro wondered how seriously he had been injured.

Javier grinned when his brother opened his eyes. "That was close, little brother! Didn't I tell you to go for his blind spot? You're lucky you got away!"

"Is he okay? Is it bad?" It was Lapiz, who looked over Javier's shoulder to inspect the mess of blood that was Lázaro's face.

Javier laughed. "He wasn't that good looking to begin with, were you Lázaro?"

Lázaro did not respond. He allowed Javier to tend to his wounds and help him out of the ring to a chair and table. Javier told Lázaro to hold the towel against his nose and then disappeared into the crowd and returned minutes later with a glass of water and a handful of cash. He gave the water to Lázaro and instructed him to rinse out his mouth. The money he counted and stuffed into his pocket.

Lázaro noticed his brother's treasured white suit was smeared with blood and that Javier didn't seem to care. "You really bet against me?"

Javier did not look at his brother. "You didn't expect to win your first fight, did you?" Now Javier beamed at his brother, and once again Lázaro became jealous of his brother's good looks. "But what a show! Especially that third round!"

Javier bought a shot of whiskey for Lázaro and another for himself. They sat together and waited for the remaining matches and were greeted by a steady stream of spectators. Many congratulated Lázaro and thanked him for a great fight, often inquiring about his injuries, and hoping he would return to the ring. These unexpected encounters were extremely satisfying. Lázaro became the center of attention and was praised and admired for a skill that he loved.

One man asked if Lázaro planned to quit his job at the cigar factory.

"Not yet," he replied uncertainly. "I don't think so. My father wouldn't approve."

The man laughed and patted Lázaro on the back. "Sounds like you're living your life trying to please your father."

The words were profound, and they were true.

His nose finally stopped bleeding, though the pain was a nuisance without the dulling effect of whiskey, and he ordered more shots which were quickly consumed. Javier commented that Lázaro would have a pair of black eyes in the morning, as the bags were already turning purple.

"There will be no hiding this from Mama and Papa."

"I don't care what they think. I fought and I lost. So what?"

Javier shook his head. "If you're trying to impress a girl then you're in the wrong town. And if you're trying to make a living, I'll advise you not to quit your job at the factory. But if you feel you've found your purpose, getting beaten to the edge of unconsciousness, then please, little brother, learn the skills of the sport."

"I know how to fight."

"But you have no idea how to box! These men train, they understand the footwork and the mechanics of throwing a solid punch. You learned to fight with children. You need to learn from a professional if you're to do this any longer."

Lázaro thought about this and though his sense of pride was powerful, he knew Javier was right. He could fight on the streets but he had no idea what he was doing in the ring. "Where do I go to learn the skills of the sport?"

Javier sat back and looked around the room. "The crew from New Orleans who are in town with Archie the Menace. They are professionals. Why don't you talk to their manager?"

Lázaro considered how he would travel all the way to New Orleans. He could get there by boat or train, but where would he stay once he was there? And how would he pay his living expenses?

They stayed the rest of the night at the table and drank whiskey until the main event ended and Archie the Menace, a giant of a man with a chubby, round frame and a bald head that melted into his shoulders sent Stomping Stan DeMartino to the mat in the sixth round.

Lázaro realized how much he had to learn. These men were champions, great athletes and he wanted to learn their ways, to be like them, to fight and to dominate. As Archie the Menace pummeled Stomping Stan in the sixth round and sent him down, the crowd became a frenzy of shouting men that made Lázaro's adrenaline surge. He decided that night that he would never be happy as a cigar maker.

Chapter 16

"Boxing? I should sell you to the circus!" Olympia stood on the porch with her fists on her hips and glared at the boys below. Lázaro's crooked nose was smeared with blood and Javier wavered in a drunken daze with blotches of red coloring his shirt and tie. "Get inside, the both of you, before I knock your teeth out!"

Lázaro climbed the steps and as he passed his mother and entered the house, Olympia slapped his backside. Javier tried to follow but Olympia stood in his way. "And why didn't you stop him?"

His jacket was folded over his arm and his hat was in his hand; his eyes sagged, tired and drunk from a long night on the town. Javier shrugged. "I'm not his father. He can do what he wants."

"Be careful what you say or I'll throw *you* out of this house!" They went inside where Lázaro sat on the couch in the parlor. Josefina was sitting on the floor reading a book, which she set aside when her brothers walked in. Javier joined Lázaro on the couch and Olympia stood before them with her fists still locked against her hips. She said to Lázaro, "If you spill blood on that couch, you will pay for a new one."

"Fine," Lázaro said and dabbed his nose with Javier's bloody handkerchief. His eyes were closed, his head hurt, and he wished she would leave him alone so he could rest.

Josefina rose. "I'll get ice and a fresh towel." She crossed the parlor and disappeared down the hallway, passing Salvador as he entered the room.

"Bring a dirty dishrag instead!" Olympia called to Josefina. "I don't want to ruin another good towel with this one's blood!"

Salvador came into the parlor with his shirt off wearing only his pants and a belt, almost ready for bed. He saw Lázaro on the couch a mess of bruises and Javier beside him with a bloody shirt. Javier's normally perfect hair was disheveled and both boys looked guilty as thieves. "Now what is all this about?" He stood next to Olympia and glared sternly at the two boys.

"He entered a contest," Javier began.

Olympia interrupted. "Let him say it."

All eyes went to Lázaro, who sighed and looked to the floor. Finally he said, "I'm not going to sit at a factory workbench all day."

Salvador and Olympia shared a glance; they had expected this moment. Inside of her anger, Olympia found that she understood, but she tried not to let it show by crossing her arms and tapping a foot. "You entered a contest?"

He nodded.

"It was a great fight," Javier said merrily. "All the men were cheering."

"Javier!" Olympia pointed at her oldest son, "If you don't shut your mouth, I'm going to break *your* nose!"

"What's wrong with boxing?" Javier asked innocently. "He's good at it, and if he keeps practicing, he can make money for the family."

Olympia asked Lázaro, "How much money did you make tonight?"

He shook his head. "None."

"Why not?"

"Because I didn't win."

Javier said, "I made ten dollars."

"You bet against him?" Olympia asked. Javier shrugged his shoulders and nodded. Olympia held out her hand. "Give me half."

Javier was surprised. "I spent it already."

"You already spent ten dollars?" Olympia said doubtfully as she took a step closer. She didn't believe he already spent ten dollars and made sure her face showed him how angry she would be if he had.

He shrugged. "Most of it."

"So you've just lied to your mother? Give me what's left." She waited with her hand extended as Javier reached into his pocket and handed her a couple of crumpled bills and some change. "Two dollars? You good for nothing fool," she folded the money into her palm.

Josefina returned from the kitchen with a fresh towel and a handful of ice, which she handed to Lázaro. Olympia said to Javier, "Your father and I want to talk to Lázaro."

Javier and Josefina dismissed themselves and went into the boys' bedroom where they sat with E.J. and listened – the walls were so thin it was impossible to avoid hearing everything that was said. Salvador moved to the couch and sat beside Lázaro while Olympia remained standing, her hands back on her hips.

Salvador said, "Let me look at your nose."

Lázaro sat back, allowing his father to inspect his face. Black bags would form under his eyes, his nose and mouth were caked with dried blood and his nose was smashed, but the bleeding had stopped. "Your nose is broken again but it doesn't look too bad. Do you still have all of your teeth?"

Lázaro clenched his teeth and opened his lips to show his father that he did.

Olympia shook her head. "You're going to come home dead one of these days, little raccoon."

Salvador said, "Lázaro, fighting and scuffling with your brothers is one thing but boxing is no way to make a living. You don't make real money unless you turn pro and you don't turn pro unless you fight constantly. In the meantime you'll break your nose, your ribs, your hands and your neck."

Olympia added, "And when you're hungry with broken hands you won't be able to work any other jobs and you won't be able to eat."

"Boxing is a life for men with no other skills," Salvador said.

"Boxing is a skill," Lázaro insisted as he held a handful of ice to his nose.

"But it is not work. How are you going to feed yourself?"

"I won't go hungry," Lázaro said. "There is a man visiting town who trains professional boxers in New Orleans."

Olympia threw her head back and forced an exasperated laugh. "You're going to waste your life on some circus clown?"

"He's not a clown."

"*You* are a clown for even considering this ridiculous stunt!"

199

Lázaro finally lost his temper and yelled, "Then why don't you kick me out of this house so I can go about my life as I please?"

Olympia pointed at him. "The only place you're going is back to the workbench so you can earn money for this family. You will do your part like every one of us."

Then Lázaro said something that not only enraged Olympia, but hurt her feelings in a way that Lázaro would regret for the rest of his life. He shouted, loud enough for the neighbors to hear, "You don't work! You don't do anything!"

Olympia's eyes opened wide and black as the volume of her voice became frighteningly lower. "What disrespect have you just shown your mother?"

Lázaro rose to face Olympia. Salvador tried to hold him back, but Lázaro broke away and stood face to face with his mother, looking down at her from above. "Papa, Javier and I work full time in the factory. Josefina is a nurse, and even E.J. is learning the trade. You stay home all day playing and bossing everyone around."

She took a step closer so their faces were inches apart. Though she was small compared to her son, to Salvador she looked as if she had risen to the same height. There was a fury in her eyes unlike any Salvador had ever seen. In a deep, controlled voice that stifled her rage Olympia said, "Are you telling me that I don't wash your clothes and keep your bed clean? That I don't fix your daily meals? That I'm not awake long after everyone has gone to sleep, and that I'm not the first to rise in the morning? When you were five and wandered over a beehive, and ran home crying like a baby, it was *my* shoulder you cried on! I was the one who treated your stings! I looked after you when you were sick, I picked you up when you fell, I carried you when you couldn't walk, and I fed you when you could not eat. And when you were an infant, and didn't know your foot from your ear, it was me who wiped your ass and cleaned you off after you had shit all over yourself! So if you think I don't do anything, then get the hell out of this house and do it yourself!"

Her eyes watered and tears fell immediately. "I am so mad I can no longer look at him," her voice cracked as she stomped down the hallway, into the kitchen and out the back. The door slammed shut and Salvador and Lázaro were left looking at each other.

Salvador shook his head as he glared at his son. "You young, stupid idiot. Why do you upset your mother like that when you know how much she does for you?" Lázaro didn't answer. He tossed the ice cubes aside and went into the boys' bedroom to find E.J., Javier and Josefina huddled at the doorway.

Javier looked at this brother with wide-eyed astonishment. "I've never heard Mama so mad!"

Josefina looked at him crossly, and E.J. was too amazed to say a word. Salvador followed him into the room. "Lázaro, go out back and apologize to your mother. The rest of you, go to bed."

But Lázaro opened his dresser drawer and reached for a fresh shirt, throwing the bloody one aside. "She said she can no longer look at me, so I'm leaving."

He was out the door before his father could stop him and headed for the saloon with hopes to catch Archie the Menace and his team before they left for the night. It was late and the saloon had closed, but when he arrived, Lázaro saw a light on in the back. He knocked on the glass window, gently at first then louder and a moment later, Lapiz appeared from the backroom, squinting across the bar at the face that peered in through the front window.

"Lázaro!" Lapiz said when he finally recognized the boy. He unlocked the door and poked his head out, and made his narrow eyes squint at the boy. He saw dark blotches under Lázaro's eyes and blood still dried around his nostrils. Lapiz laughed. "You took quite a beating, son. But what a third round! You're lucky you got away when you did. Lucky Lázaro, El Suerte. But what are you doing here so late?"

"I'm looking for Archie the Menace. What is his manager's name?"

"Ah, yes, Abrezzo. They're at the Havana Hotel. I think they leave tomorrow to sail back to New Orleans."

"Thank you, Señor. And thank you for entering me in the fight."

"Come back when you heal and we'll set you up against one of the white boys from Tampa. A Cracker against a Cuban always draws a nice crowd. And I'll pay you too!"

"I'll think about it, if I'm still in town," Lázaro said and waved goodbye. By the time he reached the Havana Hotel, it was after two in the morning. The lobby was empty and quiet and there was no one at the front desk. He decided he would wait until morning for Abrezzo and Archie's crew to check out. Not wanting to return home or miss his chance to meet Abrezzo, Lázaro collapsed onto one of the lobby's couches and fell asleep.

Olympia confronted Lázaro's accusations. The boy felt constrained by circumstance and had lashed out in anger, but there was no excuse for such disrespect. Olympia had in fact worked in the cigar factory, sweeping floors and sorting tobacco leaves when time would allow. She admitted that her presence in the cigar factory had amounted to nothing more than a few hours each month, but that did not mean she was a lazy old woman who sat at home drinking rum and playing cards. She was a mother of four whose contribution to the home surpassed any offering made by the men of her family.

"Don't be hard on yourself," Salvador told her after Lázaro had stormed out. Salvador sat on the back steps beside his wife, who had cleaned tears off her face with a handkerchief and seemed to have quickly recovered from the exchange.

"If only he knew how easy my life could have been," she said with her usual command. "I could have stayed on that property and been pampered everyday by maids. My meals, my clothes, my affairs, all of it could have been handled by someone else while I lounged in my giant bedroom and read adventure novels."

Salvador sat quietly while she talked.

"I wish I could run away from here and go back there, and take Lázaro with me so he can see what I gave up. It would make him appreciate his mother. It would make all of them appreciate me."

"He's sixteen. He will wise up soon enough. You've been a great mother."

Olympia stood and walked to the bottom of the steps, disgusted. "Enough of your platitudes." She stood with her hands on her hips, her back to her husband. Salvador watched and wondered what she was thinking.

Finally she turned to face him. "Sometimes I wish I had remained on the plantation. I should have forgiven my father. I should have stayed."

Salvador did not know what to say. He sat on the steps foolishly while Olympia walked past him, climbed the wooden boards and stepped back into the house.

When Lázaro returned to the tenements the next morning children were playing baseball in the street outside the Ortiz house but E.J., normally among that crowd, was sitting on the porch with a bucket of water beside him and a paintbrush in his hand. He pretended to paint the boards using the water, mimicking the men who painted a row of new tenement houses down the street. Lázaro scoffed at his little brother's childish antics and entered the house.

He was greeted by the smell of fresh coffee and the sound of plates clanking in the kitchen. The parlor was empty and Lázaro hurried to slip into the bedroom he shared with his brothers and found Javier asleep in bed, hung over from the night before. Lázaro moved quickly and packed a bundle of clothes into a canvas bag and retrieved a small leather pouch from the dresser drawer. Inside the pouch Lázaro had stashed nineteen dollars and some change, not enough to pay the amount Abrezzo required but enough to get to New Orleans and survive for a few days.

Beside the pouch Lázaro saw the dull knife he had purchased a few years ago. He took that and slipped it into his bag too.

"What are you doing now?" Javier had opened his eyes and was propped up on one elbow. He looked ready to collapse and fall back to sleep.

"None of your business," replied Lázaro as he fastened the buckles on his bag.

"You're going? Who are you going with?"

"Me, myself and I." Lázaro closed the drawer and turned to see Olympia standing in the doorway wearing a dress and apron. Her eyes were on Javier.

"Get out of bed, it's after ten." She walked to the bedside and tried to pull the sheets away from Javier, but he held on in protest and began a minor tug of war. Olympia dropped the sheet and Lázaro waited for his mother to address him, but she turned and left the room without giving him a single look.

Javier noticed this and cupped his hands to whisper, "You're no longer her son. She doesn't want you anymore! She said so last night after you left!"

"Liar," Lázaro did not like being mocked. "Shut your mouth before I break it."

"Clean the blood out of your nostrils at least. Gonna be a big fighter? One amateur fight and you lost to a blind man. Good luck to you." Javier pulled the sheets over himself and disappeared beneath them. Just as he closed his eyes, he was crushed by the weight of Lázaro, who dived onto the bed and attacked Javier with a series of punches to the body.

"How do you like this?" the younger boy shouted as his fists pounded his brother's back, ribs, and shoulder.

"Get off of me!" Javier yelled as he twisted in the sheets, flailing with his arms and kicking his legs to block Lázaro's advance. The weight was quickly removed as Salvador ran into the room, grabbed Lázaro by the shoulders and threw him off the bed.

"What do you think you're doing?" Salvador shouted as he stood above Lázaro, who had flopped into a pile in the corner of the room. The boy had never seen his father so angry.

Lázaro stood and grabbed his bag. "I'm going to New Orleans to be a professional boxer." He stepped around his father and into the hallway.

Salvador followed. "You've never even been to New Orleans."

"I went to Key West, I managed. I can take care of myself." Lázaro walked across the parlor where E.J. stood with water dripping from his paintbrush; the commotion had summoned him inside. "Mama told me to get out of her sight so that's what I'm going to do."

"She did not mean what she said."

They stopped at the front door just as Olympia burst into the parlor. "Oh yes, I did mean what I said! I meant every word! This boy shows no respect for his mother and now, because he is selfish and stupid, I will go back to work in the cigar factory. I will get my hands dirty and crack these precious fingernails doing manual labor, just like you wanted, Lázaro! Foolish little boy."

Lázaro scowled and then raised his voice. "When Josefina wanted to become a nurse you let her go, and she is a girl!"

"Josefina is not going to let someone beat the lights out of her," Olympia said.

"She knew nothing of being a nurse when she left. They trained her and she succeeded. Why is it any different for me?"

Salvador, like a referee mediating a bout, held up a hand between Lázaro and Olympia. "Josefina went to a place where she was taken care of. The boxing world is dangerous, filled with people who are not educated the way a nurse is educated. They only care about gambling and money and will take advantage of you every chance they get."

"Let me learn," Lázaro pleaded. "I cannot stay here the rest of my life knowing I never took his chance."

Olympia thought of her late night escape from the Cancio mansion and saw herself in this boy. In his mind the pursuit was necessary, and the consequence of staying home was eternal misery. She could not force him to stay, Lázaro needed to make the decision himself. "Do you think you're ready to handle the real world? A big boy, all of sixteen years old?"

"I'll be seventeen next month."

Olympia glanced to Salvador who seemed resigned and unable to stifle Lázaro's freewill. She felt herself become very calm as she made a prediction to Lázaro, "You will be back in Tampa in less than three weeks."

Salvador agreed but remained silent.

"Have faith, Mother." Lázaro gave her a crooked smile. His sockets were bruised black and he still had blood on his face. He looked wrecked and Olympia wished he would at least wash his face before he left.

Salvador stepped towards his boy and took him by the shoulders. "If you find you can box for a living then you have my blessing, but if this life is not for you, understand that there can be no disgrace in admitting a mistake. It can be noble to admit you were wrong and your health is always more important than your pride."

Lázaro looked into his father's eyes and waited for Salvador to release him. Then he turned and stepped towards the front door. Expecting Olympia to reach out and grab him, and attempt to keep him in the house, Lázaro was surprised when she turned and walked the opposite direction down the hall. He heard her go into her bedroom and shut the door. Lázaro glanced around the parlor and saw E.J. standing beside him still clutching the wet paintbrush, Javier in the hallway half-awake wearing undershorts, and Josefina standing behind him watching the exchange.

Lázaro nodded to his siblings and then stepped onto the porch. Salvador followed and closed the front door behind him. They started down the steps together and Salvador walked with Lázaro until they were out of earshot. Salvador handed Lázaro a five dollar bill. "Put this in your pocket. Don't tell your mother."

Lázaro took the money and looked at his father. "Tell Mama I am sorry about what I said."

"You should tell her yourself."

Lázaro looked back to the house and shrugged. It was too late. "Next time I see her, I will."

Salvador wished he could order his son to turn around and march back into the house but what good would it do? Lázaro was his own man and determined to discover his destiny. He gave his boy a gentle hug and a kiss on the cheek then they broke away and Lázaro began his journey, traveling towards Port Tampa. Salvador watched until Lázaro turned a corner and disappeared.

Chapter 17

Two months passed without any word from Lázaro, and by March of 1900 Olympia felt the family needed to compensate for the loss of his income. She went to work at the Vasquez factor stripping stems from tobacco leaves during the morning hours.

Salvador protested. "But why would you go to work? The economy is strong and so are our finances. Now that E.J. is working, we can manage."

"E.J. should be back in school," Olympia said tiredly after a long morning on the sweltering top floor of the hot factory. "And how will we pay for Josefina's wedding?"

"E.J. is a working man," said Salvador. "There is no need for him to be in school. Javier and I make top dollar at the factory, and soon E.J. will too. With Lázaro out of the house and Josefina soon to move out, there will be only four of us left. Three of us are already working! There is no need to employ a fourth!"

Olympia knew he was right, but she did not want to lose face. Lázaro's words had stung. She needed to work and to prove that daughters of rich aristocrats were not lazy women who stayed home doing nothing. "I am going to keep working," she insisted. "The money will come in useful some day, you wait and see."

Salvador waved a frustrated hand at his wife and left it alone. Olympia was being stubborn and dramatic and needed time to realize the senselessness of her ways, to end her employment with dignity.

One of the least prestigious jobs in the industry, the tobacco strippers consisted mostly of uneducated women or newly arrived Italian men. They were just above floor sweepers on the factory hierarchy, but Olympia stated that she was not concerned with status. Despite the horrible heat in the factory, which got worse as the morning wore on and the Florida sun burned through the windows, Olympia worked daily for several months and into the summer. To preserve the moisture of the tobacco leaves, the factory windows were left closed at all times, which meant the inside of the factory became humid and unbearable to a girl who had been raised indoors like Olympia.

Olympia often returned home soaked in sweat, dehydrated, with her hands sticky and callused from the monotonous, repetitive work of tearing stem after stem from cured, brown tobacco leaves. She would be home by noon, have a short rest and then move about the house making beds, folding laundry, or preparing the evening meal. It was a tiresome routine that gave Olympia little satisfaction. She was often cranky and exhausted by the time dinner was served.

"Stop trying to be a martyr!" Salvador told her. "We have plenty of money, and there is no need for you to slave away in that hot factory. One of these days you are going to collapse from fatigue, and then where will that leave you? Stay home tomorrow, get some rest."

Olympia listened silently, knowing that Salvador was right but wondering when Lázaro would return home to see her condition.

"You are trying to impress *him*?" Salvador said in disbelief after Olympia confided in him. "Lázaro is a foolish young man. There is no need to work yourself to death on his account. Stay home and rest."

Olympia shrugged tiredly, lacking the strength to argue. "Josefina's wedding is next month, and we need to make preparations."

She wiped her nose with a handkerchief and cleared her throat.

Salvador saw she was becoming sick. "After her wedding will you quit the job?" The summer heat in the factory would be excruciating by then, and Salvador hoped Olympia would end this ridiculous nonsense. She promised that she would.

Salvador hurried to the bookshelf and found Olympia's Bible. He shoved it towards her and insisted she place her hand on the book and repeat her pledge. Olympia, insulted that Salvador would mock this sacred practice, pushed the Bible away and said, "I will not take your oath. You already have my word."

Olympia continued to work in the factory into the month of June, but a week before Josefina's wedding, she finally stayed home to concentrate on her daughter's big day. There would be a dinner and a gathering of friends at the Ortiz house, after Josefina and Andres were married by Father Fernandez at St. Joseph's Church. Olympia had appointed herself the event's organizer, responsible for preparing the food, arranging the flowers, inviting the guests and ensuring Josefina's day was filled with perfect memories – all while tending to the men of the house.

Every muscle in her body felt weak and desperate for rest, and she felt herself coming down with a fever. As her body wavered back and forth between hot flashes and chills and her head ached with fatigue, Olympia took some aspirin and drank water as she worked on the wedding.

"You need rest, Mama," Josefina said as she watched Olympia dab her face with a handkerchief. "Why don't you take a long nap? I will get dinner ready."

Olympia waved a hand. "I am fine," she said even as she wondered why she felt so lightheaded.

Josefina had seen her mother get sick before. The sanitation conditions in Havana had been so bad that Olympia was almost always fighting something, but this was the first time in two years of living in Florida that her mother had been ill.

The wedding would be a traditional Cuban wedding, famous for its festivities. The Ortiz house would host the reception and would be filled with lively music and dancing. Flowers decorated the porch, food would be set out in the parlor and tables and chairs were arranged on the front lawn to host the guests and the dinner party that would follow the ceremony.

Happy to be blessed with sunny weather, Olympia spent the morning preparing food in the house, running outside to supervise the flower and table arrangements and hurrying into the master bedroom where Josefina had shut herself away to prepare. The bride's black hair was curled and decorated with lavender flowers and white ribbons. Her dress was white and covered with a white shawl, and she would carry a bouquet of flowers. As she applied makeup and perfected her hair, Josefina's smile never faded. She was more relaxed than Olympia had expected, and Olympia realized most of the wedding anxiety came from herself.

The boys were dressed in their best suits and had fresh haircuts and shaves. Javier wore a black suit with a white handkerchief in his pocket, with a white rose pinned to his lapel. Salvador and E.J. also wore black suits with white flowers, and even Juan Carlos, recently returned from self-imposed exile in Key West, had cleaned his usual rugged appearance. Olympia hardly recognized the dapper Carlito in his borrowed suit, his freshly tapered hair gelled straight back, the trimmed moustache and the bottle of red wine under each arm.

He greeted Olympia with a kiss on the cheek, and the bride's mother, realizing that the ceremony was just minutes away and that it was time to depart for the church, ran into the house to toss her apron aside, wipe the sweat from her face and freshen up.

The groom arrived at St. Joseph's wearing a sharp black suit, his thin hair combed straight back, glasses perched on the end of his pointed nose, and shoes shining in the bright June sun. There were close to fifty in attendance, and they filed into the church, took their seats and awaited the bride.

Josefina entered and took Salvador's arm, and he escorted her to the altar and presented her to the groom. Andres took her hand and they stood before Father Fernandez, the old Spanish priest familiar to even to those that did not practice, who conducted a quick and flawless ceremony. When the two were married the crowd applauded and cheered the couple.

The guests quickly vacated the church and headed to the Ortiz house where the atmosphere became loud, festive and joyous as guests brought food, desserts, beverages and gifts. The parlor had two tables pushed against the walls which quickly became filled with goodies. Using her cookbook and with help from her daughter, Olympia had prepared *lechon* – a pork shoulder they marinated for two days in a tangy *mojo* sauce and then slow roasted over night in a wrapping of palm fronds and guava leaves. Salvador sliced several loaves of Cuban bread and stacked the pieces high on a large platter. There was an assortment of fruits; mangos, avocado from the family's tree, cantaloupe, pineapple and berries, and several bottles of wine. Lapár's wife brought a pot of black beans and rice while Mendez supplied a plate of pastries. The groom's mother made a dish of baked chicken over yellow rice mixed with shrimp and peas and

Salvador insisted the icebox be stocked with bottles of cold beer for the men.

The party began right away as guests poured wine and devoured food before music and dancing brought the *fiesta* into the evening hours. The lively celebration segued into the traditional money dance, where the men of the party danced with Josefina and pinned dollar bills to her dress as a gesture of assistance to the newlywed couple.

Hours later, after the music and dancing died down and night fell, the men gathered in little groups to light cigars and discuss politics and the news of the city while women found themselves chatting in the parlor or on the front steps. Except for the brief ceremony, Olympia had not stopped moving the entire day. From preparing the food to supervising the dinner party and cleanup, she had been back and forth, in and out of the house constantly moving from one task to the next and never taking time to sit back and enjoy the day.

For Salvador and his cronies the topic of discussion was the newly-formed labor union *La Resistencia* and its dealings with the manufacturers' organized Cigar Trust. "So tell us Mendez," Salvador said. "How long can we rely on you to keep Sando's place at the Vasquez factory? The workers need your pen and they need to hear your words. They need to be warned of the threats of Americanization in the cigar industry."

Mendez smiled modestly. "Who would pass on the chance to shout Cervantes to a hundred workers for ninety dollars a week?"

Javier walked into the middle of the group and passed out cigars to each of the men. Juan Carlos asked, "What do we have here?"

"Clear Havana cigars, hand-rolled right here in the Javier Ortiz buckeye."

Salvador explained, "He's been bringing tobacco leaves home and rolling his own cigars in the kitchen. He thinks he's going to start his own cigar company."

Juan Carlos grinned. It was not an unusual practice to roll personal cigars at home and as he inspected the cigar he noticed that the wrapper was from the premium supply and the craftsmanship was exceptional. He decided to light Javier's cigar and give it a taste. As he took a few puffs, Salvador, Javier, Lapár and Mendez waited for his reaction. They burst out laughing when Juan Carlos puckered his lips like he had bitten into a lemon.

"Where did the filler leaf come from?" he asked.

Javier said, "From the Vasquez factory of course!"

"It sure doesn't taste like Vasquez tobacco."

"Only the wrapper is good leaf," Javier explained. "The filler is made up of floor sweepings."

Mendez erupted with laughter and put his arm around Salvador. "He's using tobacco droppings in his cigars! A method of cost-savings fit for Antonio Vasquez himself!"

With a smile, Juan Carlos took another enthusiastic drag from the cigar. "It definitely tastes like it's been swept off the floor!"

Salvador shook his head. "Floor sweepings are fine for practice, but if you're going to hand out samples please use the good leaf."

"I can produce more cigars this way," Javier explained. "If I sell them for a nickel apiece I can turn a profit."

"A shrewd businessman!" Mendez shouted. "Does this boy work in the Vasquez and Company front office? He sure knows the sneaky tricks of the trade!"

Javier winked knowingly and went into the house for more food. Salvador watched him and then his eye fell on Josefina, sitting on the porch swing hand-in-hand with Andres while friends crowded around and showered the couple with congratulations and good wishes. Salvador thought of how far the girl had come since her birth at the Cancio plantation twenty years ago and could not help thinking about grandchildren.

Suddenly E.J. burst out of the front door. "Papa! Come quick! Mama has fallen!"

Beer bottles were dropped and cigars tossed aside as Salvador led the charge into the house. In the parlor he found Javier kneeling beside Olympia and dabbing at her mouth with a white handkerchief. Olympia's eyes were closed and she was face-up on the floor, flat on her back, completely still with cheeks that were damp and pale. Salvador's first thought was that she had collapsed from exhaustion.

"I knew it," he muttered as Andres and Josefina hurried in. Before Salvador could do anything, the newlywed Dr. Domínguez was at

Olympia's side while Josefina stood behind him with her hands on her cheeks and her mouth locked open in a terrified O. She knew her mother had been feeling ill but saw now that it was more serious than she'd originally thought.

Salvador, thinking they would carry Olympia into the bedroom and let her rest, felt his stomach churn when Javier showed him the handkerchief he had used to wipe Olympia's face. It was smeared with blotches of red. "Mama was coughing up blood!" Javier exclaimed and the worry in his voice, the fear in his eyes was staggering.

"Bring cold water and a towel," Andres said as he touched Olympia's temples and leaned close to make sure she was still breathing. Javier rose and hurried into the kitchen while guests surrounded Olympia in the parlor and others watched through the windows, and crowded to look over each other's shoulders. Andres rubbed Olympia's neck just below her jaw. Her glands were swollen and her temperature was high. Her face was flushed and dripping with sweat, but her breathing was steady. Andres took the towel that Javier brought back and dipped it into the bowl of water that Javier carried.

He placed the wet towel on Olympia's forehead and looked up at Salvador. "We should send the guests on their way."

Chapter 18

Overwork and fatigue brought her down but when she coughed up blood and saw the red speckled handkerchief in Javier's hand, Olympia knew her condition was serious.

"Send for Hector," she told Salvador that night, after she was carried to bed by her husband and son.

Hearing Olympia call for her brother frightened Salvador. She had not seen her brother in over fifteen years and it meant her situation was more serious than Salvador wanted to believe. When Andres pulled Salvador aside the next morning and delivered his diagnosis, Salvador knew he'd need to catch the next boat to Havana.

"Tuberculosis. A form that has been latent for some time and awakened by stress, dismal factory conditions, and the generally poor health situation of this city." For Dr. Domínguez, Olympia's illness was a perfect example of why the mutual aid societies needed to build a hospital for cigar workers. "If she were a Spaniard or an American she would get the best health care in town. We can move her to my clinic in West Tampa where she can rest in a quiet environment."

A few days later, before he left for Cuba, Salvador visited Olympia's sickbed at the Domínguez clinic. Andres advised him to keep the visit short in order to minimize exposure to the pathogens. The room was ventilated with opened windows, and Salvador wore a cloth mask over his mouth and nose. He knelt beside the bed and took Olympia's hand. Her palm was cold and moist, her face was pale and glazed with sweat, and her eyes were bloodshot from the pressure of constant coughing and sneezing.

"Olympia, my love," he said gently, the mask muffled his voice to a whisper. "Josefina is going to help me with the boys until you have recovered. She will stay at the house while I'm away. The icebox and the pantry have been filled and I left some money with Javier."

Olympia nodded slowly and braced herself for a fit of coughing that she felt creeping into her lungs. After a quick inhale, Olympia exploded with a series of watery bursts that seemed to rumble from the deepest cavern of her chest. Salvador turned his head until it passed and reached to a small table beside the bed for a glass of water. He helped Olympia raise her head so she could take a sip and then she collapsed back to the pillow, exhausted and cringing in pain.

Salvador had never seen her like this and it pained him to watch her suffer. It was remarkable how quickly her condition had deteriorated, and Salvador hoped her recovery would be as swift. He dabbed her forehead with a damp cloth and tried to make his voice smile. "You should have seen me helping Josefina with the laundry yesterday." He held up his hands. "These were wrinkled like prunes and covered with suds."

Olympia nodded, too tired to reply. Her eyelids were heavy and Salvador knew she needed rest. He patted her hand and leaned over to kiss her on the forehead. "There will be a closet of fresh clothes and a bed of clean sheets waiting at the house when you return."

Now Salvador would travel to Cuba and once again set foot on the property of Olympia's father, a man who had been so incensed to learn of her unexpected pregnancy that he had attempted to murder his own flesh and blood. Though time had passed and wounds had healed, the scars ran deep. Salvador wondered if anything could remove the blemish that defined the Cancio family.

He could not imagine being estranged from Josefina the way Olympia had divorced herself from her father. Salvador remembered Olympia's painful words from just a few weeks before. "I should have forgiven my father."

Underneath the wounds and the deep resentment there existed a desire for reconciliation. A need to address the past, make peace and move on. Though Olympia had requested only the presence of her brother, Salvador heard something else and took it upon himself to broker a resolution. Olympia and Testifonte needed to see each other. The sugar planter, probably retired by now, was approaching eighty and knew nothing of his daughter's illness. Salvador believed that a father deserved to know when his child was sick, no matter how many years had passed.

He could have sent a telegram or written a letter notifying Hector and Testifonte of Olympia's condition, but Salvador believed words on a page could do little to persuade and motivate the bitter heart of Testifonte. The sugar planter required a personal plea, a direct visit from Olympia's emissary. An act of diplomacy to settle the past and cleanse the Cancio family's bad blood.

Salvador knew not what he'd say to Testifonte and Hector when he arrived, or if he'd even be allowed onto their property once he revealed his identity. Technically he was still an outlaw in Pinar del Río. Would he be arrested? Was he walking directly into death?

He knew that he couldn't go alone, so he asked Carlito to join him.

"But I will be in legal jeopardy if I return." Juan Carlos reminded Salvador that he had been banned from Cuba and had agreed to never return. "That incident with the train means I'll be going to college on the Isle of Pines."

Salvador understood his friend's caution and recognized how Carlito used the word college as a euphemism for prison. "Yes, we will be perpetrators returning to the scene of many crimes," admitted Salvador. "So I will ask Mendez if you decide you cannot go."

The idea of Mendez taking his place was an insult to Carlito's pride. And he saw that Salvador was deeply emotional for a man so often composed. The children were like nieces and nephews to Juan Carlos, Olympia like a little sister. And he would need Salvador some day. Juan Carlos knew Armando was out there, plotting, waiting for his chance. He regretted not killing the Spaniard outright. Going to Cuba with Salvador meant his friend would owe him a serious favor.

He agreed.

And so after one last visit to bid farewell to Olympia, who was more alert after three days rest, her eyes white instead of red, the two men headed to Port Tampa for a boat that would deliver them to Havana. "You haven't told her about Testifonte?" Juan Carlos asked after they had stepped on board.

Salvador shook his head, wondering if the surprise of seeing her father would be such a shock that it would reverse the healthy progress she seemed to have made. "I did not want to upset her," he explained. "She needs to rest and not sit up thinking about what she will say when she sees him." Juan Carlos shook his head, clearly not approving of Salvador's tactics but saying nothing and accepting his friend's decision.

With their hair still freshly trimmed for Josefina's wedding, they dressed in their best suits to appear as businessmen. Like respected captains of the sugar industry or charming bankers from the north. They certainly did not care to resemble the henchmen they once were. But under their jackets, buried beneath their vests and hidden by their neckties, both men preserved the cynicism to carry loaded pistols.

It had been three years since Salvador had been to Cuba and when the boat pulled into Havana Harbor Salvador noticed the differences right away. American flags flew where Spanish colors had been and made Morro Castle look like a historical marker instead of the intimidating symbol of Spanish dominance it had once been.

When they stepped off the boat and into the city, they saw commerce had returned, with signage in both English and Spanish decorating the small shops that lined the streets of Havana. Most surprising to Salvador were the blonde heads and pale Anglo faces from the north integrated with the olive features of Spanish businessmen and the black faces of old men who played dominoes on outdoor tables.

The city had been reinvigorated. Gone were the displaced peasants who lined the alleys and sent their children begging for handouts. The anguish of war had been replaced with a sense of anticipation that made Salvador's hope swell. Perhaps one day the land of his father would fly the Cuban flag and be a place where Salvador could retire and live out his last days in happiness. He missed his old home; the old factory where he had worked, the cramped apartment where he and Olympia had lived for fifteen years, the culture and diversity of the city. However, Havana had not completely recovered from decades of war, and Ybor City was still the best place to raise his children.

They rode a train into the country and through Pinar del Río, and when they arrived at the Cancio plantation they saw no quaint, family farm of the 1880's. Its borders now stretched farther into the country than they remembered. The cane fields had proliferated like a rising tide and they couldn't even see the stone mansion from the wooden fence that surrounded the property. A dirt road brought them to the main entrance on the east side where a pair of giant wooden gates tangled with wire held a sign that read:

AmeriCuba Sugar Estates
Formerly the Cancio Sugar Trust

"We shall see if time has healed the wounds we've inflicted," Juan Carlos said as they approached the entrance. Two guards met them at the gates and stared at them through the rusted wires. They resembled the bandits of old, mid-twenties with open collars and rifles slung over their shoulders, except they were likely Spaniards. The lead guard gripped the wires and rested his foot on the base of the gate and watched them seriously; the defense of Testifonte's property appeared to be his great cause in life. The second guard lurked behind him standing taller but with little curiosity.

Salvador said, "We desire an audience with Hector and Testifonte Cancio. Are they here?"

"Yes," nodded the young guard. "Who desires this audience?"

"We bring tidings from Tampa," said Salvador. "Our business is urgent."

Juan Carlos appeared above Salvador's shoulder. "It is a family affair."

The young guard thought for a moment and then stepped aside, motioning to the rear guard as he moved. "Open the gate."

"Sure thing, Raul," the tall one said as both guards pulled the gates opened and let the visitors inside. Salvador and Juan Carlos stepped onto the Cancio property and instantly their old instincts returned. Ready to draw their pistols or run for freedom if the situation took a bitter turn, the men remained constantly aware of their surroundings. Though the times had changed and the plantation had become oddly peaceful, Salvador and Juan Carlos had never been on Testifonte's land without the danger of a gunfight. It was a feeling they would never quite get used to: Cuba without war or social upheaval.

As Raul escorted them deeper into the property, the plantation's familiar sites brought memories of years past. Salvador crossed what he thought was the path where Olympia had ambushed him and demanded

219

to be kidnapped. The stone mansion came into view surrounded by a group of new buildings that had replaced the old wood frame huts dismantled or damaged by war. The cane field had proliferated, and it took twice as many men to work the fields and load sugar cane onto ox-drawn wagons.

Testifonte had remained a king, his fortress like a Citadel from Renaissance Spain, only modernized by a partnership with the American dollar. He had been lucky, and one of the few to survive the war and retain his plantation. Salvador wondered if American money would take complete control of Cuba.

Raul led them beyond the mansion to a new two-story brick building with a sign that read 'AmeriCuba Sugar' the business office for the Cuban-American sugar company. Raul instructed the visitors to wait outside while he stepped through the front entrance. A few minutes later he emerged with Hector. Seeing Hector in his mid-forties made Salvador realize how many years had passed. The son of the sugar tycoon was heavier and he wore a rich, white business suit. A flash of blue was his tie and an oversized gold ring made his left hand sparkle extravagantly. His hair was neatly cropped and speckled with gray, as was his moustache, and he appeared agitated to have been removed from business by two mysterious, urgent visitors. Hector examined the two men as he approached and recognized neither. "I am Hector Cancio," he said curiously as he shook their hands.

They were not the hands of businessmen. These men had rough palms and fingertips hardened by labor. Their faces were clean-shaven but their attempt to look like businessmen was amateur at best. Their clothes were cheap and wrinkled and appeared to have been thrown on in haste. Hector noticed the taller man's vest was casually unbuttoned and he knew instantly that these men were laborers. He became cautious as he remembered the days when bandits would disguise themselves as harmless bankers or priests, only to transform into vicious thieves.

He took a step back. "How may I help you?"

Salvador recognized Olympia's features in Hector: the rounded face, the olive complexion, the little wrinkles that formed on the forehead when she was skeptical or unsure. "Señor Cancio," Salvador bowed his head. "My name is Salvador Ortiz. My friend, Juan Carlos Alvarez. We have traveled from Tampa with news of your sister Olympia."

Hector froze in place. He had not heard from his sister in years and was staggered with the sudden memory of bandits storming the property at night with machetes in hand, the fields ablaze with the fires of torches. He recognized these men before him now. Their rugged, peasant appearance had told Hector they were not businessmen, but it was the eyes that confirmed his suspicion – that dark, distant stare that only an outlaw could have. And the name. Salvador. These were the men who had taken Olympia. His instincts told him to kick these men off the property as soon as possible, or summon the authorities, yet he was desperate to know the fate of his only sibling.

"Tell me this news," Hector said as he tried his best to remain unperturbed, and even tried to seem comforted by their presence.

Salvador tried not to think of Olympia in bed coughing up blood. He spoke quickly. "She is sick, but a visit from her family will lift her spirits and aid her revival. She asked for you."

"Olympia is sick?"

"She is at a clinic in Tampa, improving but awaiting a visit from her brother, possibly her father as well."

Hector raised an eyebrow. If his sister had sent these men to Cuba to reconcile with her family, forcing them to willingly walk onto enemy territory, then her illness must be serious. "What is her ailment?"

Salvador explained, and assured Hector that her recovery would be swift. "More important is that Olympia has realized her mistake. She told me just a few months ago that she regrets ever running away. She is ready to forgive your father."

Hector took a step back and began to pace, confronted with emotions he hadn't felt in over a decade. Salvador clearly knew much of the Cancio family's secrets. He obviously knew the darkest truths, the horrors that Testifonte had never admitted and refused to discuss. And now Olympia apparently yearned for her real family and wanted to forgive her father once and for all.

It was too much to grasp at once.

Hector invited the men inside for a glass of wine, but Salvador and Juan Carlos refused. They had come close enough, and to enter the mansion, the house they had tried to burn to the ground, did not seem right. Instead they sat around a small wooden table on the front porch. With his chin resting between his thumb and forefinger, Hector sat still for a long time and considered the startling news from Tampa.

Salvador and Juan Carlos waited quietly until Hector came to a decision and finally spoke. "I must notify my father."

He rose and entered the mansion and left the cigar makers alone. Moments later the front door swept open as if thrown aside by a powerful gust of wind and Testifonte Cancio appeared in the doorway glaring angrily at Salvador and Juan Carlos. "Who is the traitor that allowed these men onto my property?"

As Salvador and Juan Carlos stood to greet him they saw that Testifonte seemed shorter than before but not weak. The dark skin of his face drooped with sun-dried wrinkles that surrounded a pair of eyes raging with anger and curiosity. He wore a flimsy white *guayabera* and loose pants of the same color, with wisps of white hair standing upright as if he had just rolled out of bed. He looked very much like a retired sugar baron and not the slick businessman of twenty years past.

Hector tried to calm his father. "They have come from Tampa in peace, as an honorable gesture to us."

"Honorable?" Testifonte nearly shouted. He was so upset that his head physically quivered as he talked. "These men torched my land and took my daughter and then poisoned her with the seed of mongrels."

Salvador was saddened to see that time had done little to help Testifonte. The cigar maker defended himself as quickly as he could. "Don Cancio, Olympia and I are happily married with four children. Her first child, the baby, Josefina, has grown into the beautiful bride of a successful Spanish doctor."

"No Spaniard would marry such a child!"

Salvador let his head drop and said nothing.

Testifonte approached Salvador with a pair of short, laborious steps. "My son tells me my daughter has been infected with tuberculosis. Surely that was your doing."

Salvador's jaw dropped and he suddenly regretting taking the initiative to play family diplomat. Testifonte clearly was not interested in reconciliation. With his eyes on the stone patio Salvador said, "She is my wife of nearly twenty years and the mother of my children. We are a family, Don Cancio. Your family. And it is Olympia's wish that we forget the faults of the past and be together in her hour of need."

Testifonte had moved closer to Salvador so they were face to face, closer than they had ever been. "If she is so desperate to see me then why did she never come here herself?"

Hector quickly stepped forward. "Excuse my father. Your surprise visit has made him irrational, and in his old age, he sometimes says what he does not mean. Father," Hector took Testifonte's arm gently. "Would you like to go inside and lie down for awhile?"

Salvador did not want to let him get away. "Don Cancio," he said. "Your plantation has flourished. It has outlived two wars and countless torment at the hands of criminals. You have survived many hardships to the benefit of your family. You have been successful in business, you have all the money you will ever need and enough to last for generations. You are an important man, Don Cancio, and I speak not of the sugar industry. You have grandchildren who have never met you. They carry the same blood as your son, Hector. I cannot force you to return with us to Tampa, I can only extend the invitation. The choice is yours."

Testifonte calmed somewhat, though he was still agitated.

Salvador added, "What would you say to your closest relative if you knew they were about to die?"

"And what sense has a bandit who invites me into my own family? I should have you arrested for trespassing, but I'm too old to deal with fools and I will no longer negotiate with crooks." He turned and shuffled through the front door of the mansion.

Hector appeared before Salvador and Juan Carlos. "Do not leave. I intend to join you on your return to Tampa. Unfortunately my father has grown a bit senile, unable to handle the day to day management of this plantation. Often times he awakes when he should sleep and aimlessly wanders the halls of this house without reason. It may take time to convince him to visit Tampa but I will talk to him. If he decides to remain here, then I will accompany you and we will leave this island soon. Please wait." Hector turned and disappeared into the mansion.

Salvador and Juan Carlos returned to their seats and waited. Juan Carlos lit a cigar he had in his pocket and gave a second one to Salvador.

As they sat and smoked, Juan Carlos said, "His reaction was more callous than I had expected."

"He's shocked," Salvador said, surprised that a man could be so stubborn.

"You fulfilled your obligation, my friend," Juan Carlos said. "You summoned her brother and notified her father, which is all she can expect of you."

Moments later, Hector reappeared on the porch looking relieved. "My father has decided to join us."

Salvador would always wonder what Hector said to persuade Testifonte but he never asked. They returned to Havana and caught a ship to Tampa the next morning. Hector sat at the bow with Salvador and Juan Carlos while Testifonte isolated himself from the two messengers and remained alone at the stern gazing quietly across the water. He chose to speak only to Hector, through interaction limited to private whispers.

Hector explained, "Deep down I believe that he does want to see Olympia but he blames you for her flight. He may not interact with you until he speaks to my sister. He appears stubborn and heartless, but he is not that way in private. He is still in denial, overcome by disbelief and I believe curiosity is pulling him to Tampa."

He continued. "When the war started most of the sugar operations went bankrupt. My father held on for as long as he could, mainly by borrowing from the American credit markets but prices dropped so low he traded ownership of his property to an American firm in exchange for shares of their stock and a seat on the board of directors. The AmeriCuba Sugar Company was born. Now with luck and God's will the plantation will survive, and my father can protect his fortune as he retires."

Hector lowered his voice and spoke to Salvador with sincerity. "I want you to know I hold no grudge from the past. I owe you my gratitude for your consideration and for making the trip to Cuba." They shook hands.

Salvador said, "I am not proud of everything I've done in the past and I was reluctant to travel back to the plantation, thinking it was forbidden for a man like me."

"I have read Olympia's letters and know what you have told me about your family is true. I have two small children, and I hope that one day they may meet their cousins. In my eyes you are forgiven."

"You are an honorable man," Salvador remarked. "I am certain you will not be displeased with the life your sister has made."

Hector nodded. "I only hope there is some way the lost years can be replaced."

Salvador was quiet. Juan Carlos reached into his jacket and produced a cigar that he handed to Hector. "One of Tampa's finest. I rolled it myself."

Hector inspected the *perfecto*, a light brown cigar with each end rolled to a point. "Its quality cannot be matched."

Juan Carlos grinned. "You're sitting beside two of the best cigar makers in Tampa, possibly in the whole world." He lit a match and Hector leaned forward until his cigar burned with a soft, vanilla aroma.

He sat back and enjoyed a flavor that was sweet and mild. "Excellent," said Hector as he nodded his approval. "Indeed you are a talented man."

Juan Carlos ignited his own cigar and the men sat together quietly. The only sounds were the swish of water as the boat cut through the sea and the breeze of salty air. Testifonte remained at the stern and watched a seagull that had followed the boat since Havana. The last memory he had of Olympia was watching her shuffle by without Josefina in her arms, refusing to touch her father, and closing herself in her bedroom. The next morning she was gone and never returned.

Questions ran through Testifonte's mind. What would she say to him when they were face to face? What would he say to her? And how had he allowed everything to go so terribly wrong?

Chapter 19

Pedestrians ran for cover as a heavy July rain exploded onto the streets of West Tampa. The men hurried to Dr. Domínguez's clinic and huddled under the aluminum canopy that shielded the front door of the house. Inside were four hospital bedrooms, hardly enough for the local clientele.

Salvador knocked and waited and when the door slowly opened, a very tired Javier appeared in the entryway. His hair, normally in place with an impeccable shine was dry and disheveled, his shirt was wrinkled and tangled within his suspenders. Bags under his eyes told Salvador his son was sleep deprived, and not from a night of drinking and gambling but from some troubling event. Javier hadn't slept in over a day and failed to notice the entourage that accompanied his father on the rainy front porch.

"Javier," Salvador stepped into the clinic and flapped the rainwater off his clothes. "How is your mother?"

Javier took a breath. "Mama died."

His father's gasp was a sound Javier would remember for the rest of his life. It came from the gut, a reaction of genuine surprise that told Javier his father had always expected Mama would recover and live for many years.

"Early this morning," Javier said, almost whispering and making the others strain to hear what he said. "Josefina, Andres, and I were with her. She saw Father Fernandez."

It took a moment for Javier's words to register, as if the sound of his voice had not yet caught up to the movement of his lips. Salvador was stoic. He swallowed hard and then stepped forward to hug his son, who pressed his face into his father's chest. Javier cried, surprised that after hours and hours of mourning his mother's death his eyes could still produce tears.

Juan Carlos closed his eyes and Olympia's brother dropped his forehead into one hand, and reached out to grasp his father with the other. Testifonte looked weak but not overcome, confused and disappointed, still trying to make sense of everything.

Andres approached the doorway and as Javier and Salvador broke apart, he came forward to embrace his father-in-law. "I'm sorry, Salvador. Her sickness accelerated soon after you left."

"Where is she?"

Andres motioned to the back. Purple bags under his eyes and a solemn stare told Salvador that Andres had also been mourning. "She is inside and ready to be taken to the funeral parlor."

Salvador gazed down the white tile corridor where Death awaited. He wished he could dash into her room and snatch Olympia from His grasp, yet he had no such powers. Tears welled in his eyes, but Salvador wanted his family to see he was a man of strength, so he buried his grief and held the sobs.

Rain continued to fall outside, filling the dreadful silence as Andres led them down the corridor and pointed to an opened doorway. Salvador was the first to step inside and glimpse the deceased. In the center of a sterile medical room, resting on a bed of ice was the body of Olympia Cancio de Ortiz. Her eyes were closed and her hands were folded and resting over her belly. Her skin was pale with the dire absence of life and the blemish of tuberculosis.

Salvador was no longer aware of time or place; the loss of Olympia became all that he knew. As though defeated by a dark shadow, Salvador stood motionless over her body, his mind empty, his breathing nearly stopped. Expecting her to open her eyes and flicker to life at any moment Salvador waited quietly for Olympia's return.

Testifonte and Hector slowly approached, inspecting the body, trying to recognize the teenage girl who had run away. They were staggered by how much she had matured. Testifonte displayed almost no emotion and if he felt anything at all, the others could not tell. He stood above the body of his daughter giving no clues as to what he was thinking.

Salvador turned away from Olympia and faced Andres. He took the doctor's hand and squeezed. "Your work here is finished, my son. I will take her. I will bury her so others may pray for her soul."

Andres said, "Javier has organized a collection from the union to help pay for the funeral."

Testifonte finally spoke, to Andres. "You are the one who has wed the daughter of this woman?"

Andres nodded and knew right away that these two men flanking Salvador were Olympia's family from Cuba. Testifonte introduced himself and his son to the doctor and then to Javier, who was the most surprised. Javier first noticed their clothes; Hector wore an expensive suit and Testifonte, though dressed in casual attire, possessed an elegance that said he clearly hailed from money, a world of wealth that Javier knew nothing about.

Olympia had rarely talked about her family, and Javier suddenly wanted to ask them why they had made no attempt to contact Mama until now. Why had she never spoken of her brother and father? Javier knew it was not the time to pry into such matters and believed his questions would be answered soon.

When they returned to the Ortiz house, Salvador found E.J. sitting on the parlor floor with a game of dominoes spread before him. In his grief the boy had descended into his game and was concentrating on every move. When he heard the front door open and looked up to see his father he rushed to hug him. Salvador could see his son's eyes were dry and red, like Javier's had been, and that his boy had already cried for his mother.

"Where is your sister?"

E.J.'s muffled voice said, "In back, washing clothes."

"Tell her to come here," Salvador said. As E.J. disappeared down the hallway, Salvador invited the rest of the men into the house. Testifonte and Hector stepped in first followed by Javier, Andres, and Juan Carlos. The house, though modest by Hector's standards, was comfortable and not as poor as he had suspected. He helped his father to the couch and looked closely for any reaction, but Testifonte's face was grave and revealed little.

Javier sat in the rocking chair across from the couch and stared at the two rich men while Juan Carlos and Andres lurked near the door and waited for Josefina to enter. When she appeared in the hallway, Salvador could see the sadness frozen on her face and could tell she had been crying as well. When Josefina saw her father, she wanted to rush to him and fall into his arms but the sight of two strange men on the couch restrained her. She moved quietly towards her husband and waited for her father to introduce the strangers.

When Testifonte saw that the illegitimate child of El Matón had grown into a beautiful young woman who resembled her grandmother, Testifonte's wife, he forced himself to look away in shame. Rubbing his hands together he stared at the floor, humbled to be in this house and wanting very much to walk out and return home.

Salvador placed an arm around E.J. and took a deep breath. "This is a time to grieve, but we must not let ourselves be consumed by sorrow. This is a time to weep but it is also a time for strength. Our mother has gone and now we can only celebrate her life and the many things she has done for each of us."

Josefina broke down and started to sob, burying her face in her husband's chest and clutching a handkerchief in her hands. Javier felt more tears welling in his eyes and several dripped down E.J.'s cheeks as he curiously watched Testifonte and Hector.

"Right now children," Salvador said. "We have two guests. Meet Hector and Testifonte Cancio; they are your mother's brother and her father." The children now openly inspected the two men and saw the clear resemblance to Olympia. "They traveled from Cuba to be with us and to say goodbye to our mother. I know you have plenty of questions and there will be time for that. Today we will mourn our loss and pray for the soul of our mother – that she may wait peacefully for us to meet her."

Salvador surprised himself with the religious talk and felt as though Olympia was coaching him from beyond, her presence vividly beside him as she watched to make sure he said his prayers. "Testifonte, Hector," Salvador said. "This is my son, Emilio José, my son Javier, my daughter Josefina, and her husband Andres. My other son Lázaro is away in New Orleans."

For the first time in his life Salvador saw Testifonte smile. The old man grinned nervously towards Josefina and gestured to her with a quivering finger. "How long has it been since I saw you as an infant in your mother's arms?"

Josefina did not know how to respond. The circumstances of Olympia's estrangement from her family had never been explained. Olympia had only said that she married Salvador when she was very young. Josefina did notice that Testifonte, her grandfather, did not say that it was he who held her, which made her wonder if this man had ever held her at all.

Salvador sensed great tension in the parlor. Many questions needed to be asked, and there were things he did not want his children to know, but continuing to bury the past was no longer possible. He said, "We will have dinner tonight to celebrate our mother and to discuss our history."

Before dismissing himself from the family affair, Juan Carlos took Salvador's hand and gave it a double-fisted shake. Words were not needed; there was a clear understanding among old friends. They hugged, and Juan Carlos saw himself out.

Cooking soothed Josefina's grief and helped her relax. She used a recipe from Olympia's tattered, twenty-year-old cookbook – which Josefina had automatically inherited and would keep for the rest of her life. She had already decided that as the years passed it would be those light, whimsical exchanges and thoughtful debates with her mother that Josefina would miss the most. While she somberly prepared the meal, the men sat on the porch and discussed the local cigar business. A pair of Spanish aristocrats sharing the same bottle of wine with the Cuban working class made for an awkward discussion, but the uncomfortable feelings were already starting to fade.

E.J. appeared on the porch and called the men to dinner, and the family crammed around the small, round table in the kitchen to dine on roasted chicken with rice, black beans, Cuban bread and sliced tomatoes. Salvador poured wine for everyone except E.J., and the family ate quietly, patiently awaiting Salvador's story. Though no one said so, it felt like Olympia would walk through the back door and join them at any moment.

When dinner was finished and the table cleared, Salvador lit a cigar and sat back to tell his tale. He addressed his children. "I sense that you suspect something from our family's past is amiss. You are correct in that you have never heard our complete story. I will tell you now that there are certain things that will be left out, mostly for my lack of memory. Pay attention. This is a long story that started over twenty years ago." Salvador looked to Testifonte and Hector. "If you feel I have omitted something, or if you disagree with what I say, please interrupt."

The Spaniards nodded as they lit their own cigars and Salvador paused for a moment to sip his wine and collect his thoughts. "My parents were very poor peasants from the west. I know little of *their* parents, as mine were killed when I was very young. What I remember are refugees passing through our village with tales of family and friends killed by Spanish soldiers. Some of them took arms and fought back and soon, instead of peasants passing through there were rebel soldiers. I remember my father was accused of helping these men. Our home was torched one morning by the Spanish military and my parents were detained and shot. It was on that day that I was orphaned. This much of the story, you know.

"What I have told you in the past was that I ended up working in a cigar factory. I have told you that I met your mother when she was very young, when she was among the peasants. I have told you that we moved to Havana and worked sporadically when jobs were available. What I have told you so far is true." Salvador raised a finger. "But there are gaps that must be filled."

The family sat quietly as Salvador continued. "What everyone at this table must understand is that during my youth a depression dominated Cuba. There was war almost my entire life until recently. There was no economy like what you see in Ybor City. The work stoppages and strikes you see here are insignificant next to the widespread poverty of Cuba. And let me be frank, if I offend Testifonte or Hector in the process, then let me apologize in advance. It was the Spanish who were blamed for the Cuban situation.

"The Spanish took everything and left little to the Cubans. So we fought to take it back. It was a class war, a revolution against society itself. On one side, the Spanish protected their wealth and on the other, rebels did everything they could to destroy it. There was robbery, banditry, arson, and murder. It is with little shame that I will admit to you that I was involved in all of it. I stole, I kidnapped and I killed." Salvador glanced to Testifonte, who was quiet but listening attentively.

Josefina said, "What good does it do for us to know that?"

Salvador waived his hand impatiently. "You must know your history as well as you know your own face in the mirror!" Salvador realized the hypocrisy of his words as he spoke; that he proclaimed to tell his children the truth but had sworn on Olympia's Bible to never reveal the true identity of Josefina's father. He said, "I must also dispel any suspicions of the past. You, my children, will learn that you are not completely of Cuban blood but come from both sides of the bitter struggle that has lasted all of my lifetime and yours. Our two visitors deserve to hear my side of the story, and I owe it to Olympia."

Salvador glanced around the table and saw the children nodding in quiet agreement. "When I was young, not much older than Javier, I was part of a group. Not like the cigar makers' union *La Resistencia*, or any of the social and mutual aid societies in Ybor City, for these groups operate within the law. My group was a brotherhood of outlaws. We thought we were tough, but we were constantly running scared, fueled more by luck than by skill. We thought we were as much a part of the revolution as the Cuban men who called themselves soldiers. The Spanish..." he pointed to Testifonte and Hector. "They were our prey."

Hector spoke to all of the children, "Your grandfather owns a sugar plantation."

"It was from that plantation," said Salvador, "that your mother, a full-blooded Spaniard, was taken." He paused to let his children feel the impact of the words *Spaniard* and *taken* and to give Hector and Testifonte a chance to interject. When all remained silent, Salvador continued. "There was great fortune in the family of a Spanish aristocrat. Olympia was valuable to our gang because once she was in our possession we could sell her back to her father – which is exactly what we did."

Testifonte spoke for only the third time that day. "The men who ran with your father torched my crops and terrorized my home and family. It was life or death for both sides." His tone was resentful but factual, and the Ortiz clan appreciated his honesty.

"Life or death," Salvador repeated. "I have always told you: work hard or die like a dog. I would much rather have worked but there were no jobs to be had. In those days the choice was simple: live by the torch or die a starving and lonely death. We did not steal for pleasure and I

233

survived to tell you this tale because of your mother. It was Olympia who decided to stay with me and not return to her family."

Hector spoke before his father could. "She became pregnant with Josefina and decided to stay with Salvador."

"Olympia was young," Salvador explained. "When I first met her, it was apparent that she had little knowledge of the affairs of the countryside."

"I was angry when I learned she had become pregnant," Testifonte said. "I think she feared for her baby and ran away."

Now Salvador feared Testifonte would reveal the secret but saw Testifonte remained a man of few words. He did not want to address his dealings in poison and murder. Salvador talked quickly. "Olympia ran to the only people who made her feel safe. Bandits. Imagine! My outlaw band promised to keep her from harm. Olympia was worth months of food and shelter for dozens and dozens of peasants. You see, my children, when bandits plundered the wealthy Spanish, they used their treasure to feed their people. To feed you, Josefina. Money did not flow into my pockets; it merely passed through my hands. We kept Olympia safe because she provided access to Testifonte's money. We kept her because we wanted to ransom her, again and again and again. We devised plans to return her, only to kidnap her again months later. This plan failed for two reasons. One, Testifonte fortified his acreage and enlisted the help of the Spanish military to counter our threat. There would still have been a chance to execute our plans had it not been for reason number two. Olympia had no desire to return to her home." He looked to Hector. "Of what I have said, how much is true?"

Hector nodded. "You tell an accurate tale."

Salvador said, "Olympia stayed with me and among the peasants, but the Spanish army soon invaded our camp. Shots were fired, and many men who were like my brothers were killed, but Olympia, Josefina and I managed to escape."

Josefina had no recollection of this, and Salvador could see his children were fascinated by the story. They sat quietly and hung on every word. He continued. "Not until Javier was born did I completely sever my ties with my rebel brethren. I remain close to Juan Carlos, but had I not been with Olympia, I would have stayed a bandit and likely would have died fighting. You all remember the small apartment we shared in Havana. The economy had barely improved and I was tempted to leave the city and return to my roots, but at the same time I had grown. It was when I married Olympia that I finally regained my family."

Salvador sat back, finished his wine and puffed on his cigar. "The rest of the story you know. We remained in Havana for most of your lives and then moved to Ybor City. The worst part is that I never felt comfortable telling you this story, and I don't think your mother was comfortable either. But now you know, and you are what you are."

The children sat silently waiting for more but Salvador had finished. He looked to Testifonte and Hector who nodded their satisfaction. Hector said, "Such is the nature of your great country. This melting pot. You are Cubans and you are Spaniards. You come from both the upper class and the lower."

Salvador sat forward. "But make no mistake; there is great nobility among *both* classes."

The children visibly relaxed. Javier exhaled deeply and sat back in his chair. He thought of the money these men must possess. E.J. wondered if this meant his father was considered a criminal. Josefina had suspected much of the banditry in her father's past; observations of her father's best friend Juan Carlos had told her plenty. But she had never considered that her mother was a true Spaniard. The children had heard enough information to change the way they looked at their entire lives. Their mother, their father, themselves, it all looked different. It would take time to absorb the story, to review the timeline and to draw their conclusions.

Dinner adjourned. Andres and E.J. helped Josefina clear the table. Salvador, Hector, Testifonte and Javier returned to the front porch to finish their cigars. It was a quiet night in their neighborhood. News of Olympia's death had spread quickly, and those who lived closest to the Ortiz house kept silent out of respect.

Hector arranged to stay at the Tampa Bay Hotel with his father so as to not burden the family any further. As they said their goodbyes for the night to the Ortiz family Testifonte said to Josefina, "I am sorry that I missed your wedding. I have missed plenty more than that, I know. And I am sorry that I have not visited you until now."

Josefina did not know how to respond so she merely smiled and nodded. Then Hector appeared and took Testifonte's arm and helped the old man down the stairs. The Ortiz family watched them go and returned to the house for their first evening with Olympia no longer alive to bid them goodnight.

Many came to the Ortiz house to pay their respects the next day. Juan Carlos returned with Mendez, and Lapár arrived with his wife and two sons. They said their condolences and then the men went outside to discuss a labor dispute that appeared to be deteriorating.

Neighbors from all around brought food and flowers and made contributions to help pay for Olympia's funeral. Many of the cigar workers told uplifting stories of their interactions with Olympia and cried and hugged the children. There were Cuban, Spanish, and Italian people from all over Ybor City; friends from the cigar factories, vendors and store owners from town appeared and disappeared throughout the day with offerings and condolences. Even Antonio Vasquez and his wife Maria stopped by with flowers and bowed heads.

That afternoon Olympia was laid to rest at the local cemetery during a modest family funeral. Father Fernandez said a prayer for her soul before Olympia Cancio de Ortiz was entombed in a flowery plot. The marble tombstone was decorated with an oval-shaped ceramic photograph of her face. The children wept throughout the ceremony, and Salvador did not bother to stifle his emotions and let the tears flow freely.

As he stood over her grave, surrounded by the family that his daughter created, Testifonte wondered if there would be such grief at his funeral. He glanced to his left where Josefina, her face hidden by a black veil, sobbed while her husband held her hands. Testifonte felt himself becoming sick and stepped away from the scene to take a few breaths of uncluttered air. His mind ran in several directions as he thought of his wife, his daughter, his grandchildren and the fractured and disconnected family he had failed to love unconditionally.

"Can I get you something?" It was Father Fernandez, the elderly Spanish priest. To Testifonte, the priest's black robe made him look more like a judge than a clergyman.

"No," Testifonte shook his head and looked back to Olympia's plot where the family quietly tossed flowers into the grave. Hector stood off to the side, watching his father for any request for assistance. Testifonte nodded and waved Hector away then clutched Father Fernandez's elbow. "Walk with me, Father."

The priest did as he was told and slowly walked alongside the fragile father of the deceased. "What can I do for you, my son?"

They walked through the cemetery, navigating around old tombstones and sidestepping grave plots. "I don't know if there's any use," Testifonte said. "I'm too old for it to make a difference."

"You wish to confess?"

Testifonte nodded. They kept walking.

"Often times, a relative of the deceased will think it is too late to settle unfinished business. Their relative has died, what sense does it make to ask for forgiveness?"

"You seem to understand, Father."

Fernandez said, "You wish to ask for forgiveness from your daughter because you never found the time to do it while she was alive."

Testifonte stopped walking and sat on the edge of a tombstone. Fernandez stood beside him. The sugar planter felt weak, unable to hold himself up, but this priest seemed to read his mind. Testifonte's head drooped. His eyes fell to the weeds surrounding the nameless grave where they stood. "You understand me very well already, Father."

"Go on, my son."

Testifonte took a deep breath. "It has been over a year since my last confession, though there are crimes to which I have never confessed."

"Go on."

Testifonte swallowed hard, unable to look Father Fernandez in the eye. "I betrayed my family." There was a long pause as Testifonte summoned the courage to put into words something he had never been able to admit. "I poisoned my child." He actually whimpered like a boy, deflated as the words left his body. "I tried to kill my grandchild."

Fernandez stared at the frail, despicable old man before him. "These sins are remarkable, and dreadful. Your family would expect that you suffer. But to earn their forgiveness you must repent, and you must change."

Testifonte took a moment to catch his breath. "It is too late for me, Father."

"As long as you walk on God's earth it is not too late." He held his hands above Testifonte and said a prayer. "Your penance will be extensive."

Testifonte nodded. "I understand and I am ready."

Father Fernandez nodded. "Very well. Here is what God requires..."

VI.

THE COMMITTEE OF FIFTEEN
1901

Tampa Daily News

Professional Agitators Threaten Tampa Economy

Editorial by Arlen Kincaid
March 19, 1901

Is there anyone who can deny the clear antagonistic feeling among the local cigar workers? There has been no hostile action as of yet, but the manufacturers anticipate trouble. La Resistencia seems poised to act, and we urge the people of Tampa to take it upon each other to stop these anarchists and radical agitators.

The Cuban cigar makers in Tampa generally belong to La Resistencia, the most powerful union in town, an independent coalition that formed after the cigar workers' victory in the 1899 Weight Strike. Organized by immigrants, it espouses the radical political principles of Marxism and is associated with all things un-American. If Tampa could rid itself of this mischief-breeding union, the cigar industry could harmoniously and profitably proceed.

But this city is not so fortunate. Ybor City is a radical, trade union town. The solidarity of the cigar workers and the political power of La Resistencia are a combined force that one must take seriously. This is a group that met recently at the Labor Temple on 9th Avenue and unanimously resolved to give 10% of their pay to a group of striking cigar makers in Key West.

Left alone, most cigar makers are fairly good citizens, but there is another class which takes evident delight in meddling between the employer and the employed, who feels justified to derail the fair practice of capitalism. It is this class of mischief-breeding anarchists that cause differences which often result in labor unrest. Evil men, agitators and revolutionists, seek to gratify their gruesome ideals of heroism and fame by imposing upon the ignorant prejudices of the masses. It would be entirely correct for the people of Tampa to force this undesirable element to abandon their sanctuary in this city.

At the behest of these radicals who control La Resistencia, the labor union seeks to establish closed shops in Tampa, an impossible proposition. Imagine an industry where 100% of the workers are members of a single left-wing organization. La Resistencia would dominate the labor politics of this city.

We call on La Resistencia to be outlawed from all Tampa cigar factories.

And if a strike were to result, we urge the landlords of this city to evict their past-due cigar workers and for city police to close the soup kitchens. The mongrels that instigate such behavior must not be allowed to use Ybor City as a testing ground for their radical methods of sabotage and obstruction. They have developed their own means of spreading the activist message.

Fanatic, extremist publications like Gabriel Mendez's The Workers' Bulletin are popular among laborers. Writes Mendez (also La Resistencia's treasurer), "The capitalists who make a pretense of fighting us have proved worthless to the modern condition and humanity of the cigar worker. It would be a tragedy, a crime, to deliver control to their hands."

Shops like his are feverishly releasing pamphlets and handbills that are distributed to the predominantly and ironically illiterate workforce and can later be found discarded and polluting the streets of our city. The message still gets to them through lectors, street corner translators and their popular debating clubs. If a citizens' committee were to confiscate their equipment, close their shops and arrest these agitators, the economic vitality of this city would be secure.

Beware, good citizens of Tampa! There is trouble looming on our horizon! We ask every stalwart American citizen to do his part and curb these radical agitators!

Chapter 20

The Feast of St. Joseph was an Italian holiday but also a day that all immigrants knew well. Nothing was to be purchased for the celebration that honored the patron of the poor so women prepared meals from ingredients traded from neighbors and friends. Families erected altars in their homes and piled them with food and drink, and then opened their doors to visitors who circled the community and stopped briefly to sample food and pass along the gossip of the streets.

The Ortiz house was closed for the day. Salvador, Javier and E.J. prepared nothing and decided to venture into town and enjoy the day's festivities. Eight months after Olympia passed they were still not used to a house without their mother. It seemed empty without the sounds of her shuffling about the kitchen, bringing laundry in from outside, scolding her children and chattering with Josefina. Salvador often awoke in the middle of the night to Olympia's breathing and her warm body beside him only to realize that his bed was empty and cold.

The loss was especially hard on E.J. who seemed to have become more prone to tantrums as he passed the age of ten, and would often scream hysterically for his mother when being disciplined by Salvador. The Ortiz men were in need of some good, local therapy and Salvador and his boys agreed that there was no better way to sooth the doldrums, and cheer each other up, than to enjoy the Feast of St. Joseph.

They met up with Juan Carlos and Gabriel Mendez, the latter of which carried a copy of the *Daily News* which he waived disdainfully in front of the others. "They called me a professional agitator and demanded my deportation! The Crackers think they're the only Americans in this town."

Juan Carlos replied. "They can't stand that Cubans have their own community and that we're doing so well. Now throw the newspaper away – this is a day for celebration!"

MARK CARLOS MCGINTY

The crew cast aside all concerns and hurried to join the feast. Moving from house to house as their bellies filled with food and wine, everywhere they encountered the smiles and loud voices of friends gesturing wildly as they told jokes and outrageous gossip. A pair of teenage brothers from one Spanish household played guitars on their porch while friends gathered around to sing folk songs and dance their best flamenco.

As the wine flowed and the day wound into night, conversations lasted longer and became more earnest. Groups of friends gathered to discuss local political developments. A crowd soon assembled in a courtyard behind a group of cigar makers' homes, where tables and chairs were set up on the grass and cigars, beer and local rum were abundant.

Mendez started out by jumping atop the back steps to read excerpts from Kincaid's controversial editorial and was simultaneously praised and teased for being mentioned so prominently in the local English newspaper. The cigar factory *lector* took it upon himself to translate the article to the group as if he were sitting at the Vasquez factory *tribuna*. The cigar makers booed whenever Mendez was referred to as an agitator or anarchist and hissed and yelped when the article mentioned strikes. When Mendez finished reading, he tore the paper to pieces and tossed it into the angry group and then held up his hands until they calmed.

"The words of the *Daily News* should not frighten us," Mendez called out. "This is a time to discuss a collective strategy, a unified strategy for action against the oppressive Cracker Mafia." Mendez smiled as the last phrase was greeted with a mixture of laughter and booing.

Suddenly Juan Carlos sprang atop the steps of the adjacent house and hovered above the crowd not ten yards from Mendez. Rum spilled from his glass as he wavered back and forth like a happy drunk. "Did you hear the one about the guy who ordered a plate of Cuban chicken?"

The crowd murmured a collective no, curious to hear the rest.

"He told the waiter he wanted chicken and rice, but that the chicken needed to be born and bred on Cuban soil. So the waiter went to the kitchen and brought back a plate of chicken and rice. The man asked, 'how do I know this chicken came from Cuba?' and the waiter told him,

244

'because we have a chicken from every country in the back, and of all those chickens, this is the only one that was eating shit!"'

The crowd howled with laughter.

Juan Carlos held his arms open wide and savored the praise. Then he announced, "I am a capitalist!"

There was more laughter than booing as most recognized Carlito's sarcastic sense of humor. Someone playfully tossed part of the crumpled newspaper at Juan Carlos which bounced harmlessly off his shoulder. He grinned provocatively at the crowd. "I believe that all cigar manufacturers should bring back scales and institute quotas in their factories! I believe the labor union should be abolished, its leaders deported to a deserted island far away, and mutual aid should be outlawed forever!"

Now the entire crowd booed playfully as the clearly inebriated Juan Carlos preached the exact opposite of what the people believed. "Take this man off the stage!" someone shouted. More crumpled newspapers soared at Juan Carlos along with the extinguished butt of a cigar and a chunk of bread.

Mendez called out to Juan Carlos. "How do you feel about these radical agitators who threaten the economy of our city?"

"Gutless!" Juan Carlos shouted. "They should be hunted down one by one, loaded onto trains and sent to prison!" He laughed and taunted the jeering crowd.

Mendez asked, "What about the humanity of the men and women who work in the cigar factories?"

"Humanity is of no concern to me I only care about how many cigars they can produce in one day!"

More booing erupted from the crowd until an empty beer bottle flew from the mass and nearly struck Juan Carlos on the head. His reaction was slowed due to intoxication but he ducked as the bottle sailed high and struck the side of the house. Juan Carlos was suddenly angry. He reached into his jacket pocket and shouted at the crowd. "Show yourself, you lousy coward!"

He yanked a .38 revolver from his pocket and waved the pistol recklessly at the people. They gasped and many ducked when they saw the mouth of the gun swing their way. It was not another second before Salvador and two others sprang into action, hurried to the stoop and dragged Juan Carlos to the ground; Salvador cupped a hand over the .38 and snatched it from Carlito's grasp. Once they had him pinned to the ground, they noticed Juan Carlos howling with glee, the odor of rum and tobacco swarmed with each gust of laughter. The gunplay had been a prank.

"You old fool!" Salvador shouted as he pocketed Carlito's revolver. "We should tie you up and throw you into the outhouse!" Juan Carlos remained on the grass, cackling uncontrollably and clutching his side as Salvador kicked him just hard enough to produce a grunt

Again Mendez held up his hands to calm the rowdy crowd. "Brothers! Brothers and sisters! This is no place for violent reactions! Save the projectiles for the Cracker Mafia! We are here to have a healthy debate, theatrical though it may be, and discuss important matters concerning the future of labor in this city. The manufacturers are starting to industrialize. The corporation and its obsession with the dollar will soon dominate the industry and now they've threatened to abolish our union. If you are not careful, the cigar maker will be reduced to nothing more than a pair of hands and a workbench!"

There were calls of agreement from the crowd and Mendez looked to the people and asked for volunteers. "Who has something to say, a concern to be voiced, or news to share with your fellow cigar makers?"

"I have plenty to say!" The female voice belonged to Alessandria Prizzi, an outspoken Sicilian cigar worker, labor leader, and head of *La Resistencia's* strippers' union. She was known around town as an anti-capitalist who often berated anyone who she felt had strayed from the path of social unity. She was a small woman with a big personality. Standing just over five feet, her height was offset by a powerful voice rumored to be so loud that if she were on the first floor of the cigar factory, she could be heard loud and clear and the third. She was thirty-seven years of age and mildly attractive to some of the men, homely and disinteresting to others. Long and stringy black hair was tied with a plain black ribbon and covered with a black kerchief. She wore modest clothes and her hands were rough and calloused. From far or near, there was no mistake that Alessandria was of the working class.

She climbed the stoop where Juan Carlos had been and with a colorful mixture of Spanish and Italian, began a fiery invective of the cigar manufacturers. "I have no fear of those from Anglo Tampa who would vilify us as agitators and radicals. I say to them, deport me and I will only return. If the manufacturers attempt to hire anyone not aligned with *La Resistencia*, then we must strike. Our union is the backbone of our cause and we will not allow our jobs or our union to be taken by alien or transient workers who are not members of our society. No! I say to you, no!"

The crowd applauded.

Alessandria continued. "The absence of a union threatens our jobs, our livelihood and the general well being of our families! If the manufacturers abolish *La Resistencia* what is to say they won't begin hiring novice cigar makers who will work longer hours for less money? I offer my skirt to any of you so-called men who refuse to stand up to this injustice!" At that, she swished her skirt and enticed the crowd, making them cheer and shout catcalls.

"I offer a corset to any of you prissy, dainty men who can't lift a finger to fight the encroachment of the Cigar Trust, this alliance of factory owners who are harming our place in society. And to you Italians who save money so that you can leave your comrades at the workbenches and form your own companies: you are the *gabelloti* of America! I escaped these ruthless entrepreneurs who controlled rents, mills and markets when I left Sicily. And if we were born in different lands, it is not our fault. We must blot out all differences because capital is our common enemy!"

There was a hearty applause and Alessandria did not stay on the stoop long enough to savor the reaction of the people. She hurried off the steps and blended back into the crowd, disappearing into a sea of taller bodies.

Juan Carlos was back on his feet. He nudged Salvador and said loudly, "What about you, Ortiz? You are a cigar maker by trade but where do you stand politically?"

"I am a pacifist!" Salvador announced with a smile. There were a few chuckles from the crowd but most were interested to hear Salvador's thoughts. He had been among their number for three years and his face had always been welcomed around Ybor City. This was a man who had been supportive of the labor movement, especially during the Weight

Strike, but since the death of his wife, had been somewhat withdrawn and not so active in local affairs.

Juan Carlos persisted. "It is your turn, Ortiz. Take your place on stage and tell us where you stand." There was encouraging applause from the group. With the aid of the wine he had consumed that day, Salvador climbed the steps of the vacant porch and stood beside Mendez.

Salvador opened his arms to the crowd; whose alert and attentive faces made him smile. "Am I an anarchist? A left-wing socialist? Or do I descend from the uncompromising right-wing?" The crowd waited. "In truth, I am a centrist, aware of both extremes, and above all I want peace for my family."

Mendez interrupted. "How can a cigar maker loyal to the cause of Cuba Libre call himself a centrist? A centrist who understands both extremes certainly could decide that either side is right and could even decide that the cigar makers are wrong. How can you explain this, Salvador?"

Salvador answered. "In Cuba, the system did not work. We had no choice but to revolt. Here, there are higher wages, good homes, low interest rates, better social lives. There is no doubt that life is better here than in Cuba, otherwise we'd be having this discussion in Havana! The United States appears to be the best county to live – when it's business as usual. But it is difficult for our people to have a voice in this city without our labor union."

Mendez said, "Salvador, you sound as if you would settle for what you have. You sound as if your emigration to the United States was the ultimate victory. The fact of the matter is that the revolution moved from the battlefield of Cuba into the cigar factories of Tampa."

"I agree, in part." said Salvador. "We are fighting for the experience of living as well as any American family. And we should be thankful we are standing here, able to openly talk about having that fight without the threat of Spanish soldiers ambushing our gathering."

"You are sounding very much like the centrist you claim to be," Mendez said. "And this worries me, Salvador. Yes, life in America is an improvement over the prior conditions, and not just in Cuba, but in all the countries of our ancestors. But we are still oppressed. Not by Spain, not by America, but by the corporation. Capital is what threatens us directly."

Salvador raised a finger. "We do not owe any gratitude to the corporation."

"But in order to live as well as the Americans, would you have your family adapt to their ways? If there is no reason to fight the system, as you say, and these interest rates are truly so low, then how much will you yield to capitalism?"

Javier and E.J. watched closely as their father paused. Salvador had never considered how much he was willing to yield to corporate interests. "I feel the system should be used until our livelihood is directly threatened by these corporate interests. I feel that a labor strike is a desperate act to be used as a last resort. It is our loudest voice and should be contained, not abused, until it is absolutely necessary to unleash its power."

There were mixed murmurs of agreement and dissent from the crowd. Mendez said, "This is where I disagree with you, my friend. I believe our words are loudest and have the greatest impact when the voice of the minority *constantly* works against the system. Only then can the system change! And I believe our people must stick to a common strategy. We must fight as one united people and not as individual members of society."

"Yes, it's a good debate," Salvador said. "This concept of a union presents us with a dilemma: individual freedoms and the right of one person versus the greater good of his people. We can agree that we share a common cause. And I would agree with my friend, Mr. Mendez, that solidarity is essential in the fight of labor against capital."

"So then where does a centrist stand when the manufacturers threaten to abolish our labor union? Cigar makers joined *La Resistencia* as a way to secure their jobs and avoid competition with non-union workers!"

"But should we avoid competition altogether?"

Mendez threw up his arms. "You speak of capitalism at its worst! If the manufacturers outlaw our union then we must strike to protect our rights. And if strikebreakers were to arrive and take your jobs you should force them – violently, if necessary – to *leave town for good!*"

The crowd applauded and waited for Salvador's reaction: "Yes, we must protect our jobs and our society but does that mean we should fight off the competition or become better workers? We should protect our union, I agree, but first we should do everything in our power to see that a strike is not necessary. We all remember the soup lines of the Weight Strike. I had to send two of my boys to Key West so they could work and support our family. What kind of life is it when families are broken and supporting each other from different cities? When the factories are open and prosperous there is no reason for anyone to find work out of town. Surely we'd rather be with our families than to send them to Jacksonville, Key West or Havana to work for a few precious dollars while waiting for competition to disappear. Competition will be here, I hate to say it, but it is something you must all realize. Competition is something we must all deal with."

Mendez was not satisfied by Salvador's response. "So then where will you stand if the manufacturers attempt to abolish *La Resistencia* for the sake of healthy competition?"

Salvador said, "I believe cigar factory jobs should go to members of *La Resistencia* and no one else."

"So then where is your so-called competition?"

Salvador smiled and held up a finger. "I have never claimed to be a lover of competition. I *like* my job!"

The crowd laughed and Mendez smiled. Then the *lector* said, "Would you exist in a world with no labor union?"

Salvador shook his head. "Never. I am practical but I am still a cigar maker."

Mendez finally smiled. "And if our union were abolished would you support a general strike?"

Salvador nodded. "Of course I would, as a last resort."

Chapter 21

"Your idea that *La Resistencia* will be abolished is simply ridiculous," Vasquez said. "But I plan to hire whoever I want."

Lapár crossed his legs and nodded considerately. "I understand your desire to expand your enterprise, Don Antonio, but it is the position of the workforce that the factories remain closed to anyone without proper representation. No one but certified members of *La Resistencia* allowed." Lapár understood that talk of abolishing the labor union was an attempt to weaken the cigar workers both economically and politically. "As president of *La Resistencia* it is my expectation that all factories will comply with our request."

Vasquez glanced to his right where Armando Renteria sat behind his oak desk. They were in Armando's office on Fifteenth Street discussing a labor dispute that had thus far taken place outside of the factories, which is where all three men hoped it would be settled. Vasquez was in the weakest position of all. His company was barely profitable and constantly suffocated by intense competition. Tampa cigars continued to grow in popularity and more and more producers were entering the market. Many of the weaker companies were quickly put out of business or consumed by the powerful American Tobacco Company. Vasquez had already been approached by the American corporation who offered to buy his family label.

"You're not selling," Armando had told Vasquez. "This tobacco business is a family affair and we won't sell our traditions to some impersonal corporate entity."

Yet the Vasquez company's balance sheet was lopsided with debt; its cash flow was tight and its credit at risk of being revoked. The solvency of Vasquez and Company was tenuous and now the union president talked of higher wages, flexible schedules and a closed shop where no non-union workers were allowed.

"It's a preposterous request," Armando said from his desk, his eyes cold on Lapár. "You are in no position to dictate anything to Vasquez and Company. We intend to hire affordable labor."

Lapár flashed a magnetic smile that even Armando Renteria couldn't help but like. "You're dealing with the most powerful labor body in the city."

Armando smiled back. "Your union could be obsolete by next week."

The idea frightened Lapár. How would it look if the President of *La Resistencia* allowed his union to collapse in the midst of a fruitless labor talk? Lapár knew that Armando was a powerful *bolita* proprietor and had heard the rumors of Renteria's connections to the local prostitution network. For years Armando had successfully passed himself off as a legitimate investor but the wealthy crime boss was in league with the Tampa Police. Vasquez was head of the Cigar Trust and the ultimate decision maker in the room. Lapár looked to him.

"What are you willing to concede?"

Vasquez said, "Flexible schedules, as I've already said but I demand an open shop and no union activity on the factory floor."

Lapár shook his head. "I'll concede no union activity in the factory on Mondays and Wednesdays and we'll accept flexible schedules but we demand a closed shop – all employees must be members of *La Resistencia*."

Vasquez shook his head. "No union activity Mondays, Tuesdays, Wednesdays and Thursdays and an open shop."

Lapár closed his eyes and shook his head.

Vasquez looked at his watch. "We're not making any progress."

Lapár's eyes popped open. "Finally we can agree on something!" He stood and extended his hand to the cigar manufacturer. "I'm sorry we were not able to reach a settlement."

Vasquez took Lapár's hand. "I'm sorry too."

The union president looked to Armando and nodded.

Armando did not give Lapár the courtesy of moving from his desk. "It's time to tell your workers to expect non-union labor beside them at the benches – or you risk becoming the director of an illegal organization."

Lapár merely smiled at Armando's ironic statement and decided to stifle his thoughts. Here was the owner of a vast illegal gambling and prostitution network, protected by bribes to the local police, warning a respectable civil leader of the dangers of illegal activity. A laugh Lapár could enjoy once he was alone on the street if only he didn't have to take Armando so seriously. The man had the courage to follow through on his threats and a reputation for acting boldly during the night. With a gang of street thugs and a few loyal policemen at Armando's disposal, Lapár knew how dangerous the *bolitero* could be, and their failure to reach an agreement made Lapár worry greatly about the cigar makers.

Mendez awoke with the morning sun and rolled out of bed just after seven o'clock. Using water from a pitcher he kept in the small kitchen of his apartment he washed his face and shaved and then changed into his work clothes. *The Count of Monte Cristo* was the novel the cigar workers had voted on, a Mendez favorite, and he was excited to begin reading the story that afternoon. His morning ritual would continue with a trip to the corner coffee shop where he'd purchase a copy of the English language *Tampa Daily News* and the Spanish *La Gaceta* to read while he ate a pastry and drank *café con leche*.

With his copy of *The Count of Monte Cristo* tucked under his arm, Mendez stepped onto Tenth Avenue and was pleased by a sunny and dry April morning. He hoped it would not get too hot in the factory that afternoon. The summer months were upon him which meant he'd be reading from the middle of the sweltering factory heat. If only they would crack the windows and allow some ventilation the conditions would be that much more bearable. Perhaps as treasurer of *La Resistencia*, Mendez could persuade Lapár to petition for opened factory windows.

"The manufacturers will never agree to that," he could hear Lapár saying. It would be a futile effort.

Mendez arrived at the corner coffee shop and saw the usual teenage newsboy selling papers to passersby for a nickel apiece. "Good morning, Julio," Mendez reached into his pocket for change. Julio handed Mendez a copy of each newspaper and took the coins while Mendez turned towards the coffee shop and read the headline of the *Daily News*.

He dropped his novel. There would be no coffee today.

* * *

"Why don't you just come with me one time? You need it, Ortiz. At the very least it will help you sleep."

Salvador was reluctant and thought it a disgrace to Olympia to visit the girls of La Rubia but Juan Carlos would not let up. Carlito believed that a casual encounter with a prostitute was just what Salvador needed to break the doldrums.

"It's been almost a year, Salvador," Juan Carlos said as they walked to the Vasquez factory for the morning shift. Javier and E.J. lagged behind engaged in a debate over the best baseball players in Ybor City.

Salvador thought of Olympia. "I'm not ready yet."

"Whatever you say," Carlito said dismissively. "Just let me know."

They arrived at the factory and saw a group of cigar makers gathered outside the front entrance. "This doesn't look good," Juan Carlos said as they approached the group. He called out to the crowd, "What's going on?" As Juan Carlos and Salvador climbed the factory steps the crowd parted to reveal a white handbill nailed to the front door of the factory.

Juan Carlos and Salvador halted to read the notice and Juan Carlos shared an angry look with his friend. "*Coño*, Ortiz, what do they think they're doing?"

Vasquez, Capecho and Armando watched the gathering from a second floor factory window outside Don Antonio's office. "It had to be done," Armando said to the manufacturer and his accountant. "Factories can't function with that pesky labor union intact. We're back in control."

"They will surely strike," Capecho said as he bit his lip and Vasquez nodded his agreement.

"They'll do it with their union in tatters," Armando replied. "*La Resistencia* has been banned from the factories. It will soon be no more."

Vasquez watched the crowd outside and thought back to the previous confrontation with the cigar workers. The manufacturers had lost their attempt to instill quotas and weight restrictions on cigar production and the cigar workers' victory in the Weight Strike had motivated the workforce to boldly form *La Resistencia*. As Vasquez stood on the empty factory floor he hoped that the current dispute would see it dissolved.

Mendez was closest to the Martinez Ybor factory on the corner of Ninth Avenue and Fourteenth Street, and he ran that direction hoping to arrive before any workers agreed to enter the factory and work without the protection of *La Resistencia*. He heard the commotion before he rounded the corner and saw a crowd of angry cigar workers mobbed before the building's front steps shouting obscenities towards the opened factory doors.

Happy to see Lapár already among the crowd instigating their furry and provoking an uprising, an approving Mendez pushed through the crowd and approached the labor leader. Before Mendez could say anything, Lapár saw him coming and shouted, "Send our people across town to all cigar factories! Call for a general strike!"

Mendez nodded and headed north.

Juan Carlos stood atop the steps while a mob of cigar makers crowded around. He shouted loud enough for the entire neighborhood to hear. "These manufacturers will not take away our union or our brotherhood! We must never walk into that factory until Vasquez and his cohorts allow the full participation of *La Resistencia* in the labor process. We will not be abolished!"

The crowd shouted their agreement, and Juan Carlos descended from the steps to the sandy ground and picked up a fist-sized rock. He turned to the crowd, "Let them hear our voice!" He hurled the rock towards a first floor factory window, shattering the glass and provoking the crowd. Many others dropped to the ground and picked up rocks, hurling them towards the factory windows like an army laying siege to a brick castle.

"That's it!" Juan Carlos encouraged the cigar makers as factory windows were punctured by rocks and the ground became littered with broken glass. "Open those windows! Allow some ventilation in that factory! No longer will we work in hot, stuffy conditions! That's it, men!

Throw those rocks! They'll try to break our union so we'll break their windows!"

Salvador thought of how Olympia used to return from the factory exhausted, with her clothes damp with sweat. He picked up a rock and looked to his right where Javier and E.J. watched and waited to see what their father would do. He nodded to his sons and then threw his stone towards the factory. Javier and E.J. did likewise and the assault continued.

Inside the factory, Vasquez ran back and forth in a panic, watching his windows shatter, seeing his empire crumble. The bales of tobacco leaves on the first floor would be corrupted by millions of bits of glass, microscopic in size, rendering the tobacco useless. The factory would lose hundreds of man hours and thousands of dollars worth of tobacco leaves. Vasquez cursed the police for not being there, he called for the army, for anyone, but Armando stood quietly at the window and watched the frenzy down below. Juan Carlos was the leader of this group, angry and influential and unaware of the retribution that awaited him. Armando smiled. The time would soon come when he'd settle the score with the lowly cigar maker.

When Mendez arrived outside the white, wooden, box-shaped Olivia factory he saw a group of cigar makers gathered and shouting down the manufacturer, who stood atop the steps urging his workers to enter. Carlos Ramos, owner of the Olivia Cigar Company held his hands up and tried to calm the crowd that grew angrier every moment.

Mendez joined a group of fifty workers who stood hollering at Ramos, demanding their union be allowed inside the factory. "Your union will be abolished as soon as the mayor signs the decree," Ramos explained. "But you all have jobs! Come inside now and let's get back to work."

"No!" shouted the crowd. Many threw crumpled newspapers and handfuls of dirt towards the manufacturer. Then gunshots erupted and the crowd panicked and dispersed in every direction. Mendez ran east towards the Vasquez factory, ducking as loud shooting exploded behind him.

The gunmen were a pair of young Italian boys from *La Resistencia*, who fired shot after shot towards the windows of the Olivia factory with powerful Colt revolvers. They emptied their guns and reloaded, emptied and reloaded again, as people ran for cover and ducked behind palm trees and bushes. Ramos dove back into the factory fell face down on the wooden floor while his lieutenants fell beside him and covered their heads. Splinters and broken glass exploded all around them as bullets ricocheted inside the factory, leaving potholes in the walls and showering the floor with a rain of shattered lead and broken glass.

When their bullets ran out the gunmen ran south having fired over thirty shots into the walls and windows of the factory. But an American bookkeeper working inside was hit in the head by an angry bullet and was pronounced dead on the scene.

The mayor called an emergency meeting at city hall with Tampa chief of police Sean McGrath, members of the Cigar Trust including factory owners Antonio Vasquez, Carlos Ramos, and José Cienfuegos, *Tampa Daily News* editor Arlen Kincaid and investor Armando Renteria. Once the men were gathered around the conference room table, a serious and subdued mayor began the meeting by asking for an update on the morning melee from the chief of police.

"Riots of varying degree took place at eight locations throughout the city this morning but all were subdued by noon. We made a total of sixteen arrests but two Italian boys, Carmelo Ficarrotta and Antonio Albano, suspected of killing bookkeeper Philip Edwards during a shooting at the Olivia cigar factory, are still at large. My people will canvass the city until they are found."

The mayor was visibly angry. "I won't have any of this mafia activity in Tampa."

Vasquez said, "We estimate damage to property and inventory to be near one hundred thousand dollars. *La Resistencia* has called for a general strike which will cause further losses to the industry."

"Jesus Christ –" the mayor began before he was cut off by Armando.

"*La Resistencia* will be dissolved as soon as you sign a decree officially illegalizing the radical trade union." Armando produced a legal document and slid it across the table to the mayor. "By signing this document, Mr.

Mayor, you will officially outlaw all union activity in the city of Tampa, at least until it's challenged in court."

The mayor set the paper aside. "How do you plan to end this strike?"

Armando spoke for the Cigar Trust. "Strikebreakers are already on the way. Imagine a town with no union activity, Mr. Mayor, where a cigar manufacturer can hire anyone he desires, at whatever wage is necessary, without a pesky labor union looking over his shoulder and challenging his every move. We intend to act swiftly. Tomorrow the manufacturers will hire anyone who agrees to work without union representation."

The mayor glanced to Vasquez, who nodded his agreement.

"Put this down quickly," said the mayor. He slipped a shiny silver pen from his shirt pocket, and as he signed his name on the decree, *La Resistencia* became an illegal organization.

The leaders of *La Resistencia* regrouped at the Labor Temple on Ninth Avenue to review the day's events and discuss their strategy. "This is the last time we can meet like this," Mendez said to the others. "Anglo Tampa must consider us enemies of the state by now."

Lapár said, "Our walkouts have shut down half the factories in Ybor City and we made progress in West Tampa until police took to the streets and started arresting our people."

"We'll need to notify Havana," Mendez said. "And someone needs to go to Key West and gather donations from their workers."

"Who can do this for us?" asked Lapár.

There were three others in the room: Gabriel Mendez, Juan Carlos Alvarez and Alessandria Prizzi. "I am the union's treasurer," Mendez said. "Perhaps I should stay in Ybor City and manage the money we have. If this strike continues with momentum, it may be a long time before money flows from the workbenches. There is intensity among the workers like I have never seen."

Alessandria said, "I'll enlist volunteers to travel to Key West."

"Good," Lapár said. "We should expect the manufacturers to bring in strikebreakers. We should try and recruit as many non-union people as possible and convert them to our cause. *La Resistencia* must remain intact."

Juan Carlos said, "I can help recruit some new men."

Loud, piercing whistles suddenly blew and a clamor of footsteps exploded into the room. Before any of the labor leaders could react they were surrounded by six police officers with guns drawn, and Chief McGrath who shouted, "Nobody move!"

The four members of *La Resistencia* raised their hands in the air as each was approached and ordered to stand against the wall. They were searched and pistols were confiscated from both Juan Carlos and Lapár. All four were promptly handcuffed.

"You are interrupting a peaceful assembly," Mendez said. "What are the charges?"

McGrath approached the young writer and held the mayor's decree for Mendez to see. "The mayor just made it official. This is an illegal meeting. Not to mention that you are conspiring against the city, disturbing the peace and plotting economic sabotage. Sound like enough, boy-o? Or how about firing about a hundred shots into the Olivia factory and killing the bookkeeper?"

"That was not us!" Juan Carlos shouted.

"A man was killed today because of you," said the chief before he turned to his men. "Take them away!"

Salvador was home with Javier and E.J. It was lonely in the house with so many missing family members, and Salvador considered the economy of paying for a house that was large enough for six people when only three remained. A move to the affordable boarding houses with Juan Carlos might be necessary during the strike. Happy that his sons survived the day's violence Salvador sat them down to talk. "I am going to give you a real education," he said to his boys as they gathered at the kitchen table. "Years ago a cigar maker was a person who possessed special skills. He was an artisan who took pride in his work and valued his independence. He worked when he wanted and was paid very well.

"But the factory owners are starting to feel the pressure of a modern corporate transition. Many of them, including Vasquez, believe it is necessary to modernize operations to remain competitive. The practices of an earlier age are being replaced by the impersonal demands of profits and accounting. This is the root cause of the clash we experienced today."

E.J. asked, "Why is the union so important?"

Salvador smiled. "An excellent question. It is not just about work, or working conditions. As Cubans, our goals are tied to a greater class struggle, a lifelong effort to separate ourselves from the forces of colonialism and capitalism. And there is a great conundrum; to live as an individual one must rely on the support of his society. It cannot be avoided. There can be no individualism without some kind of social conformity. Only the proletariat identifies with such ideology. But Vasquez wants to open his business to people without this view, to non-union workers with American business values, who will work for less and produce more. Our union promotes solidarity and prevents a man like Vasquez from dictating how we live our lives. Can you imagine what would happen if we were reduced to permanent second-class status? Unable to prosper, stuck in one place like the blacks of this country? This is why *La Resistencia* must remain relevant. It is not about working conditions, it is about control."

Salvador looked at both his boys and asked rhetorically, "Who controls your life?" He paused to give them a moment to consider the question. Satisfied that they listened reverently he continued. "This strike will decide who controls the Tampa cigar industry. I expect it will be a long and difficult contest."

There was a knock at the front door and a man's voice. "Ortiz!"

Mendez. He let himself in and hurried to the kitchen. "Hello, boys." He was out of breath. "Salvador, I need to speak to you alone."

Salvador excused himself and led Mendez out the front door and onto the sidewalk. "What's wrong?"

"We were arrested."

"Who?"

"Lapár, Juan Carlos, Alessandria and me. For meeting at the Labor Temple of all places. The police let me go with a citation but I have to show up in court. Juan Carlos and Lapár are still in jail. They were carrying guns when they are arrested."

Salvador cursed. "This business is getting out of hand."

"I feel their lives may be threatened tonight."

Salvador agreed. "We should gather some men and head for the jail. Wait here for one moment." Salvador hurried back to the house. As he expected, Javier and E.J. were watching from the parlor windows. "I have to run out for a few hours," he told them. "Keep the doors locked and close the windows. I will be back soon."

He hurried into the master bedroom and opened the bottom dresser drawer. Inside was a .38 caliber revolver. He slipped it into his pocket and hoped it wouldn't be used.

Armando Renteria could raise enough money to purchase a majority stake in Vasquez and Company but Don Antonio would not budge. He pitched the idea of opening a branch factory under the name Renteria and Vasquez, but the manufacturer refused to sell any more ownership. Instead Armando bought small shares in other factories across town and continued his *bolita* and prostitution enterprises.

As Armando counted *bolita* proceeds in his office, McGrath arrived to collect his regular payoff. "This strike means that business will slow," Armando said.

The chief approached Armando's desk and took the envelope Armando offered. "We arrested the union's leaders, including your friend Juan Carlos Alvarez."

Armando tried to hide his pleasure. He didn't know how much the chief knew about the attack perpetrated by Juan Carlos but suspected McGrath knew enough. It was an embarrassment to the investor but now he had a chance to redeem himself.

"Thanks for the update," Armando said.

"You're welcome. We also think we found the Italian shooters."

"What are you going to do with them?"

The chief winked. "Make sure they don't shoot again." The chief let himself out.

Armando waited a few minutes and then picked up his keys. He'd lock his office and then head across town to pick up the Sanchez brothers before paying a late night visit to the county jail.

*   *   *

A five-cent trolley tide took Salvador and Mendez beyond their Latin enclave and into downtown Tampa, which was not always a welcoming experience. When they entered the city, Salvador noticed a sign above a saloon that read 'No Animals or Cubans Allowed.' The streetcar stopped two blocks from the county jail and the cigar maker and the *lector* hopped out and walked quickly to the brick building.

Two young Tampa police officers stood at the top of the jailhouse steps looking tired and bored. One nudged the other as the two Cubans approached and the two cops seemed to awake, standing up straight as their hands dropped to their belts where their pistols and clubs were within quick reach. Their nametags read Swanson and Mitchell.

Mendez called to them in English. "We demand to see Angelo De la Parte, Juan Carlos Alvarez and any other cigar maker you have jailed!"

Mitchell answered tiredly. "They're asleep. Come back in the morning."

"We will stay here until we see them."

"Why don't you go back to your families and get some rest? We expect you'll be back to work tomorrow."

Mendez glanced at Salvador and then said to the cops, "We will not leave our men at the mercy of a Cracker Mafia."

This insulted the two policemen. Swanson took a step forward and spit towards Mendez's feet. "What do you say, Pete? I think this town could use a good hanging."

Mitchell nodded. "Sure could, Bobby."

Mendez turned to Salvador. "These two are just caretakers." Mendez halted his thought when something over Salvador's shoulder caught his attention. Salvador followed Mendez's gaze across the street where three men approached the jail – two hulking bodies that flanked a tall, slim man with a beard.

"What do we have here?" Armando asked as he joined the two Cubans on the sidewalk. The Sanchez brothers positioned themselves strategically behind Salvador and Mendez. Salvador's hand moved slowly towards the pocket with his pistol while Mendez stood tall and confident.

The *lector* said, "How much did you pay the police chief to protect your lynch mob?"

Armando's eyes glowed with anger as the Sanchez brothers moved closer and towered above the two Cubans. "Son of a bitch," Armando cursed. "We should drag you out to the swamps and feed you to the alligators."

Officers Swanson and Mitchell descended from the steps, and Salvador and Mendez were surrounded. Going for his pistol would make no difference now, so Salvador took a deep breath and tried uselessly to eye an escape route. If he ran they'd catch him and throw him in jail with Juan Carlos and Lapár where he'd be at the mercy of Armando's posse.

"You're Salvador Ortiz," Armando noticed. "A friend of Juan Carlos."

Salvador held his chin up defiantly. "A *good* friend."

Armando smirked and wondered if Salvador had been an accomplice in that alley during the Weight Strike. "Perhaps you should join him in jail." Armando glanced to the police and spoke English. "These men are out after curfew, aren't they Officer?"

Swanson nodded, even though there was no official curfew in Tampa. "Sure are, Mr. Renteria. I do that believe both of these men are in violation of the law."

Armando smiled at Salvador. "And no one wants to live in a town without law and order."

Fearing that his life may be in jeopardy, Salvador took a step back and bumped into Benny Sanchez as Officer Swanson produced a set of handcuffs. Mitchell gripped his own handcuffs and moved towards Mendez as Benny grabbed Salvador by the shoulders. The cigar maker was downright frightened by these men. This was not like his bandit days when Salvador rode with the support of an army. Now Salvador only had Mendez, who was fierce with a pen, but would likely be an underwhelming foe in matters of physical confrontation.

"What a mistake," Salvador said to himself, wishing he had stayed at home with his boys. Wondering if he could talk his way out of jail, he was startled when a loud woman's voice shouted to them from down the block.

"Let them go!"

It was Alessandria Prizzi, who stomped towards the courthouse with a dozen cigar makers following closely behind her like troops marching into battle. Mendez grinned and shook his head in admiration. "What a woman!"

She had brought a trolley full of cigar makers from Ybor City to protect their leaders. Armando saw this army approaching and knew that he would not be able to get to Juan Carlos tonight.

He smiled at Salvador and Mendez. "We'll be on our way now," he said. "But I hope you'll be back to work tomorrow." Salvador and Mendez said nothing as the army of cigar makers surrounded them and the police officers stepped away, effectively turning them loose. Armando and the Sanchez brothers lurked nearby for a few minutes but eventually left the scene and went on their way.

Mendez smiled at Alessandria, who remained serious and determined. "Thank you for coming," Mendez said. Her nod was polite but unsmiling as her eyes scanned the city streets around them. The cigar makers remained outside the jail most the night, until the sun rose and the city went back to work. By morning most of them had dispersed, not wanting to risk being detained for vagrancy. Just after ten o'clock Juan Carlos and Lapár emerged safe and sound and made their way down the concrete steps, wearing the same clothes as the day before.

Juan Carlos was surprised to see Salvador and Mendez waiting for him on the sidewalk. "Ortiz! Mendez! What are you doing here?"

Salvador smiled and patted his friend on the back. "I'll tell you over coffee."

Later that afternoon the bodies of two Italian boys were found hanging from tree limbs near the swamps outside of Tampa. Their arms had been bound behind their backs and their feet were tied together. They were later identified as Carmelo Ficarrotta and Antonio Albano, the gunmen who had fired into the Olivia factory, lynched by a mob of angry citizens.

No one was ever charged with the crime.

Chapter 22

"We haven't seen you in a couple of days, Papa."
Salvador poked at his dinner. "Labor issues are keeping me occupied," he said to his daughter as he stirred his chicken and rice. The family sat together in near silence. Salvador glanced to Javier who seemed enthralled with the details of his fork, and to E.J. who divided his rice into four equal piles. Salvador set his utensils aside.

"I know this is difficult."

No reaction.

He looked to Josefina, whose eyebrows rose dolefully into a wrinkled forehead. He asked, "What are you thinking about?"

She shrugged slightly then exhaled as her eyes remained lost in her dinner. "It doesn't make any sense to celebrate Mama's birthday." Andres reached to her and patted her hand, forcing a tiny smile.

Salvador watched the others who aimed their eyes at their food. "I miss her greatly."

From Josefina, a look like she wanted to speak, followed by a quick decision to hold her tongue. She slid rice and a slice of fried onion onto her fork. Salvador glanced to his modest meal. Food rationing was underway and portions were small but Andres had provided half a chicken for the dinner that celebrated Olympia's birthday, her thirty-eighth.

Javier asked, "What would you have bought for her, Papa?"

Salvador smiled, he knew exactly. "New dancing shoes. Black."

Javier managed a smile.

"What about you?"

"A box of those lemon flavored pastries she liked."

Salvador looked to Josefina.

It took her a moment but she said, "A new adventure novel."

"E.J.?"

The boy merged his rice into two larger piles. Salvador didn't press him. He said, "It's a shame she is not here to see you off." They were several weeks into a general strike and neither side had backed down. The cigar makers were prepared for an extended standoff. After dinner Javier and E.J. would leave for Port Tampa where they'd catch an evening ferry to Key West.

When their meal had finished Andres helped Josefina clear the plates while Javier and E.J. grabbed their bags. Salvador shoveled a small pile of rice onto the edge of his plate and brought it outside for Pano. Now that Olympia was not around to stop him, Salvador could safely hand his plate over the fence and watch the dog run over and lap up every morsel in a matter of seconds.

"Good boy," Salvador approved as he retrieved the plate and stood with his boys. The roof of the idle Vasquez factory and the high water tower watched reproachfully from down the street. "Look after your brother," Salvador said to Javier. "Make sure he stays close to you."

"Of course, Papa."

Salvador set his empty plate on the porch and dug into his pocket. He handed Javier some dollar bills. "This is enough to get you started." Javier had done this before and knew to rent a room in Key West and find work right away. If the brothers were fortunate they would find jobs as cigar makers, but with the influx of hundreds of Tampa workers, the boys might have to settle for sorting leaves.

Salvador knelt and hugged E.J. then held him by the shoulders and looked into his eyes. The boy was barely eleven but stood with such confidence that he seemed ten years older. He was straight and strong and did not fear the journey to Key West or the adventure that waited. Like Lázaro, Josefina, and their mother years before, little E.J. was ready to embark into the unknown and prove his worth.

"I'll see you soon," Salvador promised, knowing E.J. needed little reassurance. "Take your bag and meet us on the sidewalk. I want to talk to your brother." E.J. did as he was told and walked to the sidewalk leaving Javier and Salvador alone by the porch. Before Javier could notice his father's move, Salvador gripped Javier's jacket and dropped something heavy into the side pocket. From the weight and shape of the object Javier knew right away that his father had just slipped him a loaded pistol. He looked to his father and awaited an explanation.

For one moment, Salvador felt like a bandit initiating a new member. "Two immigrant men have already been lynched in this dispute," he explained. "Keep it to yourself and try not to use it."

"You can trust me, Papa."

"I do," he patted his oldest son's shoulder and admired Javier. Nineteen and very much a man. "Now go."

"Wait," Josefina emerged from the house and stepped down to embrace Javier. "Be safe," she whispered into his ear. Then E.J. appeared beside them and Josefina hugged him too. With a kiss on the cheek and another on the forehead, she turned E.J. towards the street and sent him on his way.

"So long," Javier waved as he passed and then together with E.J. they starting walking to catch a trolley that would take them to the port. Josefina watched for a moment and then returned to the house. Salvador followed.

"I don't like sending my boys away," he said to Andres, who sat in the parlor sipping from a glass of red wine. Salvador took a seat beside his son-in-law, stretched out and closed his eyes.

Josefina sat in the rocking chair beside them and all were quiet for several minutes. Finally Josefina asked, "What are you going to do with this house, Papa?"

Salvador opened his eyes and stared at the ceiling. "Move out, I suppose, now that I'm alone. No need to waste money on a monthly note when I can live in the boarding houses for a few dollars a week."

"What are you going to do with Mama's stuff?"

Salvador looked to his daughter who sat forward in her chair interested to hear his answer. "I hadn't thought of that," he said. He had barely touched any of Olympia's belongings since she had died nearly one year ago. Her clothes had been washed, folded and left in the dresser and the perfumes and knickknacks on the vanity were as they had always been. Never one to pry into her affairs, Salvador felt a need to respect her privacy even in death.

"You should do something with her things. Give the clothes away to someone who needs them. Come on," she gestured to him with her finger. "Let's take a look."

They went to the master bedroom and stood in the doorway looking at the bed, the vanity, a stand-up closet in the corner and pile of books on a small table by the window. Quietly, methodically, Salvador and Josefina began to go through Olympia's things while Andres waited in the parlor, not wanting to involve himself in such an intimate family affair.

"Look," Josefina held up a book. "*Beyond the Sierra Morena.* One of her favorites."

Salvador smiled as he set a stack of Olympia's clothes on the bed. "Do you know how long she had that book?"

"No," Josefina said as she began to page through the worn hardcover novel. "Years, it looks like."

Salvador nodded. "As long as I knew her, she had that book."

"Papa, look!" Josefina pointed to a slip of paper stuck between the pages of the book. In Olympia's handwriting there was a list:

> read with E.J.
> cards with Javier
> beach with Josefina
> more time with Salvador
> apologize to Lázaro

"Remarkable," Salvador said after Josefina read the list.

"He's been gone over a year," Josefina said, and Salvador knew she was talking about her brother Lázaro.

"Maybe he met a girl."

"Have you even considered going to look for him?"

He shrugged. "He wouldn't want any of us to interfere."

Josefina groaned. "You're so stoic, Papa. You hardly react to anything."

"What am I supposed to do? Travel across the country and track him down? What do I do when I find him?"

Josefina knew her father had a point but she persisted. "Mama would have wanted you to find him by now."

"Don't invoke your mother," he said. "You have no idea what she'd want."

Josefina looked at the list and focused on the heavy, unfulfilled phrase 'apologize to Lázaro.' It stung her. She vowed that when she finally saw her brother, Josefina would apologize on her mother's behalf.

"Did you ever make it to the beach?" Salvador asked.

"Sure, all the time … Look at this!" Josefina exclaimed and slid a square photograph from the pages of Olympia's novel. She handed it to Salvador. "Is that Mama? I didn't know she went to Italy!"

It was a grainy photograph of a young Olympia, no older than thirteen or fourteen, standing before the Tower of Pisa wearing a white dress. Salvador and Josefina started quietly at the photo, both realizing that Olympia hailed from a wealthy Spanish family who could afford such extravagant adventures.

"She had family in Spain, you know, an uncle. And her grandparents." Salvador looked closely at the photograph. Olympia with her hands at her sides smiled slightly and gave the impression that she was very happy to be away from home, in a foreign land exploring her world.

"She never did much traveling," Salvador remarked sadly.

"Can I keep this picture?" Josefina asked.

Salvador nodded and put his arm around his daughter as they continued to gaze at the photo. It was one of those rare moments when Salvador remembered Josefina was not his flesh and blood, but the child of another man. He thought it unfair that the girl could not be told that both of her parents were dead. Salvador hugged her slightly as her head landed gently on his shoulder.

"Papa?" she asked quietly.

"What is it, Fina?"

"There is something I need to tell you about Mama."

Salvador tensed and prepared for troubling news.

"Are you aware of how she died?"

Still embracing his daughter Salvador tried to move his head so he could look into her eyes. "She died of tuberculosis."

"But Andres thinks she could have been killed by the conditions in the factory."

Now Salvador was no longer tense but extremely interested in what his daughter had to say. "What conditions are these?"

"The health conditions of course. With the windows always closed and that hot, damp air never allowed out of the building, the factory is a breeding ground for TB."

Salvador had heard rumblings of this before but had never considered Olympia to have been directly affected this way. He thought of his sons, of himself. Had they all been infected?

"Won't the labor strike address this issue?" Josefina asked.

Salvador sat on the edge of the bed. Here was his daughter, the competent nurse and brave champion of the sick involving herself in labor affairs. Before Salvador could summon a response, Andres appeared in the doorway.

"It's true, Salvador. Do you remember Ignacio Alarcón? He went by the nickname Fútbol. He died of tuberculosis and he worked at the Blue and White factory for years. And Bruno Braulio and José Parrilla? Both cigar workers, both killed by tuberculosis."

Salvador ran his fingers along the bed sheets as if they held some wisdom written in Brail. "It's just a coincidence."

"You've never been happy about the factory conditions," Josefina reminded him. "I always hear cigar makers complaining about the heat."

"Conditions are atrocious," Andres said. "This labor dispute could be your chance to change how the factories operate."

Salvador knew that they were both right. In the summer months the factory floor was unbearably hot with air so thick he could nearly see the fog. Windows at the Vasquez factory had already been broken and replaced, the result of an angry mob of cigar workers demanding better working conditions. But this strike was about the sovereignty of their labor union, not about conditions on the floor. As Salvador sat on the bed he wondered if it should be about both.

It was an eerie feeling to be alone in the house. Once Josefina and Andres had left for the night, Salvador poured another glass of wine, sat on the parlor couch and stared at the picture of José Martí that hung beside the door. The family had been split apart and Salvador wondered if he should have gone to Key West with his boys, or if this was the perfect opportunity to leave town and look for Lázaro. He felt responsible for his son's disappearance and wondered what Olympia would desire if she were alive.

He went to their bedroom and looked through the rest of her things: the adventure and romance novels she stacked beside the bed, her Bible, a gold necklace with a small cross, her modest wedding ring. He poured more wine and sat among Olympia's life and thought of Josefina's words. Stoic, she had said but Salvador saw his calm, passive stature as an example of strength before his family. But his oldest daughter was sharp enough to see it for what it was: a denial of grief, a dismissal of any emotion that would shows signs of weakness.

Two glasses of wine later he found himself outside the Vasquez factory.

Tuberculosis killed Olympia. And how many others? Vasquez and Renteria, Spaniards like those who had killed his parents, were responsible. The setting sun cast an orange glow across the shiny new factory windows, replaced after the riots several weeks before. Brand new windows, closed and sealed air tight.

He remembered the words of his son in law: "This labor dispute could be your chance to change how the factories operate."

Salvador picked up a rock, and threw it towards a first floor window. The sound of shattering glass was invigorating and he could hear Olympia cheering him from above.

"What do we have here?" a voice called out in English with a heavy southern drawl. Salvador turned towards the street and saw the silhouette of two approaching riders. Like shadows against the sunset they came forth on their horses, one with a shotgun propped against his hip, the other with a pistol resting in a holster. As they approached Salvador saw they were Anglo men as wide as their horses, both wearing slacks and white shirts as if their day at the office had ended and they'd removed their ties, jumped on horseback and took to the streets. It was a sight that would make El Matón laugh.

Most startling was the speed of their advance. Within moments they towered above Salvador and looked down with an impersonal hatred that smothered him and prevented him from running away. The man with the shotgun ignored his partner and spoke directly to Salvador. "Can't have you niggers out here vandalizing private property."

The other circled with his horse so that Salvador was trapped between them.

The cigar maker tried to play the innocent pedestrian. Smiling and with slurred speech, Salvador spoke Spanish. "I am just on my way to see my mother on Fourteenth Street."

The horsemen were not convinced. "We witnessed you throwing a rock through the first floor window of this here factory," said Shotgun.

Salvador's instincts told him to run. Whoever these men were, they did not intend to take him to jail but to deal with him right there. He sidestepped drunkenly but the horses moved with him. "Trying to get away?" said the man with the pistol. He looked to his partner. "What do you say, Ken? This one looks like he could use a good beating."

Salvador continued to speak Spanish. "I must hurry, I do not like to keep Mother waiting." He tried to go left but the horses converged and blocked his escape. He looked up just as the butt of Ken's shotgun slammed into his face.

Salvador was on the ground. The wine dampened the sting, but his head buzzed with a thousand trumpets and he seemed to be surrounded by the blurry legs of a dozen horses. Then Ken's boots landed in the dirt before him and a second later, the butt of a rifle smashed into the back on his head, mashing Salvador's face into the sand and knocking him unconscious.

Something tugged at Salvador's throat and choked him awake. One of his eyes was swollen shut and he opened to other to see he was in a dark forest surrounded by a musty swamp smell and the buzzing of hundreds of insects. The pressure on his throat made him gasp for breath and as Salvador tried to reach up and loosen the tension he noticed his hands had been tied together with rope.

Then Salvador was suddenly fully awake. The wine seemed to have worn off completely and he was alert and aware that the force on his throat was a noose. He was suspended from a branch with nothing but a rickety block of wood supporting his feet. His shirt was soaked with sweat almost instantly and he forced himself to concentrate on his balance to keep his feet from falling from that shaky, uneven chunk of wood.

It could not happen this way. Not here.

Not alone.

"This ought to teach a lesson to the rest of them Cubans," said Ken as he tied a rope around the stump below Salvador's feet.

"Please," Salvador gasped in English while his legs wobbled and struggled to keep his feet in place on the stump. And then Ken yanked the rope and the stump was gone. Salvador's feet dangled in empty air. He waited for the noose to tighten around his neck as he suffocated and died hanging from a branch in the middle of some deserted swamp far from town. He wondered if humans would discover his body before it was devoured by animals and if his children would be able to give him a proper funeral before laying him to rest beside Olympia.

Then his face landed on the dirt, his legs sprawled out beneath him and his pants became soaked with urine. He heard the horsemen laughing as they rode away and left him beaten and wallowing on the ground. It had been a trick. A mock execution made to scare the cigar maker out of town or back to work. His adrenaline surged and with his hands still tied behind his back and his mouth tasting dirt, Salvador Ortiz began to weep.

He remained in place for several hours – a bloody mess of mud, sweat and urine – until the shock wore off. His hands had been intentionally bound loosely so he was able to wrestle free of the ropes. As he sat up he saw he was in the middle of an uninhabited swap filled with palmettos, pools of shallow, murky water and trees weeping Spanish moss. He wondered if it was the same place where two Italian boys had been hanged weeks before.

"Who were those men?" he wondered as he stood and started making his way down a dirt path that trailed out of the swampland. Vigilantes for sure, and this city was up to no good. Salvador would have to warn the others.

It was the middle of the night and he was able to make it home unseen. Still embarrassed he wondered what Olympia would think if she could see him now. When he returned to the house and looked in the mirror he was ashamed by what he saw. There was a blood-caked gash above his eye where he'd been mashed by the heavy butt of the rifle, and a half moon bruise was forming underneath. Dried blood covered that side of his face and mud painted the opposite side. As he removed his soggy clothes he felt the bump in the back of his head. Salvador felt worse than sick and close to death. He took a tall drink of bourbon after he washed and then slept for an entire day.

He was awakened by a sulking knock the following afternoon. "Ortiz!" called a shrill voice lacking certainty. It was his Spanish landlord Castillo. Expecting to be evicted, Salvador rolled out of bed with his head throbbing and his eye swollen shut. He probably looked like a monster but he didn't care – perhaps his appearance would scare Castillo away.

When Salvador opened the door, Castillo blinked and stepped back. The landlord was a mild and portly man, always dressed in a suit, and more of a money counter than a debt collector. Knocking on doors for past due payments was the most frightening part of his job.

"You're two weeks late, Salvador." Castillo was afraid to ask about Salvador's wounds and he stepped back as if he didn't care to hear the response or collect any payment.

"Take the house," Salvador said. "I won't need it anymore." He closed the door. What use was a house so large to a man without a family? Salvador, the humble bachelor, took a drink of bourbon to ease his pain, dressed and headed into town.

He thought he'd find Juan Carlos at La Rubia and he did, playing dominoes and smoking cigars with two cigar makers. Salvador's black eye drew attention as he entered the bar and when he sat beside Juan Carlos, the latter stared open-mouthed at his friend.

"What happened?"

Salvador told the story and watched Juan Carlos grow angrier with every detail. Expecting him to throw his cigar aside and jump on the table shouting for armed revolution, Salvador was relieved when Juan Carlos merely flicked his cigar back into his mouth and concentrated on his dominoes. "You're safe in here, my friend. No Anglo would dare set foot in our sanctuary."

Juan Carlos poured rum for Salvador and introduced him to his newest friends. "Matías Rodriguez and Diego Valdivia, we call them Billy and Pirolo." Described as influential cigar makers from West Tampa, they looked like throwbacks from the bandit days. The men were rough and weathered and looked like they'd fit right in with El Matón's crew. No wonder Juan Carlos liked them so much.

A small man whose loud voice and flamboyant gestures made up for his size, Matías wore a thick moustache with coarse stubble of beard struggling to catch up. His eyes were shifty and constantly hopped back and forth between Salvador and Juan Carlos, making him look like he could snap at any moment. Known as a man who walked the streets of West Tampa distributing communist literature, Matías Rodriguez had once stood trial for murder but the case was dropped when the chief witnesses died.

Diego was a strong, hulking type who looked disengaged from the conversation and oblivious to everything happening in the saloon. His eyes were glazed as if heavily intoxicated or hallucinating but he brought a menacing presence that dared you to challenge his awareness. Nicknamed Pirolo for as long as he could remember he collected union dues in West Tampa for *La Resistencia* and was suspected in a series of robberies in Hyde Park but had yet to be arrested. He was the dutiful sidekick to Matías and known to rally groups of cigar makers through sheer intimidation.

Now Juan Carlos addressed his entire table. "How many Cubans have now been assaulted by the hands of this city? It is no longer a labor problem. It is about Cubans becoming citizens of the second, or even the third class." He turned to Salvador. "We'll pay them back, Ortiz. All in good time."

Juan Carlos tilted his head back and threw down half a glass of rum and then nudged Salvador. "I have just the medicine for you, my friend." He grinned and his rotten tooth winked at Salvador like a roguish little devil.

"What medicine is that?"

"Have some more rum," Carlito filled Salvador's glass and then placed a five dollar bill on the table in front of Salvador.

"What's this for, a doctor?"

Matías laughed and nudged Diego, who forced a chuckle.

Juan Carlos shook his head and smiled. His eyes motioned towards a staircase in the back of La Rubia.

Salvador did not need to follow the glance. "You want me to see one of the girls?"

Another nod. "It's time, Salvador."

Salvador sighed and took a hearty swig of rum. It had been less than a year since Olympia had died. Did he still need to mourn her soul?

"Feel no guilt, Salvador," urged Juan Carlos. "Just go."

Diego nodded and then pointed to the stairs, almost issuing a command.

Salvador finished his rum and realized he'd had more to drink in the last three days than in the entire last year. He didn't want to think anymore, he just wanted to have his way and be gone. "I'll pay you back," said Salvador as he took the money and headed for the stairs while Juan Carlos grinned and the men returned to their game.

It was not Salvador's first visit to a brothel. He had gone to a few when he was with El Matón, before Olympia and Josefina came into his care. Salvador's opinion of these girls was that they were of the lowest class; unfortunate to the point of emptiness, yet sassy and savvy with the dollar. Efficient and biased in their ways, as if they had experienced every man in the city and had settled, for that one moment, on you. They were soulless and worthless and yet he needed them badly.

Salvador was greeted at the top of the stairs by the madam, a boisterous Cuban woman of roughly fifty with a low neckline that thrust her bust upward for men to judge. He handed her five dollars, and she pointed to a hallway with four closed doors that looked very much like the inside of an apartment building. "Melina is free," she said. "Number two."

Salvador pushed the door open and saw a young girl sitting on the bed wearing a black negligee about to strike a long wooden match and light the cigarette that dangled from her lips. Salvador immediately thought there must be some mistake, that this girl was too young. She couldn't be any older than Lázaro.

Melina froze with her match in hand and raised an eyebrow. Even more youthful was her voice. "Gonna be hard to see me from all the way over there. Why don't you come in?"

Salvador closed the door behind him. "How old are you?"

"Seventeen," she struck her match and lit her cigarette. "So what?"

"How old really?"

"Sixteen. Is that better? Or would you like me to be fifteen?"

Sassy indeed. He said, "Either way you're younger than my daughter."

"Whatever turns you on, pal," Melina said as she laid back, her cigarette still burning in hand. She noticed his black eye but said nothing. Salvador unzipped his pants.

He thought he would struggle with the girl's youth but the shame of the act made it more appealing. Melina was charming in her lewdness and Salvador felt unperturbed and become a younger version of himself, Salvador the Bandit, spirited and agile. Her flesh was soft and unblemished by age, and her eyes welcomed him in a way that seemed she had known him many times before. The alcohol helped him last, and when it was over Salvador dressed and left her alone without giving her a look or a farewell.

Back downstairs Juan Carlos laughed and slapped Salvador on the back. He poured more rum for his friend and then inched his chair a bit closer. "Tell me, Ortiz. These men who assaulted you, what did they look like?"

Matías and Diego also seemed to be sitting closer, curious for his answer.

"Americans, not like cops. Regular citizens."

"Vigilantes," said Matías.

Salvador nodded blankly as if talk of the attack had sent him into a trance. Or perhaps he believed the attack had never happened.

Juan Carlos glanced to Matías who said, "We shouldn't be intimidated. There's a train full of strikebreakers arriving tomorrow."

"We can't let them take our jobs," Juan Carlos said. "Salvador, are you in?"

"Where is Mendez?"

"Sitting under a tree somewhere, writing a poem," Carlito said.

Matías laughed and nudged Diego again, who forced another chuckle.

Salvador sat quietly, still stuck in his trance.

"Well, Salvador? What about stopping those strikebreakers?" Juan Carlos watched closely for a sign of his old friend, the farm boy from Herrera, the one who had lost his parents and taken up arms against the Spanish. Salvador Ortiz, once again numbed by circumstance, looked to Juan Carlos and nodded.

Carlito smiled as Salvador confirmed that the bandit was back.

By three o'clock the following afternoon both Salvador and Juan Carlos had been arrested and loaded onto a train bound for Jacksonville, where they sat handcuffed side by side with two plainclothes Tampa police officers who rode alongside as escorts.

No one expected the confrontation at the train station to escalate into a full blown riot. When a gang of angry cigar makers from *La Resistencia* met a group of Havana strikebreakers on the platform, Salvador and Juan Carlos found themselves in the middle of an excited crowd. Tensions flared on both sides and within minutes the Tampa cigar workers were shouting at the strikebreakers to board the train and return to Havana while the solemn workers from Havana tried to push their way through the mob.

Punches were thrown, fights broke out, and soon a handful of police officers were among the group blowing whistles, pulling men off each other and handcuffing Tampa cigar workers. Juan Carlos was pulled to the ground by a pair of men and as he fell he noticed white men with wooden clubs – dressed in business shirts with their sleeves rolled up as Salvador had encountered – aiding the police and protecting the strikebreakers. Protecting their investment.

Salvador and Juan Carlos were taken to the jail where they were photographed and quickly placed before a judge who ordered them to be deported by train to Jacksonville.

Deported. Bound for the opposite side of the state to a city they had never been to with no contacts and no money. They sat quietly for the first hour of the journey, wondering if strikebreakers would take their jobs, and what would happen once they were released in Jacksonville.

Then Salvador said to Juan Carlos, "I hear that tuberculosis lives in the cigar factories."

"Yes?" Juan Carlos acknowledged, waiting for more.

"With the windows closed the hot air is a breeding ground for the disease."

"Welcome to 1897, my friend. That is old news." He nudged his friend. "You'll have to cheer up, Ortiz. We're not dead yet."

"No."

"We could be dead but we're not."

Salvador nodded and watched the green plains and horse farms zip by the window.

Juan Carlos said, "We're lucky to be on this train. We're lucky they didn't kill us in Tampa. I don't plan to live the rest of my life in Jacksonville, do you? The city burned to the ground three months ago, there's nothing there for us."

They were quiet for a moment. Juan Carlos glanced across the aisle to the cops, one of whom was reading a newspaper while the other dozed with his head against the window. Juan Carlos whispered, "I'll tell you what somebody should do."

"What?"

"Somebody should strike back, you know? This guy, Armando, he comes to jail in the middle of the night with a posse to kill me and Lapár. He would have done it if you weren't there, if Alessandria wasn't there. I'd be dead, Salvador. Somebody should get him before he gets us."

He sat back but watched Salvador from the corner of his eye.

Salvador suspected where Juan Carlos was headed, yet he did nothing to avoid the subject. "What are you saying, Carlito?"

Juan Carlos swallowed, glanced to the oblivious officers at his left and whispered so softly Salvador had to strain to hear. "Somebody should kill Armando Renteria."

"Not this again."

"You know I'm right. He already tried to kill me once. Once he learns that we've returned to Tampa, we'll be dead."

Salvador wasn't ready to admit that Juan Carlos was not proposing a revenge killing, but one that was necessary for their survival. And Salvador didn't dispute that once they were alone in Jacksonville they would attempt to return to Tampa as soon as they could.

"You know I'm right," Juan Carlos repeated.

He *was* right. "How would you do it?"

"We, Salvador. We're going to do it. As soon as we get back."

"How?"

"I don't know. Maybe we break into his apartment."

"Are we actually talking about this?"

"Yes."

"They will come looking for us."

"They won't even know we're in town. For all they know we're still rotting in Jacksonville."

"We won't be able to hide forever."

Juan Carlos was quiet. The train started to slow and then the screeching brakes told one officer to put his paper away and wake his partner. The cigar makers' handcuffs were unlocked, and as they were shoved off the train and into the unfamiliar city, one of the officers said, "If you are wise, you'll never again show your faces in Tampa."

Jacksonville, Florida.

A city that had burned to the ground by a fire accidentally started in a fiber factory. The business district had been completely destroyed and ten thousand citizens had been left homeless. The embers and ashes had been cleared weeks ago but Salvador and Juan Carlos were shocked to see the naked foundation of a charred city. Buildings had been reduced to pillars of concrete or empty brick shells with broken windows and missing rooftops. In some places it seemed as if only the brick chimneys had survived and everything everywhere had been scarred with the black mark of fire.

"What are we supposed to do here?" Salvador asked as they left the train station and headed towards the sounds of hammers and saws, where constructions crews bustled and rebuilt the city. The town looked like one giant construction project and there appeared to be little or no place to spend money.

Carlito said, "It feels like we've been in this situation before, my friend."

Broke, homeless and unemployed, Salvador felt as if his parents had just been killed and he was meeting Juan Carlos on the streets of Pinar del Río for the first time. But in this city there appeared to be no one to rob and no money to steal. Salvador and Juan Carlos feared they'd be stuck in Jacksonville, starving, penniless and unable to use their skills.

Until they encountered the street vendors.

Lined up along Bay Street, wooden carts carried colorful arrangements of fruits and vegetables, bread, pastries and soft drinks. Absent were the novelty merchants who sold alligator teeth and orange tree walking canes. Only the bare necessities were peddled, for there was no market for toys and trinkets. Hungry construction workers were the only clientele.

Salvador and Juan Carlos casually strolled down the boulevard and as their old instincts returned, they no longer thought of tobacco and became men of the machete and the torch. Looking over the vendors as they walked, they were surrounded by horses pulling carts of lumber and crews of workers hurrying back and forth. It was an exciting scene, an urgent and coordinated reconstruction where the citywide pounding of hammers caused men to raise their voices as they talked.

This was a place where petty crime could go virtually unanswered.

Many of the vendors had set their wagons close together, surrounding themselves with traffic and making them unapproachable for men with motives like Salvador and Juan Carlos. Then they saw their target. At the end of a long row of vendors was a small man with glasses who packed up his small pushcart for the day. Links of sausages were packed into a pair of baskets and bread was stacked neatly beside. He folded his apron and tossed it on top and then lifted his cart by the handles and started pushing it home.

There were no alleys where they could conceal themselves, no trees where they could hide, but they followed as the vendor moved south towards the St. John's River where the city had been untouched by flames. They moved swiftly and caught up to the vendor while watching over their shoulders for any witnesses. The sound of hammering created a racket throughout the streets, and once they were beside him, they pounced.

Before the vendor noticed men flanking his sides Salvador wrapped his arm around the vendor's neck and yanked him towards the ground. Juan Carlos kicked the man's feet away and down they went. Using the cart as a shield, Salvador kept the man in a tight headlock and dragged him beside one of the wheels so that they were hidden from the construction sites.

"Please," the man gasped for air as his face turned red. Salvador continued to squeeze the man's neck in the vice of his forearm and bicep while Juan Carlos searched the man's pockets. He quickly found a leather billfold filled with paper money and slipped it into his jacket pocket.

"Not everyone in this town is out of business," Carlito remarked.

"Tell Don Macarata that I was just on my way to pay him," gasped the vendor. "I wasn't trying to avoid my debt, I promise!"

Juan Carlos glanced at Salvador and realized this vendor thought his assailants were working for the mysterious Don Macarata, obviously the local boss but a man neither Juan Carlos nor Salvador had ever heard of. Juan Carlos played along. "This will keep him happy for today but someone will be back tomorrow to collect the principle."

Salvador released the man who collapsed onto the ground and wheezed while he caught his breath. The sounds of the man's pathetic gasps were shuddering to Salvador; it sounded like a dying animal. As they stood they noticed the sounds of the hammering had not ceased. No one had noticed.

"Come on," Juan Carlos said as he stole a pair of sausages and a loaf of bread from the pushcart and dashed away. Salvador followed and they cut through an abandoned lot where a few charred pillars of brick and concrete marked where a hotel stood just months before. Minutes later they had faded back into the crowd on Bay Street and were headed back to the train station eating as they walked.

Juan Carlos patted the billfold in his pocket. "The old days, Ortiz. They're back."

By the time they arrived at the train station they had already concocted their plan for Armando. "That Spaniard's dead," Juan Carlos said as he approached the station window.

"Help you?" asked the attendant.

"When is the next train to Tampa?"

"Next train leaves just after midnight, have you in Tampa by morning."

Juan Carlos set his money on the counter. "Two tickets, please."

Chapter 23

"Order! Order!" The mayor pounded his gavel to calm the assembly of angry Tampa businessmen. Those in the front of the council chamber took their seats while others continued to argue and voice their frustration. There were hundreds of men in the room; many were cigar manufacturers with their management teams, but there were also attorneys, restaurant owners, landlords, and store merchants. Armando Renteria sat in the front row awaiting the mayor's response, leader of a silent cabal with Antonio Vasquez, Antonio Junior, publisher Arlen Kincaid and police chief Sean McGrath.

The mayor slammed his gavel again and called for order as the noise finally abated and men took their seats. He addressed the assembly. "There is no doubt that we are deadlocked in a fight for control of this city."

Armando wondered what plan the mayor would present to end the dispute and suspected it would not be forceful but designed to protect his image and legacy. If Armando ever became mayor his actions would not be so passive.

"There should be no fight to begin with!" shouted Julio Baez, owner of the Flor de West Tampa Cigar Company. "Control of the cigar industry should be in the hands of the manufacturers!" The crowd greeted his declaration with a healthy applause.

The mayor answered. "*La Resistencia* has been outlawed and disbanded."

"Only on paper!" another voice shouted, generating nods of agreement from the manufacturers, including Armando.

"The workers union has been dealt with," the mayor said. "Concerned citizens have taken to the streets to urge these workers back to the benches. The police have raided their meetings, shut down their soup kitchens, and driven their agitators out of town. And we will continue to be vigilant until this strike has ended."

The crowd booed. "None of this has worked!" a man shouted. "These vagrants still clutter the streets. I encountered a group of them preaching their radical doctrine to passersby just outside city hall!"

"My bookkeeper was killed!"

"These agitators are still here," said the American accountant of a small cigar factory. "Their newspapers are still being distributed, meetings are being held under the leftist cause and they are inciting riots, for God's sake!"

The mayor began to lose control of the meeting as more stood to voice their concerns and competed for talk time. Dialogue became a shouting match and again the mayor pounded his gavel and called for order.

Armando smiled. These angry business owners were wise men. He glanced to his right where Vasquez sat quietly observing the scene. Armando wondered if his business partner would stand up to declare his position but the manufacturer remained seated, content to let others speak for the Cigar Trust. Armando shook his head and turned his attention back to the mayor.

"They should all be sent away!" Baez shouted towards the podium.

The mayor pounded his gavel and shouted, "We must be careful what we do to these men. Two were lynched by an angry mob, and that only succeeded in escalating the situation and strengthening their resolve."

There arose a great groan followed by shouts of indignation.

"Who is in control of this city?"

"We are facing a revolution from the workers!"

"Do we have a mayor or a radical sympathizer?"

The mayor threw his gavel aside and left the podium fearing this labor standoff had weakened him politically, possibly beyond repair. A solution to the General Strike of 1901 could not be settled in public and would have to be reached in closed quarters with a handful of advisors. The mayor dismissed himself and prepared for a private meeting in his office.

Armando rose and followed the mayor with Vasquez, Kincaid, and McGrath in tow. The crowd shouted them down as the city's leaders left via the center aisle and headed to the mayor's office. In the back row of the chamber, Lapár sat silently, having observed the entire meeting. His usual lawyerlike attire helped him blend into the crowd and go unnoticed.

"May I make a suggestion, Mr. Mayor?" the police chief said after all seven men were seated in the mayor's quiet office. "A bold act to send a strong message."

The mayor raised an eyebrow. "Sean, it sounds like you're suggesting these striking cigar makers be forced back to work."

The chief of police deadpanned. "I don't see what other option we have." He sat on the couch beside Vasquez and Antonio Junior. Seated in chairs by the mayor's desk were Kincaid and the head of the local wing of the Cigar Manufacturer's International Union, Tony Bello. Lurking behind the mayor's desk near the window that overlooked Tampa Bay was Armando Renteria.

The mayor sat in his chair and gripped the armrests. "We won't just start kidnapping people."

"Your honor," McGrath said. "You also can't just give into their demands."

Kincaid agreed. "Most Tampa businesses have no money coming in but the cigar workers find jobs in other cities and send money home. I fear that our cigar factories will soon follow and leave town permanently."

Vasquez said, "I know of four factories that have already shutdown and returned their operations to Havana."

Armando, annoyed that Vasquez could sound so weak and reactive, kept his eyes outside and watched the bay, waiting for his moment.

The mayor rested his chin on his fist. "Is it possible to negotiate?"

The men murmured and shifted in their seats. Tony Bello, the intelligent Spanish representative from the cigar union friendly to the manufacturers said, "The CMIU is actively trying to recruit former *La Resistencia* members but we have little to bargain with."

Armando thought Bello unimpressive; though he spoke well and came from a semi-wealthy background, Bello was another stooge of the

287

manufacturers and had little influence in city politics. Armando scratched his beard and watched two American girls enter the bank across the street. He spoke. "Negotiating will legitimize the cigar makers and inflate their stature. These men need to leave town for good."

"We just removed two of them, didn't we Sean?" The mayor looked to the chief.

McGrath nodded. "Juan Carlos Alvarez and Salvador Ortiz, two throwaways from Cuba, arrested during the riot at the train station and deported to Jacksonville."

The mayor seemed satisfied but Armando smiled and stepped forward. "Mr. Mayor, I have ownership in five cigar factories. We know that the *bolita* games have all but halted. This strike is costing all of us money. The time to negotiate has passed. It is time for action. No dead bodies to link back to us, only the disappearance of their top union officials."

The mayor sat up and clenched his armrest. "Who the hell are you to come in here and talk like this?"

Armando leaned closer to the mayor for emphasis. His voice grew heavy. "We are not here to talk about how we can revive the Tampa economy, Mr. Mayor. We are talking about whether or not there will *be* a Tampa economy."

The mayor warned him with is forefinger. "No blood for tobacco."

"Then Tampa must agree to repay our losses and Tampa can't afford to do that." Armando folded his arms and waited for the mayor's response.

The chief spoke next. "I suggest we round them up."

"I agree," Armando said and looked to Vasquez, expecting concurrence.

"I'll give the orders here," the mayor waved them off. "I want Tony, Mr. Vasquez, and you, Sean, to sit down with their top guys and find something we can agree on."

The chief persisted. "If this arbitration commission doesn't work?"

"Then I'll have to make a decision."

*   *   *

Armando left the meeting and returned to Ybor City to collect *bolita* receipts from the night before. As he visited his vendors, he counted profits that were light and dwindling with every game. Months into the strike his primary income stream was dying, and Armando was slowly going broke. He would visit the Pasaje later on and collect payments from his prostitutes, but their business had been insubstantial as even Tampa businessmen had started to cut back on nightlife.

The cigar manufacturers could sell their product worldwide as long as their inventory remained, but Armando depended almost entirely on the cigar makers, an angry bunch led by a group of radicals the mayor was afraid to overpower. Armando remembered the mayor's weakness during the Weight Strike and disapproved of arbitration, a futile attempt to resolve a violent conflict without violence.

The cigar makers needed to be dealt with decisively.

As he returned to his office for the night, he thought of ways to take complete ownership of the Vasquez factory. Rename it Renteria and Company.

Become a legitimate businessman and run for mayor.

But Vasquez wasn't selling. He intended to pass the company to his fat son Antonio Junior, as his father Florentino had done to him. With Vasquez in his way and the cigar makers out of money, Armando's future was in jeopardy. He needed a way to take care of both Vasquez and the cigar makers.

As he sat at his desk, smoked a cigar, and sipped from a glass of scotch, he searched for a way to resolve his standoff with Antonio Vasquez and put those irritating cigar makers back to work.

Then he sat up straight, inspired with an idea. A single act that would resolve both problems with one bold stroke. He grinned as he sat back and sipped his scotch, admiring his own cunning.

"A meeting?" Lapár was in Mendez's office, and together the *La Resistencia* president and *Workers' Bulletin* publisher were hearing a request from local CMIU leader Tony Bello. Bello was a newcomer in Tampa, a labor leader from New York hand-picked by the manufacturers to promote their corporate agenda. Now he had been hired to broker a meeting between *La Resistencia* leaders and the city's business owners. Lapár saw in his rival Bello a man who was happy to be where he was but underwhelming in posture and presentation. More of a messenger than a leader; a man with little clout and not someone held in high opinion by Lapár.

Three chairs were arranged in a circle in Mendez's print shop and Bello took the last seat. "Who can deny that this strike has become a great burden for both sides? The mayor has agreed to the possibility of arbitration and would like for cigar makers' representatives to meet with concerned citizens of Tampa."

Lapár and Mendez shared a victorious glance. A meeting initiated by the city was the first sign the manufacturers were beginning to capitulate. Lapár was most interested in Bello's reference to the citizens of Tampa. "Who wants to meet?"

Bello clarified. "Factory owner Antonio Vasquez, Arlen Kincaid, the chief of police and me, the head of the local CMIU."

Lapár smirked contemptuously. "The CMIU. Ha! How many members do you have in Tampa?" He knew the number was low, insignificant.

Bello smiled thinly. "The Cigar Manufacturer's International Union is the one and only legal labor organization in town."

Mendez was incensed. "Don't come in here and insult us."

Bello held up a hand and continued. "We'll meet in a neutral location, a public place where the people of Tampa can be assured that both sides are working towards a resolution."

"When?" Lapár asked.

"Tomorrow night."

"Saturday?"

Bello nodded.

Lapár glanced to Mendez for his input. The writer said, "If there is to be a meeting it will be held in Ybor City. If these concerned businessmen truly desire a resolution, they will have no qualms traveling into the Latin district."

Bello agreed. "Ybor City is as much a part of Tampa as Hyde Park or Center City."

Lapár smiled. "My friend, Ybor City *is* Tampa."

They shook hands and agreed to meet the following night at La Morena, a modest saloon on Eighth Avenue in Ybor City. Bello let himself out and then Lapár raised a curious eyebrow to Mendez. "A setup?"

Mendez shrugged. "Could be, but I'm hoping the strain of the work stoppage has become so great that they are willing to conceded some of our stipulations."

"It concerns me though," Lapár said. "We were arrested a few weeks ago. I intentionally skipped my court date. Salvador and Juan Carlos were deported to Jacksonville. Are we next?"

Mendez could not stifle his smile. "I doubt that Juan Carlos Alvarez and Salvador Ortiz will remain in Jacksonville for very long."

Respectable businessmen rarely ventured into the Scrub. While Ybor City and West Tampa were the city's immigrant enclaves, the Scrub was Tampa's identifiable black section. It was a horrible place where a Spanish industrialist like Armando Renteria had no reason to go.

The color line was visible south of Seventh Avenue at the westernmost part of Ybor City where brick streets became dirt roads and sandy paths. The Scrub was a buffer between Tampa and Ybor City, with abominable shantytowns characterized by poor sanitation and widespread illiteracy. The entire area was excluded from politics and local culture, and employment was scarce. The Scrub's inhabitants occupied the lowest rung of the social ladder – even the immigrants looked down on these people and their uncertain future.

Armando worried that if the cigar makers were not persuaded to return to work that all of Tampa would look like this. He believed that with a competent caretaker such as himself Tampa could reign for decades as the Queen City of the Gulf and the Cigar Capital of the World. Ironic, he thought, that his effort to preserve the splendor of the city brought him into the worst part of town.

Because only in the Scrub could he find Silos Calzada.

Armando considered Silos to be a local loser and just one step higher than bum. Jailed several times for marijuana and threatened with deportation until the city decided Silos was not worth the price of a boat ticket, he could be found on Seventh Avenue most Saturday nights begging for handouts from the busy crowd of amblers.

Since he had tried to sell, borrow, and swindle from nearly every citizen of Ybor City, Silos knew every face in town. Armando knew Silos was a crackpot but also an informer who was tuned into the gossip of the streets. If a petty crime had been committed, Silos could finger the culprit. He was a consistent player in the seedy subculture, wise to the street and exactly what Armando needed.

They met at Silos' small wooden shack, a rickety thing not much more elaborate than the *bohio* huts of peasant Cuba. Armando slipped him a five dollar bill, a fortune to anyone from the Scrub, and made his request. "I'm looking for a pair of recruits, a nameless duo who can be paid in pennies. They should be capable yet expendable, unassuming, with sharp eyesight untarnished by drug abuse. It will help if they are former cigar makers. And they have to be good with guns."

"Sure," Silos nodded. "I already have someone in mind."

Mendez locked his shop and headed to the Black Bean Café for an early dinner. As he crossed Fifteenth Street and headed south, he was approached by a tall, slim man wearing a dark suit and wire-rimmed glasses; his head was topped with a black derby.

"Meet us at St. Joseph's Church in five minutes."

Mendez recognized the voice. Juan Carlos. Before he could get a closer look, the man ambled across the street and started walking east on Tenth Avenue. Looking very much like a Spanish banker or accountant, Juan Carlos kept his hands in his pockets and his eyes on the sidewalk as he strolled towards the church.

Not wanting to draw attention to Juan Carlos, Mendez continued south until he reached Ninth Avenue, then turned east for a block before he turned north towards the church. Wondering if Salvador was nearby and what his disguise would look like, Mendez reached the church, a one-story wooden chapel with a modest steeple. He opened the heavy wooden doors and slipped inside.

It was cool, quiet and dark inside, dimly lit by an afternoon sun that made the stained glass windows glow in colorful patterns. A pair of tall white candles flickered at the empty altar and a small prayer station under a painting of the Virgin Mary on the right side held rows and rows of tiny candles that cast a flickering, ominous shadow on her solemn face.

There were a pair of old women praying at pews near the front, and on the left side Mendez saw Juan Carlos's derby – he was kneeling in at pew near the back. Mendez took the center aisle and sat in the next row, directly in front of Juan Carlos so that Carlito could whisper into his ear.

"Salvador is here too," he said to Mendez. The *lector* looked across the aisle and saw a man in the opposite pew, also dressed like a businessman, wearing a long coat and tie with a black hat. When he looked up Mendez recognized Salvador, who nodded and bowed his head as if he were praying.

"What have we missed?" asked Juan Carlos as he closed his eyes and bowed his head, mimicking prayer. They whispered, even though the only people who might hear were the two old women up front.

"The strike hasn't ended, but they've asked for a sit down."

"Who? Armando?"

"No," Mendez whispered and filled Juan Carlos in on the details.

"Reinstate *La Resistencia*," Carlito said. "Demand higher wages. Ortiz would ask that they improve health conditions inside the factories and allow mutual aid to flourish."

Salvador, within hearing distance, nodded his agreement.

"When is the meeting?" Juan Carlos asked.

"Tomorrow night at La Morena."

"Be cautious."

"What are you going to do?"

Juan Carlos lied. "Lay low for a couple of days, maybe end up in Key West until the strike is over. Good luck, Sandito. We'll see you soon."

Juan Carlos stood and sidestepped his way out of the pew. Salvador did the same and together the two exiles, men who had been ordered never to return to Tampa, slipped out the back door of the church and disappeared.

They walked north to the boarding house where Juan Carlos lived, removing their hats and loosening their ties before they entered, in order to look inconspicuous for the house lady who had seen Juan Carlos come and go for years. Once safely inside Carlito's room they removed their uncomfortable suits and sat down to discuss their plan. They would stay indoors for the rest of the day but tomorrow morning they would venture into town, locate and track Armando, and when the time was right – Juan Carlos had a pair of pistols tied under his bed.

"One shot in the head, one shot in the back," Juan Carlos instructed as they cleaned and loaded their weapons. When they were finished they drank rum and smoked cigars while playing dominoes, concentrating on their game as if it was the only thing that mattered, like they were not plotting the murder of a top city industrialist.

Around midnight, after their cigars were dead and the rum bottle empty, Juan Carlos rested on his bed while Salvador stretched out on the floor. They had stopped at the Ortiz house upon their arrival in town to gather some of Salvador's things and bring them to Carlito's room. The cigar maker was adamant about recovering his father's knife while he cared less about the rest of his possessions.

Now as he lay on the wood floor of Juan Carlos's room, Salvador held the knife by the wooden handle and showed Juan Carlos the dull, rusted blade. "My father's," he said. "I took it the day before he died."

Juan Carlos, half asleep, gestured towards Salvador. "Imagine if he could see what became of his son. Four children from the daughter of a wealthy Spanish sugar planter."

They chuckled. "Yes," Salvador said as he fell asleep. "There would certainly be plenty to explain."

The next morning Armando was back in the Scrub near the shack where Silos lived, sitting with the two recruits. They were in their twenties. An Afro-Cuban named Alexei and a Haitian youngster named Yadel. They appeared to be of sound body and mind, watched Armando attentively, and claimed to have worked in the cigar industry – Alexei as an apprentice cigar maker and Yadel as a stripper.

After speaking with them for a few minutes Armando was confident they could accomplish their task. Alexei, though young at the time, claimed to have fought in the Cuban War of Independence, and Yadel's slow, cunning demeanor and open disdain for the law convinced Armando that he viewed crime as a routine act of survival. Furthermore these men were destitute and willing to do anything for the right price. Armando handed Alexei an envelope.

"Two hundred and fifty dollars," he said. "You'll get the other half when the job is done."

Alexei and Yadel looked inside the envelope as Alexei thumbed the green fifty dollar bills. When Alexei smiled, Armando became aware of the boy's youth; his boyish features told Armando that Alexei was not much older than the schoolchildren or the young apprentice cigar makers in the factories. But youth was not synonymous with naivety, and these men seemed experienced in such matters.

Armando undid the latches of his suitcase. There were no documents inside, only a burlap bag which he set on the dirt floor of the shack. Inside were two Browning M1900 pistols and a box of bullets. As the assassins inspected the pistols with their eyes, Armando reached into his jacket pocket.

"The meeting is tonight," he said. "Here is your target."

He handed them a photograph of Antonio Vasquez.

Salvador and Juan Carlos awoke with the sunrise. They wore their disguises and loaded their pistols. "This is it, Salvador," Juan Carlos said. "Zero hour." He placed his alligator tooth necklace around his neck for good luck.

Salvador snapped the chamber of his .38 shut with a heavy metallic clink. "Let's go." They pulled their hats into place, adjusted their neckties and headed into town towards Armando's apartment. They spotted him just as he was leaving, dressed in casual Saturday attire of slacks and a light jacket; Armando carried a briefcase and moved swiftly along the sidewalk.

Salvador and Juan Carlos kept their distance as the Saturday morning traffic was light, but vendors and pedestrians were out and starting to fill the streets. By mid-afternoon Ybor City would be clamoring with commerce and social life. Salvador bought a newspaper for something to carry and stayed close to Juan Carlos as they followed Armando.

As he headed southwest, turning west at one corner, then south at another, Salvador and Juan Carlos thought Armando was heading for the train station. Armando's path continued southwest and they next thought he was going to the Ybor factory, but he surprised them by leaving Ybor City altogether and walking into the Scrub.

"We'd better not follow," said Salvador. "We'll stand out too much."

"You're right," agreed Juan Carlos. "Wait until he comes out."

Thirty minutes passed while Salvador and Juan Carlos lurked nearby. Salvador pretended to read his newspaper while Juan Carlos idly strolled up and down the block. They spotted Armando as he left the Scrub and hurried to catch a trolley on Seventh Avenue. Salvador and Juan Carlos followed and boarded the same trolley just as it started to pull away.

Armando sat near the front while Juan Carlos and Salvador moved by him unnoticed with heads down and hats pulled over their eyes to hide their faces. They sat in the back. There were four other passengers on the trolley sitting quietly; two men reading newspapers on one side, an older lady and her daughter on the right. As the trolley moved west along Seventh Avenue, Armando kept his eyes forward as the car cut through Ybor City's main street.

Juan Carlos and Salvador reached into their pockets for their pistols. Salvador imagined what would happen. Armando, oblivious to the men who followed, would be an easy shot for Juan Carlos. The bullet would enter his skull from behind and possibly blow out the front of his head. He would fall and die instantly, unless the bullet was defective. If Armando survived the first shot they'd need to be quick to deliver another. Or worse, Juan Carlos could misfire, forcing Salvador to step forward and fire shots of his own. Regardless of the outcome, Armando would be dead and the cigar makers would have to flee the scene without anyone having a good look at their faces.

Salvador realized he may have to leave Ybor City forever.

They left their seats and began to inch forward, aware of the conductor who seemed focused on driving. Juan Carlos began to raise his pistol towards the back of Armando's head as the streetcar slowed, but Salvador saw a flash of blue on the sidewalk. "Wait," he whispered just loud enough for Juan Carlos to hear. Carlito, trusting his friend's instincts, quickly lowered his pistol and slipped it back into his pocket, glancing back to Salvador. Following his gaze to the sidewalk, Juan Carlos saw a pair of Tampa policemen standing on the street corner, watching for vagrants or delinquent cigar makers to arrest, and hardly noticing the trolley that halted before them.

The trolley slowed to a stop with a metallic screech and Armando jumped up and hopped off, nodding to the two police officers on the sidewalk as he passed. Salvador and Juan Carlos stayed behind and sat down, keeping their heads down. As a rush of adrenaline overcame Salvador and brought an awkward sense of relief, the trolley continued on and turned left at the next corner, headed north towards the Vasquez factory, and left Armando safely behind.

As he stepped off the streetcar he recognized the two Tampa policemen as officers Reddey and Smith, two confidants of the chief who knew of Armando's affairs and always looked the other way. Armando nodded to them as he passed and stepped into Centro Español to collect *bolita* money from the night before.

He moved through town and collected payments throughout the morning, disappointed by the poor turnout. Labor disruption always hurt *bolita* but this was dismal. Even the handful of strikebreakers provided little income and some games had died completely.

The prolonged strike made the assassination of Antonio Vasquez necessary.

As he paused for lunch Armando contemplated his decision and the plan that has been set in place. The execution of his top business rival at the hands of former cigar makers cleared Armando's path to industry dominance while giving the mayor a reason to approve the removal of the city's labor leaders. It was brilliant, thought Armando. Cigar makers would be blamed for the murder, and there would be no one left to block Armando's advance. The strike would end once the mayor realized he needed to take decisive action against the labor leaders, and Armando would easily move in and takeover Vasquez and Company, then the Cigar Trust. Don Antonio's fat son Antonio Junior would inherit his father's shares, but without his father around to guide him, the boy would be easily muscled aside and see the empire his grandfather started renamed Renteria and Company.

*   *   *

Vasquez finished dinner with Maria and Antonio Junior before leaving for the meeting at La Morena. As they put on their jackets and adjusted their ties, Vasquez explained the situation to his son. "Originally we had conceded to allow union activity in the factories on Fridays only. That was before the labor union was outlawed. Surely the cigar makers will expect their union to be reinstated before they return to work. This is why we will offer them membership in the CMIU with flexible schedules."

"How will they respond?"

"I'll be lucky if De la Parte doesn't throw a drink in my face."

Lapár met Mendez at his office and together they walked to La Morena, reviewing their strategy on the way. "Our number one goal is to see *La Resistencia* reinstated with union activity allowed in the factories at least twice a week. A closed shop is really what we want but we'll need the labor union back in business first."

Mendez agreed. "What about flexible schedules, higher wages and better health conditions?"

Lapár chuckled. "Mention those and be ready for Vasquez to throw a drink in your face."

Alexei and Yadel crossed the train tracks and entered Ybor City from the south. They had studied the photograph of their target, and Armando had provided additional descriptions. Vasquez would be at the La Morena saloon on Eighth Avenue in just over an hour. Their pistols had been loaded and tested – Alexei and Yadel spent the afternoon at the beach shooting at tin cans. The request was dangerous, but the pay substantial for these men of the Scrub.

La Morena waited.

Seventh Avenue on Saturday night – the social event of the week and Salvador and Juan Carlos were stuck in the middle of it, unable to reach their target. It had been a frustrating afternoon. After the close call on the trolley, Juan Carlos and Salvador had caught up to Armando as he completed his rounds and then visited the Pasaje Hotel. Always among people, and with the streets of Ybor City growing busier by the minute, there had been no opportunity to take the Spaniard out without drawing significant attention. Carlito suggested that they trail him the rest of the night and try to get him on the way home.

Salvador agreed, and the two men faded into the busy crowd of pedestrians, shoppers, gossip-hounds and partygoers on Seventh Avenue. Despite a strike that had crippled the city's economy, the social life still beckoned. It didn't cost any money to socialize, go to a dance, or walk along the main street catching up with friends. Salvador missed his weekly date with Olympia when they would go to a dance and stay until their feet were so tired they could hardly walk home.

Spirits remained high among the immigrants, and even though they were out of work, they did not allow unemployment to hinder their enjoyment of life. The manufacturers could take away their labor union but not their attitude or zest. Salvador admired his people and saw the murder of Armando Renteria as a noble act that would preserve their pride.

They caught up to the investor as he walked along Seventh Avenue and turned north on Fourteenth Street and headed to Ybor Square. They were close to where the meeting would be held. Armando entered a small café across the street from La Morena and right beside the Martinez Ybor factory. The giant brick building towered over the café. Armando took a seat by the window, ordered coffee and a pastry and opened a newspaper.

Salvador and Juan Carlos continued walking. "This is odd," said Juan Carlos. "What is he doing here? Isn't Mendez meeting with the manufacturers' reps right across the street?"

"Yes," confirmed Salvador. "I wonder why Armando isn't attending the meeting."

"What should we do?"

"Let's stay close and keep our eye on things," Salvador said with concern. He started to wonder if this meeting was some kind of setup. "I don't like this."

La Morena accommodated an almost exclusive immigrant clientele. Rectangular shaped with a bar running down the length on the left, the smoky tavern was alive with the chatter of cigar makers and the constant click-clack of dominoes being mixed and slapped into place.

The floor was made from wooden planks with enough space between them to allow passage for roaches and mice. Square wooden tables filled the bar, and two tables nearest the picture window in front were pushed together for the evening meeting. Eight attendees arrived and introduced each other and then sat to begin negotiations. Sitting at the end of the table nearest the street, with his back to the front door was *La Resistencia* president Angelo De la Parte. Opposite Lapár at the other end of the table was Tampa chief of police Sean McGrath. Clockwise from the chief, sitting to his left was Antonio Vasquez Junior, his father Don Antonio, and Gabriel Mendez. To Lapár's left sat Alessandria Prizzi, Tony Bello, and Arlen Kincaid.

Coffee was served and everyone lit their favorite cigars as Antonio Vasquez brought the meeting to order. "Thank you for joining us tonight. Before we get into the details, I think we should establish where we are in agreement: that this strike must end." Vasquez glanced around the table and was satisfied to see unanimous nods.

The cigar manufacturer continued as his son watched closely. "Then we can also agree that a man must look after his family and that he must earn their daily meals. Would anyone disagree to this?" Heads shook and Vasquez was glad that Armando was not in the room to scrutinize the meeting. "Then it is fair to say that we all want the same thing: the means to provide for our families. We just have different ways of getting there. The manufacturers and members of the Cigar Trust choose to hire workers of all affiliations, while the cigar makers expect *La Resistencia* to be the only representation in town. What can be done about this?"

Salvador and Juan Carlos knew something was not right, which sharpened their alertness. With their hands close to their pistols they paced along the sidewalk, watching the front window of La Morena from the corners of their eyes while never losing sight of Armando in the café across the street.

They both knew that something was about to go wrong.

*   *   *

Armando waited patiently in the café. The gunmen would arrive any minute and once the shots were fired, Armando would calmly fade into the crowd that would quickly gather. Once he confirmed the death of Antonio Vasquez, Armando would slip away.

He suspected the assassins would be killed. If not on the spot, he would take care of them later with assistance from the chief. Now Armando dropped a spoonful of sugar into his espresso and stirred gently while he read the *Daily News*.

Lapár said, "We both desire prosperity, Señor Vasquez, but your methods have included beating and arresting union members, including one of the men at this table, Gabriel Mendez, who was assaulted outside his print shop during the Weight Strike. Two cigar workers, Juan Carlos Alvarez and Salvador Ortiz, were placed on a train and sent to Jacksonville after Ortiz was dragged into the woods and beaten. And of course I must mention two Italian boys who were lynched mysteriously and without trial."

The chief spoke next. "A bookkeeper was killed by those Italian boys and Ortiz and Alvarez were deported via legal court order. Most say justice was served."

The union leader puckered his lips and spat on the wooden floor while the rest of the table shifted uncomfortably in their seats. "What is the legitimacy of a mob lynching?"

The chief remained firm. "Calm your people and you will prosper. Continue in this excited state and you will only succeed in heaping more sorrow upon your friends and families."

Lapár said, "You've called us here not to negotiate a settlement but to deliver this ultimatum?"

"Call it what you will," said the chief. "It is the city's wish."

Alexei and Yadel stood on the corner of Fourteenth and Eighth. La Morena was across the street, just yards away. They looked at the photograph Armando had provided. Antonio Vasquez, cigar tycoon and head of the Cigar Trust, a powerful man in Ybor City but one who would soon be dead.

They studied his face. Pudgy and Spanish with a thinning head of hair that was nearly bald, and a pencil thin moustache. In a bar filled with Cuban workers, this man would be easy to spot.

Alexei nudged Yadel. "Let's go."

They reached into their pockets for their pistols.

Juan Carlos peered through the front window and saw Lapár addressing the group. Though his back was to Juan Carlos, the labor leader was passionately scolding the Tampa business elite. He held a pointed finger upright and shook it at the ceiling, a gesture Juan Carlos had witnessed before, usually when Lapár was angry and trying to force a point. As Juan Carlos walked casually by the window he glimpsed the chief of police and Antonio Vasquez watching Lapár with stone faces. It appeared the meeting was not going well.

Juan Carlos turned to walk towards the street and as he crossed the sidewalk, two young men passed him and headed for the bar. In one of their hands, Juan Carlos saw the unmistakable shape of a silver pistol. A Browning, one of the new semi-automatics.

Assassins!

Alexei and Yadel settled near the entrance and looked through the giant window. They spotted Vasquez right away; the portly fellow sitting near the bar's front entrance who took up almost the entire side of his table.

Their hearts pounded and their veins flushed with adrenaline that beaded cold sweat across their foreheads. It was as if time had slowed, the patrons in the bar, the pedestrians seemed almost frozen. There was no sound, no future, no past. It was the moment. They nodded to each other, ready to act and unable to predict the turmoil their actions would produce.

"Ready?" Yadel asked as the semi-automatic became weightless in his hand.

"On the count of three."

*   *   *

Juan Carlos frantically searched for Salvador, but his friend was ten feet away and looking the other direction. He could not believe what he was seeing. A set up! Two gunmen sent by the Cracker Mafia, paid with capitalist dollars to execute the leaders of the defunct labor union. He doubted he would be able to kill them both, but if he could stop just one…

He drew his pistol.

Vasquez watched as the *La Resistencia* leader continued his tirade. The front entrance was directly in his line of sight as two men rushed into the saloon with guns drawn. He saw them point the barrels at his head, saw himself pushing his chair away and falling to the ground and pulling Antonio Junior to the floor with the agility of a teenager.

The reality was that Antonio Vasquez just froze. As two tiny black gun barrels turned to him like the eyes of a monster hungry for his soul, Vasquez did nothing. Even when the barrels exploded with a roar and launched a pair of bullets at his head he sat still. It was the first slug that finally knocked him from his chair. It felt like a rock hit him just above the right ear and as he fell to the side he heard the crisp snap as a second bullet zipped past his head.

Mendez recognized the danger immediately and fell to the floor, thinking for a moment that the two gunmen were Salvador and Juan Carlos. He reached for Lapár's leg and tried to drag him down too as the gunshots erupted just yards away. The blasts were so loud and staggering that Mendez squeezed the table leg hard enough to push splinters into his palm.

Kincaid, Prizzi, Antonio Junior, and Bello also fell to the floor, and only Chief McGrath failed to cower at the sight and sound of the assault. Fueled by experience and instincts, within seconds the chief ducked below the table and pulled his own pistol from its holster. From his knees he aimed at the gunmen on the left, squeezed off a pair of shots and scored double hits to his target's chest. The force of the impact knocked Yadel back through the entrance where he stumbled and fell dead to the sidewalk.

McGrath moved his arms six inches to the right and fired again. Bullets seemed to fly in every direction as gunshots echoed throughout all corners of the bar. The air became clouded with smoke and sawdust as splintered wood and shattered glass showered the floor. The patrons screamed and ducked for cover. Mendez, under the table with Lapár and the others, had sweated his shirt clean through.

Now the second gunman turned to flee the bar, but McGrath was on his feet, determined to prevent the scum's escape. He moved surprisingly fast for a man of his age, bounding over the upturned chairs like hurdles and onto Eighth Avenue.

Juan Carlos was caught completely off guard. When the assassins stepped into the bar they immediately started unloading their weapons and Juan Carlos had little time to react. He moved in behind them with his gun raised, prepared to take them down, when someone from inside the bar returned fire. One man fell from the doorway, nearly colliding with Juan Carlos, as he collapsed onto the sidewalk.

A half second later the second gunman burst from the door and ran directly into Juan Carlos. Their bodies smashed together like rocks and with a twist of arms and legs, they fell to the pavement. The impact threw their pistols from their grasp, and Juan Carlos hurried to push Alexei away and crawl out from underneath.

"Freeze, Comrade!"

Juan Carlos was on his back and staring into the mouth of Chief McGrath's Colt .38. Alexei was on his knees beside him frozen in place with his hands in the air. The chief, oozing sweat, paused to catch his breath. He kept his pistol squarely aimed at Juan Carlos, who scowled at the police officer.

McGrath smiled. "Evening, lad. It looks like your insurrection has failed."

Salvador turned to run as soon as Juan Carlos hit the ground – there was no chance to save him once he was pinned underneath the gunman. As onlookers began to gather, Salvador instinctively took one last look at the café across and street and immediately recognized his mistake. Armando was in the window watching the action at La Morena, and when Salvador turned towards the café he was face to face with Armando. There was not just eye contact, there was recognition.

Armando now knew Salvador had returned from Jacksonville. The cigar maker had been spotted on the scene with a gun in his hand and now he needed to flee. Salvador shoved his pistol into his pocket and ran east, cutting south through an alley and into the throng of Saturday night partygoers on Seventh Avenue.

Armando joined the gathering crowd. Police officers quickly arrived and held the crowd at bay while the chief handcuffed the two offenders to each other. Armando had not anticipated the chief's swift reaction, and he was surprised to see one assassin dead and the other handcuffed to his old nemesis Juan Carlos Alvarez.

So, both of them returned from Jacksonville, he thought as he approached the scene looking for any sign of Antonio Vasquez. One objective had been met: a pair of cigar makers were in custody and would be blamed for the attempted murder. But he couldn't see Vasquez anywhere. Wondering the fate of the cigar manufacturer, Armando approached the chief. "What happened?"

McGrath dabbed his flushed face with a handkerchief. "Goddamn leaf-rollers tried to start another revolution. We have one dead, two in custody."

Armando looked for Vasquez again and saw chaos in the bar. A fog of gun smoke and sawdust, tables overturned, patrons pushing to get outside and take a look at the body or the faces of the perpetrators. Armando pointed to Yadel's body which rested face up in a pool of blood. "Who didn't make it?"

"No ID," McGrath said. "He looks like a drifter, probably a ruffian from the Scrub. Ever seen him?"

Armando shook his head as he inspected the pair of bullet wounds in Yadel's chest. One bullet had pierced his heart, the other took a lung. Two police officers arrived and covered the body with a sheet. Then Armando glanced to the perpetrators. He wasn't worried about Alexei being taken into custody – Armando had never used his own name and would take care of the Scrub denizen if he decided to talk.

He glanced at Alvarez, who was being hoisted to his feet by a pair of police officers to be taken downtown. "Alvarez is back from Jacksonville, huh?" Armando said to the chief.

McGrath shrugged. "What did you expect?"

"We need to take care of him once and for all."

McGrath raised an eyebrow and nodded silent agreement.

Armando stepped into La Morena and saw Antonio Junior on the floor kneeling beside his father, holding a bloody rag against Don Antonio's temple. The cigar manufacturer sat upright and was alert and very much alive. It looked like a bullet had only grazed his head. Armando's primary objective had failed.

He stepped back outside and found the chief. "Does the mayor know?"

"I was on my way to see him just now." The chief looked at Armando. Each man knew what the other was thinking.

"Those damn immigrants." The mayor kicked the metal railing of the mansion's front porch, though softly since he wore just his bathrobe and slippers. It was past midnight and the chief, Armando – and at his own rabid insistence – Antonio Junior had awakened the mayor to deliver news of the attempted murder. "The people of Tampa will be in an uproar when this hits the papers!"

"Kincaid will guarantee that," Armando said.

"Mr. Mayor," the chief said. "We can't negotiate when a trio of cigar makers ambush our meeting and try to kill the head of the Cigar Trust."

Armando added, "I saw a fourth man there too, Salvador Ortiz. It's a grand conspiracy, Mr. Mayor. They tried to kill Vasquez and would have surely killed the chief if he hadn't acted so quickly."

"My father is lucky to be alive!" Vasquez Junior practically shouted at the mayor.

The mayor dismissed the younger Vasquez's juvenile outburst, crossed his arms and looked to his slippers for answers. "Now what are we suggesting? You were talking about taking them off the streets for good, weren't you?"

The chief nodded. "An audacious act requires decisive retribution. We have a list of five or six of their most influential leaders. We decapitate the movement and crack down on the rank and file."

Armando added, "We have a boat."

"A boat?" The mayor squinted.

Armando nodded. "Loading Alvarez and Ortiz onto a train didn't work. Both of them returned just a few days later with guns blazing. They need to go far away. Offshore. To a place where they'll never return."

The mayor realized this could create a great burden. "No blood on our hands?"

"We're not going to kill anyone," Armando assured him. "Consider this a permanent relocation."

The chief said, "For the good of the city."

The mayor stuffed his hands into the pockets of his robe and paced.

"Mr. Mayor," said the chief. "They think they're fighting a revolution."

He glanced at the three men who had summoned him to his porch on this late August night. They were eager for action and certain their methods were just. The immigrants believed it was war and it was time for decisive action, for the good of the city. The mayor would never give such a bold order in his life.

He stopped pacing and looked at the chief. "Round them up."

Chapter 24

The Committee of Fifteen was sponsored by the mayor, though he considered himself only a figurehead – it was a political stunt to show the people of Tampa that he was in control. The real leader, the street boss, was Chief McGrath who would direct the committee on its mission of law enforcement.

Members of the committee included Arlen Kincaid, cigar manufacturer Don Antonio Vasquez, whose head was wrapped in a bandage, his son Antonito, and Armando Renteria. Armando brought his confidants Benny and Eddie Sanchez, and the chief recruited five of his most competent policemen: Roy Reynolds, Curtis Smith, Michael Hanson, Jim McKibben and Joe Reddey. Rounding off the list of vigilantes were two suggestions from Kincaid, a pair of Tampa businessmen. Harvey Blair, owner of a shipping company that operated from the port, and Richard Herd, owner of a local lumber firm. Both of these men owned significant interests in the cigar trade, and their livelihood was directly connected to the health of the local economy.

These fifteen men met in a conference room at the police station the day after the shooting and the chief of police presented a list of eight men who had been pronounced guilty by the good, law-abiding citizens of Tampa. To each of the committee members, the chief distributed a list of names and addresses with photographs and next of kin.

On the conference room wall was a hierarchy; photographs of the city's labor leaders arranged in a chain of command with Lapár at the top, Mendez and Juan Carlos directly below him with Salvador branching to the side. There were several others completing the hierarchy and the chief stood beside the photographs using them as a visual aid as he addressed the committee.

"Number one, already in custody after last night's exchange, is Juan Carlos Alvarez. A Cuban outlaw and former insurgent, he claims to have fought for the rebels during the Independence War but was later expelled to Florida. He was deported from Tampa last week but promptly returned and organized the four-man shooter team that tried to assassinate Antonio Vasquez. He's a Class A troublemaker and a cancer among the local workforce. He's currently sitting in jail.

"Number two is Angelo 'Lapár' De la Parte, union president and the de facto leader of this rebellion. He paints himself as a family man, and an educated man of reason but he is responsible for organizing the entire radical movement, from the factory walkouts to the daily agitations of our local leftist newspapers. He was recently arrested while carrying a concealed weapon and is a visible presence around Ybor City. We should have no trouble grabbing him today.

"Three is Gabriel Mendez, also known as Sandito or Little Sando. He's a cigar factory *lector*, an agitator and a mouthpiece, and a creator of radical propaganda. Together with De la Parte, Mendez is famous for a daily broadcast of rhetoric that's had a dangerous, persuasive effect on the workers. An arrest warrant has been issued for Mendez for missing a recent court date. He is also the *La Resistencia* treasurer and their top fundraiser, so taking him out should complicate the union's finances.

"Four, Salvador Ortiz, an accomplice of Juan Carlos rumored to have once been a peasant bandit and aid to Cuban insurgents. He is friends with most of the men on this chart, a quiet leader who will surely fill any leadership void. He was deported to Jacksonville with Alvarez but returned and took part in the shooting. He escaped before we could catch him. We can't take the others without taking Ortiz.

"Number five is José Plasencia, an agitator responsible for walkouts at the Cienfuegos, Charles the Great, and Ybor factories. Plasencia is another writer, the West Tampa version of Mendez, with a great deal of influence among the workforce. He's an anarchist from Havana and a vocal instigator who helped organize these recent work stoppages.

"Six is Matías Comenzamas Rodríguez. Small, loud and flamboyant, he has seven citations on record, including vagrancy, disturbing the peace, and reckless endangerment. He goes by the name of Billy. Rodríguez is notorious for distributing communist literature and once stood trial for murder but was acquitted when the star witness died.

"Number seven, Diego Valdivia. Known as Pirolo, a cohort of Rodríguez and Alvarez, he collects union dues for *La Resistencia* and rallies the rank and file. He is also the suspect of several robberies of homes in Hyde Park.

"Finally, number eight, Alexei Mirabel. This was the other surviving shooter arrested last night with Juan Carlos. His background is unknown, and his connection to the labor movement is vague. The guy won't open his mouth and has apparently taken some vow of silence. The only link we can make is his association with Juan Carlos and last night's business at La Morena. He's in custody now and we're not going to let this guy back onto the streets."

"What about the Italian woman?" asked Arlen Kincaid.

"Kidnap a woman?" Armando said. "We're not monsters."

The chief replied. "Alessandria Prizzi may be a vocal presence among the workers but she does not warrant the attention of the men we have named."

Richard Herd asked, "What are we going to do with these men once we have them?"

"That's the first order of business," said the chief. "How do we get these men and what do we do once they've been apprehended? Renteria and Blair have chartered a boat for tomorrow night, for a special mission."

"Tomorrow night," asked Vasquez. "That doesn't give us much time."

"That's your deadline. Two of the eight are already in custody," the chief said. "The other six must be taken before they can reorganize. The committee will be divided into three teams, each responsible for taking two men. You all have rosters with names, addresses and photos of the men you are responsible for arresting. Let's clean the radical element off our streets. Any questions?"

There were none. The mission was clear.

The chief handed each civilian a police badge. "You can all consider yourselves temporary men of the badge. Now let's get to work."

*   *   *

As the *La Resistencia* treasurer, Mendez oversaw how the union raised and spent its money. He managed their income and expenses and controlled all finances through a bank account in his name. When workers pooled their money to support a struggling family, or to finance a soup kitchen for the neighborhood, contributions were funneled to Mendez, who then dispersed the money appropriately.

Since he was not needed as factory *lector* during the strike he occupied himself by organizing fundraising efforts that could sustain the current standoff. Loyal cigar workers and labor groups in Key West, Jacksonville and Havana had gathered modest contributions and sent them to their fellow laborers in Tampa. Mendez received a handful of checks in the mail, totaling over three hundred dollars, more than enough to run a soup kitchen for a couple of months and help some local families with much needed medical expenses. He planned to deposit those checks at the bank on Seventh Avenue, take a few dollars to Father Fernandez at St. Joseph's and then head back to his print shop to work on the next issue of the *Bulletin*.

The shooting the night before gave Mendez plenty to write about.

He folded the checks into his checkbook, which he slipped into the inner pocket of his jacket as he stepped out the front of his shop onto Tenth Avenue. He didn't bother locking the door, and as he turned to go east on Eighth he was suddenly face to face with four men: three of them uniformed police officers.

"Gabriel Mendez?" Officer Reynolds asked.

"Who cares to know?" When Mendez saw the chief of police was one of the cops, he knew the situation was serious.

Reynolds flashed a folded piece of paper. "The city of Tampa is placing you under arrest."

"Does this have anything to do with last night?"

"You missed your court date, Señor Mendez."

Mendez ignored the contempt in the young officer's voice. He obeyed and let the policemen cuff his wrists, wondering why the chief of police was needed to arrest a man delinquent on a court date.

*   *   *

Diego was at the coffee shop on Howard Avenue where every morning he saw his friends from West Tampa. They all knew each other from the same Havana neighborhood called El Cerro, where they had been active in the city's labor movement. During more prosperous times they would meet for coffee, pastries, and breakfasts of fried eggs and rice to discuss politics, women and local affairs. Diego was early today and ordered an affordable breakfast. His *café con leche* was served with a chunk of Cuban bread which he broke apart to dunk in his coffee as he read his Spanish language newspaper.

A police badge suddenly blocked his view of the headlines. Diego followed the hand that held it and saw it belonged to a uniformed police officer whose tag said "Reddey." There was another American officer beside him whose nametag said "McKibben." Diego noticed three more men lurking at the door to the coffee shop, two American businessmen, and a Spaniard with a long, black beard.

Armando Renteria was unmistakable and Diego realized his time had come. A visit from the man with the beard meant he was in serious trouble. He looked sheepishly at Officer Reddey. "What did I do?"

Mendez was thrown into the same cell as Juan Carlos and Alexei, his arrival awakened the former. Juan Carlos sat up on his bench and rubbed his eyes. The sight of Mendez in jail was a surprise. "Now what is the meaning of this?"

"I missed my court date." Mendez sat beside Juan Carlos. He noticed Alexei sitting alone on the other side of the cell. "The chief was there."

"You were arrested by the chief?"

Mendez nodded.

"This is no coincidence," said Juan Carlos. For the first time since Mendez had known him Juan Carlos looked worried. He was no longer the angry bandit but at an isolated crook, a repeat offender at the mercy of an unforgiving city.

"What does he know?" Mendez nodded towards Alexei, who sat quietly and pretended to ignore them.

"He is as good as mute," said Juan Carlos. "He won't say a word about the shooting, or his accomplice. I know he was paid by someone, I'm not sure who, but I can't get him to admit anything."

"What were you doing outside the bar anyway?"

Juan Carlos said nothing about their plans for Armando and regretted not killing him on the trolley. "We came to protect you! We arrived at the wrong time." Juan Carlos pointed at Alexei. "I don't know who he is trying to protect, but I suspect it is the same people who arrested you. I fear we've been set up."

"I share that suspicion."

They sat in silence for several minutes.

Then an officer appeared outside the holding cell. He unlocked and opened the gate and another officer escorted Diego Valdivia into the cell. Juan Carlos stood as he watched his friend Diego, stone-faced, enter the cell and sit beside Alexei.

Juan Carlos held out his hands in amazement. "You've got to be kidding me!"

"They said the distribution of communist literature would no longer be tolerated in this city." Diego exhaled tiredly and sat back to rest against the wall. He closed his eyes.

Juan Carlos, still standing, became the angry bandit again. He jabbed a finger towards Mendez. "Wait and see, Sandito. We are being cleaned off the streets like a pack of mad dogs."

Salvador returned to the boarding house after the shooting but he didn't remain there for long. Knowing he needed to leave town right away, he returned to Carlito's apartment to gather his things: a canvass backpack with some clothes, thirty dollars in cash, a pocket watch, his pistol and his father's rusted knife.

Suddenly he was fourteen again, a fleeing orphan with no possessions except for what he carried in his pack. Salvador made his way across town to the clinic early the next morning and knocked to announce his presence before he stepped inside. "Fina!" he called for Josefina as he entered. Andres appeared in the foyer. His glasses were missing and his shirt unbuttoned at the collar – it looked like he had been up all night tending to a sick patient.

"Salvador what are you doing here?"

They embraced briefly, and then Josefina appeared at the end of the hallway. Salvador remembered it had been some time since he had seen

314

his family. They had no idea about the shooting at La Morena, or that he had been deported to Jacksonville. Salvador realized there were still scratches and bruises on his forehead and that his family was not aware of the mock lynching either.

Josefina, keen that something was amiss came forward for a closer look at her father. She saw the backpack, the scars and the urgent, almost frightful look in her father's eyes. "Papa, what's wrong?"

"I'm leaving. I'm going to New Orleans to find Lázaro."

Matías Rodríguez decided to run. He darted into the alley between Sixth and Seventh Avenues and hid behind a pair of garbage bins. He did not know exactly why the police were chasing him, but there was the robbery and rape of the widow Eva on Third Avenue, for which Matías had already denied responsibility. There were numerous petty cons and shakedowns to his credit, all enough to attract the attention of Tampa policemen, who had been chasing him since he'd been spotted loitering outside the brewery on Fifth Avenue.

Matías crouched behind the waste bins, panting and gasping for air as his clothes became sticky with perspiration. It was a hot and humid August morning, with a sun that blazed above a clear sky. His stamina was low and his body used its energy to cool itself off. Matías yearned for a glass of cold water, even a puddle to splash a few handfuls onto his face. If he could only lose these police officers, his next move would be to stop in the nearest café for a glass of lemonade.

He heard voices coming from Sixteenth Street, and a moment later two police officers appeared in the alley. They jogged past his hiding place without a glance. Searching doorways and windows of the brick buildings, the police paid close attention to the fire escapes and the rooftops. Matías could have escaped had he remained in place and let the officers pass, but he tried to make a break for Sixteenth Street.

He rose from behind the trashcans and hurried to slip into the alley and around the corner but in his haste, he knocked one of the trashcans to its side. Dozens of empty glass bottles spilled onto the ground with a terrible racket of clanking of bottles and shattering glass. The officers were nearly a block away but turned and saw Matías fleeing the scene and turning south as he reached Sixteenth.

"Rodríguez! Stop right there!" called Officer Roy Reynolds. They sprinted back towards Sixteenth where Richard Herd and the chief appeared, chasing Matías from the north. The train station was at Sixteenth and Sixth, but no train was present and there were hardly any travelers among which Matías could lose himself, so he jumped the tracks and continued south. Exhausted and unable to keep his pace for more than a block, he was tackled by Reynolds and Herd between Fourth and Fifth Avenues and handcuffed by the chief.

The Sanchez brothers received a tip on an immigrant soup kitchen that had opened in the north part of Ybor City beyond Thirteenth Avenue. One of the men on their list, José Plasencia, was rumored to be the organizer.

Benny paid the informant a dollar and with his brother, regrouped with Kincaid, Officer Smith, and Antonio Vasquez. When they arrived at the tenement, they found a noisy group socializing outside as people walked in and out of the busy house. The Sanchez brothers split from the others and covered the back in case their subject attempted to flee, while Kincaid, Smith, and Vasquez marched to the front door. The people outside stopped talking when Kincaid and Officer Smith flashed their badges and entered the house.

The noisy home became instantly silent. Moments passed and suddenly a young Latin male burst from the front door, deflected off Vasquez and nearly fell to the ground. Kincaid and Smith followed and were on top of Plasencia before he could fight while Officer Smith fiddled for his handcuffs.

Nearly a dozen cigar workers stood on the front porch and cursed the arresting officers. Once the thirty-year-old Plasencia was cuffed, Smith stood and whirled to face the group, his pistol in his hand. Smith said, "This man is a criminal and an enemy of the state of Florida. I urge you cigar makers to return to work today, or else face similar consequences."

One man on the porch replied. "There are over a thousand cigar makers waiting for management to abandon their stubborn policies so we can return to the factories. What has this man done to set himself apart? If you take him, you should take all of us!"

Plasencia was an intellectual who took pride in his clean-shaven appearance and felt these attributes gave him clout and respect. He spoke up and called to his people. "Do not worry about me! This fight will continue even in my absence. Do not return to work until our labor union is reinstated with a closed-shop!" Realizing his apprehension had been decided upon hours before, and that there was no way to prevent it, Plasencia let himself be arrested without struggle.

By afternoon Lapár had learned that armed gangs had been roaming the streets of Ybor City nabbing high-profile labor leaders one by one. Alessandria had hurried to Lapár's house and told him what she knew: that José Plasencia and Gabriel Mendez had been arrested and that Matías Rodríguez had been tackled and beaten by an armed gang near Fifth Avenue.

Lapár's wife pleaded with him. "Call off this strike and send your people back to work!"

Her argument was useless. "It is no longer a matter of labor," he explained as went to the bedroom to pack a bag. "This has become a struggle greater than commerce and industry. We are fighting for the dignity and self-respect of an entire society."

"Where are you going?"

"I'm not sure but I can't stay in Tampa. I am surprised they have not been to the house already. There is a large and extremely friendly culture in Havana. Perhaps I can stowaway on a boat."

His wife raised her hands in the air. "Stowaway! Has he gone mad!?"

Lapár's two young boys stayed near their mother, following Esmeralda like pair of ducklings as she pranced across the parlor.

"He is right," Alessandria said. "If he stays here any longer he'll surely be arrested. And only God knows what this gang has planned."

There was a loud knock at the door. The voice of a white man called out, "Angelo De la Parte, come out!"

Esmeralda grabbed her husband's sleeve and quietly begged for him to remain but he pulled away. "I will not make a scene." He turned to Alessandria. "You had better find someplace to hide. Here, in the closet."

Another knock at the door and then it opened. Lapár greeted his visitors in the parlor as though he was happy to see a Tampa police

317

officer and Arlen Kincaid stepping into the house. Behind them, the Sanchez brothers waited on the porch with Antonio Vasquez.

Lapár smiled politely. "Gentlemen, how can I help you?"

Kincaid said, "The mayor would like to speak to you downtown."

"Does it have something to do with that business last night? I thought our negotiations were proceeding smoothly when those ruffians arrived and scared everybody away. I'm very pleased that the mayor would like to sit down and close the deal."

"I have no idea what he has to say," Kincaid said.

Lapár nodded. He knew these men were not here to invite him to a friendly meeting with the mayor. They would likely rough him up on the way to the station – if taking him to the station was their plan – before throwing him into a cell to let him rot.

Esmeralda was suddenly tugging at his shirt. "Don't go with them, Angelo! It's a trick! A trick!" She looked to the porch to see Vasquez standing outside with a bandage around his head and worried that whatever violence he'd encountered would soon extend to her husband.

Lapár smiled, trying his best to maintain his confidence in front of his boys. "I'll be home before the dinner hour." Thinking of his courageous submission as an act of bravery before his sons, Lapár stepped forward.

"No," she begged as tears spilled from her eyes and dripped off her cheeks. "Don't go, Angelo! Don't go!"

Officer Smith stepped in and gently took her by the wrists. "Ma'am, don't make this difficult for your husband. He has decided to come with us voluntarily."

"Don't touch me!" she screamed at a volume so loud it startled Vasquez and the Sanchez brothers. Officer Smith backed away as Kincaid escorted Lapár out of the house; the dignified union president refusing to put up a fight.

Alessandria waited a few minutes before emerging from her hiding place. Esmeralda was crying in the kitchen as her boys watched from either side, seeming to have forgotten about the Italian woman's presence. Alessandria wondered for a moment if she should say something to comfort Lapár's wife but decided it would be useless. She slipped out the back door and headed south towards her apartment.

After they dropped Diego at the police station, Armando and his crew traveled to the northeast corner of Ybor City to the house listed as the residence of Salvador Ortiz. The front door was unlocked when they arrived and Armando peered into the empty house. He turned to Officers Reddey and McKibben. "Looks quiet. Maybe they moved out."

The officers nodded and waited for Armando.

"Let's station some men at the port and the train station in case he tries to leave town."

Salvador was a teenager again, fighting the Spanish in order to avenge his mother, his father, the village of Herrera, and El Matón. He was fighting for the people of Piro, for the cigar makers of Tampa, for Juan Carlos and Gabriel Mendez, for Olympia, and for his children. He considered killing Armando before leaving town. Would eliminating Armando end the strike and send the cigar workers victoriously back to work?

Possibly.

Juan Carlos was in custody and probably dead. Mendez, Lapár, and the rest of the group had probably dispersed throughout town. Maybe some of them had been lucky to escape to Key West or Havana before the armed gangs took to the streets to clean the so-called mongrels from the city.

Salvador would have to do it alone, and then leave town as soon as possible.

As he drifted off to sleep his last thought was of Olympia, seventeen years old and plodding through the brush with baby Josefina in her arms, having just escaped Testifonte's mansion.

He awoke early the next morning, checked his pistol, picked up his bag and money, and let himself out of the clinic before Josefina could protest.

As he walked to the train station, he encountered groups of cigar makers speckled throughout the streets, gathered in little huddles and gossiping intensely. Careful to avoid these excited groups Salvador hurried through town and arrived at the train station just before nine. He bought a ticket for the 10:00, bound for Jacksonville, Tallahassee and New Orleans.

Perhaps it was the nature of Salvador's mission that made the streets seem busier, but out-of-work cigar makers were everywhere. He hurried to Armando's office in the center of town and watched every direction for signs of police officers, and to ensure that wherever he was, there was clear access to an escape route. Moments later he stood across from Armando's building on Fifteenth Street. As the pistol grew heavy in his pocket, Salvador watched the building and waited for the investor to appear.

"You work for me, don't you?"

Salvador was suddenly face to face with a man he did not expect to see: Antonio Vasquez. He had rarely seen the manufacturer up close, and Vasquez wore a fresh bandage around his head which puffed like a tiny pillow where extra gauze covered his wounded temple. For such a casual encounter, Salvador wondered why Vasquez seemed to be inspecting him so closely, questioning every detail of his face, attempting to confirm in his own mind that this man was one of his workers.

Salvador knew he was in trouble. He didn't know exactly why, but something about this encounter was not right. Vasquez, meanwhile, knew he had only moments to have Salvador arrested but had no credibility to do it alone. Upon seeing the rogue and exiled cigar maker lurking on the sidewalk, Vasquez sent his son to find the chief or any member of the committee to assist in the apprehension. Vasquez would have to stall Salvador until Antonito returned.

Salvador answered Vasquez. "I did work for you, yes, before the strike."

Vasquez nodded, not sure what to say next.

Salvador filled the gap. "I must be going."

As Salvador started to walk away, Vasquez walked with him, looking over his shoulder in the direction his son went. "You're a respected member of the work force," Vasquez said. "Let me buy you a cup of coffee, Salvador. Perhaps we can work out some kind of agreement, a way to bring your people back to work?"

Salvador started walking faster. "Another time perhaps, Don Antonio, right now I need to catch a train. I am headed out of town to visit my son."

"How charming," Vasquez walked faster, practically jogging to stay beside the anxious cigar maker. It was clear that Salvador was keen to his motives, and Vasquez hoped he wouldn't have to tackle the cigar maker and bring him down in the middle of the city. "What time does your train leave? Fifteen minutes is all we'll need."

"I'm sorry, but I don't want to miss my train." Salvador broke into a light jog. He knew Vasquez wanted something more than a fifteen minute coffee break. He wanted Salvador arrested. Despite his size and weight, Vasquez was able to keep up. Salvador quickened his pace and opened some distance between the cigar manufacturer, knowing the plan to oust Armando had been delayed.

"He's right here!" Vasquez suddenly shouted. Salvador looked up to see Armando and the chief of police round the corner directly in front of him, less than one block away. The situation was grim. Antonio Vasquez directly behind him, the chief and Armando coming his way, Juan Carlos in jail suspected of murder and Salvador likely destined to join him.

He darted into a café and weaved among the tables, hurrying to the back with the agility of a young athlete. Armando and the chief ran to meet Vasquez outside. "Don't just stand there," shouted the chief. "Go after him!"

They ran inside, bumping into the patrons of the half-filled café and looking at every face. Armando led the way, followed by the chief and then Vasquez. They moved quickly though the café, passing by the bar and ducking into the kitchen. The proprietor, a man in his forties, and his teenage daughter turned to look as the three men entered. The chief held up his badge and asked if a man had been through there. The proprietor nodded his head and moved closer to his daughter, ready to protect her from the violence that all local citizens knew of.

"The bathroom," Vasquez said and led them out of the kitchen.

They burst into the musty men's room to find an empty cell with a trough and a commode that was unoccupied. A glass window above the sink was closed. They looked at each other for moment – no one needed to suggest that they try the room next door.

Not bothering to knock, they pushed open the door to the ladies' bathroom and saw the glass window above the sink was opened. Armando climbed to the sink and looked out the window into the alley between buildings. He saw the unmistakable shape of Salvador fleeing down the alley and turning south around a corner.

"He's there!" Armando shouted and the men clamored over each other and hurried out of the café to chase the committee's final target.

They would be right behind him soon. If only Salvador had not told Vasquez that he was headed for the train station. A stupid mistake he never would have made if Juan Carlos had been with him! He should have worn a disguise, been more cunning in his approach, and gone to Armando's earlier. Now he ran at top speed across Sixteenth Street and then south to Seventh Avenue. The train station waited on the next block. As clouds rolled in from the gulf and thunder rumbled overhead Salvador wondered if he'd be able to hide somewhere.

He checked the board when he arrived at the crowded station and saw the 10:00 was still on schedule and would leave in fifteen minutes. A voice called out, "Train thirty-two, the ten o'clock, bound for Jacksonville and Tallahassee. All aboard!"

His heart rested, his body relaxed as the sky exploded and started to pour. He reached into his pocket and thumbed his train ticket. Umbrellas opened, elbows and shoulders were everywhere as people hurried to cover themselves from the rain. Salvador had no umbrella, but he pushed towards the railcars using the rising canopy of umbrellas as further cover from his chasers.

He was not the only patron pushing for a railcar, and the crowd of people quickly flooded towards the train as if a drain had been unstopped and was sucking them towards dry safety. Salvador was bumped and knocked left and right and to his horror, he felt something fall from his pack and land on the concrete with a dull twang.

His father's knife. Salvador turned against the crowd as rain soaked him from above and blurred his vision. Dropping to the ground, Salvador crawled on hands and knees trying to locate the knife as passengers stumbled over him, stepped on his hands, called him names, and shouted for him to get out of the way.

He saw the rusty blade and the dull wooden handle sitting among a mess of puddles and shoes just a few feet away. He reached for it but was suddenly pulled to his feet by two sets of hands before he could grasp the knife. Salvador was suddenly looking at the glistening raindrops in the black beard of Armando Renteria. Handcuffs were clamped around Salvador's wrists, and as Vasquez watched with a satisfied smile, Chief McGrath announced, "You're under arrest for conspiring to murder Antonio Vasquez."

Chapter 25

The prisoners were given a dinner of ham sandwiches, apples, and water around midnight and told to enjoy their meal as it may be their last. Then, their arms tied behind their backs with rope, the prisoners were herded out of the jail and taken to a waiting streetcar, which had its lights out, the electricity having been shut off.

Salvador recognized several guards on the car as prominent men of Tampa. The Sanchez brothers, Antonio Vasquez, Arlen Kincaid and several Tampa police officers. Once all were on board the car started to move – though the lights remained off – and took them through downtown Tampa to a rank, abandoned warehouse beside the Hillsborough River.

Armando waited there with Chief McGrath as the prisoners arrived. The labor leaders were arranged in a line, and one by one Armando and the chief held a lantern to each man's face to be sure they had captured the right person before the chief ordered his team to load the prisoners onto a motor boat that waited at the riverbank. Slowly and unaided by lanterns or any source of light, the boat quietly moved along the dark river and into Hillsborough Bay, only the faint rumble of the motor marked its presence.

They arrived at Ballast Point, a beach so dark and quiet it resembled a cemetery in the middle of the night. The eight men were dragged aboard a waiting tugboat by the police officers, but Matías Rodríguez decided to put up a fight and was quickly beaten to the dirt by the fists of the powerful Sanchez brothers amid derisive jeering from the abductors on the dock. His bloody and beaten body was thrown onto the tugboat with his comrades, where he flopped to the ground like a corpse. The prisoners were quickly surrounded by members of the committee and the tug left the dock and headed into the bay where the schooner *Marie Cooper* rode at anchor with all sails set.

The men were transferred to the ship under heavy guard and only the police officers remained on board as the prisoners were taken below and ordered into the hold. Rowdy, burly men from the ship's American crew drank, laughed and played cards while they shouted insults at the Cubans.

A stiff breeze soon carried the boat to sea.

Four monotonous days passed while the kidnapped men were kept in ignorance about their fate and their destination. The heat was unbearable and the smell of diesel was nauseating. Unsatisfied by the inadequate scraps of food thrown to them by the ship's brutish crew, the prisoners became agitated and Juan Carlos spoke of a revolt, but his uprising was quickly squelched.

They were tied, blindfolded, and forced to their knees at gunpoint. The prisoners huddled together in a group, growing weaker each hour as they imaged themselves at the cusp of death. Salvador's hands had been bound behind his back with his own leather belt. His mouth had been gagged with one of his socks and the other had been used as a blindfold. His knees were raw and splintered from rocking back and forth on the boat's jagged wooden floor for miles and miles.

The blindfolds disoriented the prisoners and spoiled all concept of place or time. Minutes passed as if they were hours; the prisoners were starved, deprived of sleep, and unable even to use the bathroom. Their pants became soiled and in the humid cabin air, made a miserable stink of feces and urine.

To distract himself from his own suffering, Salvador concentrated on the musty taste of the sock in his mouth. He tried to think of his family, of Lázaro, but could not remember his son's face. Unable to stand the dank, putrid air or the infuriating heat, Salvador vomited the bile from his stomach and collapsed beside the other seven prisoners, the musty sock that gagged his mouth became soaked with stomach acid.

Finally the boat eased to a stop and the boots of several men stomped down the stairs to the prisoners' hold. A pair of hands grabbed Salvador by the shoulders and somehow his legs managed to prop him up. His soles were bare and his body supplied one last burst of strength that propelled him to his feet. He heard a metallic click and snap as someone pulled on a pistol's hammer and locked it into place. As the prisoners were herded topside, Salvador expected to be executed.

He wondered why they had waited so long. It would have been more expedient to execute the prisoners days ago, before the endless torture of the boat trip, but this was like war, his captors the callous agitators.

When he reached the top of the stairs, the dank, suffocating odor of excrement and fuel faded into a refreshing, salty breeze and the empty sound of ocean all around. His gag and blindfold were removed, and Salvador, expecting to be greeted by a blast of sunlight, was disappointed that it was nighttime and almost completely dark. His eyes were nearly useless after being confined under a stale black sock for days and he was slow to adjust to this blurry group of men that surrounded him.

He was overcome by a sudden and frightening quiet.

Salvador listened, expecting to hear a gunshot, but heard only men's voices speaking in careful, muffled English. Then it came: a pop and a flash of light. He waited for a body to slump to the deck or fall overboard with a dead splash but the sound never came.

Another snap and burst of light.

Salvador saw not a gun but a camera and flashbulb. The prisoners were being photographed one by one and when the camera flashed a third time Salvador saw his environment for a moment, frozen in a flash of light. There were six or eight guards, shadows in shadows, carrying rifles, ropes, or clubs of lumber like sinister agents of judgment. Carlito's face had become pale and angular like a soulless skull wrapped in leather. Lapár's shirt hung awkwardly from boney shoulders like an oversized sack, ready to fall off with the slightest tug.

As Salvador tried to orient himself, sensing open water all around, the cameraman suddenly appeared before him. The silver dish of the flashbulb hovered before Salvador's face like a full moon. Light exploded and stung his eyes, blinding him with white light.

Now a voice called out in Spanish. "By order of the people of Tampa, you will be landed on foreign soil, far enough away to prevent a return to the United States. Be seen in Tampa again and it means death!"

Salvador was bewildered. Having survived the grueling voyage, his life had been spared, but what punishment waited on this foreign land?

The prisoners were loaded onto lifeboats in pairs. As his eyes adjusted to the darkness Salvador found Mendez and saw the writer had managed to keep his glasses, though he had shed several pounds during the journey. The skin of his once pudgy face had tightened, and hair that was usually shiny and tidy was wild and dry. He seemed more fatigued than frightened as he was shoved onto a lifeboat with Plasencia and two police officers.

A pistol dug into Salvador's back as a hand pushed him into a different boat. Someone tossed Salvador's belt, socks and shoes into the boat as Juan Carlos joined him. They sat facing each other with an armed guard at the bow and another at the stern. Salvador and Juan Carlos locked eyes but did not speak. As the boat was lowered to the water they knew that if they survived whatever waited, a time would come when they would attempt their revenge.

As soon as their boat touched the water, the prisoners were untied, handed oars and ordered to paddle. Clouds broke overhead, and a curtain of crawling moonlight made the wave tips sparkle. More paddling soon revealed a long, low stretch of sandy beach without a single sign of human habitation.

The boats landed, the prisoners stepped onto the beach and saw the jungle stretched endlessly in both directions. Beyond the foliage loomed the dark wall of a mountain. Officer Reddey unloaded a meager supply of provisions from one of the boats: a box of soda crackers, three cans of beef, two small hams, and a gallon jug of water to be shared among eight starving men. The prisoners watched in dire silence as the boats returned to the schooner and the ship began to move away, marked by a single lantern on the deck that quickly disappeared into the darkness.

And then they were alone.

They collapsed onto the beach and started to divide one of the hams. "Okay, Sandito," Juan Carlos said to Mendez. "You know the atlas. You can read *Robinson Crusoe* in both English and Spanish. Tell us where we are and what to do."

Mendez stared blankly towards the sea and chewed a piece of ham. "We may be in Central America, Nicaragua perhaps? Your guess is as good as mine."

Everyone was silent as they gobbled their small share of meat. Salvador noticed one of them lying motionless beside Lapár. "What's wrong with him?"

Lapár raised an eyebrow and bit into his portion. "He's dead." Salvador saw how the journey had aged Lapár by five years and wondered how long the union president, the professor, would last on the beach.

Salvador looked over to the body. "Who is it?"

"Matías Rodríguez." After the beating that Matías had taken he had bled internally for most of the trip and died before he reached the shore.

Salvador rested on his back and clasped his hands over his chest. How quickly they had been reduced to seven. He wondered how long it would take to get to six. Their problems were no longer of labor struggles, social integration or class warfare. Fights against Spanish colonialism and *yanqui* capitalism were suddenly insignificant.

Salvador said, "We need to find a city, or a port where we can catch a boat."

"I still have this," said Mendez. The men saw he was holding a checkbook.

Juan Carlos threw his head back and laughed. "A checkbook! Go cash it under the palm trees and watch out for falling coconuts, you fool. What are we going to do with a checkbook?"

Mendez was serious. "If we can find our way into town we can purchase tickets on a boat. Or send a telegram to Tampa and let them know what happened."

"Ridiculous," said Juan Carlos. "How are we going to send a telegram from the jungle?"

"We send it when we find a city."

"We don't even know where we are!"

Salvador said, "We'll wait for the light of the morning, and then we can climb these peaks and have a look around."

"If we haven't been killed by poisonous bugs or wild animals," Juan Carlos said. The rest became silent and strained their ears for any clues of wildlife. All they heard was the water and the worrying buzz of a thousand mosquitoes.

"Pleasant dreams," Juan Carlos said as he laid back and closed his eyes. "You can send telegrams and climb mountains in the morning, if you survive. I'll see you then."

Salvador looked towards the ocean where the sky faded from black to purple. He realized he was looking to the east, where the morning sun would soon break.

Tampa Daily News

Perpetrators of Cowardly Ambush Deported
Along with Fellow Agitators

Editorial by Arlen Kincaid
August 7, 1901

Trouble broke out this week at La Morena when a group of ruffians took it into their heads to fire some twenty rounds into the establishment during a meeting between Tampa's civil and business representatives and the leaders of the La Resistencia labor union. One of the would-be assailants was killed in a resulting shootout with Tampa police and others – with direct links to the outlawed labor union – were arrested and taken into custody. The Daily News is pleased to announce that the instigators did not go unpunished.

It seems that feelings of ill will had been brewing for some time.

For weeks, the militant workers' union and dominant labor force in Tampa has staged a walkout of Tampa's cigar factories. But the strike was not limited to cigars: the union also organized bakers, carpenters, bartenders, waiters and laundry workers. A group of these dissatisfied men staged a demonstration outside the Olivia Cigar factory, where shots were fired into the building and a bookkeeper was killed. The two perpetrators were quickly brought to justice.

Since then, there has been widespread labor trouble. Work is suspended, and the very mention of returning to the factories has elicited insults and threats from the likes of the cigar workers.

All of the above culminated in the cowardly attempted murder of cigar factory owner Antonio Vasquez who managed to survive with a minor bullet wound. For the next day, the town was in a state of excitement as little groups of men were gathered all over the streets discussing the exchange.

A very great and cowardly crime was committed at La Morena. The good people of Tampa, of whatever nationality, have the duty to lend assistance towards the punishment of such crimes. For some weeks these gangs of bandits and their ringleaders have, by their actions, done much to intimidate the proprietors of the cigar factories and the law-abiding citizens who reside here.

At last the proprietors of the cigar factories of Ybor City and West Tampa appealed solemnly to the citizens of Tampa for aid in ridding their town of these characters. A special meeting of Tampa's business leaders was called last week for the purpose of taking such steps as might be necessary to rid our community of its lawless element. A committee of our most prominent citizens was appointed and notified these outlaws to leave at once.

There were eight of these suspects who have since been deported.

Though the strike continues, and peace and quiet have not been fully resumed in Ybor City, the removal of these radical agitators will surely have the salutary effect upon any other Cuban, Spanish or Italian citizens or anarchists who may still be lurking in our midst.

VII.

THE JUNGLE

Chapter 26

Salvador was dressed in his best suit. A black number with white pinstripes and a black and white tie, with a white silk handkerchief in the pocket. With a fresh shave and a haircut, fingernails that were cleanly cut, and shoes polished to a high shine, he was ready to enjoy the sights, sounds and smells of Ybor City's Seventh Avenue on Saturday night. Everywhere there was music, laughter, fresh baked bread, smoked fish, and simmering black beans cooked with plenty of garlic and onion. Merchants sold fresh fruits and roasted nuts to the throngs from wooden pushcarts, and friends exchanged gossip along the sidewalk.

Salvador rode his horse Chani along the excited street and navigated through the hordes of people. Olympia sat directly before him in a fancy white satin dress like the one she wore for her confirmation ceremony in Cuba. Salvador's arms were wrapped around her waist, and the horse's reins dangled from his hands. Olympia's hair was curled and decorated with flowers, and she smelled of fresh perfume.

As the couple's horse trotted down Seventh Avenue, the applauding crowd threw flowers and parted to let them through. Salvador waved modestly to the admirers and Olympia smiled radiantly with her hands folded gently on her lap. Salvador surveyed the faces as they rode through and saw even Armando Renteria and Antonio Vasquez smiled and waved. In the midst of a wall of grins and applause, Salvador saw Fortunado waving the headless body of his champion rooster above his head before he threw it towards Salvador. Then Picchu's severed head appeared in Fortunado's mouth, which he spat towards Olympia before smiling to show his blood-stained teeth. Salvador looked to his wife's lap and saw she carried a handful of chicken livers and kidneys. She happily turned to Salvador as she cradled the slimy guts. "I can take these home to Gloria and make a soup!"

A scowling Juan Carlos suddenly stepped in front of Salvador's horse and blocked its progress. He wore clean pants and a pressed shirt, like he was going to work, and his hands were dark and sticky with tobacco. Salvador pulled on Chani's reins, halted, and stared down at his friend's passive and expressionless face. The crowd became silent and watched the standoff. Salvador reached into his pocket, removed a .38 revolver and fired a shot at his friend's chest. The bullet ricocheted off Juan Carlos, hit Chani and shattered the animal like glass. Salvador fell to the ground with a thud.

Olympia disappeared and the crowd instantly turned their attention to other matters. Salvador sat on the street and brushed dirt off his suit then looked up to see El Matón smiling at him, a flaming torch in one hand and a rusted machete in the other. The grinning bandit leader thrust the torch into Salvador's side and burned through his suit, blistering and sizzling Salvador's flesh.

Salvador was suddenly wearing his street clothes, and as he lifted his shirt to inspect the wound, he saw a swarm of a hundred ants crawling across his belly. He slapped at them furiously and realized he was lying on a sandy patch of beach, sprawled face-down on top of a giant ant mound. He sprang to his feet and ran to the water, submerging himself to drown the fiery insects. Their bites had stung a spotted rash onto his skin, and the saltwater burned like acid.

When he finished rinsing, Salvador emerged from the water and saw a deserted beach and his counterparts resting in shade of jungle lining the shore. Juan Carlos slept upright against a palm tree with his arms folded and his head hanging and Salvador wondered if his friend would be better off if someone really did put a bullet through his chest.

Then Salvador thought of Mendez the bookworm and Lapár the politico, two men who were unaccustomed to the rugged outdoors. Salvador wondered how they would hinder the journey home. It was clear to Salvador that Juan Carlos was the only member of the group who could reliably survive in the wild.

Mendez awoke next, then the others. As Salvador removed his wet clothes and lined them on the sunny beach to dry, Juan Carlos stood, unzipped his pants and urinated against a palm tree before joining Salvador at the shore.

"Unbelievable," Carlito muttered as he turned to survey the jungle and the massive wall of mountain that dwarfed it.

"We need to figure out where we are," Salvador said. The first of their two hams had been consumed, and the men had been left with no tools, map or supplies.

Already a powerful heat was arriving with the morning sun.

"It is as if we are the first humans to ever set foot on this land," Juan Carlos said as he surveyed the endless tropical rainforest. "I would say this was Oriente, but we were on the boat too long to have been taken to Cuba."

"There are no mountains like this in the Caribbean."

"You know that for sure?" Juan Carlos said scornfully. "I forgot you've been to every island in the Caribbean."

Salvador ignored Carlito's jab and joined Mendez and Lapár in the shade. The two intellectuals squatted and pointed to a map they had drawn in the sand with sticks and rocks. Diego and José hovered above them while Alexei slept with his back flat against the sand nearby.

Lapár explained, "Tropical mountains like these can only be found in Venezuela and Central America. Costa Rica, Nicaragua, or Honduras perhaps. Any of those countries have plenty of sparse locations to deposit miscreants such as us."

Diego scratched his head with a pair of thick fingers. "I have been to Venezuela and this looks very much like that place."

José laughed. "You think this is Venezuela just because you have been there once and this place looks familiar?"

Lapár said, "The trip was too short for this to be Venezuela."

Diego challenged the labor leader. "You looked like you were passed out most of the trip, Lapár. Tell us, how long were we on that boat?"

Lapár paused to think, but before he could answer Mendez did. "Today is Sunday, the eleventh of August."

Juan Carlos laughed at the absurdity of Mendez's claim. "That means we were on the boat for five days. Five days without eating? I have gone five days without eating, and I will tell you, you would not be this alert after a five day fast. And it doesn't matter how many pitiful scraps of moldy ham you've eaten since landing!"

"You're exaggerating," Salvador said. "When have you ever gone five days without eating?"

Juan Carlos straightened and stepped closer. "Long before I met *you*, my friend."

"Enough!" Lapár shouted and halted the argument. "Regardless of where we are, we need to decide how and when to consume the rest of the food."

"What about him?" José pointed towards the beach where the bloated body of Matías Rodriguez grew pale on the sand.

"We bury him," Juan Carlos said. "But not before taking his shoes and clothes."

The others looked at him incredulously, but Salvador agreed. "Juan Carlos is right. His shoes may be useful." He wished he had his father's knife and cursed himself for losing it, trying to remain unruffled by his careless loss of the sacred heirloom.

After the men dug a grave and shoved Matías's naked body into the earth, Mendez rolled onto his back, exhausted and disgusted. "If Dante could see us he'd open another Circle of Hell."

They agreed to eat the second ham before it spoiled, and to regain their strength, but decided the canned beef and crackers should be saved for another day. They each sipped water from the jug, carefully rationing their portion before they broke into teams to forage for fruit and fresh water.

Salvador slipped back into his pants and socks, which were still damp, and he wore Matías's leather shoes instead of his own, setting his footwear in the hot sun to dry. The sun was unbearable, and Salvador estimated the temperature to be close to a hundred degrees. He eagerly joined Juan Carlos on a trek for fruit through the shaded jungle. The air was still hot under the dense green foliage, and just as humid, but Salvador's wet pants actually helped keep him cool. Both men had sweated through their shirts and though their clothes stuck to their wet bodies, the shirts protected their skin from the swarms of mosquitoes that followed and nipped their exposed skin.

"What do you think we should do, Ortiz?" Carlito asked. "Try to make our way through this jungle or stay on the beach and hope to see a passing ship?"

"Without a rifle we can't hunt. Without a net we can't fish." He remembered Olympia's words. *"The necessities of that lifestyle are nothing more than luxuries meant to satisfy the very desire they create."* How he longed to stand in Testifonte's mansion and surround himself with more riches than a peasant boy could ever need!

Their hunt brought nothing but bugs, branches, and roots. They returned to the beach empty handed and were appalled to see their counterparts devouring the soda crackers. Juan Carlos ran to them, his arms raised indignantly above his head. "You cannot eat everything we have!"

They stopped chewing and listened.

"We must ration our food and consume as little as we can. I do not want to spend every waking minute searching for rotten fruits and berries."

Diego's voice was muffled by a mouth stuffed with crackers. "And how many of these so-called fruits and berries did you provide?"

Juan Carlos pointed at him. "You, dear friend, are being particularly wasteful!"

Diego waved him off but Lapár stood to explain. "We are starving, Carlito. I know we need to ration our food, but we have barely eaten in days. We should eat most of what we have now and discuss rationing tomorrow."

Juan Carlos was unmoved. "You have made this decision?"

Before Lapár answered, Salvador said, "Juan Carlos is right, we need to conserve what we have. But we also need to regain our strength if we are to survive. Let's finish the crackers and one can of beef. We can save the other two cans for another day."

The men slowly started to nibble on their crackers again. Diego handed one to Juan Carlos who reluctantly took it in his hand and swallowed it in one bite. Mendez used a rock to puncture one of the tins of beef and spent nearly five minutes prying the metal apart.

After their small meal they moved into the shade to rest. As they dozed and quietly slapped at the mosquitoes, José mused. "If we could climb these mountains, we could have a look around, possibly see a nearby settlement."

"That is no small feat," Juan Carlos laughed.

José shrugged. "Just an idea."

As he began to slip into a hot, sandy sleep Salvador craved a cup of coffee with sugar. Sugar! He hadn't tasted any in more than a week. A creamy *café con leche* with a pair of ladyfingers, the last stop at bliss on the road to the end.

Salvador thought of God but not in a dogmatic sense. He wondered if the Maker could be so merciless as to lengthen their suffering. If Salvador was to die in the jungle, he hoped that Death would come disguised as sleep to greet him as a welcomed friend.

Salvador awoke hours later harassed as a powerful rain pelted his face. The rest of the men moved deeper into the jungle and crouched against the shelter of the trees as Salvador took the jug and set it on the beach to catch rainwater. For hours they were drenched in the downpour and by the time it ended, the sun was beyond the mountain, robbing them of the light that would dry their clothes.

Too tired and too miserable to squeeze the rain from their clothes, and knowing a journey for food into the dark forest was pointless, the men sat close together at the edge of the jungle. "Does anyone have a cigar?" Juan Carlos joked.

Salvador realized another unfulfilled addiction – tobacco. He had not noticed the jitters of withdrawal until that moment and craved a strong *maduro* as much as he wanted a plate of *paella* and the jug of red wine that would precede it.

As darkness fell, the sounds of the jungle became more obvious. Life was abundant in the rainforest. From the terrible buzzing of insects to the panicked scurry of small animals, the sounds of the night were an ominous reminder that they were not alone on this shore. As waves crashed to the beach and leaves and branches rustled above them under the weight of some midnight creature, the most apparent sound was the absence of man. There were no ringing trolley bells, no shouting spectators betting on gamecocks or cheering a *bolita* throw, no Spanish guitars, no gossip among neighbors and no laughter among friends.

*   *   *

340

"What about rubbing two sticks together?"

Salvador shrugged. "I've never seen that done."

Mendez nodded. "I've heard it takes a lot of practice. I wouldn't even know where to begin."

"That doesn't surprise me," Juan Carlos said as he removed his wet clothes and set them to dry on the sand in the morning sun. "I don't suppose you can remember any hints from those little adventure books you like to read?"

Mendez ignored him.

"Let's try your glasses," suggested Salvador who angled Mendez's glasses to concentrate sunlight on a small pile of leaves, but with no success.

"Good try," Mendez said as he slipped his glasses back in place. "I don't see how we survive if we remain on this beach. We need to start walking."

As Salvador inspected a pattern of tiny cuts that had appeared on his fingertips, Juan Carlos nudged him and pointed towards the pile of sand where Matías rested. The storm had eroded the grave and exposed a pair of pale, lifeless fingers.

"I hate to tell you this, my friend," Carlito whispered. "But there is still good meat under that sand."

Salvador, sickened at the thought of eating human flesh, of eating Matías, winced and shook his head.

"But you can't deny that you have already considered it."

"I'll deny it," Salvador said quickly. He moved away from Juan Carlos and joined a debate taking place between Lapár, Diego, and José. The writer from West Tampa told Lapár, "Anything is better than sitting in the hot sun swatting mosquitoes."

Lapár explained. "We don't know what's in that jungle."

"Exactly! We don't know if there's a settlement or a road or a town!"

"The mountains are miles from here, overgrown with foliage and populated by wild animals. It will be nearly impossible to navigate, and we haven't the strength or supplies to climb those hills."

"How long are you willing to wait for a passing ship?"

Lapár hadn't considered how long it would take to see a ship or how difficult it would be to draw its attention and bring it to shore. He slapped a mosquito from his neck and used his forearm to brush a curtain of sweat from his brow and finally shrugged, suspending his argument.

They opened their second can of beef and divided the portions evenly before embarking on another search of the surrounding jungle. Diego and Alexei brought back a couple of ripe, bug-ridden mangoes with hardly any consumable meat. But the bigger prize was a freshwater stream than trickled from the mountain. The men filled and drank the gallon jug and then refilled it for later. When the afternoon heat arrived, breaking at least ninety degrees, they moved out of the sun and into the shade to fight mosquitoes again.

Salvador let his mind wander hundreds of ways as the hours passed. He saw himself dancing with Olympia and playing cards with his boys. He was in a restaurant enjoying a warm pastry then standing outside, helping his father tend to their farm. He heard Ernesto's voice, "Step lively and don't look back!"

Step lively.

They could not afford to wait on this beach.

As he slapped mosquitoes and tolerated their infernal buzzing, he tried to think of Lázaro's face but could only imagine his father's wrinkled nose and dark, sun-dried skin. Agonizing over the loss of the knife, Salvador wondered if he could return to the spot where it had dropped and find it waiting.

"What's the matter with you?"

Salvador looked to Juan Carlos who stood above Alexei as the sullen younger man rested quietly. "You," Carlito's finger jabbed at Alexei. "You've said hardly a word since we left Tampa. Why haven't you told your story?"

Alexei spun his body away from Juan Carlos and rested his head against his knees. "I have nothing to say to you."

It was the first time Salvador had heard Alexei speak, and he was startled by the youthful voice.

Juan Carlos persisted as the rest of the curious men paused to listen. "You are no cigar worker and I am no fool. I know you are a hired assassin. Who are you working for?"

Alexei crawled behind a palm tree but Juan Carlos followed.

"Whoever hired you double-crossed you so why protect him? Tell me who it was!" Juan Carlos bent over and pointed a stiff finger at Alexei, just inches from his face.

The younger man, annoyed by the advance, slapped Carlito's hand away. "Get away from me."

Juan Carlos squeezed Alexei's shirt in his fists. "Tell me who sent us into this jungle!" Alexei clutched Juan Carlos's wrists and as the struggle became physical, Juan Carlos tried to yank Alexei off the ground. The younger man had leverage and he used his weight to pull Juan Carlos to the sand. Overcome by a homicidal frenzy, Juan Carlos landed a stiff punch on Alexei's chest. "Tell me now!"

Salvador and Gabriel were suddenly on top of them. They swatted at Juan Carlos's flying fists and tangled their arms in his as they pulled him away. Diego held Alexei back. The angry Juan Carlos turned his aggression towards Salvador and Mendez and tried to break from their grasp as Alexei remained calm and even started to walk away.

"Calm down, Carlito!" Salvador shouted. "It does us no good to fight!"

"He was hired to kill us, Ortiz!"

Salvador and Gabriel detained the panting Juan Carlos until he finally calmed and collapsed onto the sand out of breath and soaked with sweat. Under his breath, hardly loud enough for anyone to hear, Juan Carlos muttered, "We should have killed Armando in Ybor."

"This place is making us crazy," said Salvador.

"I feared this," Mendez replied. "The longer we are here the more we will be overcome by melancholia. As more days pass it will only get worse."

The rest of the men sat near Juan Carlos, except for Alexei who remained in isolation near the tree line. For a long time they sat in silence and perspired into their already wet clothes. Finally Juan Carlos said, "It is pointless to sit here and hope we're found."

Salvador agreed. "The more we walk the better chance we have to survive."

"There must be a village or settlement nearby," said Mendez.

The men looked to their leader for his thoughts. Lapár sighed. "If we disappear into the jungle, it eliminates any chance to be spotted. Let's try to light a signal fire and wait another few days."

"No," Juan Carlos said. He leaned towards Lapár. "No more waiting. Just because you lack the courage to explore doesn't mean the rest of us have to sit on the beach and die. We rest tonight and tomorrow morning we pack our things and enter the jungle. You have no choice, Lapár, because you are no longer in charge."

Chapter 27

Two days later they were completely lost. Mile after mile, the jungle looked exactly the same. Overhanging vines became indistinguishable from the bushes and branches that grew from the damp forest floor. As they forced their way through foliage so thick it blocked the sun, Juan Carlos slapped a branch away with his bare arm and remarked, "This is the type of travel for which machetes were invented."

The temperature was so hot that eighty degrees was a welcomed cool. Meager diets shrunk their bodies and made their clothes hang loosely from boney shoulders, and the last of the beef had been consumed. They constantly searched their surroundings for fruits or berries and were lucky to find a mango that wasn't crawling with bugs.

Salvador showed his hands to Mendez so the writer could inspect the tiny little cuts that covered his fingers. "Bats," Salvador said. "They descend at night to feed on our blood."

Mendez's fingertips had their own collection of cuts but he was more tormented by the mosquitoes that pestered him during his waking minutes. The unrelenting swarm reminded him of the locusts from the Bible. They nipped and plucked at his face until it was covered with sores, and bedded in the warm, scraggly beard he had grown. But most alarming was the condition of his feet.

With a climate so hot and humid, their shoes and socks were constantly soaked by sweat and rain. And the forest was so humid and shaded that there was no chance to dry. After climbing the rugged terrain, stepping over roots and in and out of puddles for miles and miles, sores and blisters bubbled on their feet like boiling water.

Salvador tried to ignore the soreness and swelling and found he could distract himself by repeating a rhythmic cadence as he walked. "Walk forward now and step left, step right. Walk forward now, step left, step right." He repeated this over and over in his head, day after day, even after they had stopped to rest for the night.

When he sat and removed his shoes and socks, Salvador saw the hideous condition of his feet. Blisters rose along the length, and he used a splinter to prick the sacks and let the fluid run out. It was a great relief but only temporary. The next day the skin above the blister was rubbed raw, exposing the next layer of pink and tender skin that stung with a touch. It made the walking harder still, and with his senses and awareness numbed by fatigue the journey became even more aimless.

Salvador tried to remain patient and unruffled and found it became difficult to talk to his comrades. Their days became long processions through the jungle with periods of rest where the only necessary words were, "Shall we go on?"

With an occasional handful of sour berries providing their nourishment the endless journey continued even as thunder rumbled overhead and poured sheets of rain across the treetops. For one frightening moment Salvador considered suicide as the only means of terminating a trial with no end.

Finally they reached the top of a ridge and peered through the leaves to see green treetops that flowed like a valley of rolling foliage. They had wandered deep into the hills, far from the ocean, and could see no signs of civilization. They halted and sat on some rocks to rest.

Salvador tended to Alexei's blisters while the rest of his comrades partnered off to mend each others' feet. Of all the men in the party, Alexei had spoken the least. Salvador knew it had something to do with his involvement in the shooting at La Morena, and Alexei's obvious allegiance to the other side, but Salvador tried to remain positive and neutral.

"How are your legs?" he asked while he popped one of Alexei's blisters with a splinter.

"Sore," he said.

"Mine too," Salvador said. "But the soreness in my muscles can't compare to the cramping in my stomach. What would I give for a warm Cuban sandwich and a cold beer?"

Alexei smiled, nodding his agreement.

Mendez watched Salvador and noticed that the cigar maker seemed pleasant and cheerful even during moments when Mendez was absolutely sure they would die. As he sat and stretched his legs, Salvador wished for flat ground – roots, rocks and bulges in the dirt forced him to squirm and rest in awkward positions while his legs tried to recover.

They were brought to their feet by a sudden yelp so piercing and desperate it could have come from man or beast. Then a growling was followed by the unmistakable sound of a man screaming for God's mercy. They ran towards the sound and saw José rolling on the ground and kicking furiously at a spotted leopard that had locked onto his foot, twisting it violently as if trying to tear it free.

Forgetting their fatigue, the others reached for anything they could find and started hurling it at the leopard. Salvador threw a small rock but missed, so he clawed handfuls of dirt from the forest floor and flung them at the animal. Mendez took a fallen branch and swung it towards the leopard's head, landing several weak blows that did nothing to stop the animal from tearing into José's flesh.

But Juan Carlos dove on top of the leopard and beat the animal over the head with a baseball sized rock, landing three solid blows that caused the animal to release José and disappear into the foliage.

José fell immediately into shock; his skin lost color as his eyes rolled back and extinguished their flicker. The flesh of his ankle had been torn raw, making the blisters on his feet seem like painless freckles. The ground surrounding José was littered with the bones and fur of a small carcass – José had stumbled onto the leopard's territory and interrupted its meal.

Salvador wrapped the mangled ankle with his leather belt which he pulled tight to constrict the endless stream of blood pouring from the wound. José was losing blood but a worse danger, which Salvador did not mention, was any decayed meat stuck in the leopard's teeth. If José didn't succumb to excessive blood loss he would likely contract gangrene and die.

An hour later, once José was calm and resting with his wounded leg elevated and the bleeding slowing to a manageable trickle, Juan Carlos pulled Salvador aside. "He's dead, Ortiz."

Salvador agreed but didn't want to endorse whatever Juan Carlos was about to propose. "He deserves a chance."

"He can't walk until his leg heals and there is little chance that it will. If he can't walk then none of us can. We are stuck here Salvador, with hardly any water and no food."

"Give him time to rest and make his peace."

Darkness arrived, the forest cooled, and a tremor of night chills engulfed José. Salvador curled into a ball nearby and shuddered at the endless clicking and chattering of José's teeth, and realized how wet the ground was. Salvador lay in a damp spot of earth and nursed sores on his shoulders where his wet shirt had chafed his skin. As he swatted at bugs and feared the return of the angry leopard, Salvador wondered how long José would last. He almost talked himself out of covering José with the extra shirt they had taken from Matías, hoping that the shock and cold would kill the man and end his suffering. But for the sake of his own rest and sanity, Salvador crawled to José and covered him with an extra, damp layer. It did little to lessen José's shivering and the men were awake for most of the night.

When the sun rose Salvador knelt to inspect José's wound. He tried to remain passive as he removed the dressing and saw the rash of pink and red flesh surrounded by infected purple welts. It reeked of blood and putrefaction, and Salvador could not stop his gag reflex. He turned away from José to dry heave, and when he looked back and locked eyes with the sickened man, José knew from Salvador's reaction that the wound was deadly.

"I didn't think his condition would deteriorate so quickly," Mendez said after Salvador quietly updated the others. The *lector* flopped onto a rock beside Salvador and Juan Carlos while Lapár, Diego, and Alexei sat exhausted on the dirt near José. Salvador watched the withered and drained *La Resistencia* president and wondered if any union member would elect Lapár after seeing him in this exhausted condition.

Juan Carlos shook his head. "Already fatigued and malnourished, with hardly a vitamin in his system to fight the infection. José has no chance."

"We can wait and see if he improves," Mendez suggested.

"Not likely," said Juan Carlos.

"Or we can try and carry him."

"Sure," Juan Carlos leered. "We can hire the strongest man in the world."

Mendez knew it was a futile suggestion. He hung his head, preparing to mourn the certain loss of another friend. "Gangrene is a nasty ailment, one for which only a single treatment exists."

If José was to live, his leg would need to be amputated below the knee.

By the next morning the black vines of infection had climbed his leg and wrapped around his knee, sprouting into his thigh. José seemed to sleep, barely breathing and only lifting his head slightly to sip water. The rest of the men sat quietly, too hungry and too fatigued to contemplate the loss of another. They let their minds drift aimlessly.

Finally Salvador walked to the pile of bones in the leopard's lair and found a curved rib roughly four inches long. Using the flat side of the rock where he had been sitting, Salvador began to grind the bone back and forth.

Mendez appeared beside him. "What are you doing?"

"Sharpening this bone."

Shuddering at the thought of a clumsy, bloody operation, Mendez asked, "What for?"

Salvador concentrated on sharpening the bone and stopped to poke the pointed tip into the pad of his forefinger. He felt along the edge. Satisfied that his tool would do the job, Salvador stood and walked towards José.

Mendez called after him. "You're sure you don't want to discuss this?"

Salvador knelt beside José as the rest of the men watched tiredly, unwilling to intervene or assist. Even Mendez, resigned to Salvador's deed, plopped onto the dirt and said a prayer.

"José," Salvador whispered. The young writer from West Tampa forced his eyes open. They had lost color and were as pale as his face. Here was a man, a man Salvador hardly knew, but a man nonetheless. When he gazed upon José, Salvador saw defeat, the eyes of a man who wondered if his misery would ever end.

"José," Salvador said again. "Your life was not meant to end on this spot."

José tried to nod his head but choked on his own throat and strained a pair of sputtering coughs.

Salvador continued. "None of our lives were meant to end here. There are seven of us, José. Six of us are relatively healthy. Six of us have a chance to make it home."

José exhaled, and the last bit of will left his body. He seemed to slump further into the dirt, as if his body had already started returning to dust.

"Are you a man of the Lord?"

José shook his head.

"Then you desire no prayer?"

He shook his head again.

Salvador produced the sharp, pointed bone. "Thank you for choosing a noble end, my friend. Your counterparts appreciate your courage."

It was over before José could protest. He gasped as blood rushed from his throat, and quickly lost consciousness. A minute later he was dead, and his six companions were liberated.

They buried his body under a shoddy blanket of rocks and dirt that made for a sad departure. The leopard or any jungle creature would arrive soon after the men had departed and would make a meal of José's remains. Mendez stood above the grave and removed the *La Resistencia* checkbook from his pocket. "Did anyone know his date of birth?"

No one did so Mendez wrote on the back of a check, "José Plasencia, died on September 10th, 1901." He folded the check and placed it at the head of José's grave and stepped away. With empty stomachs and aching feet covered with sores, they started walking with little idea of where they were headed or what danger they'd encounter next.

Chapter 28

"Walk forward now and step left, step right. Walk forward now, step left, step right. Walk forward now and step left, step right. Walk forward now, step left, step right."

For several days Salvador spoke only to himself, repeating his cadence in his head as he walked. They hardly ate, and when they couldn't find any sour bananas or ripe mangos they resorted to capturing insects. Using the jug to catch rainwater, they shuffled through the jungle without purpose or place, their feet so raw and sore the soles had gone numb with pain.

Aside from their physical deterioration, Salvador observed a mental decline that became more severe each day. The loss of José had crushed their morale. Lapár, who had been strong when they first landed, had tired quickly and often lagged at the end of the group during their meanderings. Salvador tried to think of his family but had trouble remembering their faces. He saw Olympia's brown eyes and the white ribbons decorating Josefina's hair, but his sons seemed to blur into a single person. "I can't remember their names," he mumbled but felt no guilt.

No one spoke of Salvador's decision to end José's life. He interpreted their silence as a mark of reluctant approval.

During a day that was relatively cool and nearly free of bugs, the men were able to cover ground and rest. When they finally sat in the brush to rest, they passed the water jug back and forth, too weak and depressed to speak. Time passed uneventfully and then Juan Carlos suddenly sat up straight and still, like a dog hearing a small animal rustling nearby. "Does anyone hear that?"

The rest of the men strained their ears and heard an unmistakably familiar and invigorating sound: the trickle of running water. Juan Carlos jumped to his feet and smiled for the first time in weeks. "A river!"

Without waiting for his counterparts Juan Carlos dashed into the trees and ran towards the rushing sound. The rest followed him to the edge of a sharp, rocky drop-off where the sound of rushing water grew louder and more intense. Over the edge of the cliff was a fifty foot ravine where a vibrant stream of waterfalls and rapids flowed between a pair of jagged rocky walls.

The bursting rapids were a sight so foreign, the echoing crash of water so magnificent that the men felt cleansed of their fatigue and injected with new life. Their strength surged as they moved along the edge of the ravine looking for a way to reach the water's edge.

"It likely pours into the Gulf of Mexico," Mendez said. "We can follow the river from here and as the ravine descends to sea level we're almost guaranteed to encounter civilization." Then he smiled at Salvador. "Next week I will be sitting in the Red Pelican coffee shop on Tenth Avenue with a fresh cup of creamy *café con leche* with extra sugar, some Cuban bread, and a nice hand-rolled cigar. Later I'll order a plate of steaming black beans and rice topped with fresh chopped onions and a side of crisp, oily *platanos*. At night, a hot Cuban sandwich and a cold beer. Make that three cold beers, with a nice dark *maduro* for dessert. And then Catrina will join me in my bed to fulfill my wildest dreams."

Salvador grinned and asked, "Who is Catrina?"

"I don't know, but she will be perfect!"

After a night of healthy rest they awoke to a dark and foggy morning that muffled the rush of the river below. They finished the last of the water in the jug and found nothing to eat, but the river was a reminder and an unspoken sign that they were on their way home.

Quickly the group broke camp and began their walk along the edge of the ravine. Juan Carlos lagged at the rear next to Alexei. "Your boss will be happy to see you once we make it back to Tampa."

Alexei dismissed Carlito. "I have no boss."

Juan Carlos smirked. "Of course! Not after he double crossed you and dropped you here with us. If you tell me who he is, I will help you pay him back."

Alexei said nothing and increased his pace to keep up with the rest of the group.

Juan Carlos persisted in a calm, even-tempered manner. "Why don't you tell me his name was Armando Renteria? And that he hired you to assassinate Lapár, and Gabriel Mendez and any other labor leader you happened to encounter?"

"No."

"But you and your partner couldn't shoot straight, so you hit Antonio Vasquez instead. No wonder they banished you to this land. So who was it that hired you? Renteria? The police chief? The mayor?"

Alexei tried to walk faster but Juan Carlos reached out and grabbed his elbow.

"Tell me who it was!"

Alexei whirled and chopped at Carlito's hand. "Don't touch me again."

With a natural, instinctive reaction, Juan Carlos slapped Alexei right across the cheek so violently that both men were temporarily stunned. Shock quickly became rage as Alexei lunged for Carlito's throat with both hands, but the cigar maker backed away and took a boxing stance, savoring the chance for a fist fight.

Diego and Mendez suddenly appeared between them and as Mendez pushed a stiff arm into Juan Carlos's chest to hold him back, Diego locked Alexei in a bear hug. Lapár stood dazed to the side.

"Save your strength!" commanded Mendez.

Juan Carlos shouted at Alexei, "Who are you working for?"

"I'm tired of being your scapegoat!" Alexei shouted back.

"Then tell us what happened! Tell us who paid you to run into La Morena with guns firing!"

Alexei had had enough and knew there was nothing to lose. "I was hired," he finally said, "by the man with the beard. He came into the Scrub and paid us to assassinate a man named Antonio Vasquez, the wealthy tobacco man. Our bullets did hit him, right in the head, and I would have gotten away clean if you hadn't been there!"

The rest of the men stood and watched Alexei, stunned that his target had been Vasquez and not the labor leaders. Stunned that Armando could be so ruthless as to plot the execution of his closest business partner, yet completely understanding his motive.

"Liar!" Juan Carlos shouted. "Armando hired you to murder Lapár!"

"It makes sense, Carlito," Lapár said. "Armando would want Vasquez out of his way so he could take ownership of the company and the Cigar Trust. It makes perfect sense."

Juan Carlos looked to Salvador expecting a dissenting opinion, but Salvador agreed with Lapár. "Save it for when we get home," Salvador said. "Save it for Armando."

Juan Carlos pushed Mendez away and walked away from the group. "I don't believe it."

"You don't have to believe it right now," Mendez said. "Let's keep following the river. We're getting so close!" He started walking and the others followed while Juan Carlos stood behind for a moment, kicked the dirt and then jogged to catch up. His eyes remained on Alexei. Juan Carlos could not believe that this skinny degenerate from the Scrub was responsible for the sores on their feet, the cuts on their hands, the bug bites all over their faces, and the pains in their stomachs. And to think that the rest of his counterparts seemed somehow willing to forgive the malice that had brought them here. Had they all gone mad? Was Carlito the only one with a sense of virtue? They walked with Alexei as if he was one of their own. Their mascot. Yet he could be leading them into another trap.

For the sake of his brothers, their families, and all the working men of Tampa, Juan Carlos could not let Alexei's crime go unpunished. He broke into a sprint, rushed past Salvador and Mendez, and caught up to Alexei. He heard the shouting, his comrades begging him to stop, but he ignored them and grabbed Alexei around the neck in a powerful headlock and punched him hard in the lower back.

Mendez tried to rush forward and intervene, but Salvador grabbed his forearm and held him back. Before the writer could question Salvador's block, Juan Carlos had dragged Alexei to the edge of the ravine.

The boy from the Scrub gasped for breath and tried to orient himself. Alexei knew he was near the cliff, but his feet dangled over thin air and furiously kicked for ground that wasn't there. He was falling.

"No!" shouted Mendez as he watched Alexei disappear over the edge. He dove to the ground and tried to reach over and catch Alexei, but it was too late. Juan Carlos was beside him panting. He seemed mighty and appeared to have grown a foot taller as he stood above the world with adrenaline surging. Here was a man who believed he could hurl boulders.

"What have you done?" cried Mendez as the others stood in horror. Only Salvador signaled his approval. As Mendez howled that Juan Carlos had gone mad, Salvador gave Carlito a subtle nod and knew his friend felt no remorse. Juan Carlos was energized, determined to make it home and finish a job that had started in Tampa.

Chapter 29

Salvador never questioned Carlito's decision to kill Alexei, and Mendez never questioned Salvador. Lapár stood dumbfounded at the back of the group and Diego, who had grown a bit delirious, saw Juan Carlos not as a killer but as a warrior with an almost mystical presence. A man who had killed another human as easily as God sweeps the wind across the sea.

"When we return to Tampa," Juan Carlos told Salvador, "Armando will never expect that we're coming. We can surprise him and get him before he knows we're in town."

Salvador kept pace with Juan Carlos and repeated his cadence. "Walk forward now and step left, step right. Walk forward now, step left, step right."

They walked at the front of the column, leading their men along the river with vigor that the others found difficult to match.

"If only we had a boat." Salvador said as they found themselves standing at the edge of the river. While the others hurried to the water's edge and knelt to scoop and pour cold water over their faces, Salvador and Juan Carlos stood beside them like military captains surveying the opposite bank for signs of the enemy.

"No signs of civilization here," Juan Carlos said as he knelt to drink the freshwater. They refilled their jug and sat at the riverbank to rest. Salvador caught a small turtle which they killed and ate raw, sucking the meat from its skin as if it were chocolate from a candy wrapper. After an hour of rest, Juan Carlos slapped Salvador's shoulder. "Let's keep going."

Bounding over the rocks and roots with unbridled urgency and new life, Juan Carlos moved along the riverbank while the others fought to keep up. As the river ran into the jungle, the area became as peaceful as night where the only sounds were the chirping birds and the trickle of water running over the rocks.

They arrived at an ominous giant black rock that grew like a monument from the bank of the river. Resembling a man's face, the shape rose thirty feet high, standing long and narrow with two jagged pockets near the top resembling eyes, a protrusion just below for a nose and a base that sloped outward like a chin. It was only a rock but all five travelers were startled by the sinister and unmistakable shape.

Juan Carlos noticed their apprehension and laughed. "Why the frowns, friends? It's nothing more than a geological accident."

"It looks like a face," said Mendez.

Diego examined Juan Carlos, who stood beside the rock confident and unperturbed, enhancing his godliness. Diego wondered if he was hallucinating. Or perhaps all of them were hallucinating? How could this random group of rocks form a natural shape that resembled a man so much that it appeared to have been sculpted?

"It doesn't look man made to me," Juan Carlos said.

Lapár nodded. "Yes, it does. This was no accident."

"That's only good news," said Juan Carlos. "Civilization is near!"

Diego, wondering if he was really seeing a face in the rock, realized that his mind was fatigued. He noticed an obvious change in his perception. He was not looking at things rationally. He knew his reality had been distorted, but even that awareness was starting to slip away. This strange rock formation was like some evil idolatry; a haunting mark of the devil, a warning to stay away, to turn back, to run from this place.

The jungle seemed to have grown darker, the river more treacherous.

And Juan Carlos was prepared to ignore this omen and lead the group into further peril. As they walked beyond the sinister formation, Diego followed with an uncanny feeling that evil spirits were present.

The energy and excitement that came with the discovery of the river quickly faded as the men wandered inland to avoid the muddy banks. Here the water grew distant, and they struggled to forge a path that kept the river in sight. Salvador's thoughts returned to his family, and he was dimly aware that they had all abandoned him, but he couldn't remember where they had gone or if they would ever come back to the jungle and be with him.

Then something happened that changed everything. They emerged from the jungle and spotted, cutting along the surface of the river and moving rapidly downstream, a man in a canoe.

They all saw him; a small man with dark skin, black hair and a white short-sleeved shirt. If they were in Ybor City, the man would have resembled any of the thousands of cigar makers. He paddled without vigor, letting the current carry him down the river. Juan Carlos knew that if he didn't give chase, the man in the canoe would be carried away and with him, a chance to survive.

"Hey!" Carlito shouted and broke into a sprint along the riverbank. Reinvigorated, he hopped over rocks and roots with the agility of a dancer and the speed of a rabbit.

Salvador was close behind, also yelling and waving his arms but the current had spirited the canoe away as quickly as it had appeared. Like Juan Carlos, Salvador was overcome with urgency, as if letting this canoe escape would be the same as saying goodbye to life itself. Salvador surprised himself with his ability to move over the terrain so quickly. It felt like the fatigue and hunger had disappeared and he had been suddenly blessed with the coordination of a champion athlete.

The boatman shrank to a tiny speck far away, but they saw where he had parked his canoe on the opposite shore. He hopped out, threw his oar inside, and started to drag the boat into the forest without knowing he was being followed by five desperate castaways.

Juan Carlos stopped and looked back to the group. Pointing to the opposite shore, he shouted, "Cross here!" He did not wait for a response but hurried to the water and stomped into the river. Salvador hesitated, thinking of snakes and alligators and all the unseen, deadly creatures of the water, but ignored the risk. He entered the water and followed.

Mendez, Lapár, and Diego reached the shore, and Lapár waded in after Salvador. He was not a strong swimmer, and he clumsily kicked and paddled but managed to stay afloat and inch along. Mendez was next, but he stopped short of entering the water when he saw Diego standing stupidly on the shore.

"Diego, what are you waiting for?"

Diego did not budge. He merely stood on the riverbank and watched Juan Carlos swimming furiously across the river. Mendez caught the strange look in Diego's eye. A look of bewilderment, almost as if he was angry, mistrusting the man's motive for crossing the water.

Mendez, still looking over his shoulder at Diego, took a step into the water and pleaded. "Come *on*, Diego. The others have nearly reached the opposite side!"

Diego was frozen in place with his eyes on Juan Carlos. He shook his head.

"What's wrong, man?"

Diego, with a disapproving look, pointed towards Juan Carlos. "That one thinks he is some kind of god."

Mendez almost laughed. "Stop talking nonsense and get into the damn river!"

Again Diego shook his head. The fatigue and the hunger, the loneliness and the uncertainty had finally taken their toll. All rational thought had died. Diego could no longer see clearly, and no longer knew he was hallucinating. Juan Carlos was not a man like everybody else but like a serpent leading them to poisoned fruit. Diego took a step away from the river.

Mendez still stood with both feet in the water, waiting for Diego to join him. "What the hell is wrong with you?"

Diego said nothing. He turned and ran back into the rain forest and then disappeared through a dark curtain of foliage.

"Diego!" Mendez called after him, but when he saw Juan Carlos and Salvador climbing onto the opposite riverbank, and Lapár nearly halfway across, his instincts told him to abandon Diego and follow the others.

"Diego!" he called again but knew it to be hopeless. His choice was to follow Diego into the rainforest and convince him to rejoin the group – and risk finding himself alone and lost – or dive into the river and let Diego fight his insanity and fend for himself. The choice was easier than Mendez expected it would be, and he felt no guilt when he turned to the river and submerged himself into the cool, murky water.

Juan Carlos removed his sopping wet shoes and socks. After he dumped the water from his shoes, he slapped his soaking socks against a rock until they were only damp. Salvador sat beside him and did the same. Lapár struggled with the last half of his swim, surprised at how difficult it was to swim with shoes on, especially after being weakened by hunger and fatigue. Mendez was soon beside him and helped Lapár paddle the last few yards until all four of them had gathered on the shore.

Juan Carlos was already standing and ready to continue the pursuit as Lapár and Mendez removed their shoes and socks. Salvador asked, "What happened to Diego?"

Mendez said. "He ran the other way."

Salvador looked across the river for Diego. "He did what?"

Mendez shrugged. "He just ran. He went crazy or something. I don't know what happened."

Salvador nodded, indifferent to this news.

"We'll have to leave him behind," said Juan Carlos. "Let's go!"

No one disagreed. All of them had been so overwhelmed with hunger and fatigue that their survival instincts spoke louder than their loyalties to each other. Diego had decided to survive on his own, and not one of them felt any remorse letting him attempt exactly that.

There was a faint but clear groove in the dirt where the light canoe had been dragged through the forest. As they followed the path they were greeted by the welcoming smell of embers. Salvador was reminded of the open-fire kitchens at his father's farm in Cuba and the village of Piro. The pleasant autumn aroma of man-made smoke grew stronger and stronger until they could hear the crackling of fire and the faint voices of men. Stopping below a short ridge of dirt and roots they listened and heard a language they did not recognize.

Juan Carlos smiled at his friends, eager to announce their presence but cautious to expose them to this unseen group. How many were there, and how would they react to the sight of four strange travelers on their territory?

Salvador whispered. "I don't think we should disturb them. What if they're savages?"

"Or worse," said Mendez. "They could be cannibals."

"What should we do?" asked Juan Carlos.

Salvador shrugged. "Just listen."

As quietly as they could, they gathered along the edge of the ridge and leaned against the dirt wall. Right above them a group of natives ate and talked and tended to their fire. Several minutes passed and Lapár, who was fluent in several languages, shook his head and said, "There is a bit of English in there, fragments really, roots. But I've never heard this language before."

Salvador whispered to Juan Carlos. "If we ever make it back, we're going to kill him." He thought of the two white men who had dragged him into the woods and tortured him with a mock lynching. "We will not let anyone bully us ever again."

A smile started to break across Carlito's face but it quickly faded. He froze and slowly raised his hands above his head, for the group was suddenly looking at three young men holding muskets. In their twenties, with light brown skin that held a mixture of Indian and Anglo, they wore loose shirts, pants and sandals. Tightly gripping their muskets, they aimed at the four travelers in defense of their territory.

Silently, the natives motioned for the four castaways to move away from the wall and follow a trail that would have otherwise gone unnoticed by the four tired men. They climbed to the top and saw a small campsite where four more native men stood with rifles drawn. The cigar makers from Tampa were face to face with the indigenous people of the region. They were the Miskitu.

VIII.

YBOR CITY
1901

Chapter 30

Javier tried to understand all that had happened between his mother and father. A thief and terrorist of the upper class, Salvador had seduced Olympia from her home at the tip of a machete and the young maiden, living all those years with an apparent aversion to her family, had never returned to her wealthy home.

What had really happened at that plantation so many years ago?

What secret was so terrible that forced Salvador to withhold from his children a vital ingredient of their past? The reason their veins were mixed with equal portions of opposing enemy blood. While Olympia remained quiet, Salvador had taught his boys that Cubans were virtuous and brave, and that Spaniards were greedy and oppressive. Spanish soldiers had killed Salvador's parents. That meant Javier's grandparents would have been mortal enemies of each other. What did that mean for Javier and his siblings? Unable to choose a side, Javier was certain of one thing: he missed his mother terribly.

He pictured her moving across the kitchen, preparing the evening meal for her family, though she was never a great cook. Javier valued the private time he shared with her after the dishes were washed and the younger children had settled for the night. They'd bring out the cards or dominoes, or sometimes just sit and talk. To the men his age, Javier projected the image of a young man who loved nightlife, fancy clothes, and women who could dance, but he never ceased being his mother's oldest son.

Now his time to grieve had passed. He could not wake up crying at night like his eleven-year-old brother E.J. Tears were for women and children but not men. Javier was nineteen and wanted to show his younger brother that Ortiz men grow up strong.

E.J. did not understand the gravity of his father's revelation, and as he rolled cigars in their adopted factory in Key West he asked Javier, "Papa said he stole Mama. Does that mean Papa went to jail?"

"No, E.J., he was just trying to stay alive. Stop asking questions." E.J.'s persistence annoyed Javier. "Do you realize you're costing me money? Every minute I have to explain something to you is another minute I'm not rolling my own cigars."

"Sorry," E.J. said scornfully and concentrated on his cigar. Halfway into his apprenticeship, E.J. had nearly perfected his craft, and Javier was eager to see his younger brother graduate and become an official cigar maker. He would be released from inspecting his younger brother's product and could concentrate on his own work.

They had been sharing a room in Key West for the last month while working at a local cigar factory and saving money to send home to Salvador and the striking Tampa cigar workers. While rumors of kidnappings, shootouts and murder flowed into Key West from the north, Javier believed that the low morale among the Tampa workforce would lead to an unfavorable end to the 1901 General Strike.

Something else troubled Javier: after a month in Key West he had not heard from his father. A letter finally arrived from Josefina and explained why.

> *Dear Javier,*
>
> *I wish that I could send good tidings from Ybor City but unfortunately our situation is grim. We have been challenged with a serious scenario. Our father is missing. Several people witnessed the abductions of the labor leaders at the hands of some local army of citizens. Along with your father, several others are missing, including Gabriel Mendez, Juan Carlos and Angelo De la Parte. An article appeared in a recent edition of the Tampa paper with a proclamation that these men have been deported but to where, no one knows. The families have petitioned the mayor's office for answers, even traveled to Tallahassee to see the governor, but neither the state government nor the mayor's office has responded. I plan to personally visit the district attorney.*

Despite these drastic events, the labor boycott of the factories has not ended. The strike is still going strong, thanks to donations and to dedicated workers like you and E.J.

I suspect that by now you will have a strong desire to return to Ybor City but I must stress the futility of such a decision. It is important that you and E.J. remain in Key West. You are responsible for your brother and must earn your daily bread. There is no work in Tampa. Stay where you are and I will send frequent updates and call you home as soon as such a call is feasible.

Listen hard for gossip of our father's whereabouts, and pray that he returns safely. The grace of God is with us. I know we will all be together soon. Until that day, I remain...

Your loving sister,
Josefina

E.J. watched as Javier wrinkled his brow and let his mouth hang open. "What does it say?"

Javier mulled the letter. He paced across the wooden floor of their musty, cramped apartment while E.J. watched and searched for some clue to the letter's subject. Feeling their situation was about to change again, E.J. asked, "What does it say?"

Javier stopped pacing and without returning E.J.'s glance he folded the letter and stuffed it into his pocket. "Pack your bag. We're leaving."

They returned to a comatose city nearing depression. Traffic at the port was light with no incoming tobacco shipments or outgoing loads of finished cigars. Gone were the rowdy street orators and labor demonstrations, and the sidewalks were free of vagrants. The taverns and coffee shops, often the scene of loud, crowded commerce had been reduced to quiet shells of industry.

The boys rode a trolley to West Tampa and walked the rest of the way to Andres's clinic. Josefina greeted her brothers at the door with hugs. "I don't know what you think you can accomplish here, Javier. No one knows where he is. The latest rumor is that they were taken to Brazil, but the day before the story was that they were deserted in Nicaragua.

367

There is even a crazy version of their fate which placed them on a barren shore of Africa!"

"There has to be someone in town who knows more than they've said."

Josefina laughed. "And you're going to make them talk? You should be in Key West working. The cigar workers in this town are dead broke and can't even afford to open soup houses. With no money to pay for health care, our clinic has been nearly empty, and even I am hoping the cigar workers surrender and return to work."

The loss of Salvador and the city's labor leaders had been a devastating blow to *La Resistencia*. Javier no longer cared about the work stoppage and would go along with whatever the cigar workers decided. "I guess you have extra beds?"

Josefina smiled. "Are you asking me if you can stay here?"

Javier returned the smile. His sister knew him well. "Just for a few days."

"I hope you don't plan to take Papa's place, Javier. The men who took him are ruthless."

"I do not seek vengeance."

She nodded. "I know. Where do you plan to start looking?"

"Is Alessandria Prizzi still in town?"

Josefina shrugged. "Never heard of her."

"If she's here, I'll find her."

Josefina fixed a small lunch for her brothers and then Javier headed into Ybor City to see what had become of the old house on Nineteenth Street. "The landlord has probably evicted you and rented the house to someone else," warned Josefina, but Javier insisted on starting his search at their former home.

"Be careful," she warned as Javier left the clinic. "This town in unforgiving."

Javier smiled. "I have never forgiven a soul."

His father's handgun rested in his pants pocket.

The house had been without tenant for over a month, and Javier wondered if the Ortiz family had already been evicted. The front door was locked, and all of the windows were closed. He tried to look inside, but the curtains had been drawn.

Songo stood on his porch next door with Pano beside him, the dog's tail wagging furiously. "The landlord came and locked the place up, said the rent was past due."

Javier asked, "What did he do with our stuff?"

"I think he left it inside. There's been no one to rent it to since everyone has left town. I think he's just waiting for one of you to return and pay the rent."

"Thanks, Songo," said Javier. "See you later."

Songo called to them. "I almost forgot to tell you, your brother was here!" He grinned happily, satisfied to be breaking the news.

Javier turned and froze. "Lázaro?"

Still grinning. "He came by yesterday."

Javier felt his pulse surge. He tried to look calm. "Do you know where he went?"

"I think to the boarding houses to find a room."

"You're sure it was Lázaro?"

Songo chuckled. "That crooked nose is one of a kind!"

Javier went to the boarding houses near Eighteenth Street which rented bedrooms and provided three daily meals to tenants for a small fee. Javier picked one at random and knocked on the door. The lady of the house answered and inquired if he was seeking tenancy.

"No, Señora," Javier apologized politely. "I am looking for my brother. A young man just younger than me named Lázaro."

"No, no one here named Lázaro," she said. Javier thanked her and moved on. He searched three more and then found one with a Cuban proprietor in her seventies, with a black dress and white shawl named Isabella.

"Yes," said Isabella. "Lázaro is here." She invited Javier inside and pointed him to the kitchen where a young man with long black hair sat the table eating a plate of black beans and rice.

"Señor Lázaro, you have a visitor," said Isabella before she left the kitchen to give the brothers their privacy.

369

Lázaro turned and saw Javier for the first time in more than a year. Javier could not believe what had become of his brother. Lázaro's hair hung below his shoulders, uncut for months. He had a thick moustache and a growth of beard badly in need of a trim. His eyes held a dire stare that made him look five years older. Javier suspected it was the same look his father had worn when he had roamed the mountains of Cuba with El Matón.

Javier could not contain himself. "Thank God!" he exclaimed and hurried to his brother. Lázaro rose and they embraced longer than they had ever hugged before. Javier broke away and held his brother by the shoulders at arm's length to gaze into his eyes. There was so much Lázaro needed to be told, so many things had happened in the last year. Javier did not know where to begin.

Above all, Lázaro was relieved to be home and with family. "It's good to see you," he said. The brothers stared at each other for a moment, overwhelmed by the sudden reunion.

"Mama died," Javier said abruptly.

Lázaro gasped and Javier was reminded of the surprised gasp his father had made when learning the news over a year ago. Lázaro made almost exactly the same sound.

"I'm sorry, but I know of no other way to tell you."

Lázaro wondered if he had heard Javier correctly. "What do you mean?"

"She died right after you left. Tuberculosis."

Lázaro's mouth was open. He slumped into this chair. "She died?"

Javier sat beside him.

"Right after I left?" Lázaro asked.

Javier nodded. "Very suddenly. She was exhausted, and then she got sick on the day of Josefina's wedding and collapsed."

"*She died?*"

Javier said nothing.

Lázaro took a moment to contemplate this news. He had missed his mother's funeral in order to pursue personal desires. And his final exchange with her had been bitter and personal, and he had later vowed to apologize for insulting his mother and hurting her feelings. How could he ever be forgiven now?

Javier read his brother's concern. "A lot has happened since you have been gone."

Lázaro nodded. "We have a lot to catch up on." He ordered a second plate of black beans and rice from Isabella, and once Javier had been served the brothers updated each other while they ate.

Javier started with the good news of Josefina's marriage to Andres; that they operated a clinic in West Tampa where Josefina worked as a professional nurse.

Then Lázaro asked, "Where is Papa?"

Javier took a breath. "Papa has disappeared."

Lázaro stared at his brother. "You can't be serious."

But Javier's stone expression told Lázaro that he was.

"What do you mean he's disappeared?"

Javier explained the circumstances of the strike, and updated his brother on the local rumor that a group of men had seized the immigrant strike leaders and sent them overseas.

Lázaro asked, "How do you know if any of this is true?"

"I don't, but if Papa has been deported I intend to find out where."

Lázaro believed Javier would do everything he could to discover their father's location. "Now that I'm home," said Lázaro, "I'll help you any way I can."

Javier smiled, happy to have an ally. "Tell me about your adventures and what has brought you back home."

Lázaro took a deep breath and recollected his journey. "The Ortiz family has been cursed. I did not return with fortune or glory. From the day I left Tampa I found nothing but bad luck. The fight promoter named Abrezzo claimed he would train and mold me into a prize fighter. He made me believe I'd become a champion. All I needed to do was pay a small fee and assist his workers at his gym in New Orleans. For the first three weeks I did nothing but sweep floors and haul laundry.

"I was broke from the time I arrived until the time I left, and I'm still broke today. This Abrezzo, a so-called manager, was nothing more than a low-level hustler, a swindler who entered his fighters in matches and kept most of the proceeds. He had two or three fighters who showed promise and fought regionally but I spent most of my time helping Abrezzo train these men. I served as a sparring partner for a middleweight who outweighed me by twenty pounds. I took a beating almost every day. Abrezzo kept telling me I had a lot of talent but needed to improve my footwork, or that my punches were almost fast enough and just needed time to develop, or that with a little more upper body strength I would be powerful enough to fight at the Pelican Athletic Club, and hold my own with the local middleweights.

"Abrezzo was nothing but sweet-talk. He charmed me and made me believe I could be a winner while I was nothing but a punching bag for his A-list fighters. And after two months, I knew it."

Javier could not help but feel a bit angry. "Yet you stayed away for another year. Why didn't you come home? Why didn't you write?"

"When I left Tampa, I believed that I would waltz back into town with bags of money and tales of success. I was nowhere close to either and pride got the best of me. I could not send news of failure so I sent no news at all."

"How long did you give into his flattery?"

Lázaro shook his head. "One day I was sparring with Tex Sullivan, a middleweight from Ireland, when I broke two fingers in my right hand. Pow! A short hook to his jaw and it felt like my whole arm shattered. It never properly healed." Lázaro showed his hand to Javier where the knuckles of his first two fingers were crooked, the skin tightened and scarred.

"I was out of the ring and out of business. Abrezzo wouldn't pay for a doctor, but he still expected me to spar if I was going to hang around. I couldn't even sweep because of the pain. I was useless because a dozen other boys who wanted to be fighters were willing to haul Abrezzo's trash. He kicked me out and left me with my clothes, my shoes, and a cheap pair of boxing gloves. My only other possession was the knife I'd carried with me since Tampa.

"That knife only helped my bad luck continue. I was out on the streets, hungry and broke. I had nowhere to go, no friends in town, I couldn't even buy a stamp and mail a letter home. So I went to a place where I knew I'd find money. There was a bar down the street from Abrezzo's gym where they threw craps and bet on card games until sun up. That knife gave me false confidence, the boldness of some tough guy who knows how to take care of himself. But I was stupid, Javier. Stupid."

Javier was already shaking his head. "Don't tell me."

"You won't believe how stupid I was. I chose some man who I thought was a weakling. This man, who I watched during the night, had been winning over and over again at craps. He carried with him a handful of cash and peeled the bills off one after another, only to collect handfuls in return. This man appeared frail in the bulky suit that he wore. The brim of his hat covered his face but had I seen the coarse look in his eyes, I may not have been so brave. I thought for some strange reason that he was some lone man passing through town, who stopped at a bar and got lucky. He was in fact, a member of the syndicate that ran the boxing and gambling rackets in New Orleans."

Javier still shook his head. "What happened?"

Lázaro continued, "I followed this man outside and when I thought we were alone I attacked from behind. I wrapped one arm around his neck and held his head in a vice-lock, and with the other hand I held the point of my knife at his throat. 'You are making a giant mistake,' he said but I didn't listen. I took his money, threw him to the curb and disappeared as fast as lightening."

Lázaro threw his head back and laughed. "Oh, the fortune I thought I had earned! I had a handful of cash and the whole city before me. I thought I had conquered the world! But not even ten minutes had passed, before I could even count what I had taken, and I was tackled by four men. They took the money and beat me senseless." Lázaro pulled his lower lip away to show his brother where two molars were missing. "I'm lucky they did not kill me."

"You mindless hoodlum," said Javier. "Lázaro, that has to be the dumbest thing you have ever done. What kind of an idiot are you?"

Lázaro hung his head and nodded shamefully. "I was desperate and foolish."

Javier repeated a phrase their mother had used, "We should sell you to the circus."

Lázaro said, "I left town immediately. I hitched a ride on a train and found myself among a group of hobos. They were a ragged bunch and they smelled terrible but now I was among them. I acted tough and told them plenty of lies about my life in New Orleans, and my days fighting Spaniards in Cuba Libre."

Javier snickered. "You fought in the war? I didn't know about that!"

"These men wouldn't know and I did what I thought was necessary."

"Did it work?"

"No. One of them asked about the worst thing I ever saw during the war. I had nothing to tell them, so I made up a story of how I once survived a battle where one hundred men were slain. Their blood covered the battlefield. One of them even had a bullet hole through his eye. None of this was true but I thought it would scare them into leaving me alone. Instead, they laughed. I didn't know if it was because they knew I was lying or for some other reason but they soon started telling me about the terrible things *they* had seen.

"One of them had fought in the American Civil War and told countless tales of bloody battlefields, amputations and disease. Another said he had seen a man cut in half at the waist by the wheels of a train. Then there was a third, who told me of finding his mother dead in her cellar half eaten by rats.

"It was embarrassing to hear their true stories after making up my own. These were men who had experienced life, real life. Soon, somewhere into North Carolina I started to walk. I hopped off the train and just started walking, all the way through the state of Virginia."

"You walked through the state of Virginia?"

"It took eighty-nine days. I went door to door begging for food and even ate a crushed candy bar that I scraped off the pavement. I don't think I'll ever be able to eat another chocolate bar again. Somewhere near Washington I boarded another train and wondered what turns in life had forced me to literally pick my food off the street. I pondered this all the way to New York City."

Javier's eyes widened. "New York City!"

Lázaro smiled. "The greatest city in the world! It is like nothing you have ever seen. Unimaginable! The size of ten, maybe even twenty Havanas!" Lázaro told his brother of the city's vast layout, the tall buildings, the crowded streets, the countless ethnic groups, the speed at which the city moved, the music, the art and the food. "It is a great city that I intend to visit again and again."

374

Javier was impressed. Lázaro's departure from Ybor City a year ago had seemed foolish and immature, but he had returned having seen the greatest city of America, something Javier had often dreamed about. He begged Lázaro for more.

"Unfortunately, my luck did not change once I reached New York," said Lázaro. "I was no better off than I had been in New Orleans. I found a job at a restaurant, hauling trash and cleaning up, washing dishes, but I couldn't write home. I had nothing to show for my efforts. I had proven nothing. I became depressed and spent some time with the bottle."

"What about boxing?"

"I tried. There were a few fights but nothing that paid enough to live on. I fought no one special, learned nothing new except for some English, met a girl and like a fool, I trusted her and paid for it later. Lived in a crummy apartment in New York's version of the Scrub.

"One day I realized I did not like it on my own. I was homesick, I was broke and I was sorry I'd left my family. With the money I had I bought a ticket on a steamer to Jacksonville and then traveled by train to Tampa. And here I am."

Javier looked upon Lázaro with new respect. His younger brother had matured ten years. For a boy to become a man he must first admit to his mistakes and Lázaro had been open and honest about his failures. Men are proud and often find it difficult to accept failure and discontent. Failure was not something Javier liked to admit to; he doubted it was pleasant for his father. Admitting and accepting defeat was certainly not possible for someone like Juan Carlos. Lázaro had grown unpredictably wise and for a moment, Javier felt like the younger brother.

Javier said, "I'm glad you're home."

"I'm sick of telling lies," replied Lázaro. "But I haven't given up on my dream. I will still become a boxer. I only came home because I'm hungry and broke, but when I'm ready, I'm going back out."

They finished their lunch without another word.

"I can't believe Mama died." Lázaro set his utensils aside and stared at his empty plate.

Javier pushed his plate away. "Would you like to visit her?"

Lázaro took a moment to decide but nodded that he did. Javier took Lázaro to the cemetery, and the younger brother stood silently beside the plot and gazed reverently at the ceramic photo of his mother that decorated the tombstone. There were a thousand things he wished he could tell her: stories of his adventures, apologies for his actions, and plans for his future. He knelt and said a short prayer then stood as Javier approached.

"This business about Papa must be settled," Javier said. "If he's still alive we may be the only people who can find him."

Lázaro nodded and agreed.

Javier extended his hand. "Let's vow that our father will not end up in this grave beside Mama before his time." They shook on it and then left the cemetery and headed into town to begin their search.

Later that afternoon the brothers heard on the street that the President of the United States, William McKinley, had been shot by a radical leftist. He would die six days later and be succeeded by a hero of the Spanish American War, Theodore Roosevelt.

Chapter 31

After the failed attempt to assassinate Antonio Vasquez, the paranoid cigar manufacturer enlisted the protection of a bodyguard: his pipsqueak son Antonio Junior. The boy had no training in self-defense or the use of firearms; he had probably never even been in a fight. Armando shook his head at another thoughtless decision by the inept Antonio Vasquez, baffled that the manufacturer had managed to stay in business for so long.

Armando turned his attention back to the labor relations meeting, where Alessandria Prizzi addressed the Cigar Trust. "*La Resistencia* has been officially dissolved and the cigar workers are prepared to return to the factories under management's conditions."

It was news the manufacturers were relieved to hear: an official surrender from the highest ranking member of the defunct labor union. Vasquez asked, "How soon can your people return to work?"

Prizzi started to answer, but the president of the CMIU local, Tony Bello, answered for her. "The factories will be filled by Thursday."

Vasquez sat back and grinned at his colleagues. Armando, Capecho, Kincaid and Cienfuegos nodded. Capecho took notes. Armando started to calculate *bolita* proceeds. The General Strike of 1901 had ended with a victory for the manufacturers. The strike began with an effort to marginalize *La Resistencia* and had resulted in the complete obliteration of the radical labor union.

Bello said, "We've made arrangements for the Cigar Manufacturer's International Union to absorb former members of *La Resistencia* so those workers will not go without representation. We plan to introduce these blue labels." He held up a small blue sticker decorated with the union's emblem. "We will fix these labels to all boxes of cigars that are union made."

"Great," Vasquez said. "We are happy to tolerate a union that is more centrist."

Bello nodded and understood that the CMIU was the preferred union of the manufacturers only because *La Resistencia* had been so extreme. Now that it was the only union in town and represented nearly all the Tampa workforce, the CMIU would receive more scrutiny than before. Vasquez dismissed the two labor representatives and turned to the members of his inner circle.

"Thank God." He sat back and lit one of his Don Florentino cigars. "I had to cash in the insurance policy on my building to pay my nervous creditors and avoid all-out financial failure." If the strike did not end by the end of the month, Vasquez and Company had been prepared to fold.

"No worries now," Armando said as he lit his own cigar and waited while the others followed suit. The men sat back and puffed their *puros*, savoring their long, hard-fought and debilitating victory. "I know our methods were extreme, but I hope none of you feel any remorse. It was the removal of those labor leaders that broke the will of the workers, turned the tide of this dispute, and put us over the top."

No one spoke as they smoked their cigars and pondered the fate of the eight men who had been kidnapped and taken to the coast of Honduras. Armando gazed out of the corner of his eye to Antonio Vasquez. What would he need to do to stick the manufacturer and his fat son on a boat and ship them overseas too?

Factory doors opened the next day, and the workers returned in a somber procession. The galley of Vasquez and Company was only half-full as many of the workers were still being called back from other towns. Javier, Lázaro, and E.J. filed into the brick building with a defeated group desperate for work, needing the money to feed their families. *La Resistencia* had been dissolved, and the fight for ideological purity that led to its demise no longer mattered.

Scales and weight restrictions had also been instituted in the factory, undoing all progress made during the Weight Strike of 1899. A major setback for the workers – they had lost their union and the benefit of personal samples of tobacco. Now, with new and aggressive daily quotas and no free cigars, the cigar makers sulked in failure.

"Life goes on," Javier said to his brothers. As they sat at the wooden benches and mashed their brown tobacco leaves into dolls they missed Gabriel Mendez, who no longer occupied his chair atop the *tribuna*. He had been replaced with a younger, more reserved *lector* named Paolo Vargas, a reader homegrown in Tampa, educated in Latin schools and the son of Cuban immigrants.

"I don't care for this guy," Lázaro muttered. He had kept his hair long but his beard had been trimmed and he wore a thick, black moustache like Calixto García. As he listened to a reading from Vargas he felt the *lector* lacked the passion of Mendez. He missed the colorful inflections that Mendez brought to his readings and Vargas's voice carried poorly across the floor.

"He's the product of a failed undertaking," Javier replied. "A consolation prize for the losing side." The rest of the cigar makers knew that Vargas failed to fill the void left by Mendez, and served as a stark reminder that the original *lector* had been kidnapped and deported along with the rest of their outlawed union's leadership.

"Hey, Ortiz."

Javier turned to the voice behind him which belonged to an older, dark-skinned cigar maker named Manny.

"I heard about your father. If there's anything I can do, let me know." Manny nodded, showing his appreciation.

"Thank you, Manny." Javier said politely and went back to his work.

The worker beside Javier, a large Cuban man in his thirties nicknamed Big Guava nudged Javier's elbow. "I heard they took them to Central America and left them for dead."

Javier nodded. "I've heard that too. Any truth to it?"

"Who knows?" Big Guava shrugged. "I also heard the mafia was involved."

"The mafia?"

"Uh-huh. The Cracker Mafia, led by the man with the beard." He used a pudgy hand to stroke an imaginary beard.

"You mean Renteria?"

Big Guava nodded. "The man with the beard who runs this town."

"Tomorrow is their first payday, and sales have been staggering. Local businesses have reopened their doors fulltime, and our vendors have started selling chances. We should see a steady increase in interest as we approach the weekend." Armando had invited El Gallego to his office to discuss the first *bolita* throw in months, which was to take place that Saturday at La Rubia.

"These bastards always fall for the same old trick," Gallego said, his bushy hair and wide grin always a welcome sight to Armando. Gallego referred to the practice of hedging their bets – painting a number on a lead ball and placing it amidst the hundred clay *bolita* balls used for each throw. They didn't think of this clever practice as cheating but a way to minimize their losses and offset the proceeds claimed by winning *bolita* tickets. Armando and Gallego had been doing it for almost two years, and the Cubans had no idea they were being swindled.

Armando slapped his partner's shoulder. "It feels good to be back in business!"

In the evenings Alessandria was usually found at the debate clubs or the Cuban social club across from the Martinez Ybor factory, but with half the workforce still out of town she remained on the porch of her shotgun house and chatted with her neighbors while chomping on a thick, *robusto* cigar. She did not recognize Javier Ortiz as he approached the porch.

"Alessandria?" Javier called.

She stayed on her porch rocking chair with her hands folded over her belly, her cigar dangling from her mouth. "Come closer so I don't have to shout!"

Javier placed a foot on the bottom step. "I'm Javier Ortiz. Salvador Ortiz was my father. I was hoping we could talk."

Alessandria removed the cigar from her mouth and held it between two fingers. "Terrible what happened to your father, to the whole damned lot of them. What can people like us do about it? We've gone to the mayor; we've gone to the police. We're totally powerless."

"My sister said they were going to petition the district attorney."

"No one in this town is talking. They're worried the Committee of Fifteen will return and punish anyone *perceived* to be causing trouble.

Keep a low profile, boy. Don't give them a chance to finger you as a radical."

He climbed the steps and squatted beside her chair. "I've heard a lot of rumors," he kept his voice low so the neighbors could not hear. "They were taken to Africa, or the Caribbean, or murdered and buried. I've heard a lot of things since I've been back. But you were close to my father and the rest of the men. What do *you* know?"

Her teeth snatched the cigar from her fingers. "Don't expect me to be an accomplice in your little game. I'm lucky they didn't get me the first time, and I'm not so sure they'll stay away just because I'm female. Your father is probably dead in some jungle somewhere, and I'm sitting here safe and alive. I intend to stay alive."

"Of course," he said. "But is there anything you can tell me? Anything at all? Who took them? Where did they take them? Who else can help me?"

"Boy," she pulled from her cigar and blew a cone of smoke into the air. "Everyone knows your boss was the man behind it."

"Vasquez?"

She nodded and chomped on the cigar. "Vasquez and his boss. You know who pulls the strings in this town. You know who runs the show."

"The man with the beard."

She nodded. "If anyone knows what happened to your father it's him."

"Señor Renteria?"

"Who's asking?"

Javier stepped into Armando's office and approached the desk. Lázaro stayed behind and lurked just inside the door. "Javier Ortiz," he introduced himself and motioned towards his brother. "My brother, Lázaro."

Armando looked at them with indifference, not linking the name Ortiz to the labor leader who had been deported to Honduras. He inspected the brothers and saw that Javier was good-looking compared to the other one, whose face seemed crooked in every way, from his uneven eyes to his bent nose. A burly, black moustache hung dirtily over an awkward, drooling sneer and slumping shoulders made Lázaro appear stupid and clumsy. Yet his dark eyes and an athletic build toughened his look. These boys were serious about something.

The industrialist locked a stack of papers in his desk and fiddled with his keys, ready to lock his office and head out for the evening. "What do you want?"

Javier swallowed, nervous to confront the bearded man. "I'm trying to find my father, he has disappeared."

Now he remembered. Ortiz. Salvador Ortiz, who was probably rotting on some deserted beach hundreds of miles away. Armando feigned ignorance as he closed his briefcase and pushed his chair into his desk. "Never heard of him. Sorry I couldn't help."

Armando tried to walk past Javier but the elder Ortiz sidestepped and blocked his exit. Taken aback by the young man's courage, Armando stood face to face with Salvador's son and looked down at him. Armando was two inches taller, and his eyes scolded Javier for the infraction, but from the corner of his eye Armando noticed Lázaro had taken a step closer.

Javier said, "My father was friends with Gabriel Mendez and Angelo De la Parte. Everyone in town has heard those names."

There was something about this boy that Armando liked. Perhaps it was his confidence, because if Javier was afraid, Armando couldn't tell. Trying to gauge the danger he was in and deciding it was minimal, Armando gently tapped Javier on the chest with his keys. "I recognize those names and I think I may know of your father, sure. But what does this have to do with me?"

Javier felt his heart throbbing in his temples; the adrenaline gave him strength, even as he stood on the turf of this influential man. He summoned his courage and thought of his father, starving and alone somewhere far away. "Several of this city's labor leaders were kidnapped and deported."

"My boy," Armando said irritably. "What do you want?"

"I want to know what happened to my father."

"Hire a detective." Armando tried to get by but again Javier blocked his exit. Armando became agitated and wondered what these boys had planned. "Son, you have no idea what you're doing." He gave Javier an arrogant smile. "Do you?"

Javier inhaled deeply and noticed Lázaro now stood almost directly behind him. Armando seemed to have grown taller, his eyes seemed darker. Javier wavered before the powerful town boss, realizing suddenly that he had underestimated Armando's authority.

Finally the bearded Spaniard seemed to relax. A small smile broke and he said gently to Javier, "My boy, I am dismayed that your father has vanished, but you have entered the office of a respected Tampa business leader. Now if you don't turn around and walk yourself out, and take your brother with you, then I will make arrangements that will prevent you from ever walking again."

He waited but the boys didn't move – the long-haired brother watched with an icy stare while Javier nervously held his ground. Armando continued, "There are men who can be threatened and men who cannot. I am a respected captain of industry, a personal friend of the chief of police, and I can walk into the mayor's office any time of day and tell him exactly what I think. You may have talked yourself into believing that courage and acts of gallantry can intimidate a man like me, but I can assure you that you've misjudged your influence in this town. I don't expect to see you around here ever again. Now ..." He leaned in close and hissed. "Piss off."

Javier froze, frightened, and didn't know if he should reply or turn and leave quietly. Lázaro thought otherwise. Perhaps it was the confident smirk on Armando's face, or the rich suit that he wore, or the way he bragged about his political connections. This was the type of man responsible for so many of their struggles: the empty plates, hundreds of displaced families, the poverty and the sickness.

Like he had done so many times before, Lázaro lost his temper. Pushing through Javier he lunged for the Spaniard, surprising Armando with his quickness, and pushed the industrialist against his desk, bracing him there with his body weight. The tip Lázaro's knife disappeared into Armando's beard.

"One chance, then I cut." Lázaro squeezed Armando's neck with his free hand. "Where's Salvador Ortiz?"

Armando gasped as Lázaro tightened his grip and pressed the knife into Armando's throat. Cupping his hands around Lázaro's wrists,

Armando tried to pull them away but the boy was strong – his grip was solid.

Stunned at his brother's bold action, Javier removed the pistol from his pocket and clumsily let it dangle in his hand while he stood at his brother's side, watching Lázaro hold Armando by the throat so tightly that veins bulged on Lázaro's forearm.

Lázaro coiled the knife in the gold chain that Armando wore, and with the flick of his wrist, yanked it back with a snap. The broken necklace slipped to the floor as Lázaro dug the knife in deeper, nearly puncturing the delicate skin of Armando's neck. "What did you do with our father?"

Armando's eyes bulged. He managed a breath and spoke with a cracked voice. "You'd better kill me now because if I see either of you in this town again I will kill you both."

"Oh, no, Captain," Lázaro shook his head. "It's not wise to threaten me when I'm in this state of mind." He felt a gentle hand on his arm.

Javier whispered. "Don't."

Lázaro hesitated. Armando looked into his eyes, his hands still cupped around Lázaro's wrists, bracing and ready to counteract. Beads of perspiration had formed on the boy's forehead as he seemed to come to his senses and realize he had nearly killed a man.

"Come on," Javier pleaded and tugged at Lázaro's arm.

Finally Lázaro released Armando as Javier wrapped both hands around his brother and pulled him away from the shocked investor before Armando had time to react. Another yank from Javier and the boys fled through the front door and ran away.

Armando was stunned at their audacity. *Brave boys*, he thought as he watched the brothers hurry away from the building. *Brave and stupid.* They'd pay for this incident. He had three choices: sending a group to kidnap them and drag them into the swamps for a mock lynching, hiring an assassin to take them out, or killing them both himself.

He rubbed his neck as he pulled himself off his desk and then squatted to the floor to recover his broken necklace. He picked the gold chain off the floor and let it dangle from one hand. Inspecting the small, golden cross that hung from the necklace, he considered its meaning and the reason he wore a symbol of the Lord. Shaking his head at the close encounter and nearly laughing at the courage of the Ortiz boys, Armando coiled the chain into a small ball and shoved it into his pocket.

The first payday in almost three months meant that La Rubia was crowded with cigar makers awaiting the first *bolita* throw since the 1901 General Strike began. Ticket sales had been overwhelming vendors all over town – boutiques, restaurants and taverns sold stacks of chances to eager players for the first throw on Saturday night. With the workers returning to the benches, the economy had been instantly energized, which made Armando Renteria the happiest man in town. The majority of the money that exchanged hands in *bolita* would eventually find its way into his pocket.

"How are we doing?" Armando asked Gallego as they met behind the bar at La Rubia. The *bolitero* had brought the Sanchez brothers with him, to help with crowd control and to watch for those pesky Ortiz boys.

"Life has returned," Gallego smiled. "Receipts are nearing an all-time record! I'm expecting a huge turnout tonight."

Armando nodded and glanced around the tavern, which was starting to fill with early afternoon patrons. Cubans, Spaniards and Italians, nearly all of them cigar workers, were arriving earlier than normal and filling their bellies with beer and rum. The smell of burning cigars created a spicy, chocolate aroma.

"What's the magic number?"

Gallego smiled as he checked a sheet of paper on the bar. "Looks like there is one number that hasn't received a single wager. Thirty-seven."

Armando patted Gallego on the back. "Play the percentages and we can't lose."

By nine o'clock the bar was packed with cigar workers. Betting would be open until nine-thirty, and the throw was scheduled for ten. Javier and Lázaro arrived to socialize with their coworkers and purchased their own tickets. Javier chose number forty-two on a whim, and Lázaro bet on eighty-three, the year of his birth. Javier bought two bottles of beer and they found a pair of seats at a table, thinking nothing of the Sanchez brothers lurking nearby. "Do you think we should go back to Cuba?" Lázaro asked.

Javier squinted into his beer. "Why?" He wondered if Lázaro wanted to hide from Armando, something Javier had been thinking about since they ran from his office earlier that day.

"To find our grandfather. The one who is rich."

Javier laughed. "What is your plan? To walk up to him and beg for a handout?"

"I don't know," Lázaro shrugged.

They drank their beers and inspected their surroundings. The bar was full and more were arriving by the minute. The throw was a half hour away, and as the bar grew noisier, the cloud of cigar smoke thickened and hung near the ceiling. Ojos Negros suddenly appeared beside the brothers, his black eyes peering at them from dark, sunken sockets. "Have you heard any word from your father?"

Javier shook his head.

Ojos nudged Javier's shoulder. "If there's anything I can do, let me know. All the workers are pulling for them. They'll make it home soon enough, you wait and see."

"Thank you," Javier said, appreciating the words of confidence.

Now Gallego entered from the back room and announced, "Two minutes, then all bets are off!" He went towards the chalkboard that hung on the back wall and updated it with the latest *bolita* statistics. Armando appeared nearby.

Javier elbowed his brother and they lowered their heads to hide their faces. Javier saw those two Spanish hulks had followed Armando and lurked beside him. "Bodyguards," muttered Javier.

A rush of patrons made last minute bets. Tickets, coins and dollar bills waved above the crowd. It grew rowdier and noisier as players made their final wagers and Gallego announced the close of bets. "All bets are off! All bets are off!" The crowd settled as men went back to their drinks and good luck charms, and awaited the throw.

Keeping careful watch over Armando, Lázaro asked, "Should we leave?"

Javier shook his head. "Not yet. He hasn't noticed us."

"What if he does?"

"He might not do anything." Both of the boys were armed, and as long as they were among their fellow workers they felt safe. Getting home might be its own challenge.

Anticipation built as one hundred *bolita* balls were displayed on a wooden table under the chalkboard. Players came by with their good luck charms in hand and waved them over the numbers they had bet. Soon Gallego appeared with a red silk sack that would hold all one hundred balls. He held the sack open as Armando took the wooden tray and poured the little white balls into the sack. Then Gallego tightened the drawstring and tossed the bag into the crowd. The first *bolita* throw in three months was underway.

The crowd cheered and waved their lucky charms as the sack passed from man to man. Javier and Lázaro stayed in the shadows, using the patrons to shield themselves from Armando and his goons. When the bag made it back to Gallego, he stood on the platform and held the sack above his head. After one last shake he reached for the bottom and felt a handful of balls through the silk. As expected, he found one that was heavier than the others, pulled this ball away from the rest and tied a string around it. Then he produced a small knife and cut that ball out of the sack, letting the winning ball slide into his hand.

"Thirty-seven!" he announced and held up the winning ball.

There was an outburst of groans and disappointed grunts. No winner emerged, and the players soon turned their attention away from the game and back to their dominoes and drinks, engaging in conversations on politics, labor, and world affairs. Javier and Lázaro crumpled their losing tickets and tossed them to the floor before joining a group of cigar makers in a discussion about the new quotas.

Almost immediately Lázaro noticed Armando watching him from across the bar and saw the Sanchez brothers pushing through the crowd. Lázaro patted his brother on the shoulder, pointing with one hand while he reached into his pocket with the other. Javier followed his brother's gaze and saw Armando looking his direction.

"Shit," Javier whispered. He felt his pocket where his pistol rested and prepared to draw it and keep it low and hidden.

Benny led Eddie through the crowded bar. "Take them into the alley," Armando had instructed. "I'll meet you outside." Benny was ten feet from Javier. The bar was filled with men who talked loud, drank beer or rum and laughed as they blew cigar smoke and gambled.

Javier backed up instinctively. He didn't realize it but the small pistol was in his hand. Lázaro stood close to his brother with his knife held tightly in his fist. His eyes switched back and forth between the advancing Sanchez brothers and Armando.

Benny's eyes locked on Javier. Two men were in his way so Benny sidestepped them and came face to face with the young cigar maker. Benny halted, and froze when he saw the small black mouth of a pistol watching him from Javier's hip. Benny's eyes moved from the pistol to Javier.

Javier shook his head subtly, warning Benny to remain halted. Eddie stopped and stood behind his brother realizing something was wrong. Javier glanced to his right for Lázaro but found him pushing through the patrons, heading towards the back, towards Armando. Eddie saw this too and peeled from Benny's side to follow Lázaro.

Benny and Javier stood watching each other. Javier kept his pistol pointed at Benny while Benny stood awkwardly in place, his hands before him. He didn't know if he should raise them above his head, or if Javier was bluffing and would falter at the moment he needed his pistol the most.

"Just take it easy," Benny said. "Mr. Renteria wants to talk to you outside."

"Do I look stupid? I follow you outside, and I'm a dead man." Javier glanced towards Lázaro and saw his brother had nearly reached Armando, who stood across the bar watching.

"Back off," Javier said.

Benny took a step closer, ready to call Javier's bluff. Big Guava and Ojos Negros suddenly appeared on either side of Javier with their eyes on Benny, warning him to stay in place.

Lázaro reached the back where the only thing that separated him from Armando was the table that held the wooden tray and the sack of one hundred *bolita* balls. Lázaro grabbed the table with both hands, leaned forward, and hissed at Armando, "You sissy, you need bodyguards to protect you from a couple of orphans? Why don't we settle this right here, you and me?"

Gallego appeared beside Armando, looking almost bored. He still held the winning thirty-seven ball in his hand. "My boy, do you have any idea who you're talking to?"

Benny took another step closer to Javier. He didn't think the boy would use the pistol and he wasn't worried about the pair of cigar makers who flanked either side. "Just a few words outside," Benny said. "No one wants to hurt you."

Javier glanced to Benny and then to Lázaro. Benny saw his chance. While Javier looked the other way, Benny pounced. His right hand went towards Javier's face to block the boy's view while the other hand reached for the pistol. He underestimated the boy's reflexes. Faster than Benny moved, Javier slipped into the crowd and out of Benny's reach and Big Guava and Ojos Negros blocked the path of the advancing Sanchez brother.

Javier darted through the crowd until he was right beside Lázaro. Now some of the nearby patrons noticed a confrontation and halted their conversations to watch.

Armando said to Lázaro. "Let's settle this like men. Why don't we all step outside for some fresh air?"

The Sanchez brothers were now within reach and prepared to grab the boys. Lázaro pulled his knife, spun in place and thrust it towards Eddie's throat, halting the giant in place. "Don't you fucking move!"

Javier raised his gun and pointed it at Armando as gasps arose from the crowd.

The noise in the bar died. Most of the customers saw the pistol and backed away, watching with shock as the standoff unfolded before them. Eddie Sanchez had his hands up, and Lázaro's knife was mere inches from his throat while Javier's pistol pointed at the *bolita* kingpin. Benny Sanchez was directly behind Javier, wondering again if this was a bluff or if he should act.

"Call him off," Javier said to Armando and motioned behind him to Benny. "Call him off!" he yelled, and Armando nodded to Benny who took a step back and gave Javier some room. Eddie did the same. If Armando was at all frightened, he hid it well. His expression was a mixture of boredom and concern. The rage Javier expected was not there.

The crowd waited.

"Eight men were abducted recently!" Javier shouted so all could hear. "Eight immigrant cigar workers. Writers, leaders, fathers, and brothers. *Our* father!" he shouted and slapped his chest, and then waved his hand over all the patrons. "Your *brothers!*" He trained his eyes on Armando and pointed with his pistol. "This man knows what happened to the eight. This man is responsible."

Now the patrons began to murmur among themselves. They looked to Armando and awaited a response. As he glanced across the crowd, Armando noticed their stern eyes. Not demanding, but questioning, as if they expected to hear Armando's side of the story before they reacted.

Armando smiled and tried not to look humiliated. "The boy has clearly suffered some trauma and has gone a bit crazy." He said to Javier, "You have lost your mind."

"Tell us what happened to the eight," Javier demanded.

Again Armando looked over the crowd. Gallego broke the tension. "Why don't the four of us go back to my office and discuss this? That way everyone else can get back to their drinks while this is settled."

Not a single person moved.

Armando sneered towards Lázaro, who held his knife towards Eddie. Armando said, "We only need to talk to the older brother. The ugly one can stay here."

That was enough for Lázaro. He tucked his knife into his pocket and with a roar he grabbed the wooden table and flipped it over. A hundred clay *bolita* balls spilled to the floor and rolled under the feet of the customers. Lázaro lunged for Armando, ready to beat him down with bare fists, but Gallego dove between them and blocked Lázaro's advance. Eddie Sanchez reached in from behind and grabbed Lázaro by the throat while Armando backed against the wall and watched as Javier covered him with his pistol.

The crowd was silent.

Lázaro's adrenaline surged. He stabbed his elbow backwards and connected squarely into Eddie's gut and knocked the wind out of the giant. Eddie fell away coughing and Lázaro turned back to Armando, but Gallego was again in his way.

Lázaro pushed hard with both arms and forced Gallego back to the wall. Gallego hit it with a thump and dropped the winning *bolita* ball. The heavy lead ball made a loud clang as it hit the wooden floor, a sound that caught everyone's attention. It was not the sound of clay striking wood but a deeper, heavier thud that sounded metallic.

The ball rolled across the floor and stopped at Javier's feet. The unusual sound had caught his ears too. He squatted, picked up the ball and noticed right away that it was much too heavy to be made from clay.

All action had ceased. Even Lázaro turned his attention to the thirty-seven ball in Javier's hand, suspecting as did every man in the bar, that the throw might not have been honest.

Javier held the heavy number thirty-seven and turned to Lázaro. "Hand me your knife." They traded weapons and Javier used the blade to scrape a flake of white paint off the ball. Under the paint, Javier dug into the soft lead and shaved off a shiny, silver slice of metal. Great shouting erupted among the nearby cigar workers and like a ripple the rest of the bar instantly learned the winning ball was a fraud.

Javier held the ball above his head. "The winning ball is made from lead! We have been swindled!" He pointed to Armando, who stood against the wall watching his empire crumble. Javier shouted. "He's running a scam!"

The patrons started to shout. Crumpled *bolita* tickets and burning cigar stubs flew towards Armando and Gallego as the two *bolita* masters were suddenly mobbed by angry players demanding refunds. Gallego tried to calm the crowd, but his voice was drowned out by angry shouting. Fearing for their own safety, Gallego and Armando tried to push through the people and find their way out of the bar, but the crowd was too thick. The angry patrons swarmed them like vultures attacking a carcass. Eddie and Benny became useless inside the horde as Armando and Gallego disappeared under the crowd.

Javier and Lázaro watched the melee unfold before them with shock, amazed that this crowd had come to life as it had. They smiled at each other incredulously as the angry patrons mobbed Armando and Gallego, and eventually chased them out of the bar like a pair of squirrels being shooed from a garden.

The crowd cheered once Armando and Gallego were gone, and Javier and Lázaro were quickly surrounded by smiling cigar workers who cheered and patted their backs. Big Guava grinned and gave Javier a hearty kiss on the cheek. "We always suspected this game was corrupt but never had the *cojones* to try and prove it." He turned to the crowd. "The Ortiz boys are heroes!"

The crowd began to chant. "Ortiz! Ortiz! Ortiz!"

Javier and Lázaro couldn't stifle their smiles. The attention and appreciation of the cigar workers was overwhelming. Though they had not accomplished what they set out to do, and were no closer to finding their father, the Ortiz brothers were responsible for a gigantic morale booster, and felt that Salvador had been oddly avenged.

Chapter 32

Armando circled through town to collect receipts from his *bolita* ticket vendors. His first stop was the Gonzalez Bakery, where he was greeted by a delicate fragrance of cinnamon and fresh baked pastries. The welcoming morning smell was ruined by the angry chirping of two old Italian women, who waved their *bolita* stubs at Porfirio Gonzalez while scolding him spitefully. Armando lurked near the front door and listened.

"What is this about a scam last night at La Rubia?" One of the displeased women asked while the other tapped her foot. "Something about a weighted ball?"

The baker appeared as irritated as the women. "You've heard what I've heard!"

"How long have you been running this scam?"

Porfirio held up his hands defensively. "I only sell the tickets!" He was flustered that so many customers had suggested him to be some kind of cheat. "I'm telling you, if you come into the bakery and want a ticket, I will sell you a ticket. I have nothing to do with the throw. I have never even *been* to a throw!"

The two women looked at each other and then placed their tickets on the counter, demanding their money be refunded. "For every game played with a weighted ball."

Porfirio took their tickets and shook his head as he dug his hand into the cash register and slammed the metal drawer shut. He slapped a handful of coins on the counter and watched them wobble in circles. "That's two weeks' worth of refunds. Are you going to buy anything from the bakery?"

The women counted their money, seeming satisfied, and the first one shook her head. "Not anymore. We heard of another *bolita* game that's been started by two Italian men. We won't do business with cheaters."

With that the women turned, held their noses high, and marched out of the bakery.

Porfirio watched them leave and then saw Armando standing by the door. The Spaniard approached the counter, his brow contracted into a concerned wrinkle and his left hand slightly open, awaiting an explanation. Porfirio remained frustrated as he paced restlessly behind the counter. "Armando, what can you tell me about this drama from last night? My business is hemorrhaging from refunds, and half my most loyal customers tell me they're never coming back!"

Armando had hoped to avoid the subject of the so-called swindle for as long as possible. "How many tickets have you sold for next week?"

Porfirio scoffed. "How many have I sold? None!"

"Your customers aren't happy?"

Porfirio's jaw wavered in midair. "Are you kidding? They're so upset that I'm worried I won't be able to stay in business!"

Armando smiled calmly. "You'll be fine, my friend. Your *churros* are the best in the city!"

Porfirio placed his hands on his hips and started disapprovingly at Armando. "Don't tell me you came here to collect."

Armando raised his eyebrows and nodded.

Porfirio laughed. "Thanks to you, I haven't a penny!"

Armando feared this. "Very well," he nodded agreeably and then turned to leave.

"What about my store?" Porfirio called after him. "I expect to be compensated!"

Armando stood at the door and looked back. "I'm not running a charity, my friend."

As Armando left, Porfirio shouted. "At least you could buy a pastry!"

Armando encountered similar situations throughout town. Angry customers had demanded refunds all day, and the vendors had earned barely any profits to kick back to Armando. Infuriated at being linked to a corrupt game, one store owner refused to speak to Armando when the kingpin arrived to collect.

He completed his rounds with just a few dollars in his hands and knew that as a *bolitero* he was quite possibly ruined. His primary income stream seemed dead, and he could not live off his small interest in prostitution, or his investments in the cigar industry. Returning to his office with his future in question, Armando was shamed to be heckled by a group of Cuban youths, who shouted him down as a cheat and a liar.

Safely inside his office, Armando sat at the desk and opened his ledger to take inventory. Without *bolita* he would lose eighty percent of his income and most of his strength. He owned twenty-five percent of Vasquez and Company, and now that the factory was operating at capacity he would start to receive dividends but only enough to cover basic expenses. There were his sliver holdings in the other cigar companies plus ownership in a small shipping company. These assets did not generate income and would not produce much capital were he to sell his interests. That left prostitution, a business in which Armando rarely dabbled. There were the call girls at the Pasaje who kicked back to him and several other brothels throughout Ybor City that didn't. He could move in on that world and consolidate his power, or sell his interest in Vasquez and Company to another buyer to generate the capital he'd need to dig himself out of this financial hole.

Just then his office door swung open and the chief of police entered from the street followed by a tall, curly haired American that Armando didn't recognize.

"Had a rough night, did you?" the chief stated instead of asking. He approached Armando's desk and stepped to the side to introduce his counterpart. "This is Douglas Clark, United States Attorney, Middle District of Florida."

Clark nodded gravely towards Armando. His bushy, gray hair was frozen in place, and his sharp blue suit and stern stare projected an ethical purity. Armando wondered if the black briefcase Clark carried in his left hand was filled with bits and pieces of incriminating evidence to be puzzled together.

The chief turned to Clark. "Mr. Renteria is one of Ybor City's most respected businessmen. He's an investor in our city's commerce and an ambassador for our community. If you have any questions about how this town functions, Armando has all the answers."

Clark extended his hand for the investor. "I am pleased to make your acquaintance."

"Likewise," Armando said as they shook hands. He glanced at the chief expecting to hear more.

McGrath explained. "The DA is in town to investigate some complaints that have been flowing into his office, regarding the alleged disappearance of eight leftist labor leaders."

"Yes." Clark stiffened and looked directly at Armando while he reached into his pants pocket for a small notepad. He flipped a few pages and read his notes. "It appears several crimes in this town have gone unanswered: the murder of Ramiro Ragano, the lynching of two Italian boys, the attempted murder of Antonio Vasquez, widespread prostitution, and a gambling ring centered around an illegal lottery called," Clark squinted as he awkwardly pronounced the foreign word, "*bo-lita.*"

Armando swallowed and tried to control his body language, keeping himself calm and interested. "That certainly makes for one busy afternoon."

The men chuckled, and as Clark slipped his notepad into his pocket, he smiled to Armando. "It'll likely take me and my team much longer than that."

"Certainly."

"Why don't you stop by the courthouse if you have any information or would like to talk? And please let either me or the chief know if you're going to leave town. Understand?"

Armando swallowed again. "Of course, thank you for stopping by to introduce yourself, Mr. Clark. I'll certainly help you any way I can."

"Excellent," Clark smiled and then nodded to the chief that he was ready to leave. McGrath opened the door for Clark, and before he left Armando's office, the redhead police chief turned back to the Spaniard and warned Armando by mouthing the words, "*Leave town!*"

And then Armando was alone.

The chief had aligned himself with the district attorney, and their visit to Armando was a clear warning from McGrath that the police protection Armando had enjoyed for so long was gone. It was time to leave town.

He sat for a moment to collect his thoughts and then unlocked the safe beside his desk. He removed two small stacks of cash and stuffed them into his pocket and then found the folder with his business contracts. He placed the papers on his desk and started shuffling through them, searching for his agreement with Vasquez and Company.

Monday morning in the factory Javier noticed a considerable improvement in worker morale. There were more smiles and more laughs, and the workers moved faster as they filled their quotas. One hundred and fifty cigars were required each day. One hundred and seventy-five paid a small bonus. Javier finished number sixty-five, placed it in the wooden mold, and started on number sixty-six.

Vargas read the national news from the *tribuna*, and the workers chatted quietly. The summer months were behind them, but the Florida heat meant the October sun still warmed the factory, and with no ventilation the galley remained eternally hot and humid.

Josefina Ortiz suddenly burst onto the factory floor wearing her nurse's uniform and desperately searched through rows and rows of faces. Javier saw her from his bench and was surprised his sister was in the factory...had she *ever* been inside one? He raised his hand and motioned to her, and when she saw her brothers, Josefina grinned and ran down the main aisle to their bench.

Lázaro and E.J. looked up from their work to see a smiling Josefina waving a yellow telegram before Javier. With gleaming black eyes she announced, "Good news from Havana!"

Collecting his thoughts over bourbon, Armando sat in the lounge at the Pasaje, where one drink quickly became three. Armando had no one to talk to but himself. A Vasquez and Company Don Florentino burned beside his drink. He considered how his reputation, now terribly tarnished, could be repaired.

Financially, his credit was still impeccable and he could easily take out a bank loan and invest in the local economy. Maybe he could purchase a store or a bakery, or a company that supplied materials to the cigar corporations. He wanted to own as many pieces of the world as he could get his hands on.

As he swirled his bourbon, Armando wondered: did he really believe in cigars? Did he want to own a string of factories because he thought he could improve the craft in any way? Did he love the leaf the way a tobacco farmer did? Armando smiled and admitted to himself that he cared little about the science of tobacco – he just liked the idea of someone smoking a Don Renteria.

He had enabled men to feed their families. He had herded shiftless workers back to the benches like camels too stubborn or stupid to find water on their own. His tough love had revitalized the city. If the cigar workers appreciated the things he had done he could be elected mayor!

Mayor. Was he too corrupt to run for public office? Or did his sins satisfy the profile of every elected servant? Were his crimes worse than any of the tainted methods used by other great leaders of men? Ybor City was a lawless society, but did that mean Armando's actions hadn't been a blessing for the people of this city? In his drunkenness, Armando convinced himself that helping those Ybor City families somehow made up for all of his failings.

He ordered another drink and let his mind wander.

The Ortiz brothers.

Those pesky little anarchists had ruined his business. Should they be allowed to go free and tell their tale to all of Ybor City? With the district attorney in town, could Armando risk retribution when he was already suspected of several crimes?

The solitude was heavy. He drank to his loneliness and decided to finish his business at the hotel. It was time to visit Gisela.

He waited in the hallway for nearly five minutes before she answered his drunken knocking. The door cracked open, and Armando saw Gisela's black negligee flow by as she returned to the bed and lit a cigarette.

"Your money is on my dresser."

He ignored her announcement and moved towards the bed where she sat upright with her cigarette between her fingers and a glass ashtray beside her on the mattress. Her eyes were a pair of lifeless globes. Armando stood beside the bed without a word and Gisela immediately knew what he wanted. She stubbed out her cigarette and lay back, pulling her slip above her waist.

The smell of alcohol was strong, and Armando moved like a beast intoxicated by lust. He was finished in minutes, and as he stood and dressed, he looked to the dresser where Gisela had left a small stack of bills and a handful of coins.

"Is that all?" he asked as he counted the meager sum.

She sat up and lit another cigarette. "What do you care? You're almost finished in this town, aren't you?"

Even the blind prostitute knew of his troubles. He stuffed the bills into his pocket and jingled the coins in his hand, assessing their heaviness. She was standing beside him now and used her arm to push him out of the way as she felt her way to the dresser for a bottle of perfume.

"My family owns a tobacco plantation in Cuba," he tried to sound charming, though his speech slurred and he wobbled drunkenly. "We could move down there together."

She sighed, ignoring his offer and squirted perfume on her neck. "Next time you visit, can you arrive without stinking of cigars and bourbon? Oh, I forgot, the senseless Cubans have run you out of town, so I won't be seeing you anymore."

The audacity of this young woman was astounding. Armando squeezed the coins in his hand. He felt their weight and hardened his fist. Gisela sensed a change in the room's energy and turned her head slightly to listen just as Armando's fist met her cheekbone. Powered by rage and the weight of the coins, he dealt a devastating blow that cracked bones.

Gisela felt as if her head had exploded into a bloody mist.

Then a second blow landed below her nose, dislodged a pair of teeth, and sent them to the back of her throat. She choked on the jagged, bloody pair. Disoriented, Gisela found herself coughing over her bed, choking on her stray teeth as blood poured from her nose.

Armando grabbed the thick, glass ashtray from Gisela's bed and slammed it into the back of her head. Purple blood and ashes mixed with the prostitute's long, black hair and Gisela fell face first onto the mattress, stunned by the surprise attack.

He threw the handful of coins across her wounded body and let himself out. Gisela was sprawled across the bed, bleeding and choking. Ten minutes later she was dead.

Chapter 33

Details of the remarkable homecoming became the subject of instant debate. Arguments broke out in factories, bets were placed in taverns, and the workers engaged in heated exchanges along the streets of Ybor City. The telegram from Havana proclaiming the return of four labor leaders had sparked anticipation and excitement unseen in the city since the buildup to the Spanish American War three years before. Every cigar maker in town had an opinion on where their leaders had been, and how they had managed to survive.

The Ortiz boys waited at Port Tampa with Josefina and Andres, and nearly every worker from the Vasquez factory. The steamer was due to arrive from Havana that afternoon and hundreds had turned out to welcome the return of Lapár, Gabriel, Juan Carlos and Salvador. As the hour grew closer, more and more people arrived, crowding the port as they pushed along the dock for a better view. Reporters and police were among them, and some would later estimate that a thousand spectators were on hand to witness the arrival.

Finally, as the sun started to fall into the orange horizon, a black steamer coasted into port and docked. The sea of spectators swayed towards the water like a rising tide, their heads bobbing up and down as they fought for a look at the ship.

Mendez was the first to appear atop the plank with bushy hair and a lean frame that made him nearly unrecognizable. Someone called out, "It's Gabriel Mendez! It's the *lector*!" and the cigar makers cheered for their beloved reader.

"He looks so skinny!" Javier said to his brothers as the grinning and triumphant Mendez waved at the cheering crowd and crossed the plank to be consumed by hundreds of opened arms.

Lapár was next. Enthusiastic applause greeted the union leader who had nearly given his life for his people. He seemed less vibrant than before, humbled and lacking the confidence that created his charismatic presence. As Javier inspected Lapár, he saw relief. With wife Esmeralda sobbing uncontrollably, Lapár crossed the plank and greeted his family with hugs and kisses. Husband and wife embraced and gathered their two young boys as four heads became buried together in a grateful huddle.

The Ortiz clan turned back to the boat hoping their father would be next, but as Juan Carlos appeared atop of the plank and raised his fists into the air, shaking them victoriously, they couldn't help but cheer. The scrappy Juan Carlos had been reincarnated into an excited, thinner version of himself. His hair was long and black, his moustache and beard had filled in, and he ran across the plank to enjoy the adoration of the younger workers.

Finally, a lean man with thick stubble of facial hair and a jacket folded over one arm appeared on the plank. Salvador paused to savor his freedom, to inhale the glorious Florida air and look down at hundreds of smiling faces. Knowing that he had finally reached the end of the grueling journey through the jungle, Salvador started across the plank and approached the crowd.

"Papa!" E.J. jumped up and down as he pointed at his father. Javier smiled and applauded, and Josefina was unable to suppress her tears. Lázaro was shocked to see his father so thin and watched curiously as Salvador entered the throng and was surrounded by happy cigar makers who patted his back and shook his hands.

Finally Salvador stood face to his with his family. They looked different, changed, older and wiser. The sight of their smiling faces was so overwhelming that Salvador instantly broke into tears. "Forgive me," he sobbed, embarrassed to show such weakness before his children. "But I am overcome with joy at finally seeing all of you after what I just endured."

Josefina was first to embrace him, burying her face in his chest and letting his shirt absorb her tears. "Sweet Fina," he purred as he kissed the top of her head and inhaled her familiar and gentle perfume. Salvador saw Andres standing behind her and he reached out to shake the doctor's hand. Then Salvador broke away from Josefina and found Javier in his arms.

"It's good to see you again, Papa." Javier's voice cracked as tears fell.

"Look at Mr. Macho." Salvador laughed as he brushed a tear off Javier's cheek.

He squatted to kiss E.J.'s cheek and rustle the boy's hair. "Look how much you have grown!"

Then Salvador noticed Lázaro standing beside Javier. The boy's hair was long, his eyes had darkened and he seemed stronger than Salvador remembered. Salvador thought back to their last encounter and embraced his son. "*¡Coño!* You're a man!"

Lázaro laughed at the words, feeling awkwardly proud to hear such praise. Finally, to be seen by his father as a man. "Welcome home," he said as they hugged.

Salvador kept an arm around Lázaro and smiled at the happy faces of his family. If only Olympia could be there to enjoy the reunion. Tears poured from his eyes and Salvador did not care. He realized that his family – family he had lost so many times during his life – was everything.

And then he saw Testifonte Cancio standing beside his boys. The sugar planter's face was expressionless. Testifonte was humbled to see how this community embraced a man he had once loathed, and he fought his desire to admire the former bandit. But he could not ignore the joy that this reunion produced, and came forward to shake Salvador's hand and welcome him home.

"Thank you for coming," Salvador said to Testifonte, appreciating and marveling at the planter's effort. Here is a man who can forgive the past, thought Salvador as he shook Testifonte's hand.

"Welcome home!" Hector said, and Salvador was again shocked, this time at seeing Olympia's brother among the group. Salvador had new respect for the wealthy relatives of his four children.

"I am surprised to see you in Tampa!" Salvador exclaimed to Hector as he dabbed his eyes with a white handkerchief. "I doubt that you came here just to greet my return."

"Nonsense," a smiling Hector patted his back. "We came for the party!"

Salvador raised an eyebrow. "Party?"

*   *   *

Armando experienced an emotion he had not felt in some time: guilt. The death of the prostitute was an unfortunate overreaction to his loss of the *bolita* racket, and the apparent end of his alliance with the chief of police. He knew there was no future for him in Ybor City and planned to catch a boat to Havana early the following morning.

Emptying dresser drawers was like sifting through old memories. He came across a gold-plated money clip his father had given him when he was six or seven, a pocket watch from Antonio Vasquez, a gold necklace with a ceramic painting of the Virgin Mary his mother had worn before she died, and a rosary given to him by his Aunt Margaret before his Confirmation.

He held the rosary in his hand and let the silver chain and black marble beads dangle between his fingers. Armando thought of his past, when he used to pray. He had attended weekly Mass up until his teenage years, but for some reason he had stopped.

The rosary amplified his guilt, but he could not pocket the shame. Instead he let it grow until he almost savored the feeling, and realized that the rosary was not meant to save a person from hell, but to rescue a man from himself.

He gripped a bead between his thumb and forefinger, but couldn't remember if the ritual called for a Hail Mary or an Our Father. Perhaps a visit with a priest could refresh his spirituality.

There was shouting and laughter outside and hundreds of voices filled the street. A crowd was approaching. Distracted by the noise, he tossed the rosary into his suitcase and peered out his second floor bedroom window onto Eighth Avenue. Hundreds of happy and celebrating immigrants were parading through Ybor City; their laughter made Armando wonder about the occasion. He had spent the last day drunk and hung over and was not current on local gossip. Surprisingly, he found he was no longer interested.

Tomorrow, Tampa would be old news.

Before locking up and going out for one last deed, Armando thought of the envelope he had sent to Antonio Vasquez. Filled with documents, old contracts, and one piece of news that would surely startle the cigar tycoon, it was Armando's final act of surrender to his old adversary, a man he had failed to supplant. Vasquez had likely received the envelope by now and knew that Armando would be leaving town having sold his twenty-five percent share of Vasquez and Company.

The feast began as soon as the crowd reached the banquet hall. A Cuban band played a joyous, excited tune led by the lanky Claudia, whose romantic contralto voice serenaded the patrons as they filed into the hall. Wasting no time, they people began to indulge in a measureless array of food and drink provided by local restaurants and families.

Several long tables were draped with white cloth and piled high with enough Cuban-Spanish cuisine to feed a company of Cuban soldiers. The first table held a tray of Cuban sandwiches cut in single-serving chunks that exposed thick ham, oily sliced pork, and Swiss cheese. There were a dozen loaves of uncut Cuban bread piled beside several large bowls of salad and a stack of plates. Salvador picked up a plate and gleefully inspected the salads: there was one with fresh avocados, onions, and limes, another with garden vegetables and an olive oil dressing, and another with an exotic mix of lettuce, provolone cheese, ham, garlic, and green olives. At the end of the table was a pot of *sopa china*, a hearty egg and onion soup.

Salvador inspected the main course; a trio of roast pigs glazed snout to hoof with olive oil, crushed garlic, and orange juice, each chomping a red apple. A tray with breaded steaks sat beside the pigs and there was a large bowl of *paella*, plus pots of *boliche*, *ropa vieja*, black bean soup, white rice and raw chopped onions.

The next table housed a bowl of sweet potatoes, a plate of plantains fried in olive oil and sprinkled with brown sugar and salt, and yucca covered in a tangy *mojo* sauce. There were several trays piled with fresh fruit, Cuban and Italian bread, dinner rolls, biscuits, cornbread and crackers.

Another table was cluttered with jugs of wine, bottles of rum, bourbon and beer, with cold soda, fruit juice and tea for the children, and a powerful, exotic *sangria* for the daring and tolerant. Plenty of pastries sat ready for dessert along with chocolate cake, strawberry cake, *flan de leche*, éclairs glazed with warm chocolate, biscotti of many flavors, *raspadura*, and a giant pot of hot coffee.

It was how Salvador had imagined heaven. He did not hesitate to dig in and pile his plate high with foods he had not tasted in months. Juan Carlos, Gabriel and Lapár likewise indulged, overwhelmed with the succulent aromas of sweet sugar, tangy garlic and onion, red wine, roast meat and fresh bread.

The triumphant exiles became instant celebrities. Everyone wanted to know the story of what happened in Honduras, how they found their way home, and what happened to the rest of their party. Salvador was approached constantly for details of his story but he insisted with a smile that he would recount the tale in its entirety over cigars, once his stomach was full.

Salvador and his family sat at one of the many giant round tables that covered the banquet hall and chatted as they ate. Salvador learned the strike had ended with a loss for the workers, and Lázaro began the tale of his adventures in New Orleans, New York City and elsewhere, content to save Salvador's story for after dinner.

Salvador filled his plate three times, first with avocado salad, three pieces of Cuban sandwich, and some fresh fruit. Then again for a main course of roast pork, breaded steak, fish and black beans on a bed of white rice topped with fresh chopped onions. There was laughter and music all around. Cigar smoke was already in the air, and a few folks had found their way to the dance floor, where they circled gracefully to the sound of Cuban folk music. For his third helping, Salvador had a plate of *paella*, plantains, yucca, a scoop of sweet and spicy *ropa vieja*, and another piece of greasy roast pork that he sliced off the pig with a sharp, oily knife. Finally, with a full stomach halting his movement, Salvador settled with a slice of cake and some coffee as his family and others gathered around to hear his story.

E.J. took a place on the floor beside his father. Javier, Andres, Lázaro, Hector, and Testifonte arranged their chairs in a semi-circle around the children, and Josefina sat beside her father with her head on his shoulder and an arm coiled around his.

Juan Carlos stood behind the group, and though he enjoyed his first glass of wine in three months, he wondered when Salvador would wrap this up so they could get on with their plan. The music serenaded a background of dominoes clicking and sliding across tabletops, while the cigar smoke grew thick.

Since Salvador had not consumed any tobacco in months he opted for the weakest cigar he could find – a light green *claro* given to him by an adoring cigar worker. Juan Carlos appeared with a box of matches to light Salvador's cigar while his own smoking *puro* dangled from his lips.

With his smoke burning and Josefina resting calmly against his shoulder, Salvador looked to the waiting group and told his story. He started with the day he had been arrested and the grueling boat ride across the Gulf of Mexico, then the landing on the deserted beach and the following days of disorientation, fear, starvation and loneliness as the men searched for food and water.

His family was amazed at his resilience and determination, and they noticed sores and healing bug bites on his arms, and scars on his fingertips. As Salvador told the story with a full stomach, surrounded by family, those first few days on the deserted Central American beach seemed as if they had been years ago.

He told of the many weeks spent wandering aimlessly through the rainforest and the eventual encounter with a group of young men called the Miskitu. "We learned that these people are not friendly to the Spanish, or the Hispanic, in our case. But they are friendly to the English, and thank God Lapár speaks the language! He talked to them and they quickly understood that we were no threat but were, in fact, hopelessly lost. The Miskitu are hospitable people, not jungle savages, with their own town, a place called Awastara. It had roads, a boat launch, and white houses not unlike those of Ybor City, even a Catholic church built by British missionaries.

"We were well-received. Their elected chief, a man named Mr. Haynes, made sure we were fed, clothed, and given a place to rest. The people of Awastara generally left us alone and tended to us only when we asked, or at meal times. We stayed for a couple of weeks, to rest and rebuild our strength. We learned that we had wandered into Nicaragua, to a coastal region called La Mosquitia, the Mosquito Coast. Once we had adequately recovered, we were given a boat ride south to Puerto Cabezas, a small coastal town, mostly Spanish speaking. We were fortunate to meet two Cuban men who were engaged in the fruit culture there. They supplied funds and hired a schooner that took us to Havana. Once we reached Cuba, we knew we would be home in a matter of days. That's when I sent the telegram to Josefina."

The group sat silently and marveled as the amazing story sank in. Andres shook his head. "Remarkable story, Salvador, absolutely remarkable."

"Eight were kidnapped," Josefina reminded them. "What happened to the other four?"

Salvador's smile faded. He did not want to go into the details and tarnish the joyous occasion so he said simply, "They did not make it."

The group understood, and then Javier stood and held a glass of red wine above his head. "A toast!" They raised their glasses as Javier placed a hand on his father's shoulder. "To an amazing journey and a welcome return home! May you never again disappear for three months and leave us all wondering where you are!"

The group laughed and Javier shouted, "¡Salud y pesetas!"

"¡Salud y pesetas!" The crowd repeated as glasses were clanked and drinks were downed.

The band broke into a rhythm that brought many more to the dance floor while others returned to the buffet tables for dessert, or for another plate of food, or some coffee. Men lit cigars while children began to play. Salvador and Juan Carlos sat together with Javier and Lázaro while Javier told the story of their clash with Armando and how the brothers had discovered the trick behind his *bolita* game.

"I knew that game was corrupt," Juan Carlos said as he eyed Salvador.

Javier replied, "Once he had been exposed, he was practically chased out of the bar. Last I heard he was leaving Ybor City."

Juan Carlos glanced at Salvador again and wondered when they would get on with their plan, and finish Armando once and for all.

There was another party happening across town, at the home of Antonio Vasquez. Celebrating victory with his wife and son, his factory foreman and three close cigar manufacturers, Vasquez poured red wine and toasted management's victory in the General Strike of 1901.

"To the continued prosperity of the family business!" Vasquez declared as the guests raised their glasses and congratulated each other on their triumph.

"I came close to mortgaging this house," Vasquez said as the guests picked up their utensils and cut into their dinners. Maria Vasquez had prepared a main course of roast pork, with sweet potatoes, yucca, black beans, and *paella*. As he chewed his meat, Vasquez glanced out the window to his brick factory across the street. "I had to cash in the insurance policy on that place just to stay in business."

José Cienfuegos pointed to Vasquez with his fork and grinned. "But now you're back in control. What about your investor? Where is Armando tonight? I'm surprised he is not here to toast wine and dine with us."

"His business is ruined," said Capecho. "I heard he's leaving town for good."

Vasquez smiled and glanced at Antonio Junior, who returned a subtle grin. "There is more good news." Vasquez reached to the inside pocket of his jacket and pulled out a folded sheet of white paper. "Armando Renteria is no longer an owner of Vasquez and Company. He sold his entire interest to the American Tobacco Company." Vasquez waived the letter for the others to see.

There were whistles and murmurs of surprise.

"So, Antonio Vasquez is free of the bearded shadow," Cienfuegos said. "But what sort of influence will the American corporation exert over your enterprise?"

Vasquez sipped his wine and pretended to be untroubled by the question.

With the taste of garlic and roast pork still lingering on his lips and his fingers slick with olive oil, Salvador went back to the buffet for another taste of *lechón*. He cut the roast pig with a carving knife, but the meat was so tender it fell to pieces at the touch of the blade. As he piled his plate with the oily meat, Juan Carlos was suddenly standing beside him – the dank odor of wine heavy on his breath.

"I realize you are enjoying your family, Salvador. But are you ready to go?"

Salvador saw Juan Carlos was cross and intense; his mind occupied by matters of revenge. Salvador started back to his table thinking about the Cuban bread he would use to mop the oils of his *lechón*. "Enjoy the party, Carlito."

Carlito's expression did not change. "I've enjoyed it very much but the time has come…" He whispered. "Armando."

Salvador stopped and looked at Juan Carlos. His friend's yellow tooth watched and waited for Salvador to answer. Salvador took a deep breath. "I'm out."

"What?"

"I changed my mind."

"Why?"

Salvador looked to the table and saw Josefina laughing with Lázaro, and Javier playing some kind of hand-slapping game with E.J. Andres and Hector sat among them chatting with each other while Testifonte quietly sipped coffee and observed the party. "The strike is over," Salvador explained. "The war is over. *La Resistencia* has lost and is no more. We are home now, Carlito. Let us be glad that we're home."

Juan Carlos followed as Salvador headed towards his table. "What about our agreement? Our pact? Need I remind you that there would be no party if Armando and his gang hadn't taken us – hadn't taken you from your family?"

"You heard the boys. He's ruined."

Juan Carlos was stunned and did not know how to respond.

"You're the same thug you were twenty years ago," Salvador said, not caring if he insulted his friend, and praising himself for finally giving Carlito some honest feedback. "Everyone else has moved on, but you're still living for the machete and the torch."

Juan Carlos was insulted. He could feel his heart pounding. "You'd turn your back on me, Ortiz? From me, your brother? Who has been closer to you than me?"

"Let it go."

Juan Carlos shook his head and stepped closer to Salvador. "I can't do that, Salvador. The machete and the torch are as much a part of me as your children are to you. I know no other way, and you, as my brother, should come with me tonight and settle our business with this man."

Salvador, aware that others at the party had taken notice of the confrontation, quietly shook his head. "I will not."

"Very well," Juan Carlos nodded and stood up straight. He glanced to the Ortiz family table and saw Josefina chatting and smiling with her brother Lázaro. "Perhaps tonight is a good night for Josefina to learn her true origin?"

Now Salvador did not bother to hide his rage. He sneered, and jabbed his chin towards Carlito. "How dare you?"

"She should know, Salvador. That she is not your true flesh and blood. She should know she is the product of rape, and the child of another man."

Salvador stood so close to Juan Carlos that he could inhale the very wine that lingered on Carlito's breath. "You would die before you uttered a word."

Juan Carlos grinned smugly. "Fine then, Ortiz. I see you would kill a friend before a foe."

"Get out of my sight." Salvador returned to his family and tossed his plate of roast pork onto the table, no longer hungry. His heart pounded, and he slid his chair close to Josefina, feeling a need to remain close to her for the rest of the night. He looked to the buffet and saw Juan Carlos pouring himself another glass of wine.

"What's wrong, Papa?" Josefina asked.

Salvador shook his head and tried to smile. "I think I ate too much."

She smiled and turned her attention back to Lázaro, who was in the middle of describing the speed of life in New York City.

Suddenly a hand patted Salvador's back and he turned to see Juan Carlos behind him holding a glass of wine in the air.

"A toast!" Juan Carlos announced. "To my oldest friend, Salvador Ortiz!" The others halted their conversations and turned to listen. "I stand here to praise this noble man, who became our leader while we were stranded in the jungles of Central America and saw us back to safety. To Salvador, my oldest friend, who has rolled ten thousand cigars at my side, and I at his. My oldest friend, Salvador Ortiz! From the mountains and plantations of Cuba, to the streets of Ybor City, to the cliffs and canyons of Central America; we have been through so much, good friend. And as you are surrounded by your beautiful family, I can only pay tribute to you, your loyalty, and your friendship. Thank you, Salvador, for being my friend."

He raised his glass and those who had heard the toast did the same. Only Salvador knew the sarcasm in those comments, but with his family smiling all around, Salvador raised his glass as Juan Carlos patted him on the back. They toasted with each other. "Welcome home," smiled Juan Carlos before he downed his wine, set his glass on the table and disappeared into the crowd.

As the music and dancing continued, Javier produced a deck of cards and slid his chair close to his father. "Game of casino?"

When Salvador saw Javier sitting beside him eagerly holding a deck of cards, he smiled, dismissed Juan Carlos as a drunken fool, and signaled for Javier to deal the first game.

Lázaro was hungry for more so he loaded his plate with a handful of cookies, then added some fresh fruit and bread, and saw platters with plenty of roast pig sitting in puddles of dark, greasy olive oil and roasted bulbs of garlic. He decided the hot, roasted pork oozing with *mojo* was his favorite food. There had been nothing like this in New Orleans, or anywhere he had traveled.

He set his plate on the table and moved in to cut himself a few slices of the meat but the carving knife was nowhere to be found. He figured with all the people coming through, it had been moved to another table, but it didn't matter. He used his fork to tear the tender chunks of meat off the pig and pile them onto his plate. Then he returned to his table to watch his father and brother play cards, and to tell them more about his journeys through America.

Armando sat alone in the last pew of the empty St. Joseph's Church on Tenth Avenue. Tall white candles burned on the altar and lit the quiet, hollow room. A shrine by the wall held rows of burning candles that cast dancing shadows across the ceiling. Hanging above the shrine was a painting of the Virgin Mary; her solemn face watched Armando and he looked away in shame.

He considered his crimes. Was he so wicked that God would dismiss him as an unredeemable failure? *Bolita* was illegal on paper but it was a game tolerated by all of society. The murder of Ramiro Ragano was a savvy business move, but Armando realized it required repentance. The killing of Gisela was a senseless act of rage for which Armando felt true remorse. He rolled his right hand over to inspect the sores and bruises on his knuckles, the scars of his final encounter with the prostitute.

Now he stood and walked to the shrine, removing his rosary from his pocket as he walked, and felt the small beads made of black marble. He knelt before the shrine and made the Sign of the Cross. The light of dozens of candles flickered before him and he held the rosary by the crucifix, letting the beads dangle to his knees. Armando was still for a moment, refusing to look upward and engage the Virgin's stare. Finally, he began to recite a prayer. "I believe in God, the Father Almighty, Creator of heaven and earth, and in Jesus Christ, His only Son, our Lord…"

A serpent arm slithered around his neck and crushed his throat. A blade flashed before his eyes and he felt a cool metallic razor's edge pressing against his gullet, accompanied by a strong whiff of garlic and wine.

"I'm home."

The voice was unmistakable. "Impossible!" Armando gasped.

Juan Carlos braced his body against Armando's and used his weight to put downward pressure on Armando's back, pinning the Spaniard below. He held Armando's neck tight between his bicep and forearm, squeezing as hard as he could. "How have things been in Tampa?"

Juan Carlos had trailed Armando since Fifteenth Street. Remaining in the evening shadows, Juan Carlos had been surprised to see Armando enter the church. Carlito had stood outside St. Joseph's and sneered at the hallowed symbol of Spanish authority, thinking there was no better way to end this battle than in a Spanish house of worship.

He flexed his arm and pulled it further into Armando's throat, and saw Armando's cheeks turn red, then purple. Veins bulged from his temples and Armando wiggled but managed only the slightest twists and twitches; his toes traced pathetic semicircles on the dusty floor. Juan Carlos had waited too long for this moment and his grip would not be shaken.

He whispered to Armando, "Have you ever been lost in a hot, wet, tropical jungle? Have you ever been starved and forced to drink rain water from puddles? That was unbearable, but worse than the heat and the pouring rain and the thought that we were completely lost, most horrible were the mosquitoes! The worst part wasn't every inch of your body being constantly bitten all night long by those pests. That was terrible in itself. No, what nearly drove me crazy was the *sound* they made. Have you ever heard the buzzing of a thousand mosquitoes? All day and all night, no matter where you go or what you do to get rid of it, that infernal noise follows you everywhere. That buzzing still lingers in my ears, Armando. It is a sound that can drive a man to wild, rabid, murderous insanity."

Armando tried remorse. He gasped, "I'm...sorry..."

Juan Carlos laughed. "Like hell you are." He tightened his grip.

Armando still held the rosary. He coiled the stone beads around his knuckles like armor and made a fist. Armando wondered how Juan Carlos had made it back and how many had returned with him...and how many of them were here in the church? With the blade at his throat, Armando tightened his fist and thrust it back, landing it square on Juan Carlos's temple. As quickly as the first punch came, another one landed in the same spot.

Juan Carlos was temporarily stunned. He tightened his grip on the knife and braced to slice Armando's throat but Armando pushed back with all of his might. Juan Carlos was shoved backwards, and the momentum was enough to help bring Armando to his feet. The Spaniard whirled hard, still locked in Juan Carlos's grasp, and threw them both into the table of burning candles.

They slammed into the rack, and as they fell to the floor, they brought the bed of candles crashing down on top of them. Hot wax burned Carlito's neck, arms and back as blood seeped down the side of his face and into his mouth. The fall was enough for Armando to break free of his assailant's grasp. He spun, now on top of Juan Carlos, and with the rosary still wrapped around his fist, punched Juan Carlos square in the face, breaking his nose and splattering blood.

But Juan Carlos still gripped the knife, which he slashed towards the blur of Armando above him. The knife slit Armando's forearm, and as the wounded Spaniard cocked his fist to deliver another blow, Juan

Carlos thrust the tip of the knife towards Armando's armpit and scored a direct hit.

Armando hollered in pain, and as he recoiled Juan Carlos was freed of the investor's weight. He pounced and brought the carving knife towards Armando's chest, rolling towards him and using his momentum to move on top and power his attack. He scored another hit as the tip of the knife stuck between a pair of Armando's ribs.

Juan Carlos yanked it free of the Spaniard's bones as he pinned Armando below. While Armando gasped for a breath, Juan Carlos chopped the knife down as hard as he could, plunging it four inches into Armando's chest and puncturing a lung.

Then again.

And again.

Covered in hot candle wax and both of their blood, Juan Carlos aimed for the heart and brought the knife down hard one last time. Armando coughed blood and knew he was a dead man. He felt numb, paralyzed by surprise.

Juan Carlos's adrenaline surged, and he knew he had finally bested the Spaniard. He placed the blade underneath Armando's black beard and prepared to slice. Smiling, and savoring his victory, Juan Carlos leaned in close so their faces were inches apart.

"May your Lord have mercy on your soul."

He pulled the carving knife across Armando's throat, slicing cleanly through the veins and tendons. Blood poured out of the slit like a spring, and Armando made a beastly gurgling sound as the last breath left his body. His mouth and eyes remained opened and formed a pained look of shock, looking towards the Virgin Mary, who watched from a stained glass window above.

Juan Carlos took a moment to catch his breath. The adrenaline surge caused his arms and hands to shake, but also helped to numb the pain of his broken nose. He rolled off Armando and sat on the concrete floor in a puddle of blood and broken candles. The shrine had been destroyed and Juan Carlos had blood all over his shirt and hands. The cut on his temple had clotted, but blood still poured from his smashed nose and filled his mouth, and stained his chin and neck. He rose to his feet and looked down at Armando, whose eyes were as lifeless as a roast pig's.

A voice shouted, "Get out of the church!"

Juan Carlos looked across the pews and saw Father Fernandez in a doorway beside the altar. The priest was horrified, tempted to flee but determined to defend his territory. Juan Carlos dropped the knife and held up his hands.

The priest pointed towards the main entrance and shouted again. "GET OUT OF THE CHURCH!!"

Juan Carlos slowly backed away from Armando. Fernandez remained by the altar as Juan Carlos turned and hurried out of the sanctuary. The priest rushed to Armando's side and became nauseous at the sight of the dead man lying among overturned candles. Avoiding the blood puddles, Fernandez knelt close to the body and waved the Sign of the Cross. He said a quick prayer and placed a Eucharistic wafer on Armando's lips so the dying man could pass with Christ. Then Fernandez rushed outside to see Juan Carlos running east on Tenth Avenue. The priest locked the door to the church and hurried to find the police.

Testifonte smiled as he watched Josefina talk with Andres. The music and dancing still vibrated in the background and the odor of cigars was strong. Salvador sat at a table chatting with Gabriel Mendez and Alessandria Prizzi while Javier, Lázaro, and E.J. were dispersed throughout the hall socializing with friends and fellow cigar makers.

Testifonte motioned for his son and Hector came to sit beside him. Both men smiled at each other, pleased to have made the trip and satisfied that the celebration was such a success. Hector said, "Remarkable, isn't it, Papa?"

Testifonte waved his son closer. "I'm getting tired, Hector. It's time to lie down."

Hector understood. In his old age, his father tired quickly and was always in bed by nine o'clock. Though Testifonte had enjoyed the party, it was time to return to the hotel. Hector helped his father to his feet, and once Testifonte stood, he walked to the other side of the table to Josefina. He smiled at his granddaughter and opened his hands to touch her cheeks. "You are such a beautiful young lady," he said and then kissed her gently on each side. "Your father is a very fortunate man."

"Thank you," she blushed. He offered both of his hands and she took them and held them, looking at him awkwardly while he smiled.

Testifonte said, "Tomorrow I must return to Cuba, but you and your family will remain in my thoughts."

She smiled and nodded, not knowing what to say. Then Testifonte turned and went to Salvador, who rose to greet Olympia's father. "Thank you for making the trip, Don Cancio. We're all honored by your presence."

Testifonte gently hugged Salvador. "Take care of your children. They are more important than anything."

Salvador smiled. He knew.

On the trolley ride to the Tampa Bay Hotel, Testifonte sat silent and watched the city pass. The city where his daughter had lived and died, the city of his grandchildren, and eventually, the city of *their* children.

Hector helped his father to his room and saw him to bed. As he rested, Testifonte thought of the madness with the poisoned tea. Remorse grew heavy in his heart and he remembered his instructions from Father Fernandez and the penance he had not completely fulfilled. Testifonte recited a prayer and then called Hector into the room.

"Yes, Father, what do you need?"

"Bring pen and paper!"

It was dark but light from the streetlamps would reveal to anyone that the figure hurrying north was nearly covered in blood from head to foot. Juan Carlos's face was a mess of his own dried blood and his hands and shirt were caked with Armando's. Even his pants were splattered red. He moved swiftly, remaining in the shadows and cutting through dark alleys.

The priest would surely go to the police, and then all of the Anglos would be searching Ybor City for Armando's killer, but Juan Carlos had prevailed.

Yet he was not finished. Only half the deed was complete.

First the machete, now the torch.

He jogged east for the Vasquez factory.

*   *   *

417

Officers Reddey and Smith followed Chief McGrath to the shrine and stepped carefully over the bloody footprints left by the assailant. McGrath recognized Armando immediately and cringed at the lifeless, rotten plums that were his eyes and the hideous gash in his throat.

"Can you identify him?" the chief asked Father Fernandez.

The priest nodded. "Juan Carlos Alvarez."

Chief McGrath scratched his chin. "Are you sure?"

Another nod. "He's always walking the streets running his mouth. And I did the Ortiz wedding about year ago, and Alvarez was the life of the party until the mother passed out."

The heathens had returned from exile and brought murder back to Ybor City. McGrath thanked the priest and assured him someone would arrive soon to collect the body and help clean the church. Then he led his men north, in pursuit of the suspect.

Juan Carlos approached from the south and found a brick factory standing like a castle in the darkness. The water tower formed a shadow above the roof that guarded the property like a turret. Across the street, the home of Antonio Vasquez was a king's mansion among the tiny workers' cottages. Lights were on inside, and the Don was enjoying dinner with his family and business partners.

Juan Carlos remained in the shadows and hurried to the building, avoiding the main entrance that faced Don Antonio's house, and going around to the side. He saw all was quiet, then picked up a rock and threw it at a ground floor window. Glass shattered and rang as the broken bits showered the concrete floor below. Juan Carlos kicked the jagged shards off the windowsill and slipped inside.

He stood in the basement among wooden crates filled with finished cigars and barrels of stored tobacco. It was almost completely dark in the quiet basement with only a small haze of light spilling in through the windows. The smell of fresh tobacco was strong; leaves were everywhere, piled on tables, stacked on the floor and pressed inside bale after bale. This was Don Antonio's fortune. Like the sugar fields of Cuba, this basement of tobacco was the treasure of a wealthy Spanish noble. And like the lords of the mountains fighting a revolution, Juan Carlos would see it all destroyed.

He lit a match.

As Antonio Junior dined with his father's business associates, he felt not only like the son of a cigar tycoon, but as an associate with a legitimate seat at the table. Enjoying his wine and roast pork, Antonito glanced around the table and watched the men eat. These were successful business leaders, great men, and men he would soon do business with himself. He savored the moment.

Then he saw an orange flicker outside. The factory, his future fortune, was on fire.

"The factory is burning!" he shouted. Don Antonio's head snapped towards the window. When he saw flames dancing in the factory windows, he knew instantly that the company his father had built might be out of business for good. As if a bell had sounded, all of the men sprang from their seats and rushed outside.

Smoke rose from the factory like steam from a locomotive as yellow and orange flames flickered within. A cloud of gray dominated the sky and made the air stink with the otherwise elegant aroma of burning tobacco. The fire had spread quickly throughout the basement and was completely out of control in a matter of minutes.

Antonito stood on the lawn with his father and his men, and watched the horrifying sight. They had no idea if they should attempt to fight the fire, run for help, or sit and watch the Vasquez empire collapse. Soon the wooden first floor would ignite, and then the second floor and all the worker's benches would be ablaze. The wooden interior would collapse into the basement – three floors worth of burning embers – and would leave the factory as a gigantic brick oven of smoldering coals and tobacco leaves. Even the 25,000 gallons of water in the tower would not be able to save the factory. It was already too late.

Then, at a ground floor window, Antonito spotted the silhouette of a man climbing out. The shadow fell to the ground coughing, on his hands and knees, and his shirt smoking as he choked on soot. Clearly the arsonist, this was the man responsible for the inferno from which he'd emerged, and Antonito set out running, intent on capturing the perpetrator and ensuring he was brought to justice.

Juan Carlos couldn't avoid breathing smoke and ashes as he escaped the burning basement. He climbed out of the window into the fresh air and collapsed onto the ground. The fire had spread faster than he'd expected, and Juan Carlos was forced to run from the basement or risk being consumed by flames.

His chest hurt from coughing, his lungs burned with smoke and hot ash, and his head still throbbed from where he had been punched by Armando. His whole body felt groggy and sore. The alcohol he had consumed at the party contributed to his fatigue, and he hadn't the energy to run away. Coughing consumed what little strength remained and as Juan Carlos stood and looked up to the factory, he saw flames pouring from the second floor windows. He had created an inferno. He smiled, just as he was tackled by the furious son of Antonio Vasquez.

"I'll kill you, you son of a bitch!" Antonito shouted as they wrestled on the sandy ground.

Juan Carlos coughed and choked, his throat cluttered with soot, his body too weak to put up a fight. Antonito used bare fists to beat Juan Carlos's face until it was a mess of bloody cuts and bruises. His nose was smashed to the side, his lips split in several places, and if the police hadn't arrived and pulled Antonito off Juan Carlos, he likely would have beaten the arsonist to death.

The party at the banquet hall was still swinging when a young Cuban boy ran into the hall and announced, "The Vasquez factory is on fire! The Vasquez factory is on fire!" The news quickly spread through the room, and soon people were gathering their families and rushing out of the banquet. Many of the celebrants lived near the Vasquez factory and wanted to hurry and defend their homes.

The party ended instantly. Salvador summoned his children. and feared, as his instincts suggested, that Juan Carlos was involved.

*   *   *

Don Antonio watched in horror as hot coals flew out of the factory. Burning tobacco leaves were sucked into the wind and carried to trees, and onto the roofs of nearby workers' houses, which quickly caught fire. People started to clear out of their homes and were furiously pumping water into aluminum buckets. In a few short minutes, the scene became pandemonium as people rushed in all directions, saving valuables from their burning homes, and taking their children as far away as possible while others desperately fought the fire that had already consumed an entire square block.

Even the Vasquez home, the once magnificent mansion that stood in the center of the workers' cottages like city hall, couldn't avoid the rain of fire that erupted from the factory. Soon the roof was ablaze, and like many of the Ybor City homes that were built from wood, it quickly caught fire.

McGrath and his men arrived and had taken possession of Juan Carlos, cuffing his hands behind his back. Carlito could hardly stand and relied on Officers Reddey and Smith to hold him up. McGrath looked into the arsonist's eyes. They were tired, beaten, and satisfied. The man clearly felt no remorse and was happy about what he had done. McGrath wanted to give him a punch in the stomach – for killing Armando, for starting this fire and for returning to Ybor City in the first place – but it would be a useless act.

He thought of District Attorney Clark and the investigation, and the big mouth of Juan Carlos Alvarez. In this business it was all or nothing.

McGrath signaled to his men. "Take him to the swamps."

Salvador arrived at the fires with his family and the rest of the party. The Vasquez factory was a fireball, and the interior had collapsed upon itself with an explosion of embers and bursts of orange and yellow sparks. The wood-framed tenement houses that bordered the factory were also burning and were so close together they allowed for the fire to easily jump from house to house.

A quarter of Ybor City was in flames, including the original Ortiz house. Salvador watched as flames poured from the window where he and Olympia had slept. The swinging bench on the porch, where he had spent hours with his wife, now hung only on one end as it was eaten by fire.

Firefighters from the city of Tampa arrived with horse-drawn water pumps. A small bucket brigade passed water from man to man in an almost useless attempt to douse the flames. Salvador and his sons joined with every able bodied man to help fight the fires. It was a clear night, with no chance of rain, yet a thunderstorm seemed like the only thing that could save the city from total destruction.

Juan Carlos was thrown against a tree. Three Tampa police officers and Antonio Junior surrounded him as he leaned against the trunk to steady himself.

The chief stepped up to him. "No need to beat a confession out of you, is there, lad? Scum like you would be proud to admit to another killing." Juan Carlos said nothing; his body had been so wounded it was nearly numb. His eyes were almost swollen shut and his lips were lacerated and bloated. The chief said, "We warned you about returning to Tampa."

Officer Reddey coiled a rope around the arsonist's neck.

The entire city had been mobilized to fight the fires. Volunteers came from every area of Tampa; horse-drawn pumps had been stationed along the bank of the Hillsborough River should the fire continue its westward march. Housing was sparse to the north of Ybor City so the effort concentrated on stopping the fire from moving south, which would save most of Ybor City's economic center. As Salvador and his sons helped carry water buckets, Andres and Josefina organized a triage to treat the injured.

Juan Carlos Alvarez stood on a block of wood with a noose lassoed around his neck. To the south, a black cloud of smoke a mile wide rose above the city. The fire had grown into a monster whose size Juan Carlos could have never predicted, nor intended. The smell of embers made him grin and he raised his arms to the heavens, evoked the spirit of El Matón, and shouted, "Long live the torch!"

The block was kicked from under his feet, and his neck snapped in place. His body twitched, his bladder emptied, and the body of Juan Carlos Alvarez swung lifeless as the fires raged on.

Chapter 34

The city reeked of charred lumber and smoldering coals. Flakes of gray ash fell from the sky like snow, and the northeast corner of Ybor City looked like it had been devastated by war. The fire had lasted into the morning and finally died just after sunrise. The heroic effort of hundreds of men had contained the flames, saving the greater part of Ybor City, but the tenements to the northeast had been reduced to twenty-four square blocks of black soot. Three had died fighting the fire, and another eight were unaccounted for.

Over a hundred homes had been destroyed, including the Vasquez mansion and his factory, the wooden Olivia cigar factory, a local bakery, a church and several stores and restaurants. Hundreds of cigar workers were suddenly homeless and unemployed. It would take a massive contribution from the community to house them until they could find new accommodations.

The mayor arrived in the morning to survey the damage and immediately declared an emergency. Every available horse drawn wagon, cart, wheel barrel and shovel was summoned to begin clearing the wreckage, and a huge cleanup began. All hands were mobilized for the volunteer effort. Cubans, Spaniards, Italians and even Anglos joined together, and more arrived from nearby towns to provide food and to help the Tampa citizens remove the ruins of Ybor City.

Salvador stood with his three sons on the sidewalk before the charred remains of their house on Nineteenth Street. He thought of the family *bohío* in Herrera, Cuba, torched by Spanish soldiers before it collapsed into a pile of burning palm fronds. It was the same culture war, the same conflict that had now brought the Ortiz house to the ground.

"I'm sorry, Papa." Javier said.

"It's just a house," Salvador said as he put his arms around Lázaro and E.J. "I'm glad everyone is safe. "

"You don't understand," Javier continued. "We had paid the lease up to date and were going to surprise you by moving back in. All of our stuff was in that house."

Salvador appreciated his boys' efforts. "Those are just a bunch of things we don't need." He smiled at his boys. "I've been homeless for three months. What's one more night?"

The body of Juan Carlos Alvarez was discovered hanging from a tree limb the following afternoon by a pair of land developers and was cut down and taken to the funeral parlor to be prepped for burial.

The fate of Armando Renteria soon reached the streets of Ybor City, where the cigar workers began whispering that Juan Carlos had been responsible, not only for the death of the Spanish thug, but for the fire that had consumed their city.

"After three months in the jungle," Javier would say. "Can you blame him for being so bold?"

Some were angry with Juan Carlos while others praised his bravado. As was the custom among the working class, heated debates broke out over his death, as some argued that he got what he deserved while others claimed the lynching was unjust.

When Salvador was asked for his opinion, he would wryly say, "Carlito didn't go crazy, he knew exactly what he was doing. There was simply no stopping Juan Carlos." But as the years passed, Salvador softened his tone and would affectionately remember his friend. "He was a wild lion among moderate men. With a mind of his own, he was a loyal comrade, a dear friend, and a lord of the mountain until the end."

Two weeks later, after the ashes and rubbish had been cleared, District Attorney Clark took depositions from Salvador, Lapár, and Gabriel and completed his investigation. Federal indictments were delivered to the five police officers involved in the kidnappings, plus Benny and Eddie Sanchez, Arlen Kincaid, businessmen Harvey Blair and Richard Herd, chief of police Sean McGrath, and the mayor of Tampa, who immediately resigned from office.

Antonio Vasquez and his son had been spared by the grand jury on account of favorable depositions from the three Cubans. They explained how Vasquez and his son had been manipulated and forced into their position, and that ringleader Armando Renteria had conspired to have Vasquez murdered.

But Don Antonio had bigger worries. His factory had been left uninsured, and the fire had literally destroyed everything he owned. Maria Vasquez could do nothing but fall to her knees and sob as men worked tirelessly to fight the uncontrollable inferno. She had been forced to abandon the house, and had only been able to fill her arms with the items she could carry. Some clothes were saved, plus a few knickknacks, and a handful of family heirlooms, but most of what they had owned was gone.

"We'll rent a house in West Tampa until we're back on our feet." Don Antonio assured her with a mix of shock and anger. Vasquez was broke. He had nothing but the money in his bank account, which was a modest amount for a man of his reputation. If he had opened a branch factory in Jacksonville, as planned, he would likely still have been able to operate. The 1901 General Strike had delayed his company's expansion long enough to put it out of business. Without the strike, his company would have survived. The manufacturers had bested the workers in that confrontation, but in the end Vasquez had lost.

And it had taken just one rogue worker to put him away.

It didn't take long for Vasquez to learn of Armando's attempt to have him killed. It shocked the manufacturer and made him question his own perception. His so-called business partner had actually plotted his murder, and Vasquez had never known. Had he been that naïve? He should have sold the company to Armando when he had the chance. Now he had to accept his inability to achieve the greatness of his father, and be content to live a modest life.

Antonio Vasquez would ponder his decisions for as long as he lived, which was a long time. After the family moved to West Tampa, Don Antonio and his son found work at the Juan la Paz factory. Don Antonio became the factory foreman, his son an accountant. For the next twenty years, they worked alongside each other in the West Tampa factory.

Vasquez spoke little of Armando Renteria, and chose to remember him simply as "a vital component of Tampa commerce."

Antonio Junior eventually left the tobacco business and married the daughter of a local banker, going to work as a vice president for the lender. Don Antonio Vasquez became an old man and died of kidney failure a few months after the stock market crash of 1929. Maria joined him six months later.

Lapár ran for president of the Cigar Manufacturer's International Union in Tampa but lost a landslide election to Tony Bello. Suspecting a rigged outcome, Lapár realized he was no longer the good natured, charismatic personality the cigar makers had known during the Weight Strike. His confidence and allure had been frightened away by his three month trial in the jungle, and it was not hard for him to decide to leave Tampa. No longer the leader of anything, he took his wife and two sons and retired to Havana.

For several years, Lapár taught mathematics in Havana and attempted to live a quiet life. He closely watched Cuban politics, and stood among a crowd of proud Cubans when the American flag was lowered, and the Cuban flag finally hoisted above Havana in 1902. Lapár considered it a sham transition, a farce marked by bribery, extortion and sporadic violence, but it was better than living under the power of a foreign country.

He quickly saw that the tobacco struggle was not limited to the workers in Tampa. He watched the 1902 Havana Apprentices' Strike innocently from the fringe and admired the labor movement's fight to demand that Cuban workers be hired instead of Spanish. The strike became violent and ended miserably for the Cubans, but Lapár remained a silent observer, favoring his simple family life over the energy and excitement of the streets.

When local leaders sought his advice, Lapár could not deny his passion; a need to rally unfortunate people, to stand above them and motivate them into action, and to drive change for the good of the common man. He began to advise the labor leaders. At first his words were laced with warning but as time passed, and the memory of his days in the jungle receded, Lapár grew more confident in his activism.

Over the next decade Lapár helped organize strikes for bus drivers, box makers, plumbers, carpenters, and railroad workers. He joined Cuba's labor leaders on speaking tours that took him all over Havana, and as far as Santa Clara. He was such an influential force, that in 1916 he became a daily concern of Cuba's first dictator, General Mario García Menocal, and was assassinated by one of Menocal's agents on Good Friday, 1916. While Lapár was leaving a union hall and hurrying across town to meet with a prominent member of the Liberal party, someone with a small caliber pistol caught up to him at close range and shot a bullet into the back of his head. It entered behind his left ear and ripped a tunnel through his brain. Lapár died moments after he fell to the street.

Salvador learned of Lapár's death from Gabriel Mendez. "A fitting end for Lapár," Salvador said. "He fought for organized labor until it killed him, and he would have had it no other way." Salvador imagined Lapár rushing from one meeting to another along the streets of Havana, while working towards the greater benefit of the working class. After his death, Lapár became a local martyr for a short period. Others followed his work and carried on where he had left off. Many were more charismatic, some were more effective, but none of them had called Salvador Ortiz a friend.

On the night of the great fire, Gabriel Mendez and Alessandria Prizzi discovered a mutual infatuation for one another. She saw him differently than she did before his abduction. He was still the impressive factory *lector* and intellectual bookworm she had always known, but those dreadful months in the jungle had transformed him into a rugged adventurer in her eyes. A brave survivor of great peril.

Mendez saw himself changed in a different way. The labor movement and his newspaper were no longer as important as the need to enjoy what was left of his life. He had once dismissed the pursuit of women as an unnecessary distraction and a burden on his work. But at the welcoming banquet, he saw Alessandria not as a fiery Italian labor leader who once offered her skirt to any man who dared to side with management, but as a passionate, likeminded female who was young and willing to share herself with a man like Mendez. He spent that first night back in Tampa at Alessandria's apartment and never left. They were married four months later.

Mendez said little in public about his experience in Honduras. After the death of Juan Carlos, he recognized the wisdom in toning down his rhetoric and left the anarchy to other radical voices. He became a more

429

moderate writer and started another workers' newspaper with a new name: *The Twentieth Century Employee*. It was not long before he returned to the *tribuna* as a *lector* in the Martinez Ybor factory on Ninth Avenue.

After the fire, Salvador, Javier, E.J. and Lázaro moved into a row of tenement houses in West Tampa. Salvador was hired as a cigar maker at the Balbin Brothers Cigar Factory, but due to the abundance of recently unemployed cigar workers from Ybor City, there were not enough jobs for Salvador's boys. Instead, they found work in the huge construction effort that took place in Ybor City. New homes needed to be built where the old ones had burned, this time with aluminum roofs instead of pine.

The boys learned how to be carpenters and then painters as the new tenement houses were given fresh coats of white paint. They stayed busy throughout the winter and into the spring as Salvador continued to roll cigars and live in West Tampa. For the first few months of 1902, life was simple, until Hector Cancio visited Ybor City with news that would change the lives of the Ortiz clan forever.

"My father has died."

"I'm sorry to hear that," replied Salvador. He wasn't sure if he should console Hector with a hug or a pat on the shoulder so he merely stirred his coffee and waited for Hector to continue.

"He died in his sleep, but the night of your party, he summoned me to help revise his last will and testament. He left one third of his fortune to you."

Salvador choked on his coffee. He wiped a drop off his chin with his sleeve. "One third of his fortune?"

Hector nodded. "He had originally intended that it go to Olympia but after she left and the years passed, he wrote her out. He recently had a change of heart and amended his will."

Salvador never knew that charity was a condition of Testifonte's penance. Or that he had given a sizable portion of his wealth to local schools and churches.

The total amount Salvador claimed was $912,000, an absolute fortune, enough to buy a pro baseball team. Hector presented a check written to Salvador, which the cigar maker promptly deposited into a bank account. He did not tell his children about the money right away.

Salvador returned to Cuba with Hector and attended the funeral service for Testifonte. The sugar planter was cremated and his ashes were spread across the plantation by Hector, Salvador, and Hector's teenage sons Ricardo and Pablo.

Years later, Hector Cancio died at the age of sixty-three, during a boating accident off the coast of Santa Lucía. What should have been a relaxing Saturday fishing expedition became a holiday tragedy when a storm arrived, seemingly from nowhere, and capsized the fishing vessel. The men spilled into the Gulf of Mexico and as the boat sank it brought Hector down with it. His body was never found.

His sons, Ricadro and Pablo Cancio, grew up to be corporate sugar tycoons as wealthy and as powerful as their grandfather Testifonte. They enjoyed a long life on the Cancio plantation, where they married and raised their families. But in 1959, political upheaval forced them to flee Cuba with their families and leave their property behind. The families built new homes in Miami, Florida to await their return to the island they would always call their home.

Salvador dreamt constantly of the possibilities. He had more money than most of the Spanish businessmen from Ybor City, and he wanted to use it wisely. On some days he thought of taking a trip around the world and spending a week in every major city. He could start with New York and take a boat across the Atlantic to London, and then Madrid, Paris, Rome, and the Far East, Tokyo and Hong Kong. On other days, the time and trouble it would take for such a trip made him consider betting all his money on cards and *bolita*. But in the end, Salvador settled on a more practical scenario and came up with the idea to help Javier and E.J. buy their own company.

For years Salvador had watched the Italian cigar makers save their wages and, one by one, leave the factories to open their own grocery stores, bakeries, cafés, and tailor shops. While the Cubans immediately spent their extra money on trips or parties, the Italians were diligent savers who thought long term. The idea came to him while listening to Javier and E.J. talk about painting houses in Ybor City.

Old Man Cuesta owned an operation that painted the new houses that had sprouted in place of those lost in the fire. Cuesta's company, called Cuesta Paints, employed dozens of painters who canvassed Ybor City and coated the new tenements with layers of white paint. New homes were also being built in the growing West Tampa side of the river, and Cuesta had contracts to paint most of those houses too.

But Cuesta was nearly seventy with grown children, and had often talked of retirement, and spending time with his grandchildren. Salvador approached Cuesta and told of his inheritance, and two months later, Cuesta Paints became The J. and E. Ortiz Paint Company.

Finally learning of Salvador's financial situation, the boys wondered why they had to work at all, but Salvador scolded them. "Work hard or you will die a worthless, lazy dog!" The boys obeyed their father, and their business practically ran itself, becoming a profitable endeavor that presented Javier with plenty of opportunities to indulge in new clothes, liquor, gambling and women.

Lázaro wanted no part of his brothers' business, and would refuse any handout that Salvador might offer. In 1903 he turned eighteen and returned to New York City, intending to continue his boxing career. A year later he was completely broke and destined to the life of an amateur, so he returned to Ybor City and joined the local amateur boxing circuit. He continued to work in the cigar factory alongside his father but eventually lost all interest in the craft and settled for sporadic work sweeping floors, or washing dishes in restaurants, while sparring with more successful boxers.

As a fighter, Lázaro never amounted to anything more than average but his respect for the sport never died. He remembered his last argument with his mother and remembered her warning that he would waste his life as a circus clown of the boxing industry. If she could see him now, she'd stand before him with her hands on her hips and say, "I told you so."

He had always regretted his vile accusation that his mother was a stay-at-home-do-nothing who contributed little to the Ortiz family. How he wished he could undo that crime! If he hadn't run away to pursue his misguided dream, he could have been with her when she died and had the time to repair the damage he'd done. It was a feeling that tore at him almost every day, until Josefina showed Lázaro Olympia's copy of *Beyond the Sierra Morena.*

"Look," she said as she slipped a piece of paper from the book's pages. She pointed to Olympia's list, where their mother had written the words 'apologize to Lázaro.' He was stunned, and somewhat relieved.

"Mama was always hard on herself," Josefina said. "She probably wanted to talk it over with you, to help you understand how hard she worked for us."

Lázaro was finally satisfied with an odd sense of closure.

He never married and never had a steady mate or a serious girlfriend. He spent most of his days in gambling joints, at the track, or at jai-alai. His main pleasures in life became bourbon, tobacco, gambling, and his lackluster boxing career. Lázaro moved from cigars to cigarettes and never dropped the habit, dying of lung cancer in 1931 at the age of forty-six.

In 1905, Josefina decided that it was time for Javier to think about starting a family. She did not want to see him become a creature of the casinos and gambling dens like Lázaro, so she introduced Javier to one of her fellow nurses from the hospital, a young Spanish girl named Celia, who six months later became his wife.

While Javier continued to run a successful painting company with E.J., he spent his profits enjoying his life and his family. He and Celia would have a boy and later, a girl, and Javier was proud to be one of the first in Ybor City to own a Model T Tin Lizzie. While he chugged his family across town in their new automobile, E.J. bought shares in a small cigar factory, and with an investment from Salvador, purchased a delivery company, and a plot of land north of Tampa. By the age of twenty-two, E.J. had become a successful businessman who was building a small, profitable empire in Ybor City.

Javier had some interest in broadening his business. He started a buckeye factory and sold his own brand of cigars one year but eventually became more interested in raising his children and investing in his family. He died in 1923, at the age of forty-one, in an on-the-job accident. Javier and another man were painting the outside of a new four-floor building in downtown Tampa and stood on a scaffolding high above the sidewalk while they coated white paint on the trim near the roof. With his paintbrush in hand, Javier took a step back to inspect his work but his stride went too far, and he fell backwards over the edge and plunged sixty feet to the pavement. He died the following morning in the hospital with Celia and his two children at his side.

E.J. took complete control of the business and lived a very long life. He spent most of his twenties working and earning money, had a knack for predicting market fluctuations, and excelled at managing money and people. He kept his costs low and was careful to never overextend. As a result, E.J. was able to save a lot of money. He did not marry until he was thirty, old by local standards, to a Cuban girl whose father worked at the Balbin Brothers cigar factory in West Tampa with Salvador. They dated the traditional way, with chaperones, and celebrated a Cuban wedding, even though E.J. was admittedly half Spanish.

He would have three children with Nora, all girls. He taught them their history and maintained close ties to their grandfather Salvador, who visited them almost every day. E.J. made sure his girls received the best education, both in school and the world at large. Two of his daughters would grow up to be schoolteachers and the third would follow Josefina and become a nurse in a local hospital.

In his later years, after his daughters were married with children of their own, and E.J. had sold his assets and retired, he would often sit in the café at Círculo Cubano with a cup of coffee and reminisce with old men on the things they had seen in their lives. They would discuss everything from The Spanish-American War to Sputnik and never tired of retelling old stories and experiences.

Emilio José Ortiz died peacefully in 1967 at the age of seventy-seven.

The health conditions in the factories would always trouble Salvador, and the factory owners remained opposed to any type of organized health care collective. Workers pooled their money and created a mutual aid society, a fund that would cover health care expenses for any participating worker.

For as long as Salvador had known his son-in-law, Andres had been passionate about starting a private immigrant hospital in Tampa. But his

Spanish social club, El Centro Español, had vigorously opposed entry into what the club described as 'uncharted territory.'

"What if I donate the money to build this hospital?" Salvador asked Josefina.

She felt guilty about accepting such a large sum from her father, which she described to Andres as "free money."

Salvador tried to convince her otherwise. "Your grandfather wanted to reacquire lost years with his family, but time is not something that can be stored or borrowed like money. This is Testifonte's way of saying he's sorry. Remember, this money would have gone to your mother had she been alive. It would have eventually passed to you through her."

Josefina still felt strange accepting such a large amount of money from a man whom she regarded as a stranger. Andres thought her feelings were bizarre. "Cast your guilt aside," he declared. "Is it your fault your grandfather was successful and saved a lot of money?"

"Of course not," she admitted.

"There are few who would disapprove of you taking this money, and many who would call you silly if you did not. Imagine the hospital we could build!"

Josefina wondered what her mother would want her to do. "Take it and be happy," she heard Olympia say. "To hell with what anyone else thinks." Eventually, and with no reluctance, Josefina accepted Salvador's gift of $100,000.

Led by Andres, a large faction of Spaniards loyal to the idea of private medicine seceded from Centro Español and formed Centro Asturiano. In Tampa, Centro Asturiano started in a two-room wooden building on Seventh Avenue, but when it came time to start the hospital, Josefina gladly paid for Centro Asturiano to lease the vacant St. James Hotel on Tampa Street and convert it into a temporary facility. When the club's membership approved construction of a modern hospital, Josefina paid for a portion of the building and equipment and by 1905, the Centro Asturiano's hospital was the most modern and best equipped hospital in all of Florida, with a pharmacy, an x-ray machine, an operating room, sixty beds, and a staff of seventeen doctors and nurses, including Josefina and Andres.

That same year, Josefina gave birth to her first of three children; a boy named Ignacio Salvador Domínguez Ortiz. Over the years, Centro Asturiano became as important to Josefina and Andres as the cigar factories were to Salvador. The club was financially secure and had progressive values that attracted over three thousand members. In 1914 the club built a new clubhouse on the corner of Nebraska and Palm Avenues, which soon became known as one of the most beautiful buildings in the south. An architectural masterpiece built of stone, with a grand staircase out front and high arched windows, the building graced the skyline of Ybor City for the next hundred years and beyond.

One did not feel like a part of Tampa as an immigrant unless he was a member of a social club, and though Salvador was frequently a guest in the facilities of Centro Asturiano, he opted to associate with his fellow cigar makers and joined Círculo Cubano. The clubs provided health benefits and a gathering place to take classes, theaters for plays, cantinas for cocktails and nightlife, and a café to sit and play dominoes until the sun went down.

Andres Domínguez died of cancer in 1935. He spent his final days in the Centro Asturiano hospital alongside patients who were also fellow club members. Josefina never remarried, but she spoiled her three children and maintained her obligations to the hospital, and eventually cared for her father, who would live into his eighties.

Their experiences in the jungle of Central America had made Salvador and Gabriel close friends. Salvador eventually became closer to Mendez than he had ever been with Juan Carlos. When they were not working, they could always been seen together, playing dominoes in a local coffee shop, smoking cigars in the Círculo Cubano cantina, or at the club's boxing ring cheering Lázaro. They had a mutual respect for each other's values and ambitions – something Salvador had not always experienced with Juan Carlos, whose motives were selfish, but believed by Carlito to be essential for the good of all.

When Gabriel announced his plans to run for mayor of West Tampa in 1906, Salvador laughed but agreed to support his friend's endeavor by financing his campaign. Mendez was still a *lector*, and very well known and respected among the cigar workers. Salvador offered verbal endorsements to his coworkers. "Gabriel Mendez has our interests in mind," he said. "He will be a good mayor, as long as you remember to vote!"

Aside from his stature as one of the top readers in town, Mendez was regarded as a sort of folk hero among the working class. The workers said to each other, "This is a man who was deported to Honduras for his involvement in labor troubles, and then defied threats from the city and fought his way back into town. And he's still standing today!"

The cigar workers' vote was enough to put Mendez over the top and he quietly served one term as mayor of the immigrant township. While occupying the mayor's office was a high-profile affair that afforded Mendez many opportunities, he desperately missed reading *Moby Dick* and *Don Quixote* from the *tribuna* in the tradition of Sando Peña. It was with little regret, and great eagerness that Mendez completed his year as mayor and returned to read in the factories. The deliberations of the city council were no replacement for the shouting and laughter he could generate from a galley full of busy cigar makers.

Mendez would sit on the *tribuna* for decades; his voice remained strong and it was only when he approached seventy and his mind started to slow that Mendez finally stepped down and retired.

Alessandria died of leukemia during the Great Depression and left Mendez a widower for the last eight years of his life. They never had any children, and during his final years, Mendez ate breakfast with Salvador almost every morning and read a book a week until his eyesight failed. Slowly his memory faded. When Salvador would talk about the Weight Strike of 1899, Mendez would look confused. He did not remember the labor troubles, or the time he and Salvador bought a car and drove to New York City to see Babe Ruth during the summer of 1927. He did not even remember those four horrific months he had suffered in the jungle of Central America. For that, Salvador was envious. Eventually Mendez's mental state declined so much that Salvador told Josefina, "If he knew he was like this, he would not want to live." Mendez died quietly while sleeping, in September of 1941.

Salvador Ortiz remained a cigar maker for most of his life and died an old man. He did not sink slowly and deeply into dementia like Mendez, or die suddenly and with great surprise like Javier. He was left with plenty of time to ponder his past, the family he had built, and the future they would shape. World War Two ended, and Salvador found it baffling that he had survived into his late eighties while so many had died before their time.

Javier was Salvador's first child, the first of three sons, and had left Salvador with two of seven grandchildren. If only Javier had been more careful about how he lived his life. His indulgence in clothes, liquor, gambling and vacations amounted to a rather flamboyant lifestyle by immigrant standards. A cigar maker once, then a painter, Javier had followed life to wherever it had pushed him, hardly concerned about the future and rarely pondering his mortality. But he came through when it counted, taking his brothers to work in Key West during the labor troubles, and standing in as head of the family during Salvador's absence. Javier had left behind a wife and two children and had been a family man until the end.

Then there was Lázaro. Was Salvador disappointed in his second son? He was. Lázaro had a dream and a passion, but he lacked the talent or the mind to make it happen. He did not possess the wit to know when he should quit and move onto more practical endeavors. Perhaps that was a noble quality, something Salvador should admire. Lázaro obtained what he wanted: to become a boxer. But he was never really successful, and never very happy.

E.J. had been the luckiest and most fortunate of all. "He still comes to see me every day," a proud Salvador would say of E.J. to anyone to who listen. When he thought of E.J. running all those businesses, he couldn't help but laugh. E.J. had become a true capitalist, the type of man Juan Carlos and Alessandria might have rallied against. It was as if E.J. had risen to prominence and supplanted those Spanish cigar manufacturers, while remembering old world values and the importance of hard work. Salvador liked to think that E.J. was a boss who treated people right.

But Salvador was most proud of Josefina. She had been independent and successful from an early age. She had made wise use of her time, had never wasted a day, and had married a great man. Their three boys had grown to be handsome young men and Andres and Josefina were well respected in the community. Now semi-retired and about to be a grandmother, Josefina made regular visits to Salvador's small house in West Tampa. She usually brought him pastries, but always chided him on his health as they sat on the front porch and drank lemonade.

Salvador's family had been fully integrated into American society. His Cuban-Spanish children had married full-blooded Spaniards and Cubans, and E.J.'s wife had a little Italian in her. E.J.'s youngest daughter was dating an American boy, a sailor who had taken a job as a painter with E.J.'s company after returning from the war in the Pacific.

Salvador Ortiz often considered returning to Cuba. Decades ago, many immigrants hoped they would ride the wave of Cuba Libre back to their homeland and live in a perfect society free of aristocracy and colonialism. What wishful thinking that had been! Cuba had become an independent country, but its leadership had constantly been plagued with corruption and controversy. Salvador knew that America was the best country in which to live. And though his children were a mixture of Cuban and Spanish blood, they considered themselves Americans. None had any desire to live in Cuba. The Ortiz family was here to stay.

Salvador remembered one of the first nights the family had spent in America in 1898, at their little white house in Ybor City. Olympia and Salvador were in the kitchen of their small shotgun cottage, and Juan Carlos was over for dinner. The kids were outside the house playing, possibly exploring Ybor City, and the three adults sipped coffee in the kitchen while a neighbor nearby played Spanish guitar and sang an old folk song. His ambient singing and strumming inspired images of the streets of Old Havana. Salvador, Olympia and Juan Carlos sat quietly at the table and listened to the music with comfortable little smiles.

Then Juan Carlos rose from his chair and took Olympia by the hand. Hesitantly she rose while Juan Carlos put an arm around her. "Did they ever teach you how to dance?" Olympia smiled shyly while Juan Carlos grinned and gleefully whirled her to the sound of the music. They danced around the kitchen table while Salvador watched and smiled warmly, unable to believe he had been lucky enough to end up with Olympia.

She was beautiful in her plain white dress with her black hair pulled back into a bun. She still wore her apron, which she held with her right hand while she played coyly into Juan Carlos's exhibition. Though she had run away from home years before, Salvador realized at that moment that Olympia had made peace with her decision. As the Spanish folk tune spilled in through the window, Olympia smiled and spun in Juan Carlos's arms, happy to be where she was.

"Are you ever going to stop playing that stupid game?" Salvador awoke from his nap and saw he was sitting on his front porch. His daughter Josefina leaned down and pecked him on the cheek and then took a seat beside him on the swing. Her gray hair was tied into a bun with a blue ribbon. She pointed to the small wooden table beside the swing where a lone *bolita* ticket sat worthless.

"Seventy-two," Salvador said. "Can you guess which number they cut? Seventy-three! *¡Coño!* I missed it by just one!"

Josefina patted his leg. "I think it's time you retired from the numbers."

He smiled and watched her pour them each a glass of lemonade. She handed him a glass and then sat back on the swing. They rocked quietly.

It was the autumn of 1945.

"Have you been working in the yard?"

He nodded. Salvador had just finished cutting the grass of his house, and had picked enough oranges from his tree to fill a grocery bag, which he gave to Josefina. He looked at his daughter and imagined that Josefina looked the way Olympia would have, had she lived to age sixty-five. Older but still feisty and determined, with dark eyes that were almost black in certain light, with silver hair elegantly tied back. Then he saw in Josefina's eyes the eyes of El Matón. Salvador experienced a rare moment when he remembered Josefina was not his real child.

She had never learned the truth. The only other people besides Salvador who knew where long dead, and he considered telling her now, after all these years, the true nature of her birth. Was it not her right to know her own history?

Rocking quietly Salvador said, "The first time I came to Ybor City was with Juan Carlos. He took me to a cockfight, you know, the roosters?"

Josefina nodded. She had heard this story several times, but her father never seemed to tire of telling it, nor did he ever remember how many *times* he had told it. She patted his hand and pretended like she was hearing it for the first time.

"He bet all of his money on that bird but when he lost, Fortunado took the thing in his mouth and bit his head clean off!" Salvador shook his head and gazed to a group of children playing baseball on the brick-paved streets. "I swear I have never seen anything like that in my whole life!"

Josefina sat up and kissed his cheek. "Enjoy your pastry. I'll see you tomorrow, Papa. The yard looks pretty."

He brushed her hand gently as she rose and then watched her walk to her car and drive away. He set his lemonade on the table beside his losing *bolita* ticket and watched the boys play baseball. Salvador fell asleep a few minutes later, as he rocked gently on his bench, and never woke up. He died smiling, dreaming about Picchu the gamecock, satisfied with a hard day's work.

From the author's personal collection.

Carlos Roque
(1918 - 2007)
The author's grandfather, resting on his porch in Ybor City.

How much of the book is true?

The Headless Rooster

Is it even possible for a man to bite the head off a live rooster? It would certainly be bloodier than I described but the incident in the first chapter is almost the exact story my grandfather gleefully told me many times.

The Spanish American War

I tried to be as accurate as possible here but some things are fictional, such as Lázaro's fight with an American soldier. The circumstances of the war and the "invasion of Tampa" by U.S. Army soldiers and reporters are based on history. Did Teddy Roosevelt ever visit a Tampa brothel? Who can say for sure, but during my research I did come across that rumor.

Peasant Cuba

Herrera and Piro are fictional towns whose culture and purpose are based on the small, Cuban peasant settlements of the late 1800's. Banditry, social disorder and cultural strife against the Spanish were common. Most of the characters are fictional, with the exception of El Matón who is based on two different bandit leaders from 1880's Cuba. For some great reading on peasant Cuba, Perez's *Lords of the Mountain: Social Banditry and Peasant Protest in Cuba, 1878-1918* is filled with fascinating information.

The Church

My grandmother was a devout Catholic but my grandfather hardly ever attended Mass, and when he did he sat still and never said a word. Animosity between Cuban men and the church was a recurring theme in my research, as they identified the church with Spanish dominance.

Life in Ybor City

Since there are endless perspectives of what life was like in Ybor City, this was the hardest part to get right and I tried to get as close as I could. Many of the anecdotes in this book are based on stories from my relatives, especially my mother and grandparents and their neighbors in West Tampa. I realize that with thousands and thousands of residents, the variety of memories and experiences must be immeasurable. I tried to keep this close to my family, and share the stories (and nicknames!) that I grew up with. The dog Pano is based on the dogs that lived next door to my grandparents. My grandfather saved a portion of his dinner and fed them every day. Pano is the nickname of one of my cousins.

Labor Disputes

There really was a Weight Strike of 1899 and the cigar makers really did win. I tried to write this portion of the book as close to history as I could. The basis of the dispute, the events, and the outcome are factual, but since 100% of my characters are original, most of their actions are fictional as well. I took imaginary characters and put them in historical situations. The same can be said for the 1901 strike, which was violent, and ended badly for the cigar makers.

The Committee of Fifteen

A group of so-called radical labor leaders really was abducted and shipped to a deserted foreign coast. This has been documented in several places and served as the inspiration for this book. I felt it was a fascinating story that had never been told in a fictional context, so I wanted to write that story. The rest of *The Cigar Maker* actually grew around those famous kidnappings in 1901.

The Fire

There was a fire that nearly destroyed Ybor City but not in1901, and it was not started by a rogue cigar maker returned from exile. In fact, several fires ravaged the city in the first part of the 20th Century. The fire in *The Cigar Maker* is loosely based on those fires.

The Pasaje Hotel

The real name of a real hotel but a place that is more fictional than fact. Prostitution plays a role in this story and though I tried to portray Ybor City is the most favorable light possible, the nature of the storyline dictated that I create certain "juicy" scenarios to develop the story and my characters.

The Radical Culture

This was a big part of Ybor City and a big part of the story I wanted to tell. I was interested in the conflict that existed underneath the romantic image of a city that produced the world's best cigars. I wanted to recreate a truly epic slice of little-known American history that has rarely been explored in mainstream culture. The anarchists and radical newspapers, all true. Mutual aid, labor unions, charges of anti-Americanism, also true.

The Mayor

The mayors of Tampa during the heart of this story were Frank Bowyer and Francis Lyman Wing. The nameless mayor in *The Cigar Maker* is in no way based on either of these two men. He is completely fictional.

Labor Unions

La Resistencia and the Cigar Makers' International Union were real labor unions. Their involvement in the labor disputes depicted in the book is based on fact, but there is no truth to the CMIU being the manufacturer-friendly stooge that it is in the book. The rivalry between the two unions and the basis for the 1901 strike is based, in part, on historical fact but is mostly a fictional conflict.

The Food

Perhaps my favorite thing about Tampa is the food and I tried to include as many tasty samples as I could. It's all based on my experience growing up with a grandmother and mother who were great cooks, and my many visits to the wonderful Cuban-Spanish restaurants in the Tampa area. The celebration at the end of the book conjures memories of my grandparents' 50th wedding anniversary celebration which was filled with great food, lots of dancing and more cousins than I knew I had!

Additional Notes

In writing the story and coloring the overall feel of this book, I took my favorite elements from my favorite books and movies and then wrote *that* story. These inspirations included the writing of James Ellroy, Mario Puzo, J.G. Ballard, William Shakespeare and John Irving, the Indiana Jones, Star Wars, Godfather and Lord of the Rings movies, Apsley Cherry-Garrard's *The Worst Journey in the World*, several classic westerns and adventure movies and of course, the writing of José Martí. Despite the vast amount of information I consumed in writing this book, most of the events in this story came directly from my own imagination. Though filled with class struggle, violence and vendetta, *The Cigar Maker* is ultimately a story about family. I hope you enjoyed reading it as much as I enjoyed writing it.

Selected Bibliography

It would be impossible to cite every source of information and inspiration used in the writing of this novel, especially since many of the anecdotes, stories and personalities reached me through the colorful stories told by my relatives, and through my own experiences in Ybor City and West Tampa. However, a book based on history requires extensive research, most of which I can share with you here. I encourage you to pursue these sources for additional reading on the fascinating subject of Cuban history.

Del Rio, Emilio. *The Birth of a City: Ybor – Tampa In Pictures*. Tampa: Emilio Del Rio, 1972.

Fernández, Frank. *Cuban Anarchism: The History of a Movement*. Tucson: See Sharp Press, 2001.

Garcia, Clarita. *Clarita's Cocina*. Garden City, New York: Doubleday and Company, 1969.

Mendez, Armando. *Ciudad de Cigars: West Tampa*. Tampa: Florida Historical Society, 1994.

Mormino, Gary R. and Pozzetta, George E. *The Immigrant World of Ybor City. Italians and Their Latin Neighbors in Tampa, 1885-1985*. Gainesville: University Press of Florida, 1998.

Muniz, José Rivero. *The Ybor City Story 1885 – 1954*. Tampa, 1976. Translated by E. Fernandez and H. Beltran.

Pérez Jr., Louis A. *Cuba Between Empires 1878-1902*. Pittsburgh: University of Pittsburgh Press, 1983.

Pérez Jr., Louis A. *Lords of the Mountain: Social Banditry and Peasant Protest in Cuba, 1878-1918*. Pittsburgh: University of Pittsburgh Press, 1989.

Tampa Bay History. Volume 7, Number 2. Tampa: University of South Florida, 1985.

Thomas, Hugh. *Cuba*. London: Pan Books, 2002.

"A wonderful romp in never-land…the idea is certainly original. If you've ever been intrigued by all those conspiracy theories that are constantly emblazoned on the pages of the supermarket tabloids this will be an interesting read."

- Midwest Book Review

ELVIS AND THE BLUE MOON CONSPIRACY

by
Mark McGinty

Have you heard that NASA faked the moon landing? Well, you haven't heard it like this!

The first and only novel that tells the TRUE story of the first moon landing. Cleverly merging the Apollo 11 mission with the death of Marilyn Monroe and the assassination of JFK while explaining all those Elvis sightings. You won't find a more amusing story than this one! Winner of Honorable Mention for General Fiction at the 2003 Eric Hoffer Book Awards.

"Elvis has left the planet!"

Available at www.thecigarmaker.net and Amazon.com

http://theboogle.wordpress.com